DEAD OF NIGHT

SHADOW SECURITY BOOK ONE

RAMONA GRAY

EK PUBLISHING INC.

Edited by:
L. Nunn Editing

Cover art by
EK Designs

DEAD OF NIGHT

SHADOW SECURITY BOOK ONE

Never sleep with the client.

Tiger shifter, Grayson Scott, has never considered defying Shadow Security's number one rule. Until he meets his newest client, former celebrity turned photographer, Ryan Shepherd. She's human. And a rule-breaking temptation.

Ryan's family may crave the spotlight, but all Ryan wants is a normal life. Until a fan with a deadly obsession becomes a threat.

Her chemistry with the sexy shifter hired to protect her, is off the charts. But as their attraction grows, so does the danger.

Grayson's determined to keep Ryan safe. But with so many suspects, will the stalker outfox the shifter?

CHAPTER 1

"Grayson? Cooper asked me to remind you that the meeting is starting in five minutes."

Grayson glanced up from the computer and nodded to the receptionist. "Thanks, Daisy."

Daisy smiled tentatively before turning and leaving the cubicle. Gray's gaze dropped briefly to her ass. The auburn-haired woman had started with Shadow Security almost three months ago, and while she was excellent at her job and pretty with her long hair and green eyes, she wasn't his type. She was barely over five feet and it was doubtful she weighed more than a hundred and ten. Plus, she was human.

His human side was perfectly content to sleep with a human, but his tiger preferred shifters. He could count on one hand the amount of times he'd slept with a human. On the rare occasion that his tiger decided it liked the scent of a human female, it certainly wasn't the scent of a tiny one who was permanently anxious.

Grayson finished typing the latest report into the database. It didn't matter if he found her attractive anyway. Cooper, owner of Shadow Security firm and Grayson's boss, had been in love with Daisy from the moment she walked into the interview, looking like she was going to throw up from nerves and barely speaking above a whisper. The moody lion shifter would have Gray's balls tacked to the wall in his office if he went anywhere near their timid little receptionist.

He saved the report before standing and stretching. His height meant he could see over the cubicles into both Cooper's office and the tiny boardroom next to it. Cooper, along with Boone, Chase and Wes were already sitting at the table in the boardroom.

He frowned as he made his way over. Shadow Security was a personal security firm that had a dozen employees. He, Boone, and Wes were the best. If Cooper had called a meeting with them, something big was up.

He ambled into the boardroom, taking a seat next to Wes. The older lion shifter handed him a coffee from the tray sitting on the boardroom table. "New guy got us all coffee."

"Thanks, new guy." Gray took a sip of the steaming hot liquid.

Chase, a cheetah shifter and the newest member of the team, cracked his knuckles. "Yeah, don't mention it."

Boone grinned at Gray. "About fucking time you got here, Gracie."

"Call me Gracie again and I'll shove a stapler up your ass," Gray said without much malice.

Boone laughed and elbowed Chase. "Don't worry, kid. You'll get used to him. Grayson likes to pretend he's the baddest motherfucker in the room, but he knows who the real badass is."

Gray rolled his eyes. "I wasn't the one crying in the ring last night when he got punched in the gut."

Boone rubbed at his ribs. "That boxing shit is too old-school for me. It's all about the martial arts these days,

Gracie. Besides, I kicked your ass last week, or have you forgotten already?"

Gray just grunted as Cooper looked up from his tablet. "If you guys are done measuring dick size, I'd like to get the meeting started."

"Sorry, boss." Boone leaned back in his chair and tucked his hands behind his head as Cooper glanced at Gray. He grimaced in an apologetic way and Cooper gave him a short nod before plugging his tablet into the projector on the table. They all stared at the far wall expectantly and Cooper cursed when nothing happened.

"What the fuck?" he muttered as he scrolled through the screen on his tablet. He pushed a button on the projector before cursing again and giving up. "Wes, can you ask Daisy to come in here?"

Before Wes could stand, Daisy was hurrying into the boardroom. Gray wasn't sure if it was Cooper's cursing that had caught her attention or just her weird ability to predict whenever there was a problem in the office.

Without speaking, she stood next to Cooper. She was so short and Cooper so tall that even though she was standing, and he was sitting, their faces were almost level.

"The projector isn't working," Cooper said.

She bent over the tablet. Her long hair fell like a curtain around her face as she studied the tablet and Gray watched as Cooper bent his head toward her hair and inhaled deeply. The look of pure want on his face and the way his hands were inching toward Daisy's narrow waist made Gray certain he was about to pull her into his goddamn lap.

He stared at Wes in alarm. Daisy was like a skittish kitten. If Cooper did what he clearly wanted to do, she'd freak out and quit. Cooper wasn't the easiest guy to work for now – Gray couldn't imagine what he'd be like if Daisy left.

Wes cleared his throat just as Cooper's hands were about to curl around Daisy's waist. Cooper jerked all over and sat back in his chair. His face turned red when Daisy stared curiously at him. The scent of his lust for her filled the small boardroom. It was a damn good job that a human's sense of smell was so bad.

"Is everything all right?" she asked.

"Yes, fine," Cooper rasped. "Did I fuck it up?"

"No," she said. "You just needed to connect the tablet remotely as well." She pushed a final button and the wall lit up with an image of a vaguely familiar looking woman. "There you go."

"Thanks, Daisy," Cooper said.

"You're welcome." She left the boardroom, shutting the door behind her.

Boone raised his eyebrows at Cooper. "Jesus, boss, I thought you were going to try and nail her right in front of us."

"Shut the fuck up, Boone," Cooper said.

"You should just ask her out," Boone said. "Who knows – maybe she's into a shaggy-haired, tattooed lion shifter. I mean, I don't think it's a good look but I'm sure -"

"Knock it off, Boone," Gray said. Boone was a good guy and Grayson trusted him to have his back, but he didn't always know when to quit when it came to razzing someone.

Boone grinned good-naturedly at Coop. "If you don't ask her out, someone else is going to and then what? You just gonna pine for her from a distance?"

Cooper ignored him and turned to the picture of the woman on the wall. "Yesterday afternoon, we were contacted by a human named Christopher Noore. He's a lawyer for this woman, Vanessa Shepherd." He pointed to the woman on the wall and they all leaned in to get a better look.

4

"Why does she look familiar?" Gray asked.

"Seriously?" Boone said. "She's a celebrity and a pretty fucking popular one. How can you not know who she is?"

"You think I care about celebrity pop culture?" Gray growled at him.

"Yeah, but Vanessa Shepherd was in *Alien Hunter*," Boone said.

"So?"

Boone sighed in irritation as Chase grinned at Gray. "It was this really cheesy sci-fi show back in 2001. Vanessa Shepherd was the ass and tits of the show."

"How do you know that?" Gray asked. "Christ, were you even old enough to watch TV back then?"

"It's a cult classic," Chase said. "It ran for six seasons, and I own all of them on special edition blue ray."

"Human or shifter?" Wes asked.

Gray studied the woman. She was blonde with striking blue eyes and that puffy look of a woman who couldn't stay away from plastic surgery.

"You have to ask?" Boone said. "Since when do shifters get plastic surgery?"

Wes just shrugged as Gray said, "Does she still act?"

"Nah," Chase said. "She didn't do much after *Alien Hunter*, just a few movies that bombed and that was pretty much the end of her career. But the sci-fi nerds fucking love her. She goes to these events called Alien-Cons, they're like Comic-Cons but specifically for the *Alien Hunter* show, all over the country and draws huge crowds every time."

Cooper tapped on the table in irritation. "Listen up. Mr. Noore contacted me because they want to hire us for personal security."

"Us?" Gray said. "Since when do we provide security for celebrities?"

"Since now," Cooper growled. "You got a problem with that?"

Gray shook his head. "It's your company, you take on whatever clients you want. I'm just surprised."

"It'll be good for business," Cooper said.

"We already do well," Gray replied.

"And now we'll do even better with Vanessa Shepherd as a client."

"Why does she need security?" Boone asked.

"There's an Alien-Con coming up," Chase said.

"It's not specifically for Alien-Con," Cooper said. "Ms. Shepherd requires around-the-clock security."

"What does she need twenty-four-hour security for?" Gray asked.

"It's for her and her two daughters." Cooper swiped the tablet screen, a new picture popped up, and Chase sucked in his breath. The woman who appeared on the wall was a younger version of her mother. Her blonde hair was cut to her shoulders and she was staring over the shoulder into the camera with a 'come fuck me' look she had nailed to perfection.

"This is Ryleigh Shepherd. She's twenty-three years old, lives with her mother and her grandmother, and she's an actress as well. She's currently starring in the reboot of *Alien Hunter*."

"They did a remake of it?" Gray said.

Chase leaned forward and studied Ryleigh's picture. "Yeah, last year was the first season. It's hugely popular. She's playing the same character her mother played. They got renewed for two more seasons. They start filming season two pretty soon."

Boone slapped him on the back. "Put your tongue back in your mouth, you horny bastard. Maybe Coop forgot to tell you this part during the hiring process, but rule number one at Shadow Security – we never bone the clients."

Chase blushed and sat back in his chair as Cooper swiped to the next picture. This one was blurry and faded and taken from a distance.

They all squinted at the woman sitting on the wide front steps of a mansion. There was a large golden retriever sitting between her feet, and most of her body and the lower half of her face was obscured by his shaggy head and body. Her head was covered with a navy knitted cap, but she had the same blue eyes as her mother and sister.

"This is Ryan Shepherd. Vanessa's oldest daughter."

"Oldest?" Gray said. "She looks like she's fifteen."

"This is an old picture." Cooper consulted the binder in front of him. "Mr. Noore said he didn't have any recent ones to send. Ryan is twenty-eight years old. She's Ryleigh's half-sister. Vanessa did some modeling and Ryan's father was a photographer. He photographed Vanessa a few times and I guess they hooked up. He died of a heroin overdose when Ryan was two."

"Who is Ryleigh's father?" Wes asked.

"Some B-list actor who lives in Europe now," Cooper said. "According to Mr. Noore, he has nothing to do with Ryleigh and hasn't since she was about a year old."

"Are the daughters human?" Gray asked.

Cooper nodded. "Yeah. Ms. Shepherd isn't fond of shifters."

"Then why hire shifters for security?" Boone asked. "Daisy is the only human working here and it's not like we're sending her off to do security."

"Because we're the best in the city and Beverly Shepherd wants the best even if it means hiring shifters."

"Wait, who's Beverly Shepherd?" Grayson asked.

"Vanessa's mother. She was a popular actress herself when she was younger. She worked on a ton of movies all over the world," Cooper said.

Boone whistled under his breath. "They must be swimming in cash."

Coop nodded. "Beverly's net worth is the highest, but none of them are hurting for money." He turned to a page in his binder. "So, two days ago, Vanessa Shepherd and both her daughters received packages. Each package contained a dead raven and a note."

"Why a dead bird?" Wes asked.

"In *Alien Hunter*, Vanessa's character could turn into a raven," Chase said.

"What did the note say?" Gray asked.

Cooper flipped to another page. "It was time for the raven to fly. Now it's time for the raven to die."

"Christ," Boone said. "That's some morbid shit right there."

"So, I get why Vanessa Shepherd got the raven and why the youngest daughter did, but why the oldest daughter?" Wes said.

"She's an actress too," Chase said.

"Seriously?" Boone said. "I've never heard of her."

"She used to be an actress," Chase said. "She was in the original *Alien Hunter* as well. Played the daughter of Vanessa Shepherd's character."

There was a knock on the door and Daisy opened it and stuck her head in. "Cooper? Ms. Wilson is here."

"Thank you," Cooper said.

Daisy pushed the door open and stood back. A dark-haired woman with sleek curves and light green eyes stepped into the room. The scent of jaguar drifted to Gray and he stood up as did Cooper, Wes and Boone. Boone poked Chase in the shoulder and the younger shifter stood.

"Hello, Ms. Wilson," Cooper said.

She smiled at him. "Hello. Thank you for agreeing to meet with me."

"Of course. Please, have a seat," Cooper said.

She sat down in the empty seat across from Gray, folding her hands neatly on the table in front of her.

"This is Lori Wilson, she's Vanessa Shepherd's personal assistant," Cooper said.

"Please, call me Lori," the jaguar shifter said as they returned to their seats.

"But I thought she didn't like shifters?" Chase said.

Cooper glared at him and Chase shrank back in his chair like a chastised kitten. "Sorry, boss."

"My apologies," Cooper said to the woman.

"It's fine." She smiled at Chase. "You're right, she doesn't like shifters and," she paused, "she doesn't know that I'm a shifter."

"Seriously?" Boone said. "How do you keep that a secret from her?"

The woman pressed her lips together for a moment. "It's surprisingly easy. No one in Vanessa's inner circle realizes that I'm a shifter."

"But what about when she comes in contact with other shifters?" Boone said. "We can smell each other. You telling me that no shifter reporter or fan has ever been like 'Yo, Vanessa, why do you have a shifter as a PA when you hate them?'"

"Boone," Cooper growled. A golden coloured beard was starting to sprout on his face and his eyes had darkened to jade.

"It's a valid question," the woman said. "My job description does not require me to be in Vanessa's presence during fan conventions and we rarely book interviews with reporters who are shifters. The few times we have been around other shifters," she hesitated, "I've been lucky, I guess. As well, Vanessa's dislike of shifters is not common knowledge."

"Not that surprising," Boone said. "Half the population are shifters, if they knew she didn't like them, she'd lose a large portion of her fan base."

"If Vanessa found out you were a shifter, what would she do?" Gray asked.

"She would fire me. Immediately." Lori stared unblinkingly at him. "Which is one of the reasons I asked to meet with you here at your office. I'm asking that you keep my secret. I like my job and I don't want to lose it."

"We'll be discreet," Cooper said. "No one on our team will reveal that you're a shifter."

"Thank you," Lori said.

"We were just going over the security detail for Mrs. Shepherd and her daughters," Cooper said.

"Yes, about that." An uncomfortable look crossed Lori's face. "As you know, Ryleigh and Vanessa still live with Vanessa's mother, Beverly. Which means both of their security guards will be staying at Beverly's home. However, Ryan lives on her own."

"That's fine," Cooper said. "We'll have the man guarding her stay at her place."

"Yes," Lori said. "But Vanessa would like to know if that will bump up the cost. If so," Gray could smell her jaguar's discomfort, "she'll pass on providing protection for Ryan."

Gray's grunt of surprise was joined by Wes's. Boone's jaw dropped and he glanced at Cooper with a very clear what-the-fuck expression.

There was a moment of confused silence before Cooper

said, "The price I quoted Mr. Noore includes a protection detail for Ryan regardless of whether she is at her grandmother's home or her own."

"All right." A look of relief crossed Lori's face. "I'll let Vanessa know."

"Why doesn't Ryan deserve the same protection?" Gray asked.

"Gray, drop it," Cooper said.

"Just curious, boss." Gray turned his gaze to Lori. "She always play favourites with her daughters' lives?"

Lori flushed and stood. "Vanessa and Ryan have been estranged for many years. Now, if you'll excuse me, I have an errand I need to run." She gave them all a quick glance. "Thank you for agreeing to keep my secret."

They stood as Lori walked out of the boardroom, shutting the door behind her.

"Hey, is it just me, or is that Vanessa lady coming across as a real dick?" Boone said.

"Boone," Cooper warned, "enough."

"You can't tell me you don't agree." Boone turned to Chase. "Any idea why they're estranged?"

"Yes," Chase said. "So, you know how Ryan was in the same show as her mother, right? Well, she hated it apparently. Hated being an actress, hated being on the show and the attention, but rumour was that Vanessa wouldn't let her quit. Ryan was almost as popular as Vanessa and the fans loved her. But when Ryan turned sixteen, she got herself emancipated and she quit the show."

"Good for her," Gray said.

"The show was not nearly as popular by then anyway, but once Ryan quit, it was cancelled for good," Chase said.

Cooper closed his binder. "I'm assigning Chase to Ryleigh, Grayson to Ryan, and Boone to Vanessa. Five days on with two days off, rotating schedules. Wes and I will be your backup. I want all four of you at Beverly Shepherd's house tomorrow morning at ten. We'll meet Vanessa and her daughters and give them the rules they need to follow. Daisy will send out an email with Mrs. Shepherd's address. Any questions?"

"Just one." Boone raised his hand. "On a scale of one to ten, how bad will you feel if something happens, I have to shift to my tiger form, and Vanessa shoots me because she hates shifters?"

"Three and a half," Cooper said. "Meeting's over."

CHAPTER 2

"What do you think, Sam? Should we just blow the meeting off? We already know I'm not getting a security detail," Ryan said. "There isn't even a point to us going in there, right?"

Sam didn't reply, just stared at her with his soulful brown eyes. Ryan sighed. "Yeah, I know. There's a small chance that Ryleigh and Grandmother could change her mind."

Ryan shut the car off and stared up at the giant mansion. "I'll be fine if they can't change her mind, right? You'll totally protect me from the crazy stalker fan, won't you, Sam?"

Sam's mouth dropped open and he licked the passenger window. Ryan rolled her eyes and petted the German Shepherd's big head before climbing out of the car. "C'mon, boy."

She walked up the wide steps as Sam trotted behind her. She rang the doorbell and waited patiently. When the old man opened the door, Sam barked and weaved around his legs before licking eagerly at the man's hands.

"Hello, Peter." Ryan smiled warmly at him.

"Hello, Ryan." He bent a little stiffly and petted the top of

Sam's head before reaching into the inside pocket of his suit. Sam sat automatically, ears pricked forward and nose sniffing the air delicately as Peter produced a dog biscuit.

"Good boy," he said before handing the treat over. Sam crunched it down as they followed Peter into the cool interior. She'd grown up in this home, but as always, she immediately felt uncomfortable and out of place. She tugged at her yoga pants and then pulled on her t-shirt. It was clinging to her round belly and while normally she didn't give a second thought to her extra pounds, she was always self-conscious about her weight when around Vanessa.

She'd pulled her long dark hair into a ponytail and she wasn't wearing a lick of makeup. She probably should have made an effort, but she was going straight to a shoot after this and she needed to be comfortable. She'd be crawling around on the ground a lot and most likely sweating in this afternoon sun. Besides, it didn't matter what she looked like. She could have worn a fancy ball gown and a full face of makeup and her mother would still snipe about the way she looked. Until Ryan dyed her natural dark hair back to blonde and lost thirty pounds, Vanessa would never be happy.

"How are you doing, Peter?" Ryan asked as she followed the old man down the hallway. She knew every nook and cranny of it like the back of her hand, but she let Peter lead her to the family room anyway. Peter had been her grandmother's butler for over thirty years and his job duties were ingrained into him.

"Very well, Ryan," he replied. "How are you?"

"Can't complain," Ryan said with false cheerfulness.

He glanced at her as they stopped in front of the family room and she impulsively hugged him. He returned her hug before opening the door. "They're waiting for you."

She walked into the room and stopped so quickly that

Sam bumped into the back of her legs. He snorted and shook his head before stepping around her. He sat at Ryan's feet and joined her in staring at the five very large men standing near the floor-to-ceiling windows.

Ryan was used to strange people being in the house. Her mother and grandmother both loved to entertain and growing up there were always people milling about the house. Celebrities, powerful politicians, anyone who her family deemed worthy of their attention had graced the hallways of the house. An introvert by nature, she'd spent a lot of time in her room.

That being said, the five men standing in front of her were nothing like her family's usual guests. Nor were they anything like the usual security detail Bert, her mother and sister's manager, would occasionally hire to watch over Vanessa and Ryleigh at events.

The smallest of them was still at least six feet tall and they were dressed in identical dark suits. A quick glance at them would have brought forth images of businessmen – lawyers perhaps. It wasn't until a person took a second look that you began to suspect they weren't quite what they seemed.

Something about all five of them screamed "danger" and as her gaze swept over them from left to right, she inhaled sharply when she caught the stare of cool green eyes. They belonged to the biggest of the men – he had to be at least 6'5" - and he had short dark hair and stubble on his jaw.

A weird little shiver went down Ryan's spine when he looked her over. She tugged self-consciously at her t-shirt again. The man lifted his head, his nostrils flaring as he took a deep breath.

Right. They were shifters. No doubt he could smell her anxiety.

She crossed her arms over her torso and her face flushed when his gaze dipped to her large breasts. She immediately dropped her arms and looked away before reaching down to pet Sam's head. Her underwear suddenly felt too tight and her nipples were hard little beads against her bra.

Jesus, Ryan. Get a hold of yourself. You're acting like you've never seen a shifter in a suit before.

"You're late!" Vanessa's shrill voice broke the silence.

Ryan grimaced before smiling stiffly. "Sorry."

"You were supposed to be here at nine forty-five and it's ten fifteen," Vanessa said waspishly. She ignored the shifters standing in the room, giving them a wide berth as she walked past them. As always, she was dressed impeccably. Her crisp white pants and bright red shirt screamed elegance and she was wearing her usual heels. Her surgery enhanced breasts pushed obscenely at the silk fabric of her shirt as she stopped in front of Ryan.

"Traffic was bad," Ryan lied before leaning down to peck her cheek. The smell of whiskey washed over her, and she groaned inwardly. Fuck, Vanessa had started early today.

Vanessa sniffed angrily before staring at Ryan's clothing. "Did you have to dress like a derelict, Ryan?"

"It's comfortable and I have a shoot to go to after this."

Her gaze turned to Sam and she made a disgusted noise. "How many times have I told you that that thing is not allowed in my home?"

"It's Grandmother's home, not yours," Ryan said pleasantly, "and she's fine with him being here."

"Don't take that tone with me," Vanessa said.

Ryan didn't reply. There was no point.

She glanced again at the green-eyed shifter and another shiver went down her back. What kind of shifter was he? It had to be lion or tiger. They were the biggest shifters, right?

She wondered who he would be assigned to. Her mother or her sister? Probably Vanessa.

What if Vanessa tried to sleep with him? He looked a bit young for her, but age had never mattered to Vanessa. Last month she'd bedded a twenty-five-year-old groupie. Ryleigh had sent Ryan pictures of them sleeping in the bed.

Please God, don't let Vanessa sleep with the green-eyed beauty. Please?

Why she cared, Ryan didn't know. A man like that wouldn't be interested in someone like her. He was too fit, too muscular, too…perfect. Ryan was curvy bordering on fat and unlike most of the women in California who were bleach blondes with skin kissed golden by the sun, she had pale skin and dark hair. The gothic vampire look, Ryleigh told her once. She hadn't meant it as a compliment.

Are you forgetting something? He's a shifter. Vanessa won't touch him with a ten-foot pole.

Weirdly, relief swept through her. No, Vanessa wouldn't try and seduce the shifter. Ryan was just being dumb. Besides, it's not like the green-eyed god would be protecting Ryan. Vanessa had made it clear that unless Ryan moved back to the house, she wasn't getting security detail.

Apprehension flooded through her. Maybe she should stop being so stubborn and just move in until the threat was over. She wasn't stupid. She knew how crazy fans could get, and she didn't relish the idea of dying just because someone she didn't know decided she'd wronged them.

Maybe living with her mother again wouldn't be *that* bad.

"My God, have you gained more weight since I saw you two weeks ago?" Vanessa said. "You do realize how bad this makes me look, right? Did you even consider doing the Keto diet like we talked about? I swear, if you get any fatter, you won't fit through the door."

And just like that, death by a crazed stalker fan was the better option.

Ryan refused to look at the five handsome shifters. Nope, she wasn't going to do it. Definitely not. She was used to her mother's cracks about her weight and would have been surprised if she hadn't made a comment. But even though she knew she didn't have a chance with the green-eyed god, it didn't mean she wanted him hearing her mother harp about how fat she was. Instead, she studied her grandmother sitting in her chair by the fireplace, deep in conversation with the family lawyer, Christopher. Ryleigh was nowhere in sight.

"Where's Ryleigh?" she asked.

"Ryleigh is upstairs with Saul. She'll be here in a moment." Vanessa poured herself a glass of whiskey and kept her back turned to the shifters.

"So, she's late," Ryan said.

Vanessa scowled at her. One of the men snorted laughter before grinning at Ryan. She returned his smile as Sam nudged her leg with his nose. The man was handsome enough with his dark hair and dark eyes, but as far as she was concerned, his good looks were overshadowed by the green-eyed, impossibly broad-shouldered god standing next to him.

"Saul is giving her a steam treatment," Vanessa said. "It's been very stressful for her as of late and her skin is showing the stress."

Ryan mostly succeeded in not rolling her eyes. Ryleigh's ability to handle stress varied greatly depending on her mood. She wasn't surprised that Saul, Ryleigh's stylist and best friend, was here. Ryleigh depended on him not just for her red carpet looks, but for emotional support as well.

Vanessa wobbled her way to the sofa, collapsing on it with a soft sigh. Ryan frowned. Her mother was more drunk than she'd initially thought.

"Ryan, it's good to see you." Christopher, his silver hair glinting in the sunlight, had approached. His whole demeanor and look practically screamed lawyer from his dark grey suit and red tie to his perfectly straight, white veneers and polished wingtips. He pressed a kiss against her cheek. "You look good."

"Thanks, so do you."

"You should consider doing a skin treatment," Vanessa said from her spot on the couch. "Your skin is dreadfully dull."

"Enough, Vanessa." Beverly sank onto the couch next to her daughter, giving the glass in her hand a disgusted look.

Vanessa stared defiantly at her before taking another sip from the glass. "I'm trying to be helpful, Mother."

"No, you're being a bitch," Beverly said. "Sam, come."

She patted her thigh and Sam took off for the couch. Vanessa made a squeal of disgust, leaping up from the couch and staggering forward when Sam jumped up between them.

Vanessa tripped over her own feet, and Ryan rushed forward. She caught her mother before she could fall, wincing again at the thick smell of whiskey as Vanessa crashed into her. Still holding her drink in one hand, Vanessa pushed away from her. "Don't touch me!"

She staggered again, scowling when Ryan wrapped her hand around her upper arm. "I said don't touch me." She wrenched free of Ryan's grip and glared at her before swallowing the rest of her whiskey in one big gulp.

"Vanessa, you're making a fool of yourself," Beverly said. The old woman was still sitting on the couch. Sam's head was in her lap and he was staring up at her as she petted his ears.

"Be quiet, Mother," Vanessa snarled.

"Mommy, what's wrong?" Ryleigh swept into the room.

She wore skinny jeans and a pink coloured top that perfectly complimented her blonde hair and tanned skin. Her hair was in a neat braid and her face was a little flushed from the steam treatment.

"Nothing's wrong, my darling," Vanessa said. "Mommy is just a little tired today."

Ryleigh studied her mother before taking the empty glass from her and setting it on the credenza. "You've had enough for now."

Vanessa didn't reply and Ryleigh drifted over to her grandmother. She bent and kissed her on the forehead. "Good morning, Grandmother."

Ryan bit the inside of her cheek to keep from grinning when one of the shifters elbowed the youngest looking shifter. He was staring at Ryleigh's ass and the tips of his ears turned red when the older shifter glared at him. He dropped his gaze to the floor as Ryleigh, well aware of her audience, crossed in front of them in a slow, hip-swaying walk that invited the men to watch.

She smiled at Ryan and took her hands. "Hi, honey."

"Hey." Ryan kissed her cheek. "How was the steam treatment?"

"Divine," she said. "Saul is still upstairs if you want one."

"I'll pass."

Ryleigh studied her face. "Your skin is looking a little dull, you should get one."

"Thanks, but I'm good. I have a shoot in an hour."

"Ah." Ryleigh leaned closer and breathed, "How handsome are those shifters? Can you believe Mommy is actually letting us be protected by them?"

Ryan didn't reply. She didn't know a lot about shifters, but she knew they had excellent hearing. No doubt they could hear Ryleigh.

"Sweetie?" Christopher smiled down at Ryleigh. "Now that you're here, we're going to get started."

"Of course." Ryleigh hooked her arm around Ryan's and gave the shifters her mega-watt smile, the one she normally reserved for the press at red carpet premieres. "Hi there."

"Ma'am." One of the shifters stepped forward. He had shaggy blond hair and Ryan could see some tattoos peeking out from the collar of his dress shirt.

"So, these fine gentlemen are from Shadow Security. They'll be in charge of keeping you safe," Christopher said. "Mr. Brooks here owns the company."

The shaggy blond nodded to them. "My name is Cooper. These are my associates, Wesley Masters, Boone Jameson, Chase Stover, and Grayson Scott."

Grayson. The green-eyed god's name was Grayson. Ryan allowed herself another quick peek at him. He was studying Vanessa, a scowl deepening the lines on his forehead.

Christopher patted Vanessa's hand. "He's going to go over the rules you'll need to follow."

"Rules?" Vanessa joined them, holding one hand on Christopher's arm to steady herself. "They work for us. They will follow our rules."

"Vanessa, we spoke about this," Christopher said.

"They work for us!" Vanessa's voice was shrill enough to make Sam whine.

"That's right, we do." Cooper stepped toward her. "We work for you, Ms. Shepherd, and you've hired us to keep you safe. In order to do that, we'll need you to follow just a few simple rules. Nothing too elaborate or worrisome, I promise."

"Fine, tell me these rules," Vanessa said with a sniff.

Cooper said, "Rule number one – you don't go anywhere without your security detail. This includes…"

Ryan tuned out. She wasn't getting a security detail so

there was no point in listening. Instead, she took the opportunity to study Grayson while he was distracted by his boss. He was big, but not works out at the gym for five hours a day big. More… lean and muscular like a…

Big cat?

She smiled inwardly. She knew that shifters came in all shapes and sizes, no matter what type of big cat they were, but she'd been around enough of them to know that the tigers and lions were almost always tall and muscular, even the females.

He had to be a lion, she decided as she studied the hard line of his jaw. His whole demeanor screamed 'king of the jungle'. She wished she'd brought her camera in. The urge to photograph him was almost too powerful to deny. She'd photographed other shifters but there was something about him…

She studied his chest and the line of his broad shoulders before studying his flat stomach. It was mostly hidden behind his suit jacket. Did he have a six pack? Probably. He looked like the kind of guy who would have a six pack. Hell, they all did.

Her gaze drifted to his crotch. He would have a big dick. She'd seen a few shifter pornos in her time and the lions *always* had big dicks.

She'd never slept with a shifter. Growing up, her mother had drilled into her how disgusting and terrible shifters were. If it hadn't been for Peter, Ryan might have been brainwashed into believing her mother's lies.

She felt a wave of affection for Peter that bordered on love. Hell, who was she kidding. She did love the old man. Loved him and his wife fiercely, and she would forever be grateful for what they'd done for her.

Still, even after she'd gotten out from under her mother's

thumb, the idea of dating a shifter had made her feel a little guilty. Her mother would kill her if she knew Ryan was banging a shifter.

You're a grown woman, Ryan. For God's sake, if you want to bang the hot lion shifter standing in front of you, bang him.

"Ryan?"

She stared blankly at Christopher as Ryleigh squeezed her arm and then gave her a little shake.

"Sorry, what?" she said.

Christopher glanced at Cooper. "Mr. Brooks is talking to you."

Ryan flushed. "I'm sorry, I was… what were you saying?"

"I said that Grayson will be your security detail."

Her mouth dropped open and she stared wide-eyed at the green-eyed god. He returned her stare, those green eyes of his making butterflies flutter to life in her belly.

Ryleigh poked her in the side and muttered, "Close your mouth, Ry."

She closed her mouth as Vanessa said, "Didn't Christopher tell you? There's been a change of plans."

Christopher grimaced. "Vanessa, she needs to be protected as well."

"Be quiet, Christopher." Vanessa turned to Cooper. "Ryan will not be requiring a security detail, just myself and Ryleigh."

"Mommy," Ryleigh said. "Don't be mean."

"Hush, my darling," Vanessa said. "Ryan's made her choice and she doesn't want a bodyguard."

Grayson's gaze turned toward her. He was looking at her like she was an idiot and she supposed from his point of view she did look like an idiot. Who in their right mind refused to have protection when they'd received a death threat?

Before she could defend herself, Cooper said. "Ms. Shepherd, the price quoted for protection includes Grayson staying at Ryan's home."

A little shiver went down Ryan's back. Why was the idea of Grayson staying at her place so intoxicating?

"Then I assume your price will go down now that it's no longer needed," Vanessa said.

Cooper glanced at Christopher. The lawyer grimaced and turned toward Vanessa. "Vanessa, be reasonable."

Vanessa glared at him. "Why are you acting like I'm some sort of monster? I am perfectly willing to pay for security for Ryan, if she moves back home."

Christopher stared over his shoulder at her. "Ryan, honey, it would just be for a few weeks. Once we figure out who the packages are from, you can return to your own place."

Ryan shook her head. She wanted protection, she really did, but the cost was too high.

Your life is too high a price to pay? Girl, be reasonable.

She wanted to be reasonable, but the idea of living with Vanessa again, even in a house as large as this one... death was the better option.

"I won't," she said. "I can't."

"Ry-Ry," Ryleigh said. "Please, honey."

"No," Ryan said. "I can't live with her, sweetie. You know I can't." She glanced at Grayson, expecting to see derision and scorn in his gaze. Instead... was that admiration?

"There, you see?" Vanessa gave everyone in the room a triumphant grin. "This is entirely on Ryan. I am more than happy to keep her safe but, as usual, she's being her stubborn self."

She wandered to the credenza and poured herself another glass of whiskey. "Thank you, Mr. Brooks. Peter will show you and your other associates out, and then he'll show our bodyguards to their rooms. Please, do not touch anything in the rooms. Everything is very valuable and -"

Ryan's grandmother stood up from the couch. "Vanessa."

Vanessa took a gulp of whiskey. "What?"

"Ryan will be receiving protection as well."

"No, she will not," Vanessa said furiously. "I will not pay for her to be protected when she has been an ungrateful brat her entire life. Just once, she can -"

"You won't pay for her?" Beverly walked forward a few steps, Sam a silent shadow behind her. "The protection detail is being paid for by me. Not you. I will not allow my grandchild to be in danger."

"Mother, she'll be fine. She isn't even in the spotlight anymore, not the way Ryleigh and I are. If the stalker is going to go after anyone, it certainly won't be -"

"Enough!" Beverly's voice barely rose a decibel, but Vanessa flinched like she'd reached out and slapped her. "Ryan will have a security detail as well, and she does not have to live in *my* home to get one. Is that perfectly clear?"

"Yes, Mother." Vanessa's voice practically dripped with fury.

"Good." Beverly reached down and petted Sam's head. "Ryan, you have a client appointment, is that right?"

"Yes, Grandmother," Ryan said.

"I'll keep Sam with me. Come back and pick him up when you're finished." Beverly pointed to her cheek and Ryan crossed the room and kissed her paper-thin skin.

She wanted to hug the old woman, but Beverly hated public displays of affection. She settled for squeezing her hand and pressing another kiss against her cheek. "Thank you, Grandmother."

Beverly patted her cheek. "I'll see you later, sweet bird."

Ryan reached down and petted Sam's head. "Stay with Grandmother, Sam."

The dog sat and leaned his head against Beverly's thigh, staring at her adoringly as Beverly stroked his ears.

Ryan turned, her breath catching when she realized Grayson was now standing directly behind her. "Are you ready to leave, Ms. Shepherd?"

At the sound of his voice, her lungs did this weird thing where they forgot how to work. She stared at him as he waited patiently. Oh my God, his voice was deep and whiskey-rough, and she felt it in every molecule of her body. She was immediately hot and horny and wet. Was it even possible to be turned on by just a voice?

"Ms. Shepherd?" He raised one dark eyebrow at her, and she forced a breath into her aching lungs.

"Sorry, yes, I'm ready."

Too aware of the shifter hovering behind her, she kissed Ryleigh on the cheek and walked out of the room.

CHAPTER 3

G rayson was in trouble.
Big fucking trouble.

He stared out the passenger window of her car, dog hair covering his best suit, and the intoxicating scent of the human filling his nose.

He'd wanted her the second she walked into the room. The very goddamn second.

Thank fuck he hadn't been standing next to Cooper. As it was, he knew damn well that both Boone and Wes had smelled his lust for the human. He groaned inwardly. Wes wouldn't say anything to him, but Boone? He figured Boone would let it go sometime around the next century.

He took another shallow breath, denying his urge to turn and bury his face in the female's throat. Her skin looked so soft. All humans had soft skin, but hers looked… softer than most.

He closed his eyes and tried to concentrate on how humiliating it would be when Cooper fired his ass for banging a client. He'd never once been tempted by a client before, not once, and then Ryan came walking into the room, her tight yoga pants clinging to her round ass and a worn t-shirt that did nothing to hide the size and shape of her perfect tits.

He really wanted to see those perfect tits.

His tiger was one hundred percent on board with him screwing the little female. Grayson swallowed down the purr that wanted to come bursting out of his throat and shifted in the seat, trying to ease the pressure at his crotch. He was sporting a semi and if he didn't stop thinking about fucking Ryan, it would turn into a full-blown erection.

Of course, it would be a lot easier to not think about fucking her if he couldn't smell her arousal for him.

His tiger purred happily. It wanted him to shift, wanted to rub up against her and mark her with his scent. Not that he couldn't mark her in his human form, but in his tiger form it would be a much stronger marking. It would leave no doubt to any other shifter that she belonged to him.

Sweet Jesus. Stop it. She isn't yours.

Remember the Golden Fucking Rule: Never. Sleep. With. Clients.

He shifted again and Ryan glanced at him. "Sorry, the car is, uh, kind of small for someone your size."

"It's fine." Jesus, even her voice was turning him on. Low with a slight rasp to it that made him wonder how she would sound when she was cumming all over his cock.

He should have pulled Cooper aside and asked him to switch him and Boone. But his tiger had threatened to throw a full-blown hissy fit the moment the thought flickered into his head. Trying to keep his tiger contained in front of clients would have him on Coop's shit list for months.

Besides, he *wanted* to be the one watching out for Ryan. At least that way, he'd be at her house and not in that cold mansion with an alcoholic human who hated him, and her oversexed and most likely a total brat of a younger daughter.

Shit. They'd be lucky if Chase didn't fuck the youngest daughter. He saw the way the kid was eye banging her.

Hell, he was a little surprised that Cooper even assigned Chase to Ryleigh Shepherd. That was just asking for trouble. Of course, Cooper was so preoccupied with his own lust for Daisy, he probably wouldn't notice if Chase broke the rules.

Maybe he should have Cooper switch him and Chase.

No. Ryan's ours to protect.

She's not ours. Get your stupid striped head out of the clouds. She's a job. Nothing more.

If that was true, why was he immediately pissed off at the way her mother treated her. Not just pissed off, but also feeling immediately protective over a human he'd only just met.

Before he could dwell too deeply on that, Ryan was stopping the car and shutting it off. He looked out the windshield, frowning when he saw the park in front of them.

"Where are we?" he said.

"Oh, I have a shoot." Ryan unclicked her seat belt. "I'm a photographer."

"The shoot is here?"

She nodded. "Yeah, my client wants some outdoor shots and this park has some areas with great lighting. It's not golden hour great, but I have to work with my client's limitations, and they can't do early in the morning or at twilight. At least it's a cloudy day."

He had no idea why it was good that it was cloudy, and he didn't care. What he cared about was keeping her safe, and it would be impossible in a place like this.

His hand shot out and curled around her wrist when she reached for the door handle. Her arousal, which had started to fade a bit, flared back into life and he bit back his groan as her cheeks flushed. "What are you doing?"

He concentrated on his job and not on how much he wanted to bend her over the hood of her car and fuck her right there in the open. "Were you not listening to Cooper's rules?"

"No, sorry. I tuned out because I thought I wasn't getting protection. Why don't you give me the Cliff notes version?"

He sighed. "Wide open spaces like this are a no go without prior approval and planning. It's impossible for me to protect you in an area like this without backup."

"Okay, well," she tugged absently at the end of her pony-tail, "that does make sense and after this, I promise to follow the rules, but -"

"You'll follow the rules starting right now," he said.

Her look of irritation was surprisingly cute. "I can't cancel on these clients."

"Yes, you can. Call or text them and reschedule."

"No," she said.

He gave her his best 'you will do exactly what I tell you' glare. "Yes."

She blew her breath out. "Look, I promise I'm not trying to be difficult, but I absolutely cannot cancel on these clients."

"You're not wandering around that park," he said. "Anyone could be hidden high in a tree, ready to take you out with a well-placed shot to the head. Do you understand?"

She winced, her face paling a little, and his tiger growled angrily at him. Let him growl. He was trying to keep her safe. "Call the client and cancel."

Her arousal was gone, in its place pure anger. She yanked her arm free and pulled at her ponytail again. "I am not canceling. This is not up for debate. If you want me to sign a waiver or something that says I understand the risks and that I know I'm breaking the rules, I will. That way if I do get murdered by some crazed psychopath hiding in a damn tree, your job is safe, and your conscience is clear."

Mother of God. Had he ever met such an infuriating human in all his life?

He glared at her. She glared back. Seconds turned into a minute. A minute turned into two.

He muttered a curse and unclicked his seatbelt. "Fine. But you'd better be prepared for me to be practically on top of you the entire time."

Her face turned red and her gaze flickered to his crotch before she looked out the windshield. His stiffy threatened to come back and his tiger made a growl of need.

Fuck, he was not suddenly picturing how she might look with him on top of her. Her legs parted around his hips, her pussy stuffed full of his cock while those fucking perfect tits bounced with every hard thrust he made.

His tiger roared with excitement and distracted by his totally inappropriate fantasy, he missed his chance to stop her from getting out of the car. She slammed the driver's door and yanked open the back door to grab a large backpack and a round black fabric case.

He climbed out of the car and shut his own door, moving around to her side as she locked the car and stuck the keys into a zippered compartment on the backpack.

"Wait," he said.

She stared at him impatiently but waited as he studied the park. It was a nice one with a grove of trees that provided a shaded area, over a dozen picnic tables, a large jungle gym and other play equipment for kids, and a small building that housed bathrooms at the opening to the park.

He could hear the faint sound of water and he lifted his head and inhaled deeply. A tiger's sense of smell wasn't as sharp as some big cats, but he could still smell the cleaning agent they used in the bathroom, the fried chicken that the family setting up their picnic at one of the tables carried in a reusable grocery bag, and the fainter scent of the pond that must have been behind the grove of trees.

"Why are you inhaling like that? Can you smell bad guys?"

Her question wasn't mocking, more curious.

"No. But if someone was carrying a gun, I might be able to smell it."

"Really?" Her look was one of fascination.

"Sometimes. The metal and the bullets have a unique scent."

"Interesting. But how would you know it wasn't just the gun you're carrying that you smell?"

He gave her a startled look, his hand automatically reaching inside of his jacket to touch the handle of the gun he carried on a shoulder holster.

"Your jacket gaped a little when you got in the car," she said in answer to his silent question. "Why do you carry a gun anyway? You're a lion shifter, right?"

"Tiger."

"Huh," she studied him, "you're so big, I would have guessed lion. So, why the gun? Wouldn't you just shred the bad guys with your pointy claws?"

"When Cooper first started the security firm, it didn't take long to realize that human clients felt more," he paused, "protected if we carried guns. Even as shifters. So, we carry guns."

"Oh. Do you ever use them?"

"Sometimes."

"I suppose it might be faster to take a bad guy down with a gun than shifting and tearing him apart. You'd still be stripping off your clothes to shift in the time it takes to fire a gun."

His lips twitched as he fought not to smile. "If we have to shift to protect someone, we don't worry about our clothes."

"Right, of course. So, do you work in a clothing allowance into your fees for all the clothes you wreck when you shift?"

This time the smile busted free. "When providing security, the best thing to do is avoid a situation where we have to shift to protect a client. Prevention not reaction is key. This photo shoot of yours is a prime example of what not to do."

She shrugged. "So, you want me to sign that waiver now? Or maybe a video recording?" She pulled her phone out of her pocket, hit the video button and held it in front of her face, staring directly at the screen. "I, Ryan Moonbeam Shepherd, do solemnly swear that I knew all the risks of doing my job in an open park and that I refused to allow my security detail, Mr. Grumpy Puss, to stop me. If I die, it is entirely my fault and there is no one to blame but me. Oh, also, if I die, don't you dare take my limited-edition *Buffy the Vampire Slayer* figurines out of their boxes, Ryleigh, or I swear I'll come back and haunt your ass."

She hit the button to stop the video and stuffed her phone back into her pocket before giving him a wiseass grin. "There? We good?"

"Your middle name is Moonbeam?"

"Depending on who you ask, my father was either a pothead or a hippie. Either way – I'm stuck with Moonbeam as a middle name."

"I've heard worse," he said as she heaved her pack onto her back and picked up the round zippered bag in one hand.

"Oh yeah? Like what?"

"Dolores." He scanned the area around them as they walked across the parking lot and through the park entrance.

"Dolores isn't that bad. A little old fashioned for a girl, maybe, but -"

"Dolores is *my* middle name."

She snorted loud laughter that shouldn't have been adorable but was. "You're kidding me."

"No."

"Seriously? Your middle name is Dolores?"

"Yes," he said.

"Grayson Dolores Scott. It has a nice ring to it. Why did your parents name you Dolores?"

He kept his big body right next to hers as they walked past the picnic area and toward the grove of trees. "My mother had a sister named Dolores who died when they were young. My dad promised her if I was a girl, they would name me Dolores. After giving birth to me, there were some complications and my mom had to have an emergency hysterectomy. So, they gave me the middle name Dolores."

She adjusted the pack on her back. "See, here I was getting ready to mock you for your middle name and then you tell me a sad and very sweet story like that."

He scanned the trees as they approached them. "How much further?"

"Just past the trees," she said. "Near the pond."

He moved even closer, his arm brushing against hers, and ignored his tiger's delighted purr. "Stay right beside me, please."

She glanced up several times as they walked through the trees toward the pond. He didn't actually believe that there was a crazed stalker sitting up in the trees, but it wasn't his job to *believe* it was possible, it was his job to *assume* it was possible.

As they walked out of the trees, she smiled cheekily at

him. "Hey, we made it through the dark and scary forest in one piece. Go Team Dolores, am I right?"

She held up her fist for him to bump but he was staring at the people clustered in a small group near the pond. He put a hand on her upper arm just above her elbow – fuck, her skin *was* soft – and pulled her to a stop. "Are those your clients?"

"Yes."

"Who's the big guy?" He studied the man standing behind the wheelchair. He had a shaved head and he was covered in tattoos and – Grayson sniffed the air – he was a leopard shifter.

"Mark's nurse." She shook off his hand with an air of impatience. "C'mon, we're already late."

They walked toward the group of people. Grayson studied the thin brunette standing next to the man in the wheelchair. She had a toddler on her hip and the little girl was staring solemnly at him. The toddler's fine brown hair hung in ringlets and was pulled away from her face with a pink ribbon. The ribbon matched the pink of her dress. White ankle socks and black Mary-Janes completed her outfit.

"Hello, Ash." Ryan set her equipment down and gave the woman a kiss on the cheek. "Sorry I'm late."

"Hi, Ryan. That's okay. We were running a little late ourselves."

Ryan turned and bent to kiss the cheek of the man in the wheelchair. Even if Grayson couldn't see the man, couldn't see the grey pallor to his skin and how his body was wasting away, he would have known he was sick. He could smell it on him. The vinegary scent that a person with cancer always had.

His tiger made an uneasy whine. Below that vinegar smell lurked the sickly-sweet scent of death.

"Hi, Mark. How are you feeling?" Ryan asked.

"Good." The man's smile was pale. The skin on his cheekbones was stretched tight and gave him the look of a talking skeleton. "Thank you for squeezing us in. We know your schedule is booked solid."

She took his hand and squeezed it gently. "Of course."

She returned to her equipment and unzipped the round black bag. She pulled out three oval-shaped light reflectors - white, gold and silver – and laid them on the grass before opening her camera bag. "Grayson, this is Ashley, Mark and their daughter Sierra. That cool glass of water in the scrubs is Oren." She winked at Oren who gave her a small grin. "This is Grayson. He's, uh, a friend."

"Nice to meet you," Grayson said.

"You as well," Ashley replied before setting Sierra on the ground. She immediately ran over to her father and climbed into his lap. She leaned against his narrow chest and he smiled down at her before kissing the top of her head.

Ashley walked over to Ryan who was putting a lens on her camera. "We'll start with some photos of just Mark and Sierra and then do some family shots. All right?"

"Yes." Ashley's eyes were watering, and Ryan reached out and took her hand.

"No crying, love. We're making happy memories today, right?"

Ashley nodded and used her thumbs to stem the tears that were dripping down her cheeks. "Yes. Happy memories. Thank you, Ryan. You have no idea how much this means to us."

"I'm happy to help." Ryan brushed away a tear that Ashley had missed. "Let's get started."

"How long does he have?" Grayson's voice was low, barely audible above the hum of the air conditioning and Sam's panting in the back seat.

After her photo shoot was over, she'd picked up Sam from her grandmother's house before heading home. She merged off of the freeway and took a left toward the quieter suburban neighbourhood she lived in.

"The doctor thinks maybe two to four weeks." Her gut twisted.

Grayson glanced at her. "You okay?"

"Yeah. But that's why I couldn't cancel."

"I know," he said. "What kind of cancer does he have?"

"How did you know he had cancer?"

"I could smell it," he said.

She swallowed and stared out the windshield. "Stage four pancreatic cancer. He's only thirty-six years old."

"That's awful," he said.

"It is," she replied.

"How long have you been friends with them?" he asked.

"We aren't really friends. I'm friends with Oren, and he introduced me to them last week."

His big body twitched in surprise.

"What?" she said.

"You seemed close to them."

She shrugged. "I like to make my clients comfortable with me. If they're relaxed and happy, I get better shots."

"So, you're one of those social extroverts," he said.

She laughed. "Actually, I'm an introvert. But I love photography and I love taking pictures of people, so I put on my extrovert face when I'm at work."

He gave her an admiring look. "It's a pretty good face."

She reminded herself he wasn't complimenting her on her

37

looks. "Yes, well, thanks for being understanding about why I couldn't cancel."

"Thanks for recording that video absolving me of any blame."

She laughed. "Are all tiger shifters funny, or just you?"

The crooked smile he aimed her way was possibly making her panties wet. "I think that might be the first time in my life I've been called funny."

"What are you normally called?"

"Brusque, stiff, serious, adorable pussy cat."

She laughed again and he said, "That last one is just my mom. Well, and occasionally Boone."

The name Boone sounded vaguely familiar, but before she could ask who Boone was, Grayson said, "I have to admit, I'm a little surprised at how agreeable you're being about protection."

She frowned at him before turning right onto her street. "Someone's threatening me, why wouldn't I be agreeable with the guy who's in charge of keeping me safe?"

He shrugged. "You'd be surprised at how many of our clients are resistant to our rules."

"The rules are in place for a reason," she said.

"And just like that – you're moved up to my favourite client list."

She grinned and parked in her driveway before shutting the car off. "That seemed easy."

He didn't reply. He was staring out the windshield at her modest home and she was suddenly self-conscious. "What?"

"This wasn't what I was expecting."

"Why? Because of my grandmother's house? Not all of us need to live in huge palatial-like mansions with crystal chandeliers and marble floors."

"It just seems small."

"It is small. Small and perfect," she said. "It's just me and Sam so why do I need anything bigger? It's a waste of space and resources."

He'd hit a nerve without realizing it and she told herself to rein it in. It wasn't his fault she hated any kind of reminder of her lavish childhood lifestyle.

"No boyfriend?" He didn't look at her, but she blushed anyway.

"No."

Was it just her or did his broad shoulders relax just the tiniest bit? Probably her imagination. "Aren't you going to ask me about a girlfriend?"

"I know you're into men."

"How could you possibly know that?" she said.

He just shrugged. "Am I wrong?"

"No, but that doesn't explain how you knew. Wait, do straight people have their own unique smell?"

"Something like that."

It was obvious he wasn't going to say anything else. She opened the door and stepped out of the car. He did the same and she leaned back into the car and popped the trunk so he could grab his stuff. She opened the back door and Sam jumped out, running over to pee on the rose bush planted next to the side of the house.

"Sam, no," she said. "Stop peeing on the roses."

The dog chuffed in an apologetic way as she grabbed her camera bag and her reflector bag and carried them toward the house. Grayson followed closely, scanning the yard and the street, a black leather satchel and a small suitcase in his big hands.

They climbed the porch steps. He set the satchel and suitcase down and held out his hand. "Key, please."

She handed her keys to him, and he opened the door. He

stepped inside and inhaled before scanning the narrow hallway that led to her kitchen and living room area. She followed him in, and he held out one big hand. "Stay beside the door while I do a sweep of the house. If you hear me shouting for you to go, you go. You get in your car and you drive. No waiting for me, no coming to investigate. You go. Clear?"

"Yes," she said.

"Do you have a basement?" he asked as he stared down the hallway to the living room.

"No. First door on your left is a half-bath. You can see the stairs at the end of the hall right before it opens up into the main living area. The kitchen is to the left of the living room, separated by an island. The back door leads out onto my deck and fenced yard. My bedroom is at the top of the stairs, guest room is to the right, guest bathroom is next to the guest room. The door to the left of my bedroom is my studio."

"I'll be right back." He handed her the keys.

She watched as he checked the half-bath before walking down the hall. He paused at the entrance to the combined kitchen/living room and looked right into the living room and then left into the kitchen. He moved fast and oddly delicately for such a big man. She assumed that was the tiger in him. He moved to the kitchen, stepping around the island, and she heard the back door open. She put a staying hand on Sam's collar when he tried to head toward it.

"Stay," she murmured.

He whined but settled back on his haunches, resting his head against her thigh. She stroked the thick fur of his throat as Grayson disappeared upstairs. He didn't have his gun out and she didn't know if that made her more or less nervous.

A few minutes later, he was back. "All clear."

"Good." She picked up her equipment and carried it

toward the stairs as he grabbed his bags and followed her. "So, you know where the guest room is. Make yourself, uh, comfortable. There are extra towels in the linen closet in the bathroom."

"Thanks."

Was he staring at her ass as they climbed the stairs? Did she *want* him to stare at her ass?

Sam pushed past her on the stairs, knocking her off balance. She grabbed for the handrail, but Grayson's hard hand was already on her bicep, steadying her.

"You okay?"

She swallowed, staring at the way his long fingers curled around her skin. They were a little rough, she hadn't noticed that earlier, but now it seemed like that's all she noticed. How would those rough fingertips feel against her nipples or her clit?

Grayson let go of her abruptly and took a step backward down the stairs. "Hey, you okay?"

"Yes. Thanks. Sam's a menace on the stairs."

The menace was sitting at the top of the stairs, his tail sweeping back and forth, and his mouth open in a wide doggie grin.

She climbed the rest of the stairs and she and Grayson parted ways at the top. She put away her camera and headed to her bedroom. She used the washroom and washed her hands before staring at herself in the mirror. She was tempted to put on a little makeup, maybe take her hair out of the unflattering ponytail, and change into a pair of jeans, but she resisted. He'd already seen her looking her frumpiest, so what did it matter?

Besides, he wasn't here to bang her, he was here to protect her.

Think of how well he could protect you from your bed.

41

She rolled her eyes and headed down the stairs. She normally had a healthy amount of self-confidence when it came to how she looked, but there was something about Grayson that made her wish she looked like she used to.

That pissed her off, and when she got to the kitchen and saw Grayson laying out what suspiciously looked like small cameras on the island, she stared frostily at him. "What are those?"

"Cameras," he said. "I'm installing some outside and a few inside."

"No," she said.

"They're for your protection."

"I don't care. No cameras in the house."

He laid the last one on the island and zipped up the leather bag. "There won't be any in the bathrooms or your bedroom."

"There won't be any cameras in my house, period."

"This isn't negotiable, Ryan," he said.

"You're damn right it isn't." She folded her arms across her chest. "You can install cameras on the outside and that's it."

She could see him studying her, trying to figure out the best way to reason with her, and it just pissed her off more. He shoved his hands into his pockets and said, "This isn't my call. It's Cooper's. He wants the cameras in the house so we can monitor -"

"No," she said.

His frustration was evident. "What happened to 'the rules are in place for a reason'?"

"I'll agree to every rule except this one. No cameras in the house."

"You can't just pick and choose what rules you want to follow. That isn't how this works," he said. "Your choice is cameras in the house, or I leave, and you explain to your grandmother why you're not longer under our protection."

She straightened her spine and called his bluff. "It was nice meeting you, Grayson. You know where the front door is, please show yourself out while I call my grandmother and let her know her invoice from Shadow Security will be less than she thought."

He stared at her across the island, his nostrils flaring, and what sounded like a low growl rumbling out of his chest. Let him growl. She wasn't afraid of him.

"Fine," he finally said before stuffing the majority of the cameras back into the leather bag, "but you are officially off my favourite client list."

CHAPTER 4

"Shit." Cooper pushed a couple keys on his laptop and glared at the screen. Maybe if he just willed it hard enough, the video feed would pop up.

Nothing happened and he muttered a curse before trying another key. The screen went black and panic flooded through him. He rolled his chair back, holding his hands up and letting loose with a string of curses that echoed through his office.

His door opened and Daisy stepped into the room. "What's wrong?"

"I broke my laptop."

She headed toward him and he mentally prepared himself for her sweet scent, the heat of her body, the way she bit at her bottom lip when she was really concentrating.

"Let's see." She bent over his laptop and he stared at her ass in her tight skirt before closing his eyes. His hands itched to pull her into his lap, to press her against his dick and let her feel how much he wanted her.

Instead, he gripped the arms of his chair and said, "How bad is it screwed?"

"It isn't," she said.

He opened his eyes, releasing his breath when he saw the familiar background picture of him standing at the Cliffs of Moher.

Daisy craned her head to stare at him. "You okay?"

"Yeah, was just mentally trying to come up with an explanation to my accountant for why I had to buy a third laptop in one year."

She smiled a little – fuck, he loved it when he could make her smile – and said, "What are you trying to do?"

"Get the video feed up for Ryan Shepherd's place. I had the feed for the grandmother's mansion up and running and I have video feed of the outside of Ryan's house, but nothing inside."

"Okay, give me a minute." She turned back, her tiny hands flying over the keyboard as she did…something.

He hated how often he looked incompetent with computers in front of Daisy, but he loved that it gave him an excuse to be close to her. He leaned forward and inhaled. The anxiety that always clung to her was a little less today. He wanted to tell himself it was because she wasn't as afraid of him as she used to be, but truthfully, it was probably because it was just the two of them in the office right now. The more shifters that were here, the more anxious she got. Why the hell a woman so obviously afraid of shifters would take a job working with a dozen of them, he didn't know.

He wouldn't ask though. He couldn't ask. He had a feeling she'd bolt if he tried to ask any personal questions, and if he didn't see Daisy on a regular basis, his lion would lose his shit.

His lion growled in agreement, then urged him to pull Daisy into his lap. He ignored its clamoring. If he did that, she'd run screaming from the office and he really would never see her again.

"So, it isn't anything you've done," Daisy said. "There's no feed because Grayson hasn't set up the cameras for inside the house."

He frowned in thought. Why the fuck hadn't Gray set up the inside cameras. He reached for the phone on his desk, muttering a curse under his breath. Fuck, he loved his cell phone but hated that he couldn't remember a goddamn phone number anymore. Before he could grab his cell from his pocket, Daisy recited a phone number.

"Is that Gray's number?" he asked.

She nodded and he said, "How did you know that?"

"I memorized everyone's cell number at the office, just in case." Daisy straightened and stepped away, putting a little distance between them that made his lion grumble out a complaint.

"I seriously need to give you a raise." He was only half-joking, but it earned him another smile.

"I highly doubt memorizing a few numbers is raise worthy."

He grinned at her and picked up the phone. "Tell me that number again, and I'll bring you a coffee tomorrow morning."

"Deal," she said.

"Hey, Cooper." Gray switched his phone to his other hand and paused at the bottom of the stairs.

"You planning on hooking up the inside cameras anytime soon?"

He pinched the bridge of his nose and backed away from

the stairs and into the kitchen. He didn't think Ryan could hear him – the door to her studio was closed - but he wasn't taking any chances.

"She won't agree to them," he said.

"You're fucking kidding me. She understands that they're for her protection, right?" Coop said.

"Yeah, it's a no go. She's adamant about it."

Cooper sighed into the phone. "Great, she's gonna be one of those fucking clients."

"Actually," he automatically rushed to her defense, "she's been good so far. It's just this one rule that she's refusing to follow."

He could hear the creak as Cooper leaned back in his office chair. "Fucking celebrities. You'd think they'd be used to being in front of a camera all the time."

A light bulb went off in Grayson's head. "Maybe that's why she doesn't want the cameras in her house."

"Yeah, maybe," Cooper said. "Everything else going all right?"

"Fine. Nothing of concern so far. You getting the feed from outside the house?"

"We got it. You gonna need a vehicle?"

He thought about Ryan's cramped little car. "Yeah. The MKX if it's available."

"It is. I'll have Mave drop it off in the morning."

"Thanks, appreciate it."

"You got my number, call me if you need anything."

"Will do, boss. Thanks."

He ended the call and shoved his phone into the pocket of his jeans. He'd changed into a t-shirt and jeans before installing the cameras outside. By the time he was finished, Ryan had retreated to her studio. He'd unpacked the rest of his clothes and put his toiletries in the guest bathroom.

His stomach growled, reminding him why he'd been about to go to Ryan's studio. He walked down the hallway, his tiger was weirdly anxious and restless, and knocked on the door to her studio.

"Come in."

He opened the door. Ryan was sitting cross legged in an office chair, staring at the large screen in front of her. There was a photo from today's shoot on the screen, and she made a slight adjustment to it as Sam stood up from the dog bed in the corner. He stretched and then ambled across the room to lean against Gray's legs. He petted the dog's head, scratching behind his ears and down the side of his neck.

Ryan continued to stare at the screen. "What's up?"

She was still pissed at him. He could smell it coming off of her in waves. He decided, and his tiger agreed with him, that he preferred the smell of her arousal.

"You hungry? It's almost six."

"I really need to get these edited," she said. "I'll eat later. But I just went grocery shopping and there's plenty of food, help yourself to whatever you want."

He hesitated, tempted to try and cajole her into joining him. "You really should eat. You worked through lunch."

"I will later," she repeated.

"What about Sam?" He stroked the dog's head again.

"I fed him while you were installing the cameras outside."

"But you didn't eat?" he said.

"I'm not that hungry."

Her stomach growled loudly in direct dispute to her claim. The tips of her ears turned red, but she leaned forward and clicked to the next photo. "Thanks, Grayson."

He knew a dismissal when he heard one. Feeling a little disgruntled, his tiger even more restless and upset, he headed toward the door. Sam followed him out into the hallway. Gray shut the studio door and, Sam at his heels, returned to the kitchen.

The dog stood at the back door and Gray let him outside before opening the fridge and rummaging around in it. There was a container of leftover roast beef and he pulled it out as well as some condiments and then looked in the pantry for bread. He made two sandwiches and bit into one as he took a container of carrot sticks out of the fridge. He set the second sandwich on a plate, added some carrot sticks next to the sandwich, and grabbed two bottles of water from the fridge before finishing off the rest of his own sandwich.

He let Sam inside and then drank half of his water before carrying the plate, a napkin, and the other bottle of water upstairs. He knocked on the studio door and at Ryan's impatient, "Come in," he opened the door and walked toward her.

He set the plate, the napkin, and the bottled water on the desk beside her. She stared at it before giving him a look of surprise. "You made me a sandwich?"

"You need to eat." He headed toward the door as Sam flopped down on his dog bed in the corner again.

"Grayson?"

He paused in the doorway. "Yeah?"

"Thank you."

"You're welcome."

GRAYSON SAT UP IN BED, PLACING HIS TABLET ON THE BED beside him. It was just after midnight and while Ryan was being quiet as she crept down the stairs, he still heard the subtle creak of each step under her feet.

He glanced at the tablet, feeling a little bit like a creeper when Ryan's face stared back at him. He closed the website and locked his tablet before getting out of bed. So, he'd been googling Ryan, what was the big deal? She was a famous celebrity, lots of people googled famous celebrities.

You've never been the star-struck type, asshole.

No, he wasn't, and he still wasn't. Ryan was his client and any extra information he had about her would only help him protect her better.

Bullshit.

His tiger huffed in agreement with his inner voice. He ignored both and slipped out of his room. Ryan had spent the entire evening in her studio while he sat bored out of his mind in the guest bedroom. It was the boredom that had driven him to pick up his tablet and start googling Ryan. Nothing more.

He'd fallen into a rabbit hole of *Alien Hunter* useless trivia and facts. Although most of it was about the current reboot of the cult show, there was plenty of information to be found on the original and on Ryan and her mother.

He stopped at the bottom of the stairs. Sam trotted out of the kitchen and he leaned against Grayson's legs as Grayson stared at Ryan. She was standing with her back to him at the counter, a knife in one hand and a block of cheese in the other.

He stared at her ass, wondering how it would look when she was naked, on her hands and knees, and he was balls-deep inside of her pussy. Beautiful, he decided. Her ass was the perfect size and shape, and just picturing it stuck up in the air, his fingers gripping those firm round cheeks as he fucked her hard, gave him an immediate erection.

"If you want some cheese, now's your chance, fuzzball." Ryan waved the block of cheese in the air.

He walked forward, leaning against the island to hide his erection, and said, "I don't like cheese."

She jumped, the knife clattering to the counter and

muttered a curse under her breath. She glanced at him, frown lines deep across her forehead. "You scared the hell out of me."

"Sorry."

She turned back and sliced off some cheese. Sam had left him to sit at her feet and Ryan dropped a piece of cheese into his open mouth. "Who doesn't like cheese?"

"Lots of people don't like cheese."

"You're the first person I've ever met who doesn't like cheese." She sliced off another piece and popped it into her mouth. "And I've met a lot of people."

"I bet," he said.

She opened the fridge and grabbed a bottle of water before raising a brow at him. He nodded and she grabbed a second and tossed it to him. "Sorry I woke you up. I tried to be quiet, but I imagine you have super sonic hearing, huh?"

"I was still awake, but I would have woken even if I wasn't."

She took a swig of water and wiped her mouth. "I shouldn't be surprised. Tigers are nocturnal."

He grinned. "True, but not all tiger shifters are nocturnal."

"Really?"

"Yeah. My mom is in bed every night by nine and awake at five."

She toyed with the label on her water bottle. "Did you get in trouble with your boss for not setting up the cameras inside the house?"

"No. But if you've changed your mind, I'll set them up tomorrow."

"I haven't," she said flatly. "I spent most of my childhood being watched and now I value my privacy. The thought of cameras in my house makes me feel sick to my stomach."

"I get it," he said.

She studied him intently before relaxing a little. "Thanks. I'm not trying to be difficult."

"I know you aren't," he said. "Did you finish editing the pictures?"

"Yeah. Normally I don't edit them this soon after a shoot, but…"

She rubbed at her temple, looking tired and a little sad. He ignored his tiger's demands to soothe her and said, "It was a really nice thing you did for them."

"You sound surprised," she said.

"Do I?"

She sighed. "No, not really. Sorry. My family doesn't have the reputation for being the nicest celebrities in the business, so I'm a bit sensitive."

"Do you miss acting?" he asked.

"God, no." Her emphatic reply was accompanied by a full body shudder of revulsion. "Being an actor is just about the worst job an introvert can have. I would never have become one if my mother hadn't forced me into it."

"Is that why you emancipated yourself at sixteen?"

"Yes. Did you watch the original show?"

"No. I don't watch a lot of TV or follow pop culture. Your mother looked vaguely familiar when Coop told us about the job, but I didn't know who she was."

She smiled a little. "Don't mention that to my mother."

He laughed. "I won't. Has she always hated shifters?"

"Yes," she said bluntly.

"Do you know why?"

"Nope," she said. "She has never given a reason, just spewed toxic venom about them to us whenever she was given the chance. If it wasn't for Peter and Mary, I'm sure Ryleigh and I would hate them too."

"Who are Peter and Mary?"

"Peter is my grandmother's butler and Mary is his wife. Mary used to be Grandmother's housekeeper. She's retired now, but she still comes by the house a lot to see Grandmother."

She didn't say anything else and although he was intensely curious, he didn't pry. "How does your grandmother feel about shifters?"

She thought for a moment. "She's… neutral on the subject of shifters."

"So, your mother doesn't get her hatred for us from your grandmother?"

"No. But to be fair, my mother hates a lot of things without any real reason for it."

"It's strange that she would hire shifters for protection considering how much she hates us," he said.

Ryan peeled off a piece of the label and rolled it into a ball between her fingers. "I imagine it was a combination of Christopher's influence, and her wanting the very best people looking after Ryleigh."

"But not you?"

"I won't let her run my life anymore and there are consequences to that decision," she said.

"Not providing protection to her own child against a death threat is a little extreme, don't you think?" he said.

"That's Vanessa," she said with a shrug. "So," her small smile at him made his tiger purr happily, "how much googling of my family have you done?"

"A lot," he admitted. "You look really different now."

The smile dropped from her face and he could smell her embarrassment. "Yeah, well, I got tired of dyeing my roots and making myself sick trying to stay thin."

He immediately felt a little ashamed for his callous remark. "I didn't mean -"

"I know what you meant," she said. "Trust me, you think when a guy finally recognizes me, he doesn't immediately comment on how *different* I look? Guys prefer me blonde with a stick-thin body, I get it."

She tossed her half full water bottle into the sink and stalked past him. He grabbed her arm and she glared at him. "Let go."

"I prefer the way you look now."

"Let go or… what?"

He stepped closer, until his chest was almost touching her arm. She was on the taller side for a woman, but she still had to tilt her head to look up at him. He studied her bright blue eyes, his tiger roaring happily when her pupils enlarged, and the sweet scent of her arousal drifted to him.

"I like the way you look now." His voice had lowered to a rasp, and the smell of her lust intensified.

His cock responded, pushing against the fabric of his jeans until it was nearly painful. He studied her mouth. When it parted and the tip of her tongue darted out to brush against her upper lip, he burned with the need to claim, to take, to fuck.

He released her arm and wrapped the silky soft strands of her ponytail around his hand. He tugged lightly, forcing her head back until the long length of her throat was exposed. He studied the pulse point at her neck, at the way it fluttered and jumped against her pale skin.

"Such a pretty human." His voice had lowered and thickened, more animal than human now, and his cock was a raging hot length of stone. Had he ever wanted to fuck a woman this badly in his life?

"Grayson?" There was lust in her voice but also the tiniest bit of fear.

He made himself release her. Made himself step back and

put some space between them before he simply threw her over his shoulder and carried her to the closest bed. Hell, the way he was feeling, he'd bend her over the damn island and fuck her right there.

Yes! his tiger growled. *Take the female. I want her.*

Knock it off, he snapped. *She's a client. We don't fuck clients.*

He dragged in a breath before rubbing his hand across his cheek. He was dismayed to feel the rough hair against his palm. Christ, he was starting to shift. No wonder she was afraid.

"I'm sorry," he said. "I didn't mean to frighten you."

"You didn't." She licked those full lips, her gaze still on his face. "Are you all right?"

"Yes."

Take the female. She wants to be fucked.

Shut up! he snarled at his tiger.

It retreated with a sulky whine.

"What is he saying?"

"What?" he said.

"Your tiger. You were talking to him, right? Your eyes turned a different green and your pupils, uh, turned to…" she waved her hand in the air, "you know… cat eye pupils."

He blinked at her. "You know about that?"

"Well, it's not really a secret is it? When shifters talk to their cat, their eyes change. Doesn't everyone know that?" she asked in confusion.

He could still smell her arousal and he took another step back. Christ, the lack of blood in his brain was making him act and sound like an idiot. "Yeah." He set his water bottle on the island and walked toward the stairs. "It's late. Good night, Ryan."

"Good night, Grayson."

CHAPTER 5

"This is a nice car." Ryan ran her hand over the leather interior.

"It's a company car." Grayson turned left and settled back in his seat, one hand on the steering wheel as he stared out the windshield.

She hadn't argued when Grayson said they were taking his SUV. She loved Sam but it was kind of nice to sit in a vehicle that wasn't covered in a layer of dog hair.

She studied her hands as Grayson drove toward the coffee shop. She was tired and feeling a little on edge, but when Ryleigh had texted her about coffee this morning, she'd said yes.

She *always* said yes.

Denying her baby sister wasn't exactly her greatest strength.

She shifted her gaze to Grayson for a quick five seconds before looking at her hands again. It was no wonder she was tired. She'd slept maybe a couple hours last night. She'd been too worked up, too...

Horny.

She sighed and fidgeted in the seat. Yeah, horny was an apt description. But could you blame her? The way Grayson had looked at her, the way he'd sounded when he said he preferred the way she looked now, had lit her up like gasoline on a bonfire.

Her panties had been soaked almost immediately, and she knew that Grayson could smell her arousal. She thought she'd be embarrassed, and she was, but there was a bigger part of her that wondered if he liked it.

Wondered if maybe he would do more than just touch her hair and call her pretty.

Ryan, enough!

Grayson's nostrils were flaring, and his hands tightened on the steering wheel until his knuckles went white. Without looking at her, he opened his window about halfway, despite the heat outside and the a/c on in the car.

Fantastic. She was turned on again and he knew it. This wasn't humiliating at all.

It was his fault, she decided a bit grumpily. Him and his stupid super sonic hearing. If he hadn't been in the room right next to hers, maybe, just maybe, she could have masturbated last night like a normal, healthy woman and relieved some of her pent-up lust.

But the idea that he would hear her touching herself made her want to cringe. So, instead, she'd tossed and turned all night and had a weird dream about petting a tiger on a cruise ship.

Desperate to take her mind off Grayson and her brand-new desire to see him naked, she said, "I'm surprised that Ryleigh's bodyguard is letting her go out in public for coffee."

"Your sister agreed to wear a," he paused, "disguise.

Quite readily, actually." He gave her a quick glance. "We were expecting her to be a bit more of a…"

"Pain in the ass?" She grinned at him.

"Difficult client," he settled on.

"She can be difficult," Ryan admitted. "She's stubborn like our mother and impulsive like her dad and that can be a bad combination. But she actually wears a disguise a lot when she goes out in public, especially since the reboot got so popular."

"Does your mother?" he asked.

"Not really. Most of the time if she's going out, it's because she wants to be recognized," she said.

Grayson pulled into the parking lot and parked in front of the coffee shop. He shut off the engine and pulled his phone from the inside pocket of his jacket. Today, he was dressed casually in a pair of jeans, t-shirt, and leather jacket. She wasn't sure how it was possible, but he was even hotter in casual clothes than the suit he wore yesterday.

She watched as he texted for a few seconds before tucking his phone back into his pocket. He unclicked his seatbelt and turned to face her. "Okay, there are a few rules while you're in the coffee shop."

She unbuckled her own seatbelt. "So, my idea of sneaking to the bathroom and ditching you by climbing out the window is probably a rule breaker, huh?"

A smile crossed his face. "Definite rule breaker."

She relaxed in her seat. "Tell me your rules."

"Do not leave the coffee shop without me for any reason. Stay where I can always see you. Chase, Wes and I won't be right at the table with you and your sister, but we will be close by. If you see anyone or anything that makes you nervous, wave at me."

"What if I actually do need to use the restroom?" she said.

"I'll escort you to the restroom and do a quick sweep before you go in."

She wrinkled her nose. "Yeah, that's not gonna look weird at all."

He shrugged. "My priority is keeping you safe, I don't care what it looks like."

"So, I know that Chase is Ryleigh's bodyguard, but who's Wes?" she asked.

"He works for the firm. Because it's a public space, we're adding some extra security."

"Wow, you guys are really…thorough."

He shrugged again. "We believe in being prepared."

"Isn't that the Boy Scouts motto?" she asked teasingly.

"Would you believe that I was a Boy Scout?"

Shit, he was adorable when he grinned like that.

"You still have your sash with all your badges, don't you?" she said.

"Maybe."

She laughed as Grayson scanned the parking lot before opening his door. "Stay in the car, please."

She stayed where she was as Grayson got out and shut his door. He studied the parking lot and the front of the building before walking to her door and opening it. She slid out of the SUV and Grayson shut the door and locked the vehicle before putting one hand in the small of her back. Another wave of lust went through her – crap, she was in so much trouble – but if he smelled it, there was no indication.

"Should I expect people to come near you and ask for autographs?" he asked.

"Not usually. I rarely get recognized by the general public. If they're, like, a super fan of the original show… maybe. But it's rare."

"All right."

"Why do you ask?"

He stared down at her. "Because if a stranger is coming up to you, it's my job to stop them."

"Right, but I mean…it could be a fan."

"It could also be someone trying to kill you."

She chewed on her lip, realizing for the first time just how difficult Grayson's job was. She suddenly felt guilty about agreeing to meet Ryleigh at a public place.

He inhaled. "What's wrong? Why do you feel guilty?"

"I should have told Ryleigh to come to my place for coffee. I'm making your job much harder than it needs to be," she said.

"You can't live your life as a hermit, even if you are an introvert." He smiled at her. "It's fine, Ryan. If someone does approach us, step behind me and wait while I assess the situation. All right?"

"Yes. But promise me you won't break a fan's arm or something… the paparazzi would go insane."

"I can't make that promise," he teased.

She laughed and he pressed lightly on the small of her back to get her moving.

"Stay right next to me, please." He was all business. The teasing grin was gone from his face and his gaze constantly scanned the parking lot as they walked toward the front door. He opened the door and ushered her inside. She took a quick look around the coffee shop, spotting Ryleigh despite the dark brown wig and eyeglasses she was wearing.

She walked over to her table, acutely aware of Grayson directly behind her and sank into the chair next to Ryleigh. "Hey, sweetie."

"Ry-Ry!" Ryleigh turned her cheek toward her, and Ryan kissed it. "How are you?"

"Good."

"I got you your coffee already." Ryleigh slid the paper cup toward her.

"Thank you." She glanced behind her, but Grayson had already moved away. Not far. He, Chase and the older shifter from her grandmother's house were sitting at a table only a few feet away. They had a clear view of both her and Ryleigh and a clear view of the door. They looked relaxed enough, but she didn't miss the way all three of the shifters' gazes were constantly moving around the coffee shop.

It was steady but not super busy in the small café and Ryan took a sip of her coffee before smiling at Ryleigh. "So, how are you?"

"Bored out of my skull." Ryleigh made the perfect pout. "I mean, it's not like Chase is refusing to allow me to leave the house, but it's sooo complicated now."

She rolled her eyes. "Even if I agree to wear a disguise, Chase has to get, like, approval from his boss and then they have to make sure there's another shifter available to go with us."

She sighed dramatically before taking a sip of coffee. "I think they're going a little overboard."

"They're not," Ryan said. "They're being paid to keep us safe."

"I know." Ryleigh studied the three shifters before grinning at Ryan. "So, your guy is super cute for an old guy."

"He's not old and keep your voice down. They have excellent hearing, remember?"

"Pfft," Ryleigh waved her hand in the air, "there's too much background noise for them to hear us." She studied the shifters before smiling and waving at them. Chase waved back but Grayson and Wes didn't move.

Ryleigh made a low snort. "The really old one – Wes - is,

like, super creepy. He barely spoke a word in the car over here."

"Okay, one, neither Grayson nor Wes is old," Ryan said in a low voice. "Grayson's probably my age or a little older and Wes looks like he's in his forties. That's not old, Ryleigh. And two – not talking a lot doesn't make a person creepy. It just makes them quiet."

Ryleigh grinned at her. "Spoken like a true introvert."

"How is Mom doing with her bodyguard?"

"Fine." Ryleigh made a careless shrug. "She's barely left her room since they arrived. The guy protecting her is Boone, and he spends most of his time standing guard in the hallway outside her bedroom door."

"She must have a stash of liquor in her room again," Ryan said.

"She does." The happy-go-lucky grin on Ryleigh's face slipped. "Her drinking is getting worse."

"There isn't much we can do, sweetie." Ryan took her sister's hand and squeezed. "We've tried how many times to get her into rehab? We can't force her to go."

"I know. It's just – she's drunk like all the time now. When she bothers to show up for a meal, her and Grandmother fight through the whole thing. It's seriously bringing me down. Filming for the second season starts soon and Saul says he's never seen my skin and hair looking so drab. It's the stress, Ry-Ry."

"You should move out, honey. Get your own place. You're too old to be living with Grandmother now."

Ryleigh shrugged again. "I'm not like you. I don't want to be alone, you know? I'd be lonely in a place by myself."

"You could stay with me for a bit," Ryan said. She cringed inwardly, hoping her dismay at the idea of Ryleigh living with her didn't show on her face. It wasn't that she didn't love her sister, she just really valued her privacy and Ryleigh had a way of… taking over a space.

"Uh, that's sweet, but God no," Ryleigh said with a laugh. "You need your own space because you're a weirdo introvert, and no offense to Sam, you know I love him, but the idea of having dog hair on everything… ugh. Besides, your place is way too small for me. Like, seriously, honey, you have sooo much money. Buy a mansion for God's sake."

"I don't need a bigger place. It's just me and Sam." Ryan glanced at Grayson. "Well, and Grayson."

Ryleigh leaned forward with a salacious look on her face. "So, you hitting that yet, or what?"

"Ryleigh! Keep your voice down." Ryan wanted to smack her baby sister. "They can hear you."

"So, that's a yes then?"

"No, it is not a yes." Ryan took too big of a sip of coffee, wincing when the scalding liquid burned her tongue. "He's my bodyguard, nothing else."

"You want to bang him like a screen door though," Ryleigh announced with delicious satisfaction.

"I am going to straight up murder you. You know that, right?" Ryan said between gritted teeth.

Ryleigh giggled, her blue eyes dancing with mischief. "You gotta loosen up, Ry-Ry. When was the last time you got laid?"

"That is none of your business."

"I'm just saying," Ryleigh glanced at Grayson, "he's sexy as hell and you're all alone in that tiny house of yours. Things…happen."

"No *things* are going to happen," Ryan said. She stared suspiciously at Chase and then at Ryleigh. "You are not sleeping with that kid, are you?"

Ryleigh's grin was cheeky and infuriating. "What is it you told me? That it's none of your business?"

"Ryleigh, they are here to do a job," Ryan said. "Don't distract him by flirting."

"There's nothing wrong with a little flirting. You should try it every once in a while," Ryleigh said. "Besides, you can't expect me not to flirt with Chase. He's super cute and I'm so damn bored."

She made a dramatic motion with her hands. "Chase has a crush on me, I can tell."

"Everyone has a crush on you," Ryan said. "You're the most famous actress on television right now."

Ryleigh's smile was so bright it could have guided lost sailors back to shore. "I am, aren't I?"

Ryan laughed, her irritation with her baby sister disappearing under a wave of affection. "Yeah, you are."

"It's so great. I love being me." Ryleigh made another preening little smile.

Before Ryan could reply, the door to the coffee shop opened and a crushing wave of tourists flooded in. She grimaced as, laughing and talking loudly, they crowded toward the cashier to order their coffees.

As they passed by their table, she automatically ducked her head, even though she was certain none of them would recognize her. Even after all these years, old habits died hard. Her skin was starting to itch, and her pulse was kicking it up a notch, and she had to stop herself from standing up and just fleeing the coffee shop as more people crowded in.

She wasn't an agoraphobic, but she hated crowds, hated having so many people in her personal space.

She let go of her coffee before she crushed the paper cup, and stuck her hands into her lap, curling them into tight fists. She was fine. No one would recognize her. She was fine.

As more and more tourists crowded into the tiny café, her panic grew. Why had she agreed to go to this coffee shop? It was right on a popular bus tour route and tourists were always showing up. Beside her, Ryleigh was tapping on her phone, completely oblivious to Ryan's growing distress.

You're fine. Do not flip out. It'll only make things worse.

A woman with a bright pink *Hello Kitty* backpack and wide hips, jostled into her as she passed by. "Sorry!" she chirped cheerfully before passing on by.

Her nails digging into her palms, Ryan dragged in a breath. It wasn't nearly enough oxygen, but she couldn't seem to get her breathing to slow down, couldn't seem to get her heart rate back to a normal rhythm.

Oh God, no. Having a panic attack right now would be the worst possible timing.

The weight developing on her chest grew heavier, the talking of the tourists grew excruciatingly loud, and the tapping of Ryleigh's phone was a rhythmic beat that threatened to drive her mad.

Shit.

"Ryan, take a deep breath." Grayson's big body crouched in front of her, one heavy hand sliding around the back of her neck and cupping firmly as his face appeared in front of hers.

He squeezed her neck, his low voice somehow drowning out all the other sounds in the café. "One deep breath, Ryan. Take just one deep breath for me, honey."

She stared at him, her hand clutching at his when he placed it over her fist. His thumb rubbed the side of her neck as he linked their fingers together and he smiled encouragingly. "One deep breath, honey. That's all I want."

She sucked in air, her nostrils flaring as she filled her lungs deep.

"Good. Now release it."

She let it go in a harsh rush. Grayson rubbed her neck again. "Do it again."

She took in another breath and then another, staring at Grayson as her heartbeat slowed. His big body kept tourists from jostling her, his intense gaze demanded her attention, and she could feel the bright edge of panic slowly receding.

"Good," he said. "Better?"

"Yes, thank you."

"Okay. If you're up to it, you're going to stand up for me and then we'll walk out of here nice and slow."

She shook her head. "No, I need to stay."

He frowned. "You don't."

"I do," she said. "My therapist says it's a good idea to work through the-the panic and then try and stay for a while in the situation that made me panic."

Grayson glanced at her sister. She was still staring at her phone and hadn't even noticed him. Ryan wasn't surprised. She loved Ryleigh, but her sister was a bit insensitive when it came to anything that wasn't directly about her.

"Are you sure?" Grayson asked.

"Yes. I'm better now. Thank you. That, uh, helped a lot."

"You're welcome." He gave her neck one final gentle squeeze before letting go of her and standing. His motion finally caught Ryleigh's attention and she glanced up from her phone.

Her I'm-adorable-and-I-know-it smile fell firmly into place. "Hi there. We haven't formally met. I'm Ryleigh."

"Grayson." He shook her hand before staring at Ryan again. "You sure you're okay?"

A line creased between Ryleigh's eyebrows, almost hidden behind the glasses she was wearing. "Why wouldn't she be okay?"

Her gaze switched to Ryan. "Ry-Ry? What's wrong?"

"Nothing's wrong," Ryan said. Her sister had no idea about her panic attacks, and she planned on keeping it that way. "Grayson just, uh, had a question he needed answered."

"Oh," Ryleigh brightened, "well, you're asking the right person. Ryan is simply brilliant. The smartest person I know. And so pretty, don't you think?"

Great. The last thing she needed right now was Ryleigh playing wingwoman.

"We won't be too much longer," Ryan said before Grayson could reply. "Thank you again."

He studied her for a moment before turning and pushing his way through the now crowded café to their table. He sat down, continuing to stare at her, as Wes leaned over and spoke into his ear.

"He's intense," Ryleigh said.

"A little," Ryan replied.

Ryleigh leaned back in her chair, studying the crowd of people milling about the café. She stroked absently at the dark wig she was wearing. "How good do you think these guys are at their job?"

"What do you mean?" Ryan asked.

Ryleigh shrugged. "Just wondering if they're worth the money that Grandmother is shelling out."

"Whatever you're thinking, stop," Ryan said as fresh alarm bells went off in her head.

An impish grin crossed Ryleigh's face. "There's no harm in finding out if they're worth the cost, Ry-Ry."

"Ryleigh, don't -"

Ryleigh pulled off the dark wig she was wearing with a flourish and sat it on the table. Her long blonde hair was in a low bun and she pulled out the elastic, smoothing her hair before taking off her glasses and setting them next to the wig.

Her smile widened as she waved at the woman who had

slowed to a stop next to their table. "Oh my God, are you…
are you Ryleigh Shepherd?"

"I sure am," Ryleigh said.

"Oh my God, I love you!" The woman squealed like a
rusty hinge, the sound drilling into Ryan's skull.

"Aren't you sweet," Ryleigh cocked her head at her.
"Would you like an autograph?"

"Yes! Oh my God, yes! Oh shit, I need paper. I need some
paper! Who has paper?" The woman's voice was shrill and
eager, and Ryan muttered a curse when everyone in the coffee
shop looked their way.

There was a collective gasp, a murmur of excitement
went through the crowd, and Ryleigh's grin grew.

"Here we go," she said to Ryan.

"Oh fuck," Ryan said as the people surged toward them.

She stood up as Ryleigh did, trying to reach for her
sister's hand, but there was already a herd of tourists
surrounding her.

Frantic shouts filled the shop as more and more people
crowded closer. Cameras were behind held up in the air as
people tried to get a picture of Ryleigh.

A woman, her face bright red, grabbed a handful of
Ryleigh's hair and yanked on it. Ryleigh cried out in pain as
the woman squealed to another woman behind her, "Holy
shit, it's real! I thought it was a wig, swear to God, Jennifer!
It ain't a wig!"

"Ryan!" The fear in Ryleigh's voice cut through the
growing panic in Ryan's chest. She fought to get to her sister,
but the flood of people was crushing her. She was trapped
between a sweaty, foul-smelling man wearing a trucker hat
and a woman in a flowered dress wearing so much perfume it
practically dripped from her pores.

She cried out when the woman, her hands jerking wildly

in excitement, scratched her across the cheek. There was stinging pain and liquid dripped down her cheek. The man in the trucker hat raised his arms and bellowed Ryleigh's name as he surged forward. The man in front of him turned and shoved him back. Sweaty man stumbled, his elbow slamming into the side of Ryan's face.

Little flashes of light swarmed across her vision and she was immediately lightheaded. Her cheek throbbed in agony and she swallowed down bile as she shook her head. More pain flooded through her.

She was going to die in a goddamn coffee shop. Squashed to death between a woman who'd bathed in Obsession by Calvin Klein and a man who hadn't bathed since God was a baby.

"Move!"

The loud and angry growl was a soothing balm to her ears. The perfume-laden woman was jostled aside, and Ryan flailed for Grayson's wide shoulders like a woman drowning. He slipped an arm around her waist and pulled her up against him, his big body protecting her from the riot of tourists.

"Ryleigh!" Ryan gasped out when Grayson lifted her into his arms. "Help Ryleigh first!"

Grayson ignored her, turning and pushing his way through the crowd of people. She tried to get free, wiggling and squirming in his arms.

He squeezed her tight and growled, "Stay still."

"Ryleigh! You need to help Ryleigh!"

"Chase and Wes will help her."

"No!" She stared at him in panic as he kicked open the door to the coffee shop and carried her out into the bright sunlight. "Grayson, go back!"

Still ignoring her, he carried her to the SUV. He set her on her feet, clamping one arm around her waist when she tried to run back toward the café, and opened the back-passenger door before lifting her and tossing her inside. He climbed in beside her and slid across the seat when she immediately scrambled to open the opposite door. He grabbed her wrist.

"Ryan, enough!"

"Ryleigh needs help! Let go of me."

"Enough!" His angry growl made her freeze in place. He cupped the back of her neck again and slid closer until her back was pressed against the door and their faces were only inches apart.

"Please help her," she whispered.

"My job is to protect you." His voice was raspy, and his eyes had turned a bright jade, their pupils narrow slits as he stared directly at her.

There was the loud roar of an angry cat, and Ryan winced as Grayson looked out the windshield. "Stay here."

He opened the back door and jumped out. Ryan cried out with relief when she saw Chase with Ryleigh in his arms, running across the parking lot toward them. He dumped her on the seat next to Ryan and climbed in after her. Grayson ripped open the driver's side door and slid behind the wheel.

"Where's Wes?" He started the vehicle as Chase slammed the back door shut.

"Holding back the crowd," Chase said. He was panting and his dark eyes had turned bright yellow. "He should be… there he is!"

Ryan watched with wide-eyed panic as Wes came busting out of the front door of the coffee shop. He ran across the lot as Grayson leaned over and opened the door. He threw the SUV into reverse and stepped on the gas as Wes shot into the car like a bullet. He slammed the door shut and Grayson put the car into drive as the horde of tourists ran across the parking lot, screaming Ryleigh's name.

"Go, Grayson, go!" Chase shouted.

Grayson tore out of the parking lot and onto the street, barely missing a blue Camaro. The Camaro's driver honked his horn and stuck his hand out the sunroof, his middle finger jabbing into the air, the gigantic fuck you a testament to Grayson's wild driving. Ignoring him, Grayson stepped on the gas, leaving the café and the crowd of tourists behind them.

"Ryleigh, sweetie, are you okay?" Ryan scanned Ryleigh's face and body, adrenaline making her voice too loud and too high.

"Yeah, I'm okay. I'm fine," Ryleigh whispered and then burst into tears.

Ryan pulled her into her arms, hugging her hard and kissing the top of her head. "You're all right, sweetie."

She rocked Ryleigh back and forth as Chase leaned against the back of the seat. His shirt was ripped, and he rubbed at the top of his skull. "Fuck, some woman ripped out a chunk of my hair when I was picking up Ryleigh. Thank fucking Christ we brought Wes with us. We wouldn't have gotten out of there alive. What the fuck is wrong with people?"

He took a deep breath before reaching out and squeezing Wes's shoulder. "You okay, man?"

Ryan studied the older man as Ryleigh sobbed quietly into her shoulder. His shirt was hanging in tatters around his body and she could see red scratches across his arms.

"I'm good," he said.

"You sure?" Grayson gave his destroyed shirt a quick glance.

"Yeah, there were two women at the front of the mob who scratched my arms up some, but they didn't do this to my shirt. I almost had to shift to keep them back once we got Ryleigh out of the cafe."

"Fuck," Chase said. "Did you see that cougar shifter completely lose it? She shifted and tore some guy's leg open trying to jump over him to get to Ryleigh."

"Yeah, I saw it," Wes said.

Sirens wailed in the distance. Grayson stared at Ryan and Ryleigh in the rear-view mirror. Her sister's quiet sobs had slowed to the occasional sniffle. "What the fuck were you thinking taking off your disguise?"

"I'm sorry," Ryleigh whispered. "I wasn't – I mean, I didn't think…"

"No, you didn't think," Grayson snapped. "You acted impulsively, and you almost got your sister crushed to death by a mob of people."

"Stop it, Grayson," Ryan said.

"Do you have any idea how close you just came to seriously injuring or killing your sister?" Grayson carried on relentlessly.

"They were hurting me too," Ryleigh whispered.

Grayson snarled at her, his eyes flashing bright jade. "And whose fault is that?"

"Gray," Wes said quietly.

"She needs to understand that there are consequences to her actions," Grayson growled.

"I didn't mean to do it, okay?" Ryleigh started to cry again, throwing herself into Ryan's arms. "Ry-Ry, it was an accident."

"I know," Ryan said, "I know it was, sweetie. It's -"

"Don't you dare tell her it's all right," Grayson said. His hands gripped the steering wheel until it creaked. "She could have gotten you killed, Ryan."

"It was an accident." Ryan glared at him as Ryleigh sobbed harder. "Let it go, Grayson."

"Let it go? Ryan, you -"

"Enough, Gray." Wes's hand landed on his shoulder hard enough to make Grayson wince. "We can talk about this later when everyone's calmed down."

Grayson stared grimly at Ryan in the rear-view mirror. She returned his look for a few seconds before turning and staring out the window as Ryleigh continued to sob in her arms.

CHAPTER 6

"Sit down." Grayson pointed at the stool next to the island.

"I'm going to my room," she said stiffly.

"You're sitting down so I can clean that scratch on your face," Grayson said.

"I can clean it myself."

Sam was sitting between them and he cocked his head before making a low whine. Grayson took a deep breath, soothing his restless, pacing tiger. "Ryan, please."

Her stiff body slumped a little and he could see the shine of tears in her eyes. "I'm fine, Grayson."

"Let me just take a look at it, okay?"

She chewed on her bottom lip before nodding and sitting down on the stool. Sam leaned against her lower legs and she petted the top of his head. "There's a first-aid kit in the cupboard under the sink in the half-bath."

He left her in the kitchen, walking down the hallway to the bathroom and grabbing the kit from under the sink. He stared at himself in the mirror, at the way his eyes were the bright green of his cat, the pupils narrow slits.

He took a deep breath, his alarm at just how panicked

he'd felt when Ryan had been mobbed by the crowd of people still pulsing through his veins. His tiger made a low whimper of distress and he soothed it again before returning to the kitchen.

Ryan was texting at the island, and he opened the kit and removed a disinfectant wipe. She set her phone down on the counter. "That was Ryleigh. She wanted to know how my cheek was, and to make sure we got home okay after dropping them off at Grandmother's."

He snorted, and she scowled. "She's a good person, Grayson. She just made a mistake."

He ripped open the packaging and studied her cheek. "The scratch is deep."

"Yeah, everyone in California has those dangerous fake nails."

He didn't smile at her weak joke. Instead, he cupped her neck and swiped the disinfectant across the scratch on her cheek. She hissed, her body straining to get away from him. He held her tightly and, without thinking, he purred to her.

She blinked at him as he wiped the smears of blood from her cheek. "Did you just purr?"

"No." He could feel heat rising up the back of his neck.

"Um, yeah, you did."

He ignored her and finished cleaning up the blood before studying the cheek. "It's deep but I don't think it needs stitches. This though…"

He touched her other cheek, already a bruise was blossoming into life against her pale skin. She made a low sound of pain and his goddamn tiger pushed forward and purred to her again.

"That was definitely a purr." She paused. "Now you're blushing."

"I'm not blushing."

"But you are purring."

"Fine. I'm purring. It happens sometimes. It's no big deal."

She studied him. "I like it."

He clamped his mouth shut around the purr that immediately wanted to escape. Jesus, his tiger was losing its mind. "Yeah, well, it doesn't mean anything."

"Are all tiger shifters this surly about accidental purring?"

He didn't want to find her cute and funny right now. He wanted to hang on to his anger with her, but Christ, she was making it difficult.

"She could have gotten you killed, Ryan," he said.

The smile dropped from her face. "It was an accident."

"Taking off the wig and glasses was deliberate. You know that," he said.

She sighed. "Look, I told you that Ryleigh is impulsive. She doesn't always consider the consequences of her actions, okay?"

"Why are you defending her? You're scratched and bruised and you're acting like she's a toddler who has no control over her decisions or actions."

"Stop it," she said. "You don't know me or my sister, so stop right now before you say something that'll make me kick you out of my house."

"Ryan, she needs to be held responsible. You can't just let her get away with -"

"Enough, Grayson." She crossed her arms over her chest and glared at him. "Ryleigh is my sister and she means everything to me. Okay? I will defend her until my last breath. She didn't mean to hurt me. End of story."

"You're not doing her any favours by allowing her behaviour to continue the way it is."

"I said stop. You have no idea what it was like for her

growing up, and yeah, maybe she's a little immature, but she's a good person with a good heart. So, stop talking shit about her. Got it?"

"Got it," he ground out.

Her body slumped and she touched the growing bruise on her face gingerly. "One last thing. I appreciate what you did for me today, but in the future, the priority is Ryleigh. If something like this happens again, you make sure she's safe before -"

She gasped, her eyes going wide when he cupped her face and made a low growl. He bent his head until he could feel her warm breath on his mouth. "My priority is you and only you, Ryan Shepherd. My job is to keep you safe and that's what I'm going to do. There will be no arguing on this point. I'll keep my opinions about your sister to myself, but I'll also do my job."

He couldn't resist running his thumb along her bottom lip, loving the way it made her eyes darken and her arousal flare to life. "Tell me what my job is, Ryan."

She swallowed before licking her lips. "Grayson -"

"Tell me."

"Keeping me safe," she whispered.

"That's right." His gaze flickered to her bruised cheek. "The only thing I care about, the only thing that's important to me, is keeping you safe. Understand?"

"Yes."

He wanted to kiss her. He wanted to take her upstairs, undress her, and bury himself deep inside her body. He wanted to fuck her until she was moaning his name and begging him to make her cum.

Instead, he released her and took a step back. "Good. Do you like quesadillas?"

She blinked at him, her body swaying a little as she reached for the island to steady herself. "What?"

"It's almost lunch and I'm hungry. I make a mean chicken and cheese quesadilla. Do you want one?"

She licked her lips again before nodding. "Yes, please."

"YOU WEREN'T KIDDING ABOUT YOUR QUESADILLA MAKING skills." Ryan smeared sour cream on her bite of quesadilla and stuffed it into her mouth.

"I never joke about quesadillas," Grayson said so solemnly that she couldn't help but laugh again.

He removed the last quesadilla from the pan and sliced it in quarters then put half on her plate and half on his. He spread avocado across the top before spearing a bite and popping it into his mouth. "So, what's on the agenda for this afternoon?"

"Finishing up the edits on Mark and Ashley's photo shoot."

"You don't have a photo shoot today?" He drank some water before eating more quesadilla.

"No. But I have two tomorrow. One in the morning and one in the afternoon."

"Indoors or outdoors?"

"Both indoors. So, you enjoy cooking, huh?"

"I wouldn't say I enjoy it," he replied. "But when you're a bachelor, you learn to cook some easy meals. The alternative is to be like Boone and just exist on raw meat and coffee."

"So, no girlfriend?"

"No." He caught her gaze briefly before looking at his food again.

"Boyfriend?"

He shook his head, a small grin curling up his lips. "I think after last night you're well aware I'm into women."

"You could be into both."

"True," he acknowledged. "But I'm not."

She tried not to let her excitement show. No doubt he could smell it, but she didn't need him to also *see* that she was thrilled he wasn't in a romantic relationship. It wasn't like anything was going to happen between them. He was here because of his job.

He thinks you're pretty.

She could feel warmth infusing her skin. He did think she was pretty, and she couldn't deny that she liked it.

He was staring at her, his nostrils flaring as he inhaled. She cleared her throat. "Where did you learn to cook so well?"

"Cooking shows," he replied.

She laughed. "You're kidding me?"

"Nope. You can learn a lot from the Food Network."

There was silence that wasn't uncomfortable, but she cast about for something to say anyway. She didn't want this moment to end. "What kind of shifters are Chase and Wes?"

"Chase is a cheetah shifter and Wes is a lion."

"And Boone?"

"Tiger like me. Cooper is a lion shifter," he added before she could ask.

"Is that everyone who works there?"

"No. Cooper has a few other part time employees who handle some of our easier assignments. And we have an admin person named Daisy. She's human."

"What other celebrities have you protected?" she asked.

"You're the first." He licked away a bit of avocado from his lower lip. "We don't normally provide security for celebrities."

"So, why did you this time?"

He shrugged. "You'd have to ask Coop that. He's the boss, I just work here."

She smiled a little. "How did you meet him?"

He pushed away his empty plate before drinking the last of his water. "Cooper, Boone, Wes, and I were in the military together. Special forces. Coop got out and started up his own company, and then one-by-one we all joined him."

"Why did you leave the military?"

He shrugged, but there was a tenseness in his shoulders that hadn't been there a few seconds ago. "We had a mission that went... bad. All of us in the unit were tight back then, but the five of us were particularly close."

"Five?" Her stomach felt like razor blades were jostling for place in it, and she reached across the island and touched Grayson's hand. He immediately linked their fingers together, his gaze still on his empty plate.

"His name was Derek. He was a jaguar shifter and so goddamn serious all the time. Boone used to drive him crazy with his constant talking and joking, but..."

"What?" she said after a moment.

"In some ways, he and Boone were the closest. Which made it even worse when he died in Boone's arms."

"I'm so sorry," she whispered.

"We all were. There are so many rumours and false shit about shifters, but the one I hate the most is that we can't be hurt or killed or that we," he waved his free hand in the air, "can heal instantly. It's bullshit, you know?"

"I do," she said.

"Shifters are just as vulnerable as humans. I don't know where the fuck the rumour about our instant healing got started, but it isn't true. We watched Derek fucking bleed out in Boone's arms and couldn't do a goddamn thing about it."

"I'm so sorry," she repeated. He was squeezing her hand so tight that she was losing circulation in her fingers, but she didn't try to pull away. She couldn't. Not with that lost and vulnerable look on his face.

"Anyway, Cooper was already thinking about leaving and Derek's death pushed him to make the decision. After that... it didn't feel right anymore. Not without Coop and not without Derek. Boone and I left at the same time and then a year later, Wes was out.

He stared blankly at their linked fingers before shaking his head to clear it. He released her hand, frowning when he saw the white marks that were slowly turning a dull red. "Jesus, I'm sorry."

"It's okay."

He stood up abruptly. "I didn't mean to hurt you."

"It's fine."

He loaded his plate into the dishwasher before putting the pan in the sink. She massaged the feeling back into her hand as he added dish soap and ran some hot water into the pan. Sam was sitting at her feet, his tail wagging hopefully. She petted his head and then held her plate next to his face. He licked away the remnants of sour cream and cheese, his tail thumping against the floor.

Grayson turned to face her. "Is your hand all right? I'm sorry, I... okay, that's gross."

She laughed. "It's not gross."

"Your dog is licking your plate, Ryan."

"It's not like I'm going to lick it when he's done," she said.

His retching motion made a laugh come busting out of her throat. "You're kind of squeamish, aren't you?"

"I'm not getting up in the middle of the night to let your

dog out because he has raging diarrhea from the sour cream," he warned.

She slid off the stool and petted Sam's head. "He's got a cast iron stomach. Don't be such a worrywart, *Dolores*."

"Hey, I revealed that very personal bit of information under the assumption that you would take it to your grave," he said.

She stuck her fork and knife and spit-shiny plate into the dishwasher and leaned against the counter next to him. "Are you trying to tell me that none of your cat shifter buddies know what your middle name is?"

"Of course, they don't. I'd never hear the end of it from Boone. Hell, he still gives Cooper shit for crocheting."

"Cooper crochets?"

"Yeah. Says it relaxes him. Last year for Christmas, he gave me six dishcloths and a teapot cozy."

She gave in to the giggles that wanted to be free. "You're kidding me."

"I'm not. Right now, he's making Wes a granny square blanket for his birthday."

"You are talking about the big blonde dude with tattoos from my grandmother's house, right?"

"Yep."

"He crochets."

"Uh-huh."

"Well, that's very…"

"Artistic?" Grayson supplied.

"Yes, artistic," she said with another giggle.

His smile was infectious and gorgeous. She was suddenly itching to photograph him. This morning before leaving for coffee, she'd been taking pictures of Sam in the backyard. Her camera was still sitting on the counter and she reached for it, taking off the lens cap as Grayson raised an eyebrow.

"What are you doing?"

"I'd like to take your picture. Can I?"

"Why?"

"I'm a photographer. It's what I do."

"I'm not photogenic."

"Everyone says that. It's rarely true."

"This time it's true," he said.

"Just a couple quick shots… please?" she wheedled.

That adorable grin was toying at his lips again and before he could protest, she raised her camera and fired off two shots.

"I didn't say yes," he said sternly but there was amusement in his eyes.

"Sorry," she said as she flicked over to view mode on her camera screen.

"You don't sound sorry."

"You got me. I'm not sorry." She showed him the screen. She was actually pretty happy with the two pictures she got, considering that she hadn't adjusted her aperture or her shutter speed. "You're a natural. Look at how cute you are."

He grimaced. "Please tell me you didn't just describe me as cute."

"What's wrong with cute?"

"Fuzzy little kittens are cute. Chubby-cheeked racoons holding bananas are cute."

"Raccoons are not chubby cheeked, nor do they hold bananas," she said.

He took a step closer, one hand reaching out to tug on a lock of her hair. "Babies dressed up as flowers are cute."

Her breath caught in her throat when he inched even closer. She clutched her camera in one hand, staring up at him as he placed his hands on the counter on either side of her and penned her in.

"Big… ferocious… tiger shifters are not…cute."

His warm breath washed over her face and his light green eyes were dancing with amusement and something else. Something that made her stomach muscles clench and her pussy wet and her nipples turn to diamond chips against her bra.

She wanted to kiss him. She wanted to take him upstairs and do very naughty things to him.

His nostrils flared and his eyes glowed. For almost a minute, they turned a darker jade and his pupils turned to narrow slits. She waited, watching in fascination, as he spoke internally to his tiger. When his pupils returned to normal, she stood on her tiptoes and pressed her mouth against his.

He froze against her. She had a moment to think she'd made a stupid mistake before his big body pressed up against hers and his hand cupped the back of her neck. He angled his mouth over hers, his tongue pressing against her lips. She opened her mouth, moaning when he slid his tongue between her lips and tasted every part of her mouth.

Mother of God, the tiger shifter could *kiss*.

She returned his kiss eagerly, reaching behind her to blindly set her camera on the counter. She wrapped her arms around his broad shoulders and parted her legs when he pressed one thick thigh between them.

His kisses went from almost sweet to hot and demanding and… she moaned again when he rubbed his thigh against her pussy… delightfully filthy. He kissed her like a man drowning, releasing her mouth only to give her the chance to suck in a few quick breaths before he took her mouth again.

She slid her fingers into the thick dark hair at the base of his skull, clutching tightly as his hand skimmed the curve of her hip and up her waist. His fingers traced the side of her breast and below it.

She made an impatient sound of need, arching her back and rocking her pussy against his rock-hard thigh. When his big hand finally cupped her breast, his fingers finding her hard nipple through her t-shirt and her bra, she was fairly certain she would be able to cum like this. Just the hard length of his thigh against her pussy and his fingers pulling on her nipple… yep, that would work just fine for her.

His other hand moved to her face, his hand cupping her jaw. His thumb brushed across her cheek and when it touched the bruise, she couldn't stop her wince.

He pulled back immediately, moving his hand to the back of her neck and holding her firmly when she tried to kiss him again. "I'm sorry. I shouldn't have done that."

"It's fine," she said. "It's just a little tender. Come upstairs with me."

He released her and stepped away. The look on his face made her cheeks burn with embarrassment. "You don't want to have sex with me."

His laugh was weirdly bitter. When he reached down and adjusted his jeans, she stared at the obvious bulge in his crotch, trying not to drool. "Trust me, I want to have sex with you."

She reached for his hand. "Then let's go upstairs."

"I can't," he said. "Cooper has a rule – no sleeping with clients."

Disappointment flooded through her. "I won't tell if you don't."

"Trust me, it's tempting, but I can't betray Cooper like that. Look, I'm sorry, I shouldn't have -"

"Stop it," she said. "I kissed you, remember? You don't have to apologize. I should be the one apologizing for -"

He shook his head. "Don't say you're sorry for kissing me, Ryan."

She reached instinctively for her camera, fiddling with the settings as she avoided looking at him. "Maybe I could ask Cooper to switch you and Chase. If you're not actively protecting me then…"

"No." His tone turned brutal and unyielding. "I am the best one to keep you safe, Ryan. Not Chase."

She studied him, her fingers stilling on her camera. "Can Chase keep Ryleigh safe? He's really young, right? How much experience does he have? Because if he can't keep her safe, then -"

"She's safe with him." Grayson ran his fingers through his hair in obvious frustration. "Look, even if I was reassigned to someone else in your family, I still wouldn't feel right sleeping with you. You're the client and -"

"I know," she said. "There isn't an obvious work around to the problem. I'm grasping at straws because I really want to bang you."

He huffed laughter. "Ditto."

She rubbed at the back of her neck. Her lips felt swollen and hot and if she had to spend another minute staring at Grayson's damn erection, she'd go mad. "I'm gonna go do some editing in my studio. Just, uh, make yourself at home, okay?"

He nodded and cursing her really terrible, awful, stupidly bad luck, she trudged out of the kitchen.

CHAPTER 7

"What's that?" Grayson stared at the box in Ryan's hand as she walked down the stairs.

It was just after seven. Ryan had worked all afternoon and through dinner, stopping around five just long enough to grab a bowl of cereal to take back upstairs.

He'd spent the afternoon petting Sam, texting with Boone, and googling more information about Ryan. He was an official goddamn stalker now, but he couldn't help it. He was fascinated by the human, and it wasn't just him. His tiger was rapidly becoming obsessed.

He couldn't blame it. After kissing Ryan, after hearing her moan, and smelling her arousal, he could barely contain his urge to say 'fuck Cooper's rules' and take her to his bed.

His tiger purred in agreement. It tried to bust free, it really wanted to mark Ryan, and he held it back grimly.

Let me free!

No, he snapped. *You can't mark the human. One, she's a client, and two, we barely know her. We're not marking someone we just fucking met.*

His tiger retreated with a whine and he gave Ryan who

was now standing at the island, an apologetic look. "Sorry about that."

"It's fine," she said. "How many times a day do you talk to your tiger?"

He shrugged. "Depends on how much he has to say that day. Mine is on the quieter side, usually. Boone's never shuts up."

She laughed as he joined her at the island. He studied the box she'd set on the counter. "A puzzle?"

"A puzzle," she said. "Can you grab the card table that's tucked behind the couch and set it up for me?"

He peered behind the couch, grabbed the table and hauled it out. "You're going to put together a puzzle tonight?"

"*We're* going to put together a puzzle tonight."

He cocked his head at her. "You want us to put a puzzle together."

"No," she set the box on the card table and opened it up, shaking the puzzle pieces out, "what I want is for us to have sex."

"We can't," he said.

"I know that." She dragged over a chair from the kitchen table and set it down next to the card table. "Grab that other chair, would you?"

He grabbed the other chair and brought it over as she let Sam out into the backyard and then grabbed two beers from the fridge. "Can you drink beer while on duty?"

"I can have one," he said.

"Cool." She opened the beers and brought them over. She set them on the card table and folded one leg under her as she sat down. She took a sip of beer and started flipping over the puzzle pieces.

He sat down. "Seriously, Ryan?"

She leaned back and took another drink of beer. "Look,

we can sit here together for the evening in awkward boy-I-wish-we-were-having-sex-right-now silence, or we can do something creative and challenging that keeps our hands busy. Your choice."

He drank a swallow of beer. "Puzzle, it is."

"YOU'RE TERRIBLE AT PUZZLES."

Gray scowled at Ryan. "I'm amazing at puzzles."

"It's been an hour and I've got most of the outside put together. What have you done?" she said with a grin.

"I put all the red pieces in a pile together." Gray pointed at the pile of red before trying to hammer a piece of puzzle into the one beside it.

"That doesn't fit."

"It almost fits."

"Almost fits doesn't count in a puzzle." Ryan took the piece of puzzle from him. "Those pieces would never have worked together."

"They might have."

She pointed to the rounded end of the puzzle piece. "It's way too big for the hole."

"That's what she said."

Her grin was adorable and only slightly evil. "Maybe it's better that we're not allowed to have sex. Watching you try and ram that into place makes me a little nervous."

"Trust me, gorgeous, my sex skills are far superior to my puzzle skills. If I'm ramming my dick into you, it's because you're begging me to do it." He let his gaze linger on her tits, gratified when a soft blush crept up her neck.

"Are all tiger shifters this cocky?"

"You say cocky, I say confident." He grinned in amusement when she took a look at his crotch. "Hey, lady, my eyes are up here."

She rubbed delicately under her eye with her middle finger, making him laugh, before she finished the last of her beer. "Stop distracting me with dick talk. This puzzle isn't going to finish itself."

He bent over the puzzle, mentally berating himself for flirting. He needed to keep it strictly professional between them. He took a sip of beer and then said, "How many people are in the inner circle of your mother and sister?"

She cocked her head in thought before ticking off names on her fingers, "Let's see, there's our lawyer Christopher, my sister's manager Bert – he was also my mother's manager – Peter and Mary, Saul, and Lori. Saul is Ryleigh's personal stylist and makeup guy, and Lori is Vanessa's PA. Then there's the housekeeping staff. Since Mary retired, Grandmother hired a company to do cleaning, but I think they send the same people every week. But I wouldn't consider them to be in the 'inner circle', so to speak."

"The others who are in the inner circle - they all get along well with your family?"

"Yes, for the most part. Vanessa can be difficult to get along with."

"Who's the closest to them?"

She frowned. "Depends on what you mean by closest. Peter has the greatest access to them, I guess, followed by Lori and then Saul. All three of them are at the house every day. Saul is also Ryleigh's best friend, so he spends a lot of time with her. Lori is basically at Vanessa's beck and call."

"Does Ryleigh have a boyfriend?" he asked.

She pushed another piece of puzzle into place. "No."

"You're sure?"

"Positive. Ryleigh wouldn't keep something like that from me."

"What about Saul? You said they were best friends, could they be something more?"

"Nope. Saul is gay." She glanced up at him. "He and Ryleigh are really close, Grayson. He would never hurt her."

"What about Peter?"

"What about him?" She laughed in disbelief. "You met Peter. The guy is seventy-three years old and suffers from arthritis. Not to mention, he's the most honorable, wonderful man I've ever known. Why are you asking me these questions? You guys are a security team, not private investigators."

"I know," he said. "But knowing of anyone who might have a problem or a grudge against your family, helps us be more effective at our job."

Her scowl deepened. "Peter and Mary have *nothing* to do with the threat, Grayson. Stay away from them. If anyone on your team starts harassing them or even suggesting they're suspects, my grandmother will fire you so fast, your head will spin."

"All right." He kept his voice low and non-threatening.

"I'm serious. They mean a lot to our family and if you're even hinting that you think they have something to with this -"

"I'm not," he said. "I'm just trying to help, Ryan. I swear."

She took a deep breath, obviously calming herself, and said, "Sorry. I'm – we all are – a little protective of them. They're not just employees, okay? They're family and I – *we* – love them a great deal."

"Okay," he said. "What about the lawyer and the manager?"

"I doubt Christopher has anything to do with this. He's the one who urged Vanessa to get protection for us and made all the necessary calls and arrangements. As for Bert…"

He looked up from the puzzle. "What?"

"I'm not saying he did it or anything, but he and my mother do have a contentious relationship. But," she stressed, "they always have. He's been my mother's manager since we were in *Alien Hunter* and they fought back then too."

"What did they fight about?"

"Anything and everything related to Mom's career and mine." She picked at the edge of the puzzle piece she was holding. "He was really angry when I emancipated myself and quit the show and acting. They were in the middle of discussing a spin-off to *Alien Hunter* with the network that would feature Vanessa and me. When I quit, the network lost interest in the spin-off and Bert lost out on a lot of money."

"How angry was he?" Grayson asked.

"Very," she admitted. "But he's over it now."

"You sure about that?"

"Yeah. I mean, it took a few years, but he's good now. He'd already made a ton of cash off of me and Vanessa, he was just being greedy with the spin off."

Grayson shrugged. "People can hold grudges for a long time, Ryan."

"I know," she said. "But it isn't Bert. It would be stupid of him to threaten us now. He's Ryleigh's manager too and with her reboot of the show being so popular, he would lose money again if something were to happen to her."

"But if the threat is actually against you and they just sent the same message to your mother and your sister to hide that fact, then -"

"I doubt it's me." She smiled at him. "Look, I'm happy that

Grandmother demanded I have protection. I'm not stupid and I know there's the possibility that the threat is against me, but if we're being completely honest – it's more likely my mother or sister. I'm a nobody now, Grayson. I rarely get recognized in public and I haven't done an Alien-Con in years. The only reason I'm doing one this year is because of Ryleigh."

"All right. I'd still like to talk about your inner circle though. Who are you close to?" Grayson told himself he was asking her because it was for the job, not because he was itching for information on Ryan.

She cocked her head at him. "What about Lori?"

"Sorry?"

"You asked me for specificities about everyone in Vanessa's inner circle but Lori. Why?"

He stared blankly at her and she leaned back in her chair. "Is it because she's a shifter?"

He dropped the puzzle piece he was holding and leaned down to pick it up before Sam could grab it and eat it. "What do you mean?"

She laughed. "You have a terrible poker face, Grayson."

"Normally, it's very good," he said. "But you -"

"I what?"

"Nothing," he mumbled. Telling Ryan that she had him all twisted up and barely able to think straight wasn't a great idea. It might make her ask to have someone else assigned to her protection and the thought of anyone else watching over her made him feel... stabby.

You are in so much trouble, dude.

"How do you know she's a shifter?" he asked.

Ryan traced her fingers along the edge of the puzzle. "A couple of slip-ups over the years. She's careful, really careful, but I've seen her eyes change twice when she's talking to her cat. I've never said anything to her. It's obvious that she's trying to keep it a secret from Vanessa."

"It doesn't bother you that she's lying to your mother?"

She shrugged. "I know why she's hiding it and in the grand scheme of things, why would it matter that she's a shifter? She's good at her job, handles Vanessa and her moods like a damn rock star, and my mother relies on her for everything. Lori's only been working for Vanessa for three years now, but my mother would be lost without her. Lori basically does everything for her. Honestly, I won't be surprised if Lori just eventually moves into Grandmother's house. I know Vanessa has already hinted a few times that she should."

She shifted in her chair, rubbing her hand against the back of her neck. "What kind of shifter is she?"

"Jaguar," Grayson said.

"So, is that why you're not asking me about her? You smelled that she was a shifter and so just naturally trust her?" Ryan asked.

"She stopped by the office before we came to the house and asked us to keep her secret," Grayson said. "She was sincere and seemed to care about her job. But I suppose there is a part of me that thinks she isn't a suspect because she's a shifter. Guess, it's a good job I work for a security firm and not a private investigator, huh?"

She smiled at him and his tiger purred happily. He moved around a few of the puzzle pieces on the card table. "So, what can you tell me about Lori?"

She laughed. "Nothing, to be honest. I've maybe had two personal conversations with her, and both revolved around our mutual love for trash reality shows. Ryleigh would probably have more intel on her since she sees her more often."

"All right. What about your inner circle?"

"It's not very big," she said. "Like, maybe two people and I trust both of them implicitly."

"Tell me about them," he coaxed.

"Well, I basically have two best friends. You've already met one of them – Oren. He's a nurse and he's also Peter and Mary's son. My other bestie is Shay. She works in the finance industry, but she did some acting as a kid. We met on the set of a commercial when we were six and have been best friends since."

"So, I met Peter and I know he's human and I could smell that Oren was a leopard shifter, which means Mary's a shifter. Your mother had two shifters working for her without knowing it?" Gray asked.

"No, Mary is human. Oren is adopted."

"How often do you see them?"

"Shay every week at least and Oren a few times a month depending on our schedules. But they have nothing to do with this," she said.

"Anyone else I should know about?"

She shook her head and then grimaced. "I sound like such a loser."

"You don't," he said.

"As a kid I was always forced to socialize, to constantly have my personal space and my privacy violated and now…"

"Now you like your space," he said.

She sighed. "Yeah. Probably even more so than your average introvert. I just want to take pictures, spend time with the people I love, and watch trash TV when I feel like it."

"There's nothing wrong with that," he said.

"You're the only one in my life who thinks that," she said. "Everyone else thinks I'm gonna turn into a crazy old woman surrounded by cats."

He petted Sam who was sitting at his feet and resting his

head on Grayson's thigh. "Sam would probably disagree about the cats."

"Probably." She stared affectionately at the shepherd. "He doesn't hate cats or anything, but he's perfectly content being the only animal in the house."

Sam stood and wandered over to her, his tail wagging as he put his head in her lap. She stroked his silky ears and rubbed between his eyebrows. "You're mama's good boy, yes you are. The best boy in the whole world."

Christ, even her baby talk to the damn dog was turning him on. He glanced at his watch. It was only nine thirty, but he wasn't sure he could sit for another couple of hours with Ryan without trying to fuck her. The puzzle idea had been a cute one, but it sure as hell wasn't working to take his mind off of what it would be like to fuck her. Not when her scent was driving his tiger crazy with need.

Ryan stood up and stretched. He immediately looked away, his heart thumping away in his chest and his tiger purring with delight at the sight of Ryan's tits pushing against her shirt. His cock was stiffening, and in desperation, he thought of the look of disappointment on Cooper's face when he smelled Ryan's scent on Grayson. Would he hand Grayson an actual pink slip or just tell him to pack up his shit and get the fuck out of the office?

"Grayson?"

"Yeah?" He risked a look at her, ignoring his tiger's demands to coax her upstairs to his bed.

"I know it's early, but I'm pretty tired and the photo shoot is early tomorrow. I'm going to head to bed. We need to leave the house by seven-thirty, okay?"

"Sure, okay. I'll see you in the morning?"

"You bet." She headed toward the kitchen, Sam at her heels.

He stood up and followed her to the back door. "Let me check things out first, please."

She stepped back, holding Sam's collar to prevent him from darting out the door. Grayson stepped outside onto the deck, scanning the entire yard. It was dark but like all cat shifters, he had excellent night vision. The yard was empty, and he swung the door open. "All clear."

She let Sam go and stepped out onto the deck beside him, breathing in the warm night air as the dog bounded down the steps of the deck and into the back yard.

"It's a nice night out," she said.

"It is." He glanced upward at the security camera mounted to the right of the door, before taking a step sideways and putting a bit more space between him and Ryan. It was doubtful that Cooper was watching the feed this late at night, but the lion shifter was a night owl and lived and breathed his job. It was entirely possible he had the feeds up and running at his house and watching them right now.

"You okay?" she asked.

He nodded and stared at Sam as the dog sniffed along the row of bushes planted next to the fence. He would relay the information about the manager to Cooper in the morning. It wasn't much in the way of suspects, but it would be enough for Cooper to do a bit of digging into Bert's background.

Hell, if he was really lucky, Bert would be the stalker and they could get him arrested and out of Ryan's life. She'd no longer be a client and maybe, just maybe, they could explore the attraction between them.

CHAPTER 8

"Well, this place looks straight out of a nightmare."

Ryan laughed as she unclicked her seatbelt. After confirming with the security guard at the gate who they were, Grayson had followed the long and winding driveway to the mansion that sat hidden among the trees. The place was the spitting image of a haunted Victorian house and it was mildly amusing to see Grayson's first reaction to it.

He shut the car off and studied the man who was standing guard outside the large front door. She took a deep breath. He absolutely wasn't going to like what she was about to say. She was a little ashamed that she'd waited until they were parked in front of the client's house, but if she'd told him earlier, he probably would have locked her in her bedroom or something.

"Grayson?" She traced the back of her phone nervously.

"Yeah?"

"You can't go into the house with me."

That stubborn line appeared between his eyebrows and his eyes flashed a dark jade. "Like hell, I can't."

"I'm sorry, you really can't," she said. "I'm not trying to be difficult, but -"

"You keep saying that," he turned his heated gaze toward her, "but you realize you're being difficult, right?"

"I do." She turned in her seat to face him. "Look, the woman in there is a... bit of a recluse, okay? She doesn't allow strangers into her home."

"You could have mentioned this earlier," he said.

"I could have."

"But you didn't." The weird disappointment in his voice made her stomach churn.

"I'm sorry," she said. "But this is my career we're talking about. I can't just start canceling on clients."

"This is your life we're talking about," he said.

"This client is absolutely not the stalker, and she has more security in place than you think. Not only is there a security detail in the house, but there are men in the woods surrounding her home."

"I saw them as we drove in," he replied.

"You did? How?" She hadn't seen even a flicker of movement. She would never have known about the security detail in the woods if Rowena hadn't told her at a previous visit.

"I get paid to notice shit like that," he said a bit impatiently. "Ryan, I can't protect you if you keep shutting me out like this."

"I know," she said, "but it really can't be helped. The client will not want you seeing her."

"I don't need to see the client," he said. "I'll do a sweep of the house before you go in and then stand outside the room while you work." He studied the mansion in front of them through the windshield.

"You can't. She's a very private person and -"

"Ryan." He leaned over and cupped the back of her neck,

tugging her closer until their faces were only inches apart. "Let me do my job, honey."

Fuck. He was playing dirty pool what with the touching and that endearment that they were definitely not close enough for him to be using on her. But holy hell if she didn't like it. Just hearing his raspy low voice saying 'honey' made her drip with anticipation. If he kept this up, she'd have to bring a change of panties with her every time she was with him.

"Ryan, stop that."

She blinked at him, her lips parting when she realized that his eyes had turned jade and an orangish coloured beard was growing on his jaw.

"Stop what?" Her voice was breathless. Needy. Wanting.

He groaned, his hand tightening on the back of her neck. "I am about two seconds away from bending you over the hood of this car and fucking you."

"Maybe we should consider the back seat instead of the hood. Guys in the woods, remember?"

He muttered a curse, his gaze still on her lips before he released her and leaned back. She was panting and sweating like she'd just run a half-marathon. She ran a shaky hand over her mouth, wishing she had kissed him like she really wanted to. He was a great kisser, a *phenomenal* kisser, and just thinking about the way –

"Ryan," he ground out before reaching down and adjusting the front of his jeans, "for the love of God, please stop. I can smell your arousal."

She took a deep breath. "Maybe stop touching me and calling me 'honey' then."

His eyes deepened in colour, his pupils turned to slits and he went inward. Her eyes widened when he muttered, "She is not ours, stop saying that. No, you can't mark her. Stop fucking asking."

He blinked and his eyes were back to normal. She had an idea that he had no clue he'd spoken out loud. She cleared her throat. "I need to go in."

"I need to go with you."

She shook her head. "You can't. It's that simple."

"Tell me why," he said.

She picked at the cuff of her shirt sleeve. "My client is Rowena Jackson. Do you know who that is?"

"No."

"She is – was – a very famous actress about seven years ago. She was at the height of her career when," her throat tightened and she swallowed hard, "a woman threw acid in her face. The woman was jealous that her boyfriend had a celebrity crush on Rowena."

"Jesus," he said.

She nodded. "Yeah. It was awful and for those of us who are or were in the celebrity business, it was a real wake up call about how dangerous being in the spotlight can be."

She stared out the windshield at Rowena's house. "After the attack, Rowena became a recluse. Half of her face is horribly scarred, and she doesn't go out in public anymore. She's married to a great guy who loves her no matter what, but she struggles with PTSD from the attack and the way she looks now. She was very pretty before the attack and while she's still beautiful to the people who know her and love her, it's been rough for her."

A note of bitterness crept into her voice. "So much of her life and career were defined by her looks and in this business, people are... harsh."

"I can only imagine," he said.

"Rowena hired me to do some boudoir style photos as a

surprise for her husband Thomas. Doing this is," she paused, "a very big step for her and I'm hoping that it will help her embrace who she is now and be more self-accepting."

She sighed. "I know that sounds like a bunch of new age bullshit, but -"

"It doesn't," he said. "I feel for the woman, I do, but I've been hired to protect you. You are my priority. Do you understand?"

"I do," she said.

"Maybe you can ask her if I can take a quick look around. I won't go into the room she's in and I'll stay outside of the room while you take pictures. I promise," Grayson said.

"She'll cancel the whole thing if I do that," Ryan said. "It's important to me to help her."

"Are you friends with her?"

"No, not really," she said. "But I want to help her. I need to help her."

He studied her and she fidgeted in her seat when he said, "You're a good person."

"Does that mean you'll stay in the car?"

He gripped the steering wheel and stared at the house again. "Would you be willing to compromise?"

"How?"

He opened the car door and climbed out. She opened her door and stepped out before following him to the back of the SUV. He opened it and she stared at the cases. "What are you carrying in these cases?"

"Assorted things, but this one," he pulled a small silver case from the back of the pile and set it on top of one of the larger black cases, "has what I'm looking for."

He opened it and she stared at the electronic devices nestled inside. "What is this?"

"It's a surveillance system." He held up the small electronic earplug. "This goes into your ear and the neckloop goes around your neck and can be hidden underneath the collar of your shirt. This," he held up a small black square, "is a microphone with an adhesive backing that can be hidden under your collar. It will allow me to hear what's happening and the earpiece will allow me to communicate with you. If you need help, all you have to do is say my name."

She studied the equipment. "If there is a crazed stalker with a gun in the house, you won't get there in time to save me. So, what's the point in wearing this?"

"What's the harm in wearing it?" he countered.

"It feels a little… invasive."

"Your client won't know it's there," he said. "C'mon, Ryan, compromise with me. I'll feel much better about staying in the car if I can hear you."

She nodded. "All right, fine. But don't be talking to me the whole time I'm in there. I don't need your stupid sexy voice in my ear while I'm trying to work."

His grin was one part smug and two parts adorable. "You think my voice is sexy?"

"And stupid," she clarified. "Don't forget the stupid part."

He laughed, and she shivered all over when he stepped close enough to press the microphone onto the underside of her collar. His warm breath washed over her mouth and it took a terrifying amount of willpower not to stand on her tiptoes and kiss him.

"Behave," he said in that sexy, maybe-not-so-stupid voice.

"I am behaving."

"I can smell your lust."

She scowled at him. "It's totally unfair that you know immediately when I'm imagining you naked."

"Like you can't tell when I'm imagining you naked," he said.

She took a quick glance downward, gleefully satisfied when she saw the tell-tale bulge at the front of his jeans.

"Woman, I swear if you don't stop staring at my dick, I really will fuck you right here. I don't care who's watching."

"Promises, promises," she said.

He groaned and her next flirty remark was lost when his hand brushed her hair away from her ear. His chest was almost touching her tits, and she leaned forward a little until they were pressed against him.

He inhaled and muttered a curse under his breath but didn't move away. Instead, he carefully stuck the earpiece into her ear, his blunt fingers caressing the curve of her ear. Her body tingled all over from that simple, light touch, and she was pretty sure she made an embarrassing moan. Hell, her lust was so thick, *she* could almost smell it now.

"Unbutton your shirt."

His guttural demand had her immediately reaching for the top buttons. She undid two and was headed for the third when he growled, "Stop."

She unbuttoned the third one anyway and his low growl made her sex pulse against the confines of her jeans. He stared at her cleavage for a few seconds before he picked up the neckloop. He placed it around her neck and when his fingers traced down her chest to dip into her bra and stroke the soft skin between her breasts, she knew for certain she moaned.

His eyes glowed bright green and the purr that rumbled up and out of his chest made goosebumps break out across her flesh. Was purring supposed to be a turn on? Did all women get wet when a shifter purred to her? Or was she a total freak?

He purred again and she bit at her bottom lip. "Please kiss me, Gray."

His purring cut out and his look was one of genuine regret. "I can't, honey."

He buttoned her shirt and made sure the loop was hidden before he stepped away. Feeling shaky and weak, she gripped the back of the SUV as he popped a second earpiece into his own ear. "I'll set this up while you're grabbing your camera equipment."

His voice was rough and low, and she didn't need to stare at his crotch to know he was just as turned on as she was.

"Sounds good," she managed to croak out before walking to the back seat of her SUV to grab her equipment.

***

"YOU DID A GREAT JOB WITH HER."

Ryan looked up from her phone, a pleased look etched into her face. "Thank you."

They were driving back to Ryan's house and he switched lanes on the freeway. "I mean that. Even just listening, I could tell that Rowena was really nervous and you did a lot to help her relax."

Ryan fiddled with her phone cover. "I'm glad I could help her. This was important and I know that Thomas is going to love the pictures and that, in turn, will help boost Rowena's confidence."

Her phone chimed again, and she texted quickly, her thumbs moving in a blur. "Sorry, it's Shay. She wants to have drinks tonight at a bar not far from my house. Would that work or not enough notice?"

"Let me talk to Coop and confirm we can have someone else with me," Grayson replied.

"It won't get crazy like the coffee shop," Ryan said. "People don't recognize me the way they recognize Ryleigh."

"Cooper will still want another person and so do I." He glanced at her. "It's for your safety, Ryan."

"I know."

"I'll call Cooper as soon as we're home and -"

His phone rang, cutting him off mid-sentence. He glanced at the screen on the dashboard. "Speak of the lion himself." He hit the answer button on the steering wheel. "Hey, Coop."

"Hey. Where are you?" Coop's voice drifted out from the speakers in the dashboard. To someone who didn't know him, Cooper sounded normal, but Gray had been friends with the lion shifter long enough to recognize the tension in his voice.

"Just driving Ryan back from a client appointment. Why?"

"I have Mave keeping an eye on the security cams outside Ryan's house. Mailman just dropped off a box on the front porch."

Tension settled on the back of Gray's neck. He glanced at Ryan. "Are you expecting a parcel?"

"Uh, yeah, I think so," she said.

"You *think* so or you know so?" Cooper asked.

She thought for a few seconds. "I know so. I ordered a new camera bag last week."

The tightness eased in Cooper's voice. "Good."

"Before you hang up – Ryan has drinks with a friend tonight at a bar. Do we have someone available to go with us?"

"Honestly, just Grayson will be enough," Ryan said.

"No," Cooper said immediately. "Not after what happened at the coffee shop."

"It won't be like that," Ryan said. "People don't recognize me the way they recognize my sister."

"Don't care," Cooper replied. "Hold on, let me see who I have available."

They could hear the click-clack of Cooper's keyboard. Gray merged off the freeway toward Ryan's house as Cooper muttered, "Oh for fuck's sake. This goddamn computer is gonna be the fucking death of me."

Ryan glanced his way and Gray grinned at her. Cooper's issues with computers was legendary in the office. If there was a way to fuck up a computer, Cooper would find it. Usually in five minutes or less."

"What the fuck?" Cooper's voice was full of exasperation and disbelief. "Where the fuck did the calendar go? Are you fucking -"

"Here, let me help." Daisy's voice drifted into the car, a little muffled but perfectly understandable.

"Where the hell did the damn thing go?" Cooper said.

"The calendar app is in the recycling bin somehow," Daisy replied.

"I swear to fucking God I didn't put it in the goddamn recycling bin," Cooper said heatedly.

There was a pause and then Cooper said, "Sorry. I shouldn't curse in the office."

This time Daisy's reply was too faint to hear but Gray could hear the gratitude – hell, adoration was probably a better description – in Cooper's voice when he said, "Thanks, Daisy. I appreciate your help."

Ryan poked him in the thigh and mouthed, "He likes her."

His grin widened as Cooper said, "Okay, I got the calendar open. Wes is available tonight. Text him the details."

"Thanks, Coop."

Gray hit the end call button on the steering wheel and Ryan burst into laughter. "That was a… production."

"Anytime Coop has to use a computer, it usually is."

"He likes Daisy, huh?"

He turned onto her street. "How did you know?"

"Maybe the way his voice went all gaga when he talked to her," Ryan said with another laugh. "If we'd been in the same room as them, I'm pretty sure we would have seen cartoon hearts over his eyes."

He parked in her driveway and shut off the car. "You're not wrong about that."

"Does Daisy like him?" Ryan unclicked her seatbelt.

He scanned the area around her house and then opened the car door. He inhaled deeply but didn't smell anything out of the ordinary. "I don't think so. Daisy is human and... nervous around shifters."

"Seems weird that she'd take a job with shifters if she's nervous around them."

"Yes," he agreed. He slid out of the SUV and walked around to Ryan's side. He opened the door and when she climbed out and slammed her door shut, he took her hand and walked toward the porch.

His tiger purred happily when she squeezed his hand and smiled up at him. "Thanks again for being understanding about Rowena this afternoon."

"Thank you for compromising." They climbed the porch steps and when Ryan reached for the box, he said, "I'll get that, just let me check the house first."

"It's fine," she said. "It isn't heavy." She lifted it and waited patiently on the porch as he unlocked the front door. He handed back her key as Sam nosed his way out onto the porch, tail wagging and body wiggling.

"Hi, baby," Ryan cooed to him. "Did you have a good afternoon?"

Sam sniffed at the box in her arms before wandering off the porch. Gray entered the house, grinning to himself, when he heard Ryan scold the dog for peeing on the rose bush.

He checked the house before returning to the porch and opening the door. "All clear, come in."

She and Sam followed him into the kitchen. Sam stood at the back door and he walked across the kitchen to pet his head. "Didn't you just pee on the rose bushes?"

The dog whined at him and he opened the door, scanning the back yard before he let go of Sam's collar. Sam sprinted out into the back yard, barking loudly at a squirrel sitting on top of the back fence.

He could hear Ryan opening the box behind him, and he laughed when the squirrel scampered along the fence to the far post. It sat on top of it, chittering at Sam as he barked wildly at it.

"There's a squirrel tormenting Sam," he said over his shoulder.

Ryan laughed. "Yeah. That's Frodo. He's a total dick and constantly teases Sam. One time he – oh my God!"

He turned, his tiger pushing forward at the look on his mate's face. She staggered back from the box, her hands coming up to cover her mouth as her face turned the shade of crisp mountain snow.

His tiger roared angrily, the scent of Ryan's fear and disgust had the large beast immediately riled up. Gray strode across the kitchen, catching Ryan by the arms and pulling her up against his chest. She buried her face into his neck, her breath hot against his throat.

"Honey, what's wrong?"

"The box," she whispered. "It isn't a camera bag."

He eased away from her and she wrapped her arms around her body. She was shaking wildly, and her face was still void of colour. He turned to the box, pushed aside the bit of bubble wrap that was still inside it, and peered in.

"Fuck!" The curse exploded from his mouth as he took an involuntary step backward. Despite knowing that Ryan was safe, his tiger was howling with horror and he soothed it quickly as Ryan made a shaky laugh behind him before wrapping her arms around his waist.

She rested her forehead between his shoulder blades. "Are you freaked out like I am right now?"

"A little," he admitted.

"It's fake," she said. "I know it's fake, but…"

"It is horrifyingly realistic," Gray said.

"Yeah." She released her breath on a shuddering sigh. "Who are you calling?"

He hit a button on his cell phone. "Cooper."

———

"Fucking hell," Cooper said. He stepped back from the box and wiped his hand across his face. "That's goddamn creepy."

He glanced at Ryan. "My apologies for the language, ma'am."

She laughed, it was still shaky, and the tone was off. Like a piano just the slightest off tune. She wondered if she'd ever laugh normally again. "It's fine. I've heard worse."

Grayson was peering into the box again, a look of fascinated disgust on his features. She had no urge to look a second time. Seeing her decapitated head, blood dripping from the open mouth and ragged neck, just once was more than enough. She'd be lucky if she didn't have nightmares for weeks.

Cooper reached out and closed the box before setting it on the floor next to the island. "Sit down, ma'am."

"Call me Ryan," she said automatically as she joined them at the island. She sat on the stool, wishing she could reach out and take Gray's hand. Instead, she folded them into her lap and stared silently at the two men.

"Did Vanessa and Ryleigh get parcels?" Grayson asked.

Cooper nodded. "Yeah. I called Boone after I talked to you. There was a box waiting for each of them at the security booth. Boone opened both and same thing – decapitated heads of both women. Neither Mrs. Shepherd nor her daughter saw them. Boone left them at the security booth for now."

Ryan breathed a sigh of relief. Her grandmother's home was fenced and gated with a twenty-four-hour security guard posted in the little booth at the front gate. Personally, Ryan had always thought it was a little overkill. Especially after she had quit the show and she, and her mother to a certain degree, had faded into obscurity, but now she was grateful it was there.

If Ryleigh had seen the head… she shuddered all over.

"You okay?" Grayson's voice was casual, but his boss sniffed the air and then studied him in a way that made Ryan extremely nervous.

"Fine. Just very glad that Ryleigh didn't see it. So, now what do we do?"

Cooper rubbed a hand across the blonde stubble on his jaw. "I spoke to your mother on the phone while I was driving here. I recommended that she contact the police, but she refused."

"You're kidding me?" Grayson said.

"No," Cooper replied.

"Why the hell wouldn't she call the police?" Grayson

stood and paced back and forth in the kitchen with Sam at his heels. "I get that they're fake, but holy shit, severed heads – even fake ones – are not something to fuck around with. Whoever is doing this is a complete fucking nutjob, Coop."

"I know. I explained that to Ms. Shepherd, but she refused to involve the police."

Grayson turned to her. "Can you talk to her?"

Her laugh was sour. "Trust me, Cooper would have better luck convincing her than I would."

"I don't understand why she won't call them," Grayson said.

Ryan traced the side seam on her jeans. "Once the police are involved, the paparazzi find out, then the entire world finds out. It's bad publicity."

"Don't they say that any publicity is good publicity?" Cooper asked.

Ryan shrugged. "My mother doesn't think so. She's very... weird about Ryleigh and what is said about her online and in interviews. My mother didn't have a very good reputation when she was younger, and she's done everything in her power to keep Ryleigh's reputation pristine."

She pulled at a loose thread near her knee. "She wants more for Ryleigh than what she had. She didn't even want Ryleigh to do the reboot of the show, was worried that it would typecast her the way she was typecast. If word gets out that we have a crazed stalker, she believes it will affect Ryleigh's career in a negative way."

"Oh, for God's sake," Grayson said. "Your mother is -"

He cut himself off abruptly but the exasperation on his face was still clear.

"Is there a chance we can convince your mother and sister not to do the Alien-Con next week?" Cooper asked.

"No," Ryan said. "Vanessa will just point out that you

were hired for a reason and if you can't keep them safe during Alien-Con, she'll hire someone else who can."

"It's not a good idea," Grayson said. "Maybe we can get your grandmother to put her foot down again."

Ryan smiled a little. "It won't work. Grandmother is tough, but Ryleigh has her wrapped around her little finger. And Ryleigh will never back out of the Alien-Con. She and her reboot show are the hottest attraction this year, there's no way she won't go."

Grayson muttered an expletive as Cooper stared at the top of the island. "We'll get some more guys," he said almost to himself. "Frost owes me a favour, he'll loan me some men."

"Who's Frost?" Ryan asked.

"A guy I know." Cooper's tone suggested he was done talking about Frost.

Ryan bit at her lip. She didn't want to tell them but if Cooper was doing any kind of background check on Bert, he'd find it anyway.

"Ryan."

She glanced at Grayson. Shit. He knew she was hiding something. How the hell could she be this transparent to him already?

"Tell me," he said but his tone was gentle.

"It's about Bert," she said.

Cooper drummed his fingers on the island. "The manager." The shaggy-haired lion shifter turned to Grayson. "The one you talked to me about. The one who has a problem with Ryan."

"Yeah," Grayson said.

"Not has," Ryan said. "Had. As in – a long time ago. Everything's fine between us now."

"But?" Grayson said.

She sighed. "I'm sure it's just a coincidence, but before Bert became a manager he was, uh, in special effects."

Cooper leaned forward. "What do you mean... in special effects?"

"He created creatures and did fantasy make-up, stuff like that, for movies and TV shows."

"For *Alien Hunter*?" Grayson asked.

"No. He was managing at that point. I mean, he only had three clients, me and my mother and some other B-actress. But, uh, he was really good at the special effects before he quit. Like one of the best."

Cooper and Grayson stared at each other. Ryan chewed at her bottom lip. "I'm sure it wasn't Bert who made the heads."

"Are you?" Cooper asked.

"It can't be him. He's not – I mean, he isn't... it can't be him," she finished lamely.

Cooper had his phone out and was tapping on the keyboard. "I'll do the background check and then have a chat with him."

"I want to be there when you talk to him," Ryan said.

"No," Grayson replied. "If he did make the heads and he's still got a beef with you, I don't want you anywhere near him."

"It isn't him," Ryan said. "I only told you about the special effects thing because you would have found out when you did the background check on him anyway. Bert's a good guy, okay?"

"I still need to talk to him," Cooper said. "It's my job."

"You're security, not private investigation," Ryan said.

She wondered if she'd just unintentionally insulted the lion shifter, but a broad grin broke across his face. She was totally one hundred percent into Grayson but holy hell, when the lion shifter smiled it transformed his face to super-hot babe mode. Did he smile at Daisy like that? Because if he did, she would have to be crazy not to fall for him.

"Consider it a little extra value for the money," Cooper said. He stood and cracked his neck. "I gotta go. You want me to take the box?"

He nudged the cardboard box with his foot. Another involuntary shudder went through Ryan and Gray nodded. "Yeah. Take it back to the office with you. As long as we're not touching the evidence inside, the police could still maybe use it if we can convince Ryan's mother to talk to them."

"You won't convince her," Ryan said as Cooper bent and lifted the box. She, Sam, and Gray followed him to the front door.

"You talk to Wes yet?" Cooper asked as he opened the door.

"Not yet." Grayson glanced at her. "Not sure if tonight is still on or not."

"It is," Ryan said.

Grayson frowned but didn't say anything. They said their goodbyes to Cooper, and she shut the front door, leaning against it and giving Grayson a strained smile.

"I think you should cancel for tonight," he said. "Or ask your friend to come here for drinks."

"I don't want to," she replied. "I'm not going to hide away because of this, okay? I'm already an introvert, I won't let this turn me into a full-blown hermit."

A trace of a smile crossed his face. "All right."

"Besides, the place Shay wants to meet at won't be that busy. It's kind of off the beaten path." Ryan petted Sam's head.

"We'll be sitting close," he warned.

She laughed. "Trust me, once Shay sees how hot you are, you'll probably be sitting at the table with us."

CHAPTER 9

"You don't really think it's Bert, do you?" Shay leaned over the small table, her forehead nearly touching Ryan's. "He is so not the type to put a decapitated head in a box."

"No, I don't think it's him." Ryan sipped at her drink.

At the back of the bar, the band was setting up. She watched the four burly men in cowboy hats move their equipment and instruments easily across the stage in front of the dance floor.

Shay took her hand and squeezed it. "Hey, *are* you okay? I know you keep saying you are, but you must be terrified."

Ryan smiled at the slender brunette. "I'm okay. A little shook up when I first saw the head, but I'm just thankful Ryleigh didn't see hers. You know that would have traumatized her."

Shay shrugged. "I think she's tougher than she looks."

Her best friend was probably right, but after basically raising her baby sister, Ryan found it difficult to see Ryleigh as anything more than the sweet little pig-tailed girl who burst into tears at the slightest provocation.

Shay adjusted the cowboy hat on her head before taking another sip of beer. Although she was born and raised in LA, she pulled off the small-town cowgirl look to perfection. Her skinny jeans and off-the-shoulder top looked like they were purchased from one of the boutiques in Beverly Hills, but knowing Shay, they were from Target. Shay had just as much money as Ryan did, but she loved a good bargain.

Ryan adjusted her dress before sipping at her own beer. She told herself not to glance at Grayson and then did it anyway. He was tracing one finger around the rim of his soda glass, his gaze never wavering from hers. The heat in them made her very glad she took some extra time to do her hair and makeup. Not that anything would happen between them, she knew that, but it hadn't stopped her from wearing her most flattering dress or shaving above the knee.

"So, what's the deal with the older guy – what's his name again?" Shay asked.

"Who – Wes?"

"Yes. What kind of shifter is he?"

"A lion. Why?"

"Because he's hot and I'm thinking once he's off duty, I'm gonna try and convince him to come home with me." Shay grinned at her.

Ryan's mouth dropped open. "Seriously?"

"Why are you so surprised? Older guys are hot, and I like Wes's intensity. Guys that intense are dynamite in bed, trust me." Shay sent a flirty smile Wes's way. He didn't smile or acknowledge her in any way, and Shay's smile widened. "Ooh, he's playing hard to get."

"You're not into Grayson?" Ryan said.

"Oh, he's a fucking fox, but I see the way you're looking at each other." Shay waved her hand in the air. "Hell, I can feel the sexual tension from here."

Ryan cleared her throat. "There's no sexual tension between us."

There was a moment of silence and then both she and Shay burst into laughter. She took another swallow of beer, peeked at Grayson, and said, "Fine, we might want to bang each other's brains out."

"Uh, yeah, that's obvious," Shay said. "So, why aren't you? Is it because he's a shifter? Because I have to tell you – shifters are way better than human men in bed, at least in my experience. Their peens are massive and they're all about the woman's pleasure. Don't let your mother's prejudice about shifters stop you from having the best sex of your life, girl."

"It has nothing to do with my mother," Ryan said. "Gray isn't allowed to sleep with clients. It's a rule, and he has a lot of respect for his boss."

"Ooh, that's bad luck." Shay studied Grayson. "Although his integrity and commitment to his job is kind of hot."

"He's a really good kisser," Ryan said.

Shay's eyes lit up. "Shut. Up. You kissed him?"

"Keep your voice down," Ryan said. "Their hearing is incredible."

"Meh, the band is warming up, it's fine," Shay said with a wild gesture at the stage. "When did you kiss?"

"The other day. It was amazing. I asked him to come upstairs with me and that's when he told me the 'no banging the clients' rule."

"That really blows," Shay said. "I'm glad Wes isn't protecting me. I don't want anything coming between me and his gigantic lion peen tonight."

"Shay," Ryan said with a laugh, "he's not going to sleep with you."

"He might. I'm a babe and I have a great personality."

"That's true, but even though I don't know him that well, I'm pretty sure he's not into one-night stands."

Shay's pout could be seen across the bar. "Boo."

Ryan set her beer on the table. "So, how are you? How's the -"

"Ladies!"

Ryan glanced up, her smile widening until her cheeks hurt. Oren, along with another guy she didn't know, were approaching their table with drinks in their hands. She stood and Oren pulled her into his embrace, lifting her off her feet, and giving her a wet kiss on the mouth.

"Ugh, Oren." She frowned at him and he laughed before licking her cheek.

"Sorry, gorgeous."

"Stop licking me." She poked him in the side, and he set her on her feet before hugging Shay. She wiped her cheek and looked at Grayson. He was sitting up straight, the tension in his shoulders obvious. If he gripped his glass any harder, it would shatter. Wes leaned over and spoke into his ear.

She wasn't sure what had upset him. She knew he recognized Oren from the photo shoot the other day so why was he so tense?

"Ryan?"

She turned and smiled at Oren. "Sorry, what?"

"I said this is my friend, Jamie. Jamie, this is Ryan and Shay."

"Nice to meet you." She shook the man's hand.

His smile was on the shy side and she could see Shay sizing him up in her head as she pressed a kiss against his cheek. "Hi, handsome."

"Don't bother, Shay-bae," Oren said as he settled into the chair next to Ryan's and draped his arm over her shoulders. "Jamie's got a boner for that dude and only that dude." He pointed to the stage where the smallest of the four men was standing in front of the microphone as he fiddled with his guitar strap.

Jamie blushed bright red. "Shut up, Oren."

"What? Nothing to be ashamed of. Shay and I were band groupies ourselves back in the day," Oren said.

"It's true," Shay said. "We followed the Backstreet Boys across four states once."

"Jesus," Oren groaned as Jamie laughed, "you don't have to point out it was a fucking boy band."

"You need to acknowledge your shame and live with it," Shay said.

Ryan laughed as Oren said, "I still have my signed Nick Carter t-shirt."

"You probably rub one out to it every night," Shay said.

"Guilty." Oren nudged Ryan. "I see you still have your security detail." He raised his glass to Grayson. The tiger shifter gave him a short nod, the scowl on his face now seemed to be a permanent fixture.

Oren turned to Ryan. "He doesn't seem to like me much."

"He doesn't even know you," Ryan said. "How is Mark doing?"

Oren's face sobered. "Not great. It won't be much longer now. It meant a lot to Ash that you got the pictures back to her so quickly. She already has a bunch of them up around the house."

"That's good, I'm glad." Ryan took Oren's hand and squeezed it. "How are you doing?"

"Fine." Oren's smile wasn't quite truthful, but she didn't push him on it. Now wasn't the time, and besides, when you were a nurse who worked mostly with end-of-life patients, your days would rarely be good. Oren was amazing at what he did, but she often wondered how much of a toll it took on him.

She squeezed his hand again. "You look very handsome tonight."

"Thanks, doll. You're looking hot yourself. You looking to pick up a man tonight?"

"Maybe." Her gaze flickered to Grayson only briefly, but Oren still caught the look and grinned at her.

"Didn't think tiger shifters were your type."

"I don't have a type," she said. "Besides, I'm not into Grayson."

Oren leaned down and kissed her forehead. "Baby-girl, for an actress, you can't lie worth shit."

"Be quiet, you." She poked him in the ribs as the music started up. It was loud and the twang in the lead singer's voice made Ryan want to stab a fork in her ear. She hated country music, but both Shay and Oren loved it, which meant she'd been subjected to it a lot over the years.

"Time to dance." Oren grabbed her hand and pulled her to her feet.

"God, yes!" Shay bounced to her feet and took Jamie's hand. "C'mon, handsome, let's show that lead singer your sexy moves. With me as your wingwoman, you'll be plowing him before the sun rises, I promise."

Jamie turned a bright red as Oren laughed. "Never change Shay-bae, never change.'

"YOU NEED TO CALM DOWN."

Gray glared at Wes who just shrugged. "Your tiger is riled up, calm it down."

"He's fine," Gray muttered.

The older man was right, his tiger *was* riled up, but the thing was – Gray didn't *want* to calm him down. His tiger had a perfectly valid reason for being angry and if that asshole leopard shifter didn't stop manhandling Gray's woman, he would drag him off the dance floor and show him exactly what happened to shifters who didn't respect –

"Gray, enough."

Wes's voice cut through the fog of shifting and, with difficulty, he pushed his tiger back. He grabbed his glass of soda and drank the rest of it in four large gulps, the ice crashing against his front teeth. He was sweating and his body was vibrating, and he was so fucking angry.

"*Gray*! Get your shit together." Wes's big hand clamped down on his arm.

He took a deep breath, staring at the table as the music thumped and thudded. Wes's hand eased on his arm. "You good?"

"Yeah, thanks, man."

Wes leaned back and studied the dance floor where Ryan and her friends were dancing. "You know you can't sleep with a client."

"Yeah," Gray replied. "I know, but my tiger…"

"Doesn't give a shit?"

"Exactly."

A rare smile crossed Wes's face. "I've been there. It sucks."

"You wanted to sleep with a client?" Gray glanced at Wes before scanning the crowd. The bar wasn't busy, and he had a clear line to Ryan if he needed to get to her, but he hated that she was so far away from him.

"More like I've wanted someone I absolutely couldn't have," Wes replied.

Gray studied Wes's profile. "Recently?"

Wes hadn't had a girlfriend since... hell, he didn't remember Wes ever having a girlfriend. The guy was a loner and other than Gray and the others at Shadow Security, he didn't have any other family or friends. Grayson had assumed that was the way Wes preferred it.

To be honest, he didn't know Wes that well. In their unit, he and Coop were close, Boone and Derek had been close, and Wes was... well, Wes. He rarely spoke and he definitely didn't share personal information. Boone was a damn open book when it came to his life, and Gray had spent enough time with Cooper to know just about everything there was about him, but Wes kept his personal life to himself. Always had.

The fact that he was sharing anything personal was a damn miracle.

"Does it matter?" Wes said. "I can't have her. End of story."

"You know you can talk to me and the rest of the guys if you need to, right?" Gray said.

Another smile crossed Wes's face. "Yeah, I know. I'm fine, Gray. Don't get your panties in a knot."

"I'm just saying that if you need..."

His tiger roared angrily, and Gray forgot entirely about Wes. The music had changed, turned soft and slow as the lead singer crooned into the microphone. The leopard shifter had pulled Ryan into his arms and Gray stood, nearly knocking over his chair.

"Gray," Wes said warningly. "If you shift in this bar and take on that leopard shifter, Cooper will fire you."

"I'm not going to shift." Gray's voice was a low growl. "I'm moving closer because she's too far away from me, I can't keep her safe from here."

Wes sighed but didn't say anything as Gray strode across

the bar. In seconds he was standing behind the shifter and Ryan, his tiger growling with rage at the way Ryan's body was pressed against the leopard's.

The leopard stiffened, Grayson knew he could smell his rage, and then made a half-turn, his arms still clasped loosely around Ryan's waist. "Hey. Grayson, right?"

Gray smiled icily at him. "May I cut in?"

Oren eyed him before sniffing at the air. Gray's tiger made another low snarl that he couldn't contain. Ryan's eyes widened at the sound and she stepped out of Oren's arms and in between them. She rested her hand on Grayson's arm and his tiger's growl turned to a purr.

"Can you give us a minute, Oren?" she asked.

The leopard shifter nodded. "Sure. I'll order us some more drinks."

"Thanks, honey."

His tiger growled angrily at the endearment. Gray slid his arm around Ryan's waist, pulling her up tight against him as Oren walked off the dance floor.

Ryan put her arms around his shoulders, locking her hands together behind his neck. "What's wrong?"

"Nothing." He swayed to the music, his stupid tiger purring and chirping like a damn kitten at the feel of Ryan's body against his.

"Something's wrong," she said. "You were growling."

His arms tightened around her hips. "You said you didn't have a boyfriend."

"I don't."

"So, what? You and the leopard are friends with benefits?"

She stared at him, her curvy body going slack against his with surprise, before she laughed.

"What's so funny?" He could hear the sulk in his voice,

and he knew he was acting like a damn three-year-old, but he couldn't seem to help it.

"Your jealousy is stupidly adorable when it really shouldn't be," she said. "I should find it annoying as hell."

He opened his mouth to say he wasn't jealous and then shut it with a snap. He *was* jealous and it was stupid to even try and deny it. Ryan might be human, but he wouldn't be surprised if she could smell the jealousy on him, it was that damn thick.

"I'm not judging you," he said in a tone that sounded judgemental even to him, "but I need to know exactly who you're sleeping with so I can…"

"So, you can what?" Her amusement was just as thick as his jealousy.

"So, I can stop you," he muttered.

She laughed again and pressed her body a little tighter against his as he moved her around the dance floor. She put her mouth to his ear, her warm breath made his cock harden immediately, and said, "Basically what you're saying is that you get to tell me who I can fuck and can't fuck."

"No," he said between clenched teeth.

"Oh good. Because for a second there," his entire body stiffened when she licked the lobe of his ear, "it sounded like that's exactly what you were doing."

"It isn't safe for you to be with that asshole leopard tonight," he snarled. "I need to keep an eye on you, and I can't do that if you're fucking him."

Her hand stroked between his shoulder blades. He supposed she meant for it to be soothing, but it only turned him on more. He changed position slightly, letting her feel the hardness of his dick pressing against her hip.

She gasped into his ear, her arms tightening around his

shoulders. They were at the farthest edge of the dance floor now, barely moving to the music.

"Oren is pretty adventurous, maybe he'd be fine with you standing in the room while we're having sex."

Her tone was light and teasing but the mental image of her being fucked by anyone but him, sent his tiger into a frenzy. His hand slid up into her hair, threading through the long strands until he was at her scalp. He tightened around the silky softness until she gasped, and he pulled her head back so that she was staring up at him.

"You're mine. If you go anywhere near that leopard shifter's dick, I'll make him wish he was dead."

His voice was soft, pleasant even, but something on his face made the teasing smile drop from her face.

"Oren is gay," she said quickly.

He blinked at her. "What?"

"Oren is gay and we're only friends. I was teasing you."

Relief and shame flooded through him. "Only friends?"

"Yes," she repeated, "only friends."

He wanted to bury his face in the curve of her neck, inhale her sweet scent, and kiss her soft skin. Instead, he pulled her impossibly close and rested his temple against hers as he stared blankly at the others on the dance floor.

Her hands were rubbing his back again, slow wide circles that soothed his tiger. She lifted her head to murmur, "Sorry", into his ear.

"No, I'm sorry," he said. "I shouldn't have said that shit."

She leaned back so she could stare up at him, searching his face for what, he didn't know.

"You were jealous," she said, "and I liked it."

Shit. Her honesty was as much of a turn-on as the feel of her body pressed against his.

She stroked his upper back before smiling a bit sheepishly. "I teased you about sleeping with Oren because I liked the jealousy. Totally embarrassing high-school girl behaviour."

He studied her for a moment before saying, "I really want to fuck you right now."

Her entire body shivered against his and just like that, her lust was back. Thick and sweet and unbelievably tempting. She shifted against him, letting the top of her pelvis brush against his erection. When she spoke, her voice was a low sexy rasp. "I can tell."

He groaned and tightened his hands on her hips, resisting the urge to thrust against her. But, when she lifted her head and pressed her lips at the base of his throat, he palmed her perfect ass through her dress, squeezing it roughly.

She moaned, and he said into her ear, "The things I would do to you, if we weren't surrounded by people on a dance floor."

"Oh yeah?" she said breathlessly. "What kind of things?"

His tiger purred as he nuzzled her ear before giving the lobe a light nip. "First, I'd take off this dress so I could see what kind of panties you were wearing."

"What if I'm not wearing panties?"

He groaned again and rocked his dick against her, his hand gripping her hip tightly. "Fuck, woman. Tell me you're wearing panties."

She giggled. "I'm wearing panties."

He studied the people around them. No one was looking at them and he gave her ass another hard squeeze. "I can smell your arousal. Did you know that?"

Her blush was endearing, and he grinned wickedly. "Your sweet pussy is soaking wet, isn't it?"

She gasped in reply and he nuzzled her ear. "Do you want to know what I'd do next?"

"Yes," she moaned.

"I'd strip off your bra so I could finally see and taste those perfect tits of yours. I dream about them, honey. How they'd look in my hands, how they'd taste in my mouth."

Her body trembled again, and the smell of her arousal deepened. If he didn't stop this right now, he'd take her into the damn alley behind the bar and fuck her.

"I think about that too," she said. "All the time."

Her soft lips pressed against the column of his throat and he muttered a curse. The music stopped and he forced himself to pull away from her, grimacing at the pressure in his groin. Her face was flushed, and her lower lip swollen like she'd been biting at it.

"I'm sorry," he said in a hoarse voice. "I shouldn't have said that."

Disappointment flashed across her face. "I know. I'm ready to go home now."

He reached for her, "Ryan, I -"

She jerked away, making his tiger whine loudly. "Don't, please. I can't – just don't touch me right now, okay?"

"Yeah, okay."

Her smile was pale but at least she didn't look like she wanted to murder him. "Take me home?"

He nodded and followed her off the dance floor.

"SORRY THAT WE HAD TO GIVE WES A RIDE HOME FIRST," Grayson said as he followed her into the kitchen. Sam was waiting eagerly at the back door and she let Grayson check the yard before releasing Sam. He bounded out into the yard, tail wagging wildly, and she shut the door before leaning against it.

Grayson was leaning against the counter, looking extremely fuckable. His lean body clad in a tight t-shirt and jeans was a frickin' wet dream waiting to happen. She studied his mouth and then his big hands that were gripping the edge of the counter. What would it be like to have those hands on her naked body? God, did it suck that she couldn't find out, what with the whole forbidden to bang her thing. Hell, ever since they danced, he was straight up acting like he couldn't even *touch* her.

Uh, idiot? You told him not to touch you. Remember?

Well, yeah, but that was purely self-preservation. A woman only had so much willpower around a hot tiger shifter, right?

He can't touch you, but that doesn't mean you can't touch him.

She froze against the door, her gaze dropping to his crotch. Hmm, her inner voice made a good point. Sure, it was sort of a loophole, but whatever. He wasn't allowed to fuck her, but where in Cooper's rules did it say she wasn't allowed to give him a handjob or – her mouth actually watered at the thought – a blowjob?

"Ryan?"

She dragged her gaze away from his dick. "Sorry, what?"

"I said I'm sorry we had to give Wes a ride home first. He doesn't drive."

"No? That's nice." She walked toward him, completely distracted by the idea that she might have her hands on what most likely would be a giant dick.

His body tensed when she stopped only inches away from him. "Ryan, what are you doing?"

She smiled at him but kept her hands to herself for the moment. "So, you have rules you have to follow, right? No banging the client rules."

"Yes." His breath hissed out when she gave in to temptation and rested her hand against his lean abdomen. "Honey, I can't."

"*You* can't touch me," she said. "But there's no rule that says *I* can't touch you."

A small grin played on his lips, but he shook his head. "That's just semantics. Besides, I'm not into taking without giving."

"You shouldn't be so close-minded about trying new things." She traced the button on his jeans before popping it open and then tugged on his zipper.

"Fuck." The small grin was gone from his face and his eyes had gone a brilliant colour of jade. The pupils turned to slits and, while he was talking to his tiger, she took the opportunity to tug his zipper down.

He returned to her, his breathing already harsh and uneven. "Honey, you know that I want this, but -"

"Don't ask me to stop," she said. "I need this."

His hands, which had been reaching for hers, faltered and triumph went through her when he returned them to the edge of the counter and gripped it hard.

"Don't touch me, Gray," she whispered. "You're not breaking any rules if you don't touch me."

He groaned when she slid her hand inside his briefs. His cock was rock hard, and she traced the silky-soft skin of his shaft before wrapping her hand around his width. Shay was right, he was big. Big and hard and- she gave him a slow stroke – delightfully thick.

He moaned this time, a low drawn-out sound that soaked her already wet panties. She pressed her thighs together to ease the ache between her legs before stepping a little closer to Grayson.

She studied his mouth as she stroked lightly up and down

before rubbing her thumb across the wide head. Precum dripped steadily from him and she circled the head with her thumb before rubbing him again.

"Does it feel good, Gray?"

"So good," he groaned. His head fell back, and she studied the stubble on his throat as his hips thrust into her hand. "Harder, honey."

She gripped him more tightly and stroked faster. When the deep purr rumbled up out of his chest, her nipples tightened into hard buds and her stomach cramped with pure pleasure. Fuck, she could listen to him purr all damn day.

His purring grew louder as his hips rocked back and forth. She loved seeing him this way, loved watching his need grow stronger because of her and only her.

"I want to touch you," he growled out.

She shook her head. "No."

Another low growl and she gave his dick a quick squeeze before squirming her hand further down to cup his balls. "Behave, Gray."

He was white knuckling the counter now, his big body rocking back and forth as she eased her hand back up to his cock and curled her fingers around him again. When her cell phone rang in her pocket, she ignored it even though it was Ryleigh's ring.

He cracked open one eye, his body still moving to the rhythm of her hand. "Do you need to get that?'

She smiled at him before sliding her other hand up under his t-shirt and exploring the hard ridges of abdomen muscles with her fingertips. "Do you really want me to get that?"

"No," he groaned. "But if… oh fuck!"

Her questing fingers had moved higher, found one flat nipple, and given it a sharp pinch. His body jerked, his cock twitching in her hand as fresh precum spilled out of the tip.

"Like that, do you?" she said before rubbing the ball of her thumb over his nipple.

His purring grew so loud that she almost didn't hear her cell phone when it started ringing a second time. It was Ryleigh again, and her strokes faltered on his dick. Her baby sister didn't hang up and call again immediately unless it was really important.

"Ryan?" Grayson arched an eyebrow at her as she slid her hand out from his briefs.

"I'm sorry." She pulled her phone out of her pocket. "Something's wrong. She wouldn't call me twice in a row if there wasn't a problem."

She hit the answer button. "Ryleigh? What's up?"

She listened for only a few minutes, pacing back and forth in the kitchen before saying, "Okay, sweetie. I'll be right there. Just hang in there. I'm on my way."

She stuffed her phone into her pocket. Grayson had already buttoned his jeans and she yanked open the back door and whistled for Sam. He ran into the house and she locked the back door. "I'm sorry. I know it's late, but I need to get to Grandmother's house right now."

"It's fine. Let's go." Grayson held out his hand and she took it, following him out of the kitchen and toward the front door, sincerely grateful that he wasn't asking questions.

CHAPTER 10

"You think you're better than me? You are not better than me, you ungrateful little bitch!"

The scream reverberated through the mansion. In front of him, Ryan froze for a second before running down the hallway. He chased after her. His tiger was growling angrily, and he wanted to pick Ryan up and carry her out to the car. Whatever was happening here wasn't going to end well.

Ryan stopped in front of the door leading into the family room. Both Boone and Chase were standing outside of it. Chase was sweaty and pale and even Boone looked uneasy. Grayson grabbed Ryan's hand when she reached for the knob.

"It's fine." She shook him off impatiently. "Stay out here."

"What? No fucking way," he said.

"Yes, fucking way," she snapped. Her usual calm and easygoing nature had disappeared, and she looked pale and sick to her stomach. "This is a family matter, and it doesn't concern you."

He bit back his retort that it fucking well did concern him.

Just because his tiger had decided that Ryan belonged to him, didn't mean she did.

"You would be nothing without me! Nothing!" Vanessa shouted.

Ryan winced, her face paling even further. Without looking at him, she slipped inside the room and shut the door behind her.

"What the fuck are you doing here?" Vanessa's voice could have shattered the crystal chandelier hanging above them.

Ryan replied, but even with his shifter hearing, the walls and door were thick, and he couldn't quite hear what she said.

He leaned against the wall and stared at Boone. "What the hell is going on?"

"She's completely plastered," Boone said. "The woman can drink like a goddamn fish, but today..." He shook his head. "I have no fucking idea how she's even standing."

"Ryleigh tried to put her to bed about half an hour ago and Vanessa just lost it," Chase said. "Like, started freaking out. We wanted to help Ryleigh, but she told us it was a -"

"Family matter, yeah, I heard." Grayson ran a hand through his hair. "Where's the grandmother?"

"In bed, knocked out with some pretty strong pain medication. She suffers from migraines," Boone replied. "A fancy-ass doctor came by earlier and injected her with some shit that apparently put her in a fucking coma or something. As soon as she was out, Vanessa really ramped up the drinking. Apparently, Beverly keeps Vanessa's drinking under some semblance of control but with the old lady incapacitated..."

"Don't you dare tell me to calm down, you stupid fat cow!" Vanessa screeched. "You ruined my fucking life and you think you can just waltz in here and tell me to calm down?"

Grayson winced when Vanessa screamed, "You always have to call your big sister, don't you, Ryleigh? You've always hated me, always loved Ryan more, and I did everything for you! If it wasn't for me, you wouldn't even be on the show! Do you hear me?"

"Christ," Boone said before running a hand over his face. "She is a serious bitch. I'm not kidding, Gray. The shit she says to Ryleigh on a daily basis... it's bad."

Chase nodded in agreement. "Ryleigh acts like it doesn't bother her, like it's some big joke, but..."

"She's acting," a soft voice said.

Grayson turned and studied Vanessa's assistant, Lori, as she walked toward them. The jaguar shifter clasped her arms across her torso and shook her head. "Ryleigh is incredibly sensitive and everything Vanessa says to her when she's this drunk, wounds her deeply."

Behind the door, Vanessa's screaming was going on and on. Gray's tiger whimpered in misery. The sound of the woman's high-pitched squawking was driving it mad. For his tiger's sanity, he blocked out what Vanessa was saying and concentrated on Lori. "Why doesn't she move out?"

Lori shrugged. "Honestly? I have no idea."

"How often does Vanessa do this?" Chase asked.

"Once or twice a month, whenever Beverly gets a migraine and isn't around to police her drinking."

"She needs to be in fucking rehab," Boone said.

"She does, but you can't tell Vanessa to do anything she doesn't want to," Lori replied. "She'll only dig her heels in if you try."

There was another screech of outrage that made Lori

flinch. "Ryleigh tries to calm Vanessa down, but she always ends up calling Ryan."

"Why?" Boone said.

Lori hesitated and Grayson scowled. "Because when Ryan shows up, Vanessa turns on her instead of Ryleigh."

"Yes," Lori said. "But she's tough. She can handle it."

"She shouldn't *have* to handle it," Grayson said.

"I've never met a mother who hated her own kid before," Boone said.

"She doesn't hate Ryan," Lori said.

"I hate you, you wretched cunt!" Vanessa screamed. "Do you hear me, Ryan? I hate you and I wish you'd never been born! You ruined my goddamn life!"

Boone stared at Lori who rubbed at the delicate skin below her eyes. "She's not a monster, okay? She has a disease and needs treatment."

There was the sound of glass shattering and Ryleigh screamed. Grayson whipped around and grabbed the door handle, barreling into the room without a second thought. His tiger roared in pure fury and tried to push to the front as he watched Vanessa rush at Ryan with a broken bottle in her hand.

He wasn't going to get to her in time, even if he shifted. The room was too big, and they were too far away. The old woman was going to slice open his mate's throat and he would have to watch her die.

Vanessa screamed again and slashed at Ryan with the broken bottle. To his immense relief, Ryan caught her arm easily and shoved it down, squeezing Vanessa's wrist until the woman made a sharp cry of pain.

"Let it go, Vanessa," Ryan said.

"Bitch!" Vanessa shrieked at her.

"Let it go," Ryan repeated.

How the fuck she could be so calm, Grayson had no idea. Ryleigh was cowering behind Ryan, her arms wrapped around Ryan's waist and her face buried between Ryan's shoulder blades.

Ryan squeezed Vanessa's wrist again and Vanessa made another cry of pain before letting the bottle drop to the floor. It shattered on the marble floor, sending shards of glass skating across the slippery surface, and Ryan dropped Vanessa's arm.

Her mother immediately slapped her so hard across the face that Ryan stumbled back, knocking Ryleigh into the wall. Grayson was almost to them now and he reached out and caught Ryan's arm before she could fall, keeping her on her feet. Ryan reached behind her to grab for Ryleigh.

"Ryleigh! Sweetie, are you okay?"

"She's fine," Grayson said. He turned Ryan toward him, cupping her face, a growl slipping from his throat. The force of Vanessa's slap had opened up the cut on Ryan's cheek. "You're bleeding."

Ryan touched her cheek, staring at the trace of blood on her fingers. "It's fine. It's barely bleeding."

Her eyes were watering, and her chest was hitching, and he already knew her well enough to know she was on the verge of crying. He tried to pull her into his arms, but she pushed away from him. His tiger made a sulky whine as Ryan turned to her mother who was weaving unsteadily in front of them. "Time to go to bed, Vanessa."

"Fuck you, you little slut," Vanessa slurred. She turned her vacant bloodshot gaze to Grayson, "You fucking this animal? Is that it? You're disgusting."

Grayson's tiger surged forward. His fangs dropped and he

bared them at Vanessa, growling loudly. Vanessa squealed in terror and lurched backwards, tripping over her own feet and landing on her ass with a harsh thud.

"Mom!" Ryleigh slipped past them and crouched next to her, putting her arm around her shoulders. "Mom, it's okay."

"He tried to attack me," Vanessa whined. The front of her dressing gown was covered in spilled whiskey and she raised one shaky hand and pointed it at him. "He tried to kill me."

"You're wrong," Ryan said quickly. She moved to her mother, and she and Ryleigh hauled Vanessa to her feet.

"He growled at me." Vanessa was weaving so badly now that Ryan had to sling the woman's arm around her shoulders to keep her upright.

"He didn't," Ryan said calmly. She no longer looked on the verge of tears but the red mark on her cheek was deepening. It would be a bruise by tomorrow and his tiger made another rush for control. He held it back, but he knew his eyes turned jade and his fangs were still out by the look on both Vanessa and Ryleigh's faces.

"Ry-Ry?" Ryleigh whispered nervously.

"Gray, stop," Ryan said. "It's fine. Everything's fine. Don't shift."

He took a deep breath as Boone and Chase joined him. Boone clapped him on the back. "Go get some fresh air."

"No," he said. "Ryan, we need to talk."

She and Ryleigh were easing Vanessa toward the door, their shoes crunching on the broken glass scattered across the marble floor.

"Later," she said.

"Now," he replied.

She glanced back at him and he took another deep breath. "Please."

She chewed at her bottom lip before glancing at Boone. "Can you help Ryleigh get her upstairs?"

"Yes." Boone took Ryan's place and Chase followed them out of the room. Lori took Ryan's hand and squeezed it, and Ryan gave her a tired smile.

"Hi, Lori."

"Hi, love. I'm so sorry."

"It's okay. Nothing new, right?"

"Yeah." Lori sighed before staring at the glass. "I'll get a broom to clean this up."

"Thank you." Ryan hesitated and then hugged Lori.

The jaguar shifter wrapped her arms around Ryan's waist and returned the hug before kissing her forehead affectionately. "It'll be all right, love."

She left the room and Ryan turned to face him, hugging her torso protectively. She pressed her lips together. "Don't look at me like that, Grayson."

"Honey, this is abuse." He took a step toward her, hating the way she backed up. "She hurt you."

"She has a disease, a terrible one that makes her do terrible things," Ryan said.

"You can't keep doing this," he said. "Ryleigh is a big girl. She can take care of herself. Putting yourself in your mother's path of anger and hatred isn't -"

She glared at him. "Stop it. Don't say another word, Grayson. You don't know my life or Ryleigh's life."

"Then tell me," he said. "Tell me why you would let her abuse you like this."

"I don't let her abuse me," she said heatedly. "Jesus, you are not my fucking shrink, okay? You're here to keep me safe from some psycho stalker, that's it, nothing else. So, do me a favour and stay the hell out of my personal life."

She turned and stalked out of the room, slamming the door behind her. He sighed before bending and picking up the bigger pieces of glass. "You fucked that up, you asshole," he muttered.

His tiger whined in agreement.

"HOW IS SHE?"

Ryan continued to stare out the window into the darkness. "Passed out."

Lori closed the door to the bedroom and crossed to the bed. She sat down next to Vanessa and brushed a few strands of hair away from the woman's pale face. Ryan had turned Vanessa on her side and a long strand of drool was clinging to her lower lip and cheek.

With the care of a mother, Lori wiped the drool away from Vanessa's cheek and lip with a tissue before resting her hand on Vanessa's bony shoulder. "Are you okay?"

"Fine," Ryan said.

"I know how hard this is and I'm sorry."

"She has a disease, a terrible one that makes her do terrible things," Ryan recited dully.

"Love, look at me."

Ryan turned to face Lori, studying her in the dim light from the bedside lamp. "What?"

"It's okay not to be fine. You know that, right?"

Tears threatened and she blinked them back. "I know."

"Vanessa didn't mean what she said. She loves you," Lori said. "It's just, when she drinks, she..."

"Yeah, I know," Ryan repeated. She appreciated Lori's kindness, she really did, but Vanessa didn't love her and never would. But it was one thing to know that, and another thing entirely to admit it out loud.

"You should go home," Lori said. "You're exhausted and in pain."

Ryan laughed bitterly. "I need to make sure Vanessa doesn't choke on her own vomit in the night."

"I'll stay with her." Lori stroked Vanessa's hair lovingly. "Go home and get some rest."

"This isn't part of your job," Ryan said. "She already asks you to do too much, I'm not going to -"

"I don't mind," Lori said. "I promise you. Besides," she aimed a small and lopsided grin at Ryan, "your mother will pay me overtime for spending the night."

Ryan rubbed at her temples. She had the beginnings of a tension headache and her entire body ached like she had the flu. "Ryleigh needs me."

"Saul is on his way," Lori said.

Another bark of laughter escaped her throat. "Jesus, you two really didn't know what you signed up for when you were hired to work for my family, did you?"

"We love you," Lori said before glancing at Vanessa again, "*all* of you and you're good people."

"We're not good people," Ryan said wearily.

"Go home, love. Go home and get some rest and enjoy the attention of a handsome tiger shifter who is totally into you."

"He's not into me, he's just doing his job," Ryan said.

Lori smiled. "He *wants* to take care of you… let him."

Ryan moved to the bed and leaned down to press a kiss on Lori's forehead. "We don't deserve you, you know that, right?"

"Totally know it," Lori said with another smile. "Good night, Ryan."

"Night, Lori." She left the bedroom and peeked into Ryleigh's room, but it was empty. Once they'd gotten Vanessa into bed, Ryleigh had left. Ryan didn't blame her. A raging drunk Vanessa was horrifying to deal with.

Her stomach churning and her head throbbing, she paused in the hallway to stare at her reflection in the mirror hung on the wall. She leaned in, studying first the bruise on her cheek she'd gotten from the mob at the coffee shop, before turning her face to look at the cut. Although it had already stopped bleeding, she could practically see Vanessa's handprint on her cheek. Fantastic. By tomorrow she'd be sporting bruises on both cheeks.

She rested her forehead on the mirror, releasing her breath in a shuddering sigh. "Don't cry. Don't cry. Don't cry."

She rarely cried, at least not since she'd gotten away from Vanessa, but the tears wouldn't stop threatening. She didn't know why. It wasn't like she hadn't been through this with her mother and her sister before. Ryleigh called her over at least once or twice a month to help deal with Vanessa. It was par for the course.

You're upset because Grayson tried to help, and you snapped at him. You were a total dick to him and if you think he's still gonna be attracted to you after all of this, you're crazy.

She pushed away from the mirror, straightening her dress and taking a deep breath. She had fucked up any possible chance of being with Grayson after this whole stalker mess was over.

"It would never have worked with us anyway," she muttered to herself as she descended the large staircase. "We're too different."

She walked down the hallway and into the family room. Saul, with Ryleigh tucked up against him, was talking to

Grayson and Boone and Chase. She walked toward them, smiling at Saul when he reached out and took her hand.

"Hey, Saul."

"Hey, beautiful. You okay?"

"Yes." She kissed the dark-haired man's cheek before squeezing Ryleigh's arm. "You feeling better, sweetie?"

Ryleigh nodded before wiping at her cheeks. "A little. Saul's gonna stay the night with me. Right?"

She stared anxiously at Saul who nodded. "Of course, I am."

Ryleigh pressed her head against his chest. "I don't know what I would do without you."

Her phone rang and she pulled it out of her pocket and stared at the screen before glancing at Saul. A look passed between them, one that Ryan didn't understand, before Ryleigh said, "I have to take this. I'll be right back."

She hurried out of the room. Saul slipped his arm around Ryan and studied the bruise on her cheek. "Ryleigh told me what happened at the coffee shop. She didn't mean for you to get hurt."

Grayson snorted loudly behind them. Not wanting to see his anger or – worse – disgust with her, Ryan kept her gaze on Saul's handsome face. "I know she didn't. I'm not angry with her."

"That's good." He touched the red mark on her other cheek. "If the bruises aren't gone by Alien-Con, I'll work my magic and cover them for you, okay?"

She nodded. "Thank you."

"Just doing my job." He pressed a kiss against her forehead. "You stayin' the night?"

"No. Lori said she would keep an eye on Vanessa. Thank you for staying with Ryleigh."

Saul smiled and kissed her forehead again. "Anytime. Go home and get some rest. You look like shit."

Grayson growled, and Saul winked at her before turning to face him. "Ryan knows I say it with love, big guy. No need to get your panties in a twist."

"Are you ready to go, Ryan?" Grayson asked.

She nodded and turned away without looking at him. "I am. Saul, just call me if anything happens."

"Nothing will happen," Saul said. "Go on. We've got this."

HIS TIGER WAS RESTLESS. WORSE, HE WAS UPSET, AND demanding Gray go to Ryan.

"She doesn't want us with her," Gray said. "She's pissed at us."

His tiger snarled at him and Grayson pressed the heel of his hand against his forehead. He was getting a headache, both from his tiger's anxiety and his own. "We can't."

His tiger tried to surge forward, and Gray pushed him back with difficulty. A trickle of unease went through him. His tiger never tried to take control, he always bent to Gray's will in the past, and this was how many times now in the past few days, that it had tried to gain control?

He paced back and forth in his room, staring at the wall that separated him from Ryan. He wanted to go to her, but the car ride home was tense and quiet, and she wouldn't look at him. When they finally got home, she'd let Sam outside, muttered a quick goodnight, and escaped to her room with Sam in tow. He'd gone to his bedroom as well, changing into sleep pants and crawling into bed. He'd tossed and turned for ten minutes before getting out of bed to pace the room.

She needs us.

His tiger could be incredibly persuasive.

Just check on her. That's all I'm asking.

It wouldn't *hurt* to check on her. The worst that would happen is she wouldn't open the door, or she'd tell him to leave her the fuck alone.

She needs us.

He yanked open the door to his room and strode down the hallway. He rapped on Ryan's bedroom door. "Ryan? Can I come in."

There was no reply, but he heard her moving in the bed.

"Honey, I just want to talk," he said.

"Come in."

He opened the door and stepped into her room before she could change her mind. It was dark, but he had no problem seeing her sitting up in the middle of the bed. Hell, he could see the shine of tears on her cheeks and the puffiness under her eyes that indicated she'd been crying for a while.

Fuck. He was an asshole.

"Honey, I'm sorry." He skirted around Sam, who had trotted over from his dog bed in the corner to greet him and hurried to the bed. His tiger whined in dismay at the sadness and anxiety surrounding Ryan in a thick coat.

She sniffed loudly before dabbing at her eyes with a tissue. "Why are you sorry? I'm the one who needs to apologize to you."

"Apologize to me?" he asked in bewilderment. "Why do you need to apologize to me?"

"Because I was-was-was -" she hitched in a shaky breath, "awful to you," and then burst into tears.

He immediately slid into the bed beside her and pulled her into his arms. He leaned against the cushioned headboard, pressing her head against his chest and kissing the top of her head. "You weren't awful to me."

"I was," she sobbed. "You were just trying to help earlier, and I snapped at you."

He rubbed her back through her tank top and purred to her. "It's all right, honey. It was stressful and I was butting in where I didn't belong."

She shook her head before wrapping her arm around his waist and clinging tightly. "No, I don't – I mean, I appreciate you wanting to help. It's just… Vanessa is difficult to deal with when she's like that, and I didn't want to drag you into my fucked-up life."

He put a finger under her chin and tilted her head up until she was staring at him. "I want to help you. I want to be involved in your life even if it is fucked up."

He wiped away the tears on her cheeks and pulled her even closer. She blinked back more tears before sighing. "She hates me. My own mother hates me."

"I'm sorry," he said. "She's a fool."

She pressed her cheek against his chest again, her fingers curling through the rough hair. "I'm sorry I'm being such a baby. I don't normally act like this, I just…"

"Don't be so hard on yourself," he said. "Crying isn't something to be ashamed of. Besides, I'm used to this. I'm constantly having to climb into bed with Boone and hold him while he cries."

She sat up and stared at him before a grin cracked her face. "For, like, one second I actually believed you."

He smiled innocently at her. "What? I'm telling you the truth. Boone is a weeper. You should have seen him when he made Coop and me watch *A Dog's Life* with him. I thought they were gonna ask us to leave the theatre, he was crying so hard."

This time she giggled, and the sound made his tiger so happy that it purred loudly in response. She immediately pressed her ear against his chest. "I really like it when you purr."

He kept purring, the low rasp rising and falling with every breath he took as he cuddled his mate. He stroked her back and kissed the top of her head as her anxiety slowly drifted away.

"Better?" he asked after about five minutes.

"Much," she said. "It sounds stupid, but your purring is oddly relaxing. I'm actually feeling a little sleepy now and I didn't think I'd sleep at all tonight."

"Lie on your side," he said.

She did what he asked, and he spooned her, wrapping his arm around her waist and tucking her against his big body. She fit perfectly against him, her perfect curvy ass snug in his lap and their legs entwined.

He continued to purr, the sound reverberating out of his chest and she made a sound of contentment. "This is really nice."

"Hmm," he said before burying his face in her hair and inhaling deeply.

They were quiet for almost ten minutes, the only sounds in the room were his purring and the occasional whimper from a dreaming Sam.

"I hate her." Ryan's voice was low, barely loud enough to be heard over his purring. "I hate her, and I feel so horrible for hating her."

"Don't," he said. "You have valid reasons for feeling the way you do. Vanessa doesn't exactly make it easy to love her."

She snuggled in closer, wrapping her hand around his forearm and tracing his skin with her fingertips. "She's always been a bad mom. Her drinking was more under control when Ryleigh and I were kids, but we were always an afterthought to her. We lived in Grandmother's house, but she was still working at that time, and she was gone a lot on different movie shoots. Mom was doing some modeling and some small acting jobs and," her tone turned bitter, "sleeping with anyone she thought would help advance her career."

He kissed the back of her shoulder, purring again to help calm the fresh anxiety coursing through her.

"I looked after Ryleigh. It was my bed she crawled into when she had a nightmare, me she came to when she hurt herself, me who made sure she brushed her teeth and bathed and ate properly."

"Your grandmother wasn't around to help?" Grayson asked.

"Not really. She was still filming movies and she was gone most of the time. When she was home, she picked up the slack for Vanessa, but Grandmother was working on location more often than not."

She hesitated and then said, "I just wanted to be a kid and sometimes I hated having to look after Ryleigh."

"That's a lot to ask of a little kid," Grayson said.

Her fingers traced small circles on his arm. "I was eight and Ryleigh was three when Peter and Mary stepped in. I guess they'd had enough of watching us raise ourselves. They were both there every day and they just decided to look after us like we were their kids."

She craned her neck to stare at him in the darkness. "They didn't have to do that, you know? They didn't have to care about us or-or love us. But they did."

He bent his head and kissed away the tear that was trickling down her face. "I'm glad you had them to look after you."

"During the summer, when Mary knew that Vanessa wouldn't be home, she would bring Oren with her to work. The three of us would play together. In the evenings, if Vanessa didn't show up before Mary and Peter left for home, they would take Ryleigh and me with them. One time, Grandmother was shooting a movie in Australia. Vanessa hooked up with some semi-famous TV actor and spent a week at his beach house in Florida. She was gone a week and didn't even bother to arrange childcare for Ryleigh and me. I was nine years old. If it hadn't been for Mary and Peter, who knows what would have happened. They called Grandmother and told her that Vanessa was gone and not returning their calls. Grandmother was going to leave the set and come home but Mary and Peter offered to look after us. They took us home with them for the week."

Her voice turned wistful. "It was the best week of my entire childhood. Waking up every morning, knowing that Mary would be downstairs and cooking breakfast, that I wouldn't be dragged to yet another audition by Vanessa, that I wasn't responsible for keeping Ryleigh safe... it was bliss, you know?"

He hugged her tight and dropped another kiss on her forehead. "I'm so sorry, honey."

"Grandmother was so pissed at Vanessa. They got into a huge fight when Grandmother returned from Australia. She told Vanessa if she ever just abandoned us again like that, she'd call Child Services on her. She said she'd kick her out of the house and raise Ryleigh and me herself."

Her voice dropped. "I wanted that to happen. I-I hoped and prayed that Vanessa would screw up again. But she didn't. She still wasn't much of a mother, but she made sure that she did just enough that Grandmother wouldn't kick her out."

"I'm sorry," he repeated.

She smiled wanly at him. "It wasn't all bad. Like I said, when Grandmother was home, she was there for us, and we had Mary and Peter when she wasn't around. They're the reason I survived after I emancipated myself at sixteen. I lived with them until I was eighteen, and then Peter helped me find my house and guided me through the process of buying it. Money was never a problem. Bert and Christopher arranged for the money I made on the show to be put in a trust and that I would receive it on my eighteenth birthday. It was more than enough to buy the house and even now I still get residuals from reruns of the show. Mary knew I loved taking photos and she encouraged me to take photography courses and hone my skill."

Her smile turned more natural. "I have so many pictures of Peter and Mary and Oren. They were my guinea pigs and I'm the reason all three of them run when they see a camera now."

He laughed and she squeezed his forearm. "I asked Ryleigh to move in with me when I bought the house. Grandmother had retired from acting and she was home most of the time by then, but I still hated the idea of Ryleigh being there with Vanessa. She always got so mean when she drank and after the show ended, her drinking got worse. That was my fault."

"No," he said immediately. "It wasn't. Vanessa is a grown-ass adult who makes her own decisions."

"If I hadn't quit the show, or if I had agreed to do the spin-off -"

"You would have been miserable," he said. "Vanessa's feelings and wants are not more valid than your own, honey. Remember that."

"Yeah," she whispered. "Anyway, I asked Ryleigh to

move in with me, but she wouldn't. She was only thirteen, but she had already been in a couple of movies and done a few guest spots on TV shows and loved it. She'd been bit by the acting bug hard. Plus, she was getting along okay with Vanessa."

"Really?"

"Yeah. See - when I was ten, Vanessa and I started working on *Alien Hunter*. The show became popular fast, and Vanessa and I were thrust into the spotlight. I hated it, but Vanessa craved it. With the new interest in us, Vanessa started acting like a mom to Ryleigh and me. It was all for the public and the paparazzi, of course, but Ryleigh was only five and she wanted that affection and love from Vanessa. She believed it was real. It's why she defends her even now."

She was quiet for a few minutes before dragging in a deep breath. "Vanessa told me once why she hated me. She'd gotten really drunk, and Ryleigh had called me and begged me to come over. I sent Ryleigh to her room and let Vanessa scream and yell herself out. When I was putting her to bed, she told me that I was the reason my father was dead. She said he was the only man she ever truly loved, and that the stress of having a baby had driven them apart and worsened his drug use. He died of an overdose because of me, she said, and she would never forgive me for killing the love of her life."

He kissed the side of her neck. "That isn't true. Do you hear me? You aren't responsible for his death."

"I know." Her voice was robotic. "I know that it isn't true, but I still feel guilty. Isn't that stupid of me?"

"Nothing about you is stupid," he said. "I'm sorry you had such a fucked-up childhood. It isn't fair or right."

She just shrugged. "Thanks for listening to my sob story. Tell me about your childhood."

He kissed her neck again. "Tomorrow. Right now, you're exhausted and in pain and you need rest."

"Will you stay with me in the bed?" She whispered, her hand tightening around his forearm.

"Yes," he said. "I'll stay."

CHAPTER 11

"Does he do this every morning?" Shay stared out the window of the back door. "Because if he does, how has your entire neighbourhood not just been washed away by a sea of drool? When I drove up, I saw your neighbour staring out her window at him with binoculars."

"Every single torturous morning." Ryan stood next to Shay and stared greedily at Grayson as he moved into the next pose. He was standing on the back deck and she smiled a little when he used his foot to gently push Sam off the edge of his yoga mat. The tiger shifter was wearing just a pair of track pants and she studied the large muscles in his back as he switched positions again.

"Swear to God, if he moves into downward dog, I'm gonna cream my underwear," Shay said.

Ryan laughed. "I took a few pictures of him doing yoga the first couple mornings. I couldn't resist. The light and subject were perfect."

"Oh hell, yes," Shay said. "Send me one."

She eyed her best friend suspiciously. "Why?"

"I'm gonna blow it up to life size and plaster it to my bedroom ceiling so I have something to look at while I'm masturbating."

Ryan smacked her in the arm. "Gross, Shay."

"Oh please, like you haven't thought of doing the same thing."

Ryan didn't reply and Shay poked her in the side. "You know I'm only teasing, right? I'm not interested in your man."

"He isn't my man."

"But you want him to be."

"Maybe," Ryan said. They watched Gray in silence for a couple of minutes before she said, "I seriously had no idea watching a guy do yoga could be this hot."

"That's because the guys in our yoga class do not look like that." Shay leaned against the island and took a sip of coffee. "How are you not banging him, girl?"

"It's a struggle, trust me." Ryan poured herself more coffee. She should have been exhausted and depressed, she always felt that way after dealing with a drunk Vanessa, but there was a weird elation running through her and she'd slept better last night than she had in weeks.

She wanted to tell herself it wasn't because she'd been tucked up against Grayson all night, but she wasn't very good at lying. Not even to herself.

"So, your text said Vanessa was being a bag again last night?" Shay bumped her with her hip.

"Yeah," Ryan replied. "It was awful as usual. Grayson, of course, had to go with me and it was excruciatingly embarrassing."

"It's not your fault your mother is a drunk," Shay said. "Don't be embarrassed."

Ryan sighed. "I was super upset and I kind of snapped at him while I was dealing with Vanessa. Later that night though, he was so sweet to me. He knocked on my bedroom door to apologize and I was – shit, I was crying which was also humiliating – but, Shay, he was so kind and…"

"Sweet," Shay said with a soft smile.

"Yeah. Sounds weird to describe a tiger shifter as sweet, but he was. He spent the night in my bed."

"Jesus, and you still didn't sleep with him? You have the willpower of a god," Shay said.

Ryan shrugged. "Honestly? If he'd still been in the bed when I woke up, I would have at the very least given him a blowjob, but he was already up and in the shower."

"Bummer," Shay said.

"I told him a little bit about my childhood."

Shay paused with her coffee mug at her lips. "Shut the hell up, you didn't?"

"I did," Ryan said.

"You don't tell anyone about your childhood. Ever."

"I know, but it felt right to tell him. And it felt good after."

"Your therapist would be so proud of you right now," Shay said with a grin.

Ryan laughed. "Wouldn't she? I'll have to tell her at my next appointment."

"So, it's obvious that as soon as this stupid stalker mess is cleaned up, you and Grayson are gonna bone each other. Are you hoping it'll be more than just boning?" Shay asked.

"Crude, but yes. I think he wants that too."

Shay put her arm around her and gently kissed her bruised cheek. "I'm happy for you, sweetie."

"Thanks, Shay."

"What are your plans for the rest of the weekend?"

"I have a shoot this afternoon and then I'll spend the rest of the weekend," she paused, "attempting to avoid having sex with Mr. He Makes Yoga Sexy over there."

"Good luck with that," Shay said.

"I'm going to need it. The Alien-Con starts Wednesday afternoon so that'll keep us both occupied until the weekend, and he's off on Monday and Tuesday. I just need to get through today and tomorrow and then I'll have a few days where maybe I'm not constantly thinking about how nice it would be to have sex with Grayson.

"Like I said, good luck." Shay cocked her head, staring at Grayson's ass as he went into the downward dog pose. "And now I need a dry pair of underwear."

Ryan burst into laughter.

"For fuck's sake." Cooper glared at his laptop instead of throwing it across his office like he wanted to. He did not have goddamn time for a software update. Could a shifter actually feel their blood pressure rising?

He took a deep breath and yanked open the bottom drawer of his desk. The granny square he was working on for Wes's blanket was sitting on top of the ball of yarn and he picked it up gingerly before grabbing the crochet hook stuck in the ball of yarn.

He forced himself to concentrate on the crocheting as he added a round to the square. He did another one and then the final round before fastening off and cutting the yarn. He placed the granny square on top of the pile of growing squares at the back of the drawer and checked the time.

He'd come in early to the office to try and get some work

done before he had to go back to the mansion to cover Chase's shift. He shuddered at the thought of being back in the mansion. He'd gone over Saturday morning and spent the weekend covering for Boone. The idea of returning was an unpleasant one.

He didn't have time to keep crocheting but he started another granny square anyway. He'd thought it was stupid when his doctor suggested he take up a hobby to help him relax. Her suggestion of knitting or crocheting had made him snort with derision. But, early one morning, after another sleepless night, he'd found himself in a damn craft store checking out the yarn selection. A nice lady in the yarn aisle had helped him pick out yarn and a hook, a book on how to crochet, and given him a couple of suggestions for YouTube videos. Six months later, he was officially addicted to goddamn crocheting.

He sighed and continued to crochet. Maybe he'd send Wes to cover Chase and he'd cover Gray's shift with the older daughter. It was a dick move to do to Wes, but, hell, Coop was the boss. Shouldn't that mean he gets some damn perks?

The yarn knotted and he muttered another curse before picking delicately at it. He smelled Daisy's scent only seconds before she knocked on his open door. His face bright red, he turned and shoved the ball of yarn and the granny square into the drawer and kicked it shut with his foot.

"Um, hey, hi there," he said. Fuck, he really hoped she hadn't seen him crocheting.

"Morning, Cooper." Daisy smiled tentatively at him. "You're here early for a Monday."

"So are you," he said.

"I'm sorry, is that a problem? I didn't mean to, that is, I can…"

"No, it's fine," he said as the smell of her anxiety drifted to him. "It's fine, Daisy. I mean it."

"Okay," she said. "So, um, why are you here? I thought you were doing security for the Shepherd job today and tomorrow."

"I am," he said. "I just wanted to try and do a bit more research on Bert before I headed over, but my laptop is doing a software update."

"That's the manager, right?" Daisy sat down in the chair in front of his desk and his lion purred so loudly, he could barely hear her next sentence. "Have you found anything suspicious yet?"

Give her to me.

He ignored his lion's whining and wiped at the sweat on his forehead. Christ, it was getting more and more difficult to control the urge to claim Daisy as his mate.

"Cooper?"

"Sorry, what?" He looked away from her perfect mouth.

"I asked if you'd found anything suspicious."

"Oh, uh, no, but honestly, I haven't had a lot of time to do the research I want."

She crossed her legs and he studied the firm line of her calf. She wasn't wearing nylons and her skin looked silky smooth and soft. His hands itched to touch her, and he stuck them together in a tight fist under his desk as his lion purred again to Daisy.

"I could help," Daisy said. "I know I'm just the recep-tionist but I'm happy to take on extra responsibilities."

"Sure, that would be really helpful."

The immediate happiness that surrounded her made him glad he'd agreed. He inhaled deeply. It wasn't often that Daisy was this happy and the scent of her happiness was addicting to him. Would her lust smell this sweet?

You'll never know.

His good mood deflated immediately. No, he wouldn't. Daisy was scared to death of shifters. He could try and fool himself all he wanted that she was less terrified of him now, but it wasn't true.

His lion growled with displeasure. It hated that Daisy was afraid of him and was constantly pushing for him to shift in front of the timid receptionist so that it could rub up against her and show her she didn't need to be afraid.

Bad idea, he said for the thousandth time. *It'll only make it worse.*

It won't, his lion growled. *She'll be less afraid once she sees me.*

No, she'll be completely traumatized and quit. Is that what you want?

You know it isn't, his lion replied sulkily before retreating.

He glanced up, his stomach dropping when he smelled Daisy's anxiety. She was studying his eyes and while she looked relaxed enough, her hands were gripping the arms of her chair so hard that her knuckles were white.

Shit. He tried really hard not to talk to his lion in front of Daisy. Even just his eyes changing was enough to freak her out.

He cleared his throat. He'd discovered the best thing to do was ignore her tension. If he tried to ask her if she was all right or assure her that she didn't need to be afraid, it just made things worse. He'd discovered that the hard way.

"You sure you don't mind doing the research?" he asked.

She shook her head, her small body relaxing a fraction. "No, not at all. I'll email you with any relevant details that I find."

"Okay. Talk with Lusa as well. She might be able to get you some... additional information."

A brief smile curved up Daisy's perfect lips. Lusa was a cougar shifter, and their IT person. She was only twenty-four years old, but she was a damn savant when it came to finding shit on the internet. He supposed she was what they called a hacker and while Coop had no idea how she found out the information she did, he wasn't above asking her to get it for him. The oldest Shepherd daughter wasn't wrong when she'd said they were security not private investigators, but this wasn't the first and it wouldn't be the last time, that they'd helped clients with more than just security.

"I will. Before you leave, did you return Frost's call about how many men you need?"

"Shit. No, I forgot." He grabbed for his phone. "I'm already running late but I was supposed to call him on Saturday."

"I'll call him for you. How many men do you want?"

"Eight. Thanks, Daisy. This place would fall apart without you."

She smiled again, making his lion purr happily. "I doubt that, but I appreciate the thought."

YOU'RE BEING AN IDIOT.

Yeah, maybe, but he couldn't stay away from her any longer. He shifted the box to one hand and knocked on the door with the other. He waited a bit impatiently. She was home, he could see her car in the driveway. Why wasn't she answering? Was she hurt? Was she in trouble?

His tiger growled in alarm. Where the hell was Ryan?

He was five seconds away from just busting down the door when it opened. Ryan stared at him in surprise. "Gray? What are you doing here? It's your day off."

"I was in the neighbourhood." He held up the box in one hand. "I brought a puzzle."

She burst into laughter as Sam wiggled past her and barked excitedly at him. Gray petted Sam's head and Ryan said, "Come inside. We're just making dinner. Did you know Wes was such a good cook?"

Jealousy flared inside of him. "Yeah, I knew."

"You're crushing the puzzle box."

"What?"

She pointed to the puzzle. He *was* crushing it and he forced himself to relax his grip as Ryan leaned against the door jamb and grinned at him. "Did you come by on your day off because you think I'm gonna hit on Wes?"

"No," he said.

"You do," she said with another smile. "You don't have to worry. I'm not into Wes."

"I know," he said. "I missed you."

God, could he sound any more pathetic? He was completely head over fucking heels for this woman and he couldn't even hide it if he tried. He didn't want to hide it. It had been less than twelve hours since he'd left her house this morning and his tiger had been whining and bitching the entire time about going back to Ryan. He'd gone home, done his laundry, cleaned his already spotless apartment, and then gone to the gym in an effort to keep himself busy.

None of it worked. He missed Ryan and yeah, maybe there was a part of him that was just the tiniest bit worried about Ryan and Wes being alone, but ultimately it wasn't that worry that sent him back to her house.

Genuine pleasure blanketed her in a thick scent, and she smiled at him. "I've missed you too. Come inside."

He followed her and Sam into the house, and he glanced

around before leaning down and pressing a quick kiss against her mouth. "Did you have a good day?"

She touched her mouth, another smile crossing her lips, before she nodded. "It was good. I had a shoot this morning and then spent most of the afternoon editing. How about you?"

"It was fine. Did some laundry, went to the gym. Did you -"

Warm throaty laughter drifted down the hallway from the kitchen and he sniffed the air. "Is Shay here?"

She nodded before leaning in and whispering conspiratorially, "Hey, Wes is straight, right?"

"Yeah. Why?"

"Shay's totally into Wes. When she found out he was my security for the next two days, she came over immediately. She's been hitting on him for the last two hours and," she waved her hand in the air, "nothing. I mean nothing from him. Shay's a good-looking woman and she's smart and funny. When she hits on a guy, they're usually interested."

"Isn't she a little young for Wes?" Grayson said.

"Eh, age is just a number. You're way older than me and I don't care," she said.

"Hey, I'm not that much older than you."

"Just teasing," she said with that smile he loved. "How old are you, anyway?"

"Thirty-two."

"Seriously? I thought you were thirty at the oldest. Hmm, I might have to rethink my attraction to you."

He growled at her and she laughed quietly before standing on her tiptoes and pressing a second kiss against his mouth. He put his arm around her waist and deepened the kiss when she tried to pull away.

Her hands curled into his jacket and she opened her

mouth. He tasted her sweetness, their tongues teasing and tormenting before he forced himself to pull back. Her bottom lip was swollen from his kiss, and he resisted the urge to suck on it as her eyelids fluttered open.

"I'd like another kiss, please," she said in a sweet and cajoling voice.

"Ryan? Who was at the – oh hey, Grayson."

He pushed away from Ryan, wiping at his mouth almost guiltily as they both turned to face Shay. The pretty brunette grinned at them.

"Grayson, uh, is joining us for dinner," Ryan said.

"Awesome," Shay said with another cheeky grin. "The more the merrier."

"You already put a tracking app on my phone."

"I know," Grayson said patiently.

Ryan leaned against the counter as Sam sniffed at her suitcase. "Why do I need that then?" She pointed at the black rubber wristband Grayson was holding.

"Just an added measure of safety," Grayson replied.

"But I always have my phone with me."

"What if you were kidnapped and they took it from you?"

She paused and then said, "You make a fair point. I'll wear it."

He moved in front of her. "This bracelet has a tracking chip embedded in the centre of it. The chip is synced to my phone. I can set it for a certain distance, and if you go further than that distance from me, my phone alerts."

Before he could slide the bracelet over her hand, she said, "What do I get from you in return for wearing this?"

"What do you want?" He traced her exposed collarbone

167

with his fingertip and shivers of pleasure coursed up and down her spine.

"A kiss," she said. "With tongue."

"You drive a hard bargain, Ms. Shepherd," he murmured before pressing his mouth against hers.

She parted her lips immediately, sucking lightly on his tongue when he slipped it into her mouth. He groaned and one hand slid around her to cup her ass while they kissed. He kneaded it roughly as they explored each other's mouths. When he pulled away, she groaned in disappointment and tried to kiss him again.

He released her ass and took a step back. "We need to leave for the hotel, Ryan."

"Right." Ignoring the way her pussy was throbbing was proving to be much more difficult than she anticipated.

She held her arm out, trying not to shiver when Grayson slipped the bracelet over her hand and onto her wrist. She really shouldn't keep kissing him, every time they did it just got more difficult to resist him, but God, the guy could kiss and really, could you blame her for wanting to make out with him? He was hot and funny and seriously sexy. Plus, he was into her and he didn't even try and hide it, and she loved that he didn't play games.

She'd been stupidly happy when he'd come by the house on Monday night – it was almost a little scary how much she'd missed him in the twelve hours they were apart – and then he'd shown up again at her house last night. They'd sat in the living room with Wes and watched TV and even though Wes had to think it was strange that Grayson kept dropping by on his days off, he didn't say a word to her or to Gray about it. She just hoped that Wes didn't say anything to Gray's boss either.

"Ready to go?" Gray reached down and adjusted his

crotch. Smug satisfaction went through her when she saw the bulge.

He laughed and leaned down to press a fleeting kiss against the pulse point in her neck. "The smugness that radiates from you every time you see my woody, is adorable."

She grinned at him and grabbed her camera bag and her purse from the table. Her suitcase, as well as Grayson's was already in the car. Grayson had loaded them into the back of the SUV after they'd returned from dropping Sam off at her grandmother's house.

She followed him to the front door, locking it securely behind her and waiting behind Grayson as he scanned the neighbourhood. He took her hand and they walked to the car. He opened the back door and put her camera and purse on the seat before opening her front door. As she climbed in, he took a quick feel of her ass.

She laughed and settled herself into the leather seat. "Behave, pussy-cat."

"Hey, if you're gonna show off your ass in tight jeans, I'm gonna grab it." He tugged on a lock of her hair and closed the door.

"I want you to go over the rules with me," he said once they were on the freeway and headed toward the hotel.

She looked up from her phone. "We've gone over them twice."

"Just once more," he said.

She set her phone in her lap. "Once we're at the conference, I am never alone unless I'm in my hotel room. During the conference, you or one of the other two men assigned to me will always be within ten feet of me. If I have to use the bathroom or go somewhere that's not a designated location, I inform you and you'll arrange for someone to go with me."

"Good," he said. "And when you're in the hotel room?"

"I use all the door locks at all times, and I don't open the door unless I know who it is. When I want to leave, I text you and you'll come to my room to get me," she said.

"That's right. We aren't stationing men outside your rooms because your mother believes keeping a low profile is more important than your safety."

She could hear the disgust in his voice, and she reached across to pat his arm. "Guards outside the rooms aren't necessary. All of us are adults who are well aware of the dangers in opening the door to someone we don't know. Plus, it'll definitely make it easier to sneak out for a midnight pizza run with Saul and Ryleigh. Don't worry, I'll leave my bracelet in the room, so your phone doesn't alert and send you into a panic."

He growled at her and she laughed. "Relax, I'm only teasing."

"Do not take off the bracelet, Ryan. Do you understand? Not even when you're showering."

"I won't," she said.

There was silence and then she said, "Are you thinking about me showering?"

"Maybe."

She giggled and he reached over and squeezed her knee before resting his big hand on her thigh. She liked the weight of it on her leg, and she traced his knuckles with her fingers as he said, "Your hotel room is right next to Ryleigh's. My room is to the right of you and Chase's room is to the left of Ryleigh. Your mother's room is beside Chase and Boone is in the room next to her. The eight added security guys are two to a room across the hallway."

"I know," she said. "Bert told me when we dropped Sam off at grandmother's this morning."

She glanced at Grayson. "Has Cooper found anything suspicious on Bert yet?"

"Not that I know of," Gray replied.

"He won't," Ryan said confidently. "Bert isn't behind this."

He squeezed her leg again before continuing. "The lawyer guy -"

"Christopher."

"Right, Christopher – convinced your mother that the conference people should know about the threats against the three of you. Cooper spoke with the head of security for the conference and the hotel. He didn't give specifics but did convince them to add some extra security at the panel discussions, just to be on the safe side."

"That's good," she said. "Do you think the stalker guy will be there?"

"He or she could be," he said. "It's going to be busy, lots of people for them to blend in with."

"Yeah, but also easier to get caught," Ryan said. "It's hard to murder someone at a conference full of thousands of people without someone catching you."

She was only half-joking and Grayson obviously caught the scent of her anxiety because he purred soothingly to her and rubbed her thigh. "No one's being murdered, honey. I'll keep you safe."

"I'm more worried about Ryleigh," Ryan said. "I honestly think the stalker is just sending shit to Vanessa and me in the hopes of distracting security from his real target – Ryleigh. Maybe you should assign one of my extra men to Ryleigh's team. She's more popular and -"

"No," he said.

"Grayson -"

"No," he repeated. "She already has Chase and four extra men watching over her. She'll be safe."

She sighed and stared out the window. "God, I hate this. The next few days are going to be hell."

He took her hand and laced their fingers together. "Should I be concerned that you might have a panic attack?"

She shrugged, her embarrassment turning her cheeks red. "I want to say no, but I might have one. Honestly, it depends on how many people get close to me." She glanced over at him. "I'm sorry."

"Don't be. It isn't a problem. I just want to know if it's something I'll need to help you deal with."

"Are all tiger shifters perfect, or just you?"

He laughed. "Trust me, I'm not even close to perfect. Spend some time with Cooper and he'll give you a list of all the ways I fuck up on a regular basis."

She squeezed his hand. "Well, I'll be practicing all my 'don't freak the hell out' techniques my therapist taught me, so you may not have to come to my panic attack rescue."

"If at any point, you need to get away from people or need to go to your room for a break, just tell me. Okay?"

"If I left a panel or an autograph session, Vanessa would kill me. Appearance is everything to her, and me not being able to handle my shit in front of the press and fans would send her over the edge. Maybe I should do what she does and drink from a damn flask all day to keep myself calm."

"With your grandmother not there to police her, will Vanessa's drinking get out of control?" Grayson asked.

"No. Lori is staying with her in her room and she'll help keep the drinking to a manageable level. Plus, like I said, appearance is everything to Vanessa. Even her addiction to alcohol takes a backseat to it."

They were almost to the hotel and he squeezed her leg again. "You sure you're ready for this?"

She took a deep breath and nodded. "Yeah. It'll be fine, right? It's only until Saturday and most of the fans who show up will be there for Ryleigh. It's not going to be as bad as I'm imagining."

Grayson stroked her knee and she stared out the window. God, she hoped she was right.

CHAPTER 12

"**D**id you know that you growl every time a guy touches Ryan?"

"Shut up, Boone."

Boone elbowed Chase. "He does, doesn't he?"

Chase nodded and Grayson scowled at both of them. "Why are you paying attention to me instead of doing your goddamn jobs?"

He could smell a whiff of fear coming from Chase, but Boone just laughed. "Jesus, you've been in one fuck of a mood the last few days. At first, I thought it was because of being around all these humans and shifters, but now..."

"Now, what?" Gray growled.

"Now I'm thinking it's because you got a thing for Ryan."

He growled again but kept his gaze on Ryan. It was Friday afternoon and the last panel of the day had just finished. She and Vanessa and Ryleigh were doing an auto-graph session in the largest conference room. He rubbed at the back of his neck. He was bone tired and he had no idea how Ryan was managing to keep the smile on her face.

She'd been wrong about how popular she would be at the

conference. Just as many fans were eager to talk to her as they were to talk to Ryleigh, and after three days of almost constant interaction with strangers, he could only imagine how exhausted and stressed out she was.

A little trickle of pride went through him. She'd only come close to a panic attack once. It was shortly before the first photo and autograph session on Thursday morning. He'd been leading her to the big ballroom for the event, two of Frost's men walking behind them. As the smell of her anxiety grew and her body began to shake, he'd taken her hand and led her to the small alcove in the hallway that housed an ice machine and soda machine. Indicating to Frost's men to give them a few minutes, he'd pressed her into the small space between the ice machine and the soda machine and rested his forehead against hers, making her mimic his deep and even breathing until her shaking stopped and her anxiety lessened.

That wasn't all you did to help stop her panic attack.

He studied the tiger shifter that approached Ryan's table, a glossy 8x10 photo of Ryan as a teenager in one hand and an *Alien Hunter* ballcap in the other. Ryan smiled at him and made small talk as the tiger shifter stared wide-eyed at her. When the fan reached out and quickly touched a lock of her dark hair, his tiger growled angrily.

"Easy, big guy." Boone patted his arm. Gray wanted to snap at him to pay attention, but Boone's gaze was on Vanessa and his big body was tense and on alert.

"Hey, Chase, is it just me or does Gray smell like Ryan?"

"Shut up, Boone," Gray repeated.

Boone's grin widened. "I'm just saying… I can smell Ryan's scent on you."

"I'm her damn bodyguard, remember?"

"Chase doesn't smell much like Ryleigh and I know for a

fact that there isn't a hint of Vanessa's scent on me," Boone said.

Gray ignored Boone's teasing. Of course, he smelled like Ryan. A guy couldn't make out with her for a few glorious minutes in the space between an ice machine and soda machine and not *not* smell like her. Her arousal had been intense enough that he wasn't surprised her scent still lingered on him. When they finally had sex, their scents would probably linger on each other for *weeks* after.

You can't have sex with her.

No, he couldn't. So why did he keep fucking torturing himself by making out with her?

His tiger purred happily at the memory. Kissing Ryan, cupping her breast and whispering into her ear all the dirty things he wanted to do to her was an unexpected but incredibly pleasant way to help ease her panic attack.

It didn't do much for the worst fucking case of blue balls he'd ever experienced, but that was a small price to pay to keep his mate happy.

Our mate, his tiger said happily.

Shit, now he was referring to her as his mate too. He wanted to blame his tiger, but it felt right to call Ryan his mate. He hadn't even slept with her for God's sake. He and his tiger were losing their damn minds.

She's ours. And if they keep touching her, I'll kill them.

Stop it, he said to his tiger. *She's not interested in them. She's just being polite because it's her job.*

He knew that was true, but it fucking bugged him watching all the male fans who wanted to touch her or hug her. Hell, yesterday, one of them had even managed to press a kiss against her mouth before Ryan could step back. His tiger had gone fucking apeshit and only Grayson's superior control had stopped it from forcing the shift.

He shuddered at the thought of what would have happened if he had shifted and torn the man's throat out. These feelings of possessiveness, the almost undeniable urge to mark his mate, was completely foreign to him. He both loved it and hated it.

"I don't know about you two assholes, but I will be very fucking glad when this shitshow is over," Boone said. "Every fucking fan that comes up to them could be the stalker. Us being ten feet away isn't going to do jackshit when it comes to protecting them. They should have cancelled the damn conference."

"There was absolutely no way we could do that." Bert had joined them, and he frowned at Boone. "Most of the fans bought their tickets months ago. To cancel the conference would have been career suicide for Ryleigh."

"And that's all you care about, right?" Grayson said. "Afterall, if Ryleigh doesn't have a career, you don't have a job."

The stout man stiffened. "No, but it isn't just Ryleigh's career that would be jeopardized. What about the other actors on the reboot? Or the crew? They rely on their jobs to feed their families, Mr. Scott. Ryleigh, as well as Vanessa and Ryan, realize that. Cancelling the conference and potentially starting a fan backlash is risking the jobs of hundreds of people who work on the show."

Gray didn't reply and Bert made a snort of derision. "You're being paid to keep my girls safe, not to comment on things that are none of your concern. Remember your place, please."

Gray's tiger roared at the idea that Ryan would in anyway belong to the balding manager. Gray kept his gaze trained on Ryan but bared his teeth in a snarl. "Call Ryan your girl again and I'll -"

"You know," Boone's hand clamped down on Gray's arm, "I heard a real fucking funny joke the other day. Have you heard the one about the shifter who got fired because he couldn't keep his fucking mouth shut?"

Gray shut his mouth as Bert smiled stiffly at them. "After the final Q&A panels tomorrow morning, Vanessa has requested that both Ryan and Ryleigh join her for a meeting with Henry Washings. The meeting will last approximately half an hour to forty-five minutes."

"It's not on the schedule," Gray said.

"No, it isn't, but sometimes schedules change," Bert said. "Mr. Washings is a highly-respected director who wants to do a biography on Vanessa. He wants both Ryan and Ryleigh to participate in the biography so it's imperative that they're at the initial meeting."

Grayson snorted loudly and Boone squeezed his arm before muttering, "Shut it, you idiot."

"Ryleigh and Ryan need to be at the Willow conference room by eleven," Bert said. "Make sure they're not late."

He walked away and Gray snarled, "What a fucking asshole he is."

"Actually, he isn't," Boone said. "He's been pretty cool to us, hasn't he, Chase?"

The younger shifter nodded. "Yeah. Ryleigh loves him too. She says nothing but good things about him."

When Grayson didn't reply, Boone clapped him on the back. "I know you got a thing for Ryan, but rein it in, buddy, before it gets your ass fired. I love you, but when you're jobless and homeless, I'm only letting you couch surf at my place for a month max."

"I don't have a thing for Ryan," Gray said through gritted teeth.

"Chase, you ever seen a shifter so in denial in your life?" Boone said with a laugh.

Chase grinned, his gaze roaming the crowds of people. "Nope."

Grayson growled again as a man, his hands shaking with excitement, grabbed Ryan's hand and shook it so enthusiastically that she winced.

Boone laughed. "Nope, you don't have a thing for her at all."

"OH MY GOD, I'M SOOO TIRED." RYLEIGH COLLAPSED ON THE couch in her suite, kicking off her heels and putting her feet on the coffee table. "Saul, honey, I'll give you a thousand dollars to rub my feet."

"Sweetheart, ain't no one need money that badly," Saul said with a laugh. "Ask your sister to do it."

"No," Ryan said. "Not a chance."

"Both of you suck," Ryleigh said with the perfect pout.

Saul studied Ryan's cheeks, the bruises still hidden beneath his artful makeup job despite the long day, before kissing her forehead. "I'll come to your room around eight tomorrow to do your makeup, okay?"

She nodded. "Yes, thank you, Saul. I appreciate it."

"You bet." He walked across the room and leaned down to give Ryleigh a kiss. "See you at nine, sweetheart."

"Okay, honey. Have a good sleep."

Saul left the hotel suite and Ryleigh patted the couch beside her. "Sit with me, Ry-Ry."

Ryan glanced at the time. It was only nine-thirty, but she was dead tired. She wanted to go back to her own hotel suite, have a hot bath and crawl into bed. Hell, she was even too tired to masturbate to the lovely little fantasy about banging Grayson in the shower she'd concocted during one of the slower Q&A panels.

"Sweetie, I'm tired," she said to Ryleigh.

Ryleigh pouted at her. "Please? You know I hate to be alone."

"I know, but -"

The knock on the door interrupted her. She glanced at Ryleigh, adrenaline kickstarting in her belly. "Are you expecting someone?"

"No."

"It's just me," Saul said through the door. "I forgot my phone."

Ryan opened the door and Saul smiled apologetically before snagging his phone off the narrow table the TV sat on. "Sorry."

"You'd forget your own dick if it wasn't attached to you," Ryleigh said with a grin.

Saul shot her the bird. "I always remember the really big stuff. Good-night, ladies."

Ryan sat next to Ryleigh as Saul left for the second time. Ryleigh rested her head on her shoulder. "I'm exhausted."

"Me too."

"Mommy's been doing okay with the drinking, huh?"

Ryan shrugged. "She was drunk during the panel and the autograph session tonight."

"I know, but the fans couldn't tell. And it was the first time since the conference started. I figured we'd have to peel her off the floor at the panels," Ryleigh replied.

Ryan rubbed at her forehead. "God, I hate these things."

"I know you do. Thank you for doing this one. I know it's super difficult on you. Are you getting enough alone time to recharge?" Ryleigh kissed her upper arm and snuggled closer.

Ryan hid her shock. She knew that Ryleigh loved her, but her baby sister was also seriously self-absorbed. The fact that she even acknowledged that Ryan needed alone time was a little surprising.

"It's been all right," she said. "I have the evenings to myself so that helps."

"Oh? Grayson hasn't been staying in your hotel room with you?" Ryleigh said innocently.

"Why would he?"

"He's your bodyguard."

"Chase is your bodyguard," Ryan waved her hand in the air, "and I don't see him in your hotel room."

"Yeah, but Chase isn't into me the way Grayson is into you," Ryleigh said. She paused and giggled. "I mean, he's *into* me because most guys his age are, but he's not obsessed with me like Mr. Tall, Dark and Intense is obsessed with you."

"He's not obsessed with me," Ryan said. "Sometimes the shit you come up with, Ryleigh, I swear."

Ryleigh sat up. "I'm not dumb nor am I blind, Ry-Ry. I see the way he looks at you."

"We're just friends," she said. Ryleigh wouldn't deliberately try to get Grayson fired, but Ryan could see her spilling the beans about Grayson's "obsession" in front of Chase or Boone. What if they told Cooper? Grayson would be fired.

At least you'd get to fuck him then.

She scowled at her inner self. Grayson loved his job, that was plain to see, and wishing he'd get fired just so she could scratch her itch was a terrible thing to wish for.

"Yeah, just friends," Ryleigh snorted.

"Ryleigh, don't be talking about me or Grayson in front of Chase or Boone. Do you understand? There's nothing going on between us. Nothing. Keep your mouth shut about us."

Ryleigh blinked at her. "Fine. God, relax. I'm not going to say anything about your bodyguard having a crush on you."

They sat in silence for a minute or so before Ryleigh said, "Besides, it was Wes who told Boone who told Chase who told me that Grayson came over to see you on both of his days off. So, why is he making you sit alone in your hotel room?"

"Those guys are worse than teenage girls when it comes to gossiping," Ryan said.

Ryleigh laughed. "I was a little surprised. That Wes dude is, like, the quietest guy on the planet, usually. Anyway, why isn't Grayson spending the nights in your room?"

"Because we're just friends," Ryan said. "Drop it, okay?" She could hear the anger in her voice, and she rubbed at her forehead again. She was angry and disappointed and taking it out on Ryleigh which wasn't fair.

Ryan didn't expect Grayson to spend the night with her or anything, but she didn't know why he spent the evenings in his hotel room instead of hanging out with her. She'd thought he would, especially after Thursday morning when they'd had a weirdly hot make-out session between an ice machine and a soda machine, but he hadn't shown up to her room Wednesday night or Thursday night. She didn't expect tonight to be any different.

She touched the rubber bracelet around her wrist, hoping Ryleigh didn't see the sadness and the loneliness on her face. It was stupid to be lonely. She'd always loved her alone time and after an entire day of extroverting, she should have been welcoming the silence and the peace of no one in her space. Instead, she'd sat on the couch, staring at her phone and wondering why Grayson was avoiding her.

"Ryan, honey, are you okay?" Ryleigh touched her face.

Before Ryan could reply, Ryleigh's phone chirped. She

snagged it out of her pocket and read the screen. Ryan had never seen such happiness on her sister's face before and she leaned over to try and see the screen. "Who are you texting with?"

Ryleigh turned the phone away before she could see it. "Just a friend." She tapped out a message, her thumbs a blur on the keyboard.

"Who?" Ryan asked.

"I told you – a friend."

"What's her name?"

Ryleigh scowled at her. "Why are you being so nosy?"

Ryan studied her for a moment. "Why are you being so secretive?"

"I'm not."

"Then let me see your phone." She reached for it and Ryleigh shoved her hand away before standing up and moving away.

"Stop it, Ryan."

More than a little curious, Ryan stood up. "What are you hiding, Ryleigh?"

"I'm not hiding anything." Ryleigh's phone chirped again, and she glanced at the screen. "Weren't you heading back to your room? You're tired, remember?"

"Tell me who your friend is," Ryan said.

"No."

"Yes."

Ryleigh glared at her, all the sparks of good humour gone from her face. "You're my sister, not my keeper, Ryan. I don't have to tell you shit."

Ryan twitched in surprise. "Ryleigh, what is going on with you? It's not like you to keep secrets from me."

"I'm not," Ryleigh said. "It's no big deal, okay?"

"If it's no big deal, then just tell me your friend's name."

"Oh my God,' Ryleigh rolled her eyes, "you are friggin' impossible, I swear. You're always in my business, always acting like you know what's best for me. Well, guess what? I'm an adult and I don't need you or anyone else telling me how to live my life or -"

There was another knock on the door and Ryleigh stalked toward it. She whipped it open. "For God's sake, Saul, what did you forget... who the hell are you?"

Ryan, still standing near the couch, stared past Ryleigh at the blonde-haired man. He was wearing an *Alien Hunter* t-shirt, a pair of black jeans, and both of his hands were folded neatly behind his back.

"Ms. Shepherd, I'm your biggest fan."

The man's voice was low and pleasant, but all of the hair stood up on the back of Ryan's neck. She sprinted toward the door. "Ryleigh! Shut the door! Shut the door right -"

Ryleigh made a squeak of pain as the man reached out and grabbed her around the neck. He spun her around and Ryan's blood formed jagged glaciers when he placed the large hunting knife at Ryleigh's throat.

"Move forward please," he said to Ryleigh.

Her face the colour of spoiled cottage cheese, Ryleigh took a few hesitant steps forward. The man kicked the door shut with his foot and smiled in a pleasant way at Ryan. "Hi there. I'm your biggest fan as well, Ms. Shepherd. My name is Steve. It's so wonderful to finally meet you, Ryan. May I call you Ryan?"

Ryan, her gaze on the knife at her sister's throat, nodded. "Yes. It's-it's nice to meet you as well, Steve."

He smiled and stroked Ryleigh's hair with his free hand. "You smell really good."

"Ryan," Ryleigh whispered.

"It'll be okay, honey," Ryan said. "Just stay still."

"Don't worry," Steve said. "I would never hurt you, Ryleigh. You're… precious to me. I've been waiting so long to meet all of you. It's been my biggest dream since the show started."

He giggled boyishly and kissed Ryleigh's cheek. "The original show, that is. I mean, don't get me wrong, I'm a big fan of yours but it was your mother and your sister who first captured my heart. I was so sad when the show was cancelled."

Ryan, her heart a banging, shrieking drum in her chest, tried to calm her breathing. "We were sad too, Steve."

"Were you though?" Steve cocked his head at her. "It's your fault the show was cancelled."

"That's right, it was my fault," Ryan said. "So, why don't I exchange spots with Ryleigh? What do you say? It's me you're angry at, not her."

Steve frowned at her and fresh fear sent shards of ice floating through her blood. "I'm not angry. I know why you did what you did, Ryan. I understand, you know? Better than anyone. I had an overbearing mother, just like you did. It's why I wanted to meet you and your sister, why I wanted to tell you just how much alike we are. My mother was an alcoholic bitch who tried to control my life too."

"I'm sorry to hear that, Steve," Ryan said. Somewhere in the back of her head, an old clip from some crime show surfaced in her brain. *Keep him talking, say his name a lot, make him think you're friends. Win his trust.*

She took a step closer, fighting against the adrenaline that made her knees so wobbly she could barely stand. "Hey, Ryleigh has a fan thing she has to go to, but why don't you and I go for coffee? Just you and me, Steve. We can talk about our mothers and how awful they are. What do you say?"

He laughed, and Ryleigh gasped when the edge of the knife pressed against her throat. "I want all three of us to be together, Ryan. Ryleigh needs our protection against your mother, doesn't she?"

Ryan took another wobbly step toward him. "No. Vanessa loves Ryleigh very much. She's good to her. She-she doesn't treat Ryleigh like she treated me, or your mother treated you."

"Bullshit." Steve's voice was still low and pleasant. "Your mother is a bitch to you and Ryleigh. Don't lie to me, Ryan."

"I'm not," Ryan said.

"You are. People like your mother and my mother are incapable of being good to anyone." He kissed Ryleigh's cheek again. "My mother had an accident when I was nineteen. A terrible, terrible accident. We lived on a farm, isolated, the closest neighbour miles away. My father left us when I was only a small boy. I couldn't blame him. My mother never stopped nagging him, she was drunk almost every night. I wrote him a letter once and asked him why he didn't take me with him, but my mother watched the mail and stole the letter he wrote me before I could read it. Wasn't that awful of her?"

"Very awful," Ryan said. She glanced to her left. Chase's room was right there. If she screamed loud enough, he'd come check on them.

And Ryleigh's throat would be cut, and she'd be dead. Is that what you want?

She shuddered all over as Steve stroked Ryleigh's hair for a second time. "My mother was leaving for work and she stopped at the end of the driveway to check the mail. Only, she forgot to put her car in park because she was drunk, and it rolled forward and pinned her against the oak tree right next to the mailbox. She was pinned there for hours, Ryan. Hours. Can you imagine what that must have been like? The terrible pressure against your body, knowing that you were dying, being trapped like a rat in a cage."

"No," Ryan whispered.

Ryleigh was crying silently, her hand clenched tight around her phone, and Ryan tried to give her a calm look. It was impossible. She'd never been so afraid in her life.

"She screamed a lot," Steve said matter-of-factly. "I heard her, screaming and pleading and begging for me to come help her. I told the police that I didn't hear her. That I was in my room with my headphones on and didn't hear a single cry. They believed me. Why wouldn't they? I was her son, if I had heard her crying, I would have helped."

Ryan swallowed down the bile rising in her throat as Steve smiled at her. "She deserved to die the way she did, screaming and shrieking with piss and blood running down her legs and her intestines oozing out of her back. She deserved it, Ryan. It was her time to die. Just like it's the raven's turn to die."

"Please," Ryleigh moaned. The tears were flowing down her cheeks and Steve made a low sound of comfort before kissing at the moisture.

"Shh, Ryleigh, don't cry. I don't mean you."

He stared at Ryan in an almost apologetic manner. "I probably shouldn't have sent the dead birds to all three of you, but I just…"

He drifted off, staring blankly at the floor, one hand tugging at his t-shirt, and his face growing slack and unanimated.

"Ryan?" Ryleigh whispered.

"It's okay, honey," Ryan said. She took another step forward and then one more. She was almost close enough to touch Ryleigh now. She reached for Ryleigh's wrist, freezing in place when Steve's hand clenched around his t-shirt and his head popped up.

Awareness flowed back into his face and he shook his head before pressing the blade against Ryleigh's throat until a thin trickle of blood appeared. Ryleigh cried out and Ryan held her hands up.

"It's okay, Steve. You don't need to do that."

"Take a step back please, Ryan."

She stepped backwards, still holding her hands up. "I'm sorry. I didn't mean to upset you."

He sighed like a librarian being interrupted during story time. "Where was I? Right... I probably shouldn't have sent the dead ravens to all of you but sometimes my head... sometimes it isn't right, and I do things that I don't understand. You know?"

"I do know," Ryan said. "I understand."

"I knew you would. Did you like my other gift to you?"

"I loved it," she said.

His body relaxed a little. "Good. I've always been artistic. For a while, I even imagined I might go into special effects, that I might get a job working with stars like you. I would have been really good at it. I wasn't sure what to send you, but then – it just hit me, and I knew that you would love it."

"I did," Ryan said. "It was – the detail was incredible."

"The head looked just like you, didn't it?" he said eagerly.

"Yes."

"Did it frighten you when you opened the box?" His tone turned sly.

"Yes," she said. "A little."

"How about you, sweetie?" He patted Ryleigh's arm. "Did it scare you when you saw your head?"

"Y-yes," Ryleigh whispered.

"Good." Steve made a brisk little nod. "Okay, enough chit-chat. Time to go." He reached down and pried Ryleigh's phone from her hand and threw it on the floor. "Ryan, leave your phone too, please."

"Where are we going?" Ryan set her phone on the table next to the TV.

"First, we're going to stop and get your mother from her room, and then the four of us are going to leave."

Ryan licked her dry lips. "Leave for where?"

"My farm." His tone turned dreamy. "You'll like it there, Ryan. It's so pretty and quiet. I won't be interrupted while I'm teaching your mother what happens to shit-stains like her who abuse their kids. No interruptions and," he smiled sweetly at her, "no one to hear her scream."

CHAPTER 13

*G*o to her room.

Grayson jabbed the mute button on the TV, rolled off the bed and stalked over to the balcony doors. He jerked them open and stepped out into the heated night air.

Go to her room.

Would you shut the fuck up for one goddamn minute? He snarled at his tiger. *We can't go to her room.*

She needs us.

No, she needs alone time and rest, Grayson replied. He gripped the balcony railing and stared at the sea of lights emanating from the surrounding buildings. He wanted to go to Ryan, wanted it desperately, but if he did...he'd mate with her.

His tiger roared with happiness at the thought and Grayson shut it down quickly. *No, we can't. For the last time, shut up about it.*

His tiger didn't respond, and Gray squeezed the railing before closing his eyes. He was doing the right thing, but he missed Ryan like crazy. He was with her all day long but not *really* with her and he missed their alone time together.

Acting completely professional around her at all times just seemed to increase his need for her. But even if he could spend the evening with Ryan without tearing off her damn clothes and mating with her, she needed some down time. She was an introvert who was spending all damn day being an extrovert. She needed space and quiet, not him in her personal space.

Just for a few minutes. I need to see my mate.

His tiger's whining was unsettling. His tiger never whined, never begged or pleaded for anything. Hell, it rarely asked him for anything, always seemingly content to go with the flow. Until Ryan.

I need her.

When Grayson ignored him, his tiger growled and tried to surge forward. Tremors wracked Gray's body, and his hands pulled at the railing until the metal squealed in protest. His pupils flickered from round to narrow rapidly and he made a low sound that was half groan and half growl.

With effort, he stopped the shift. His tiger retreated with a growling whine that hurt his head. He rubbed at his temples and muttered, "I'm sorry, but we can't."

His tiger refused to respond, sulking like an overgrown kitten, and Gray slumped against the railing. He honestly wasn't sure how long he could keep his tiger contained. It's obsession with marking Ryan grew stronger by the day.

He pulled his phone from his pocket. It would be easier if he could talk to Coop about this. Cooper had been fighting his own attraction to Daisy for months, no doubt he'd have some suggestions on how to control the urge to shift and mark his mate.

He was on the verge of calling Coop when his common sense kicked back in. He couldn't talk to his best friend about this. If Coop even suspected Gray had a thing for Ryan, he'd have Wes watching her and Grayson doing admin work at the office before he could even protest.

He was stuffing his phone in his pocket when it buzzed and the ding that was connected to Ryan's GPS tracker went off. His heart kicked into high gear and he stared at his phone. Fuck, it was the app for the bracelet.

"Go on, knock," Steve said.

He gestured toward the door with his free hand and Ryan, her hand trembling, knocked on Vanessa's door. Steve was standing behind Ryleigh and he kissed her cheek again before smiling at Ryan. "Be a good girl now, or your sweet baby sister will have a knife lodged in her kidneys."

Ryleigh whimpered quietly and Steve shook his head. "Shh, sweet one, nothing will happen if you're a good girl."

"Who is it?" Lori said.

Steve nudged Ryleigh. Ryleigh cleared her throat and said, "It's Ryleigh. I need to talk to Mommy."

The door opened and Lori stared at Ryan in surprise. "Ryan? What's up?"

"Hey, Lori, uh, can we come in? We need to talk to Vanessa."

Lori stepped back, opening the door wider. "Come in, but Vanessa isn't exactly up for visitors. She's in her bed passed out and - wait, who are you?"

She studied Steve, her nostrils flaring, as Steve shut the door with his foot. Lori sniffed the air almost delicately, her gaze flickering to Ryan. "Why are you and Ryleigh afraid? What's -"

"Fuck, you're a shifter," Steve said.

He shoved Ryleigh to the floor, she cried out with surprise

as she fell face-first into the carpet as he lunged for Lori. Lori grunted in pain, her hand clamping down on her right arm. Ryan could see blood pouring out between her fingers and Lori snarled at Steve, her fangs dropping.

Before she could shift, Steve grabbed her by the hair and slammed her head-first into the door. Lori dropped immediately, her body crumpling like a flower as she flopped back on the carpet. Her eyes rolled up in her head and Ryan could see a goose egg already rising out of Lori's hair just past her temple.

Ryan started forward and Steve shook his head. He pointed the blood-covered knife at her before reaching down and grabbing Ryleigh under the armpit. He hauled her to her feet, and she made a groan of disgust when he used her shirt to wipe Lori's blood off the knife.

"Get your mother, please," Steve said calmly.

"Lori is bleeding. I need to stop the blood before she bleeds out," Ryan said.

Steve stared at the pool of blood growing under Lori's arm. "She's fine," he said dismissively. "It's only a flesh wound. Hurry up and get your mother."

"Steve, please, just let me tie a tourniquet so -"

"I said get your fucking mother and let's go!" Steve snarled at her. "Don't make me hurt Ryleigh. I don't want to, but if you don't get your fucking ass moving, I will, Ryan. Do you understand?"

Ryan staggered back, nodding frantically and holding her hands up. "I understand. Don't- don't be angry. I'll get Vanessa and we'll leave."

Licking her dry lips, she stumbled toward Vanessa's bedroom. Steve and Ryleigh were walking behind her and Ryan glanced at the bracelet around her wrist. How far had Grayson set the distance? She wished she'd asked him.

If it even works.

It would work, it had to. She touched the bracelet as she opened the bedroom door and stepped inside.

What if he's in the shower and doesn't hear it?

She shut her inner voice down immediately. If Grayson was in the shower, she and Ryleigh and her mother were dead. Simple as that.

She studied the bedroom, barely hearing Vanessa's loud snoring, as she tried to decide if there was something in the room she could use as a weapon. She considered the bedside lamp as she bent over Vanessa and shook her roughly.

Won't work. It's bolted to the table.

Fuck. She shook Vanessa again and her mother muttered a curse before rolling onto her back. There was an empty bottle of whiskey lying on the bed next to her. Ryan stared at it. The glass looked heavy and thick and it would make a suitable weapon. Before she could reach for it, Steve said, "You thinking of trying to hit me with that bottle, Ry-Ry?"

She froze before turning and staring at him. Steve smiled at her. "Ry-Ry, that's what little Ryleigh calls you, right?"

Ryan didn't reply and Steve tugged playfully on Ryleigh's hair. "That's your nickname for your big sister, isn't it?"

"Y-yes," Ryleigh whispered.

"So cute. Just know, *Ry-Ry*, that I can cut your sister's throat before you even reach the bottle." Steve nuzzled Ryleigh's cheek before giving Vanessa a disgusted look. "Get her up."

"I'm trying," Ryan said. She shook Vanessa harder before lightly slapping her cheek. "Vanessa, wake up."

Vanessa eyes opened and she stared blearily at Ryan before pushing at her. "Fuck off."

"Vanessa, sit up." Ryan yanked her mother into a sitting

position. Vanessa swayed back and forth, and Ryan groaned inwardly. She was completely plastered.

Steve rolled his eyes. "Surprise, surprise, she's drunk."

"We have to leave her," Ryan said. "She can't walk like this."

"You'll get her up and walking," Steve said, "or watch me carve my initials into Ryleigh's cheek." He ran the tip of the knife over Ryleigh's smooth cheek.

"Ryan," Ryleigh whispered.

Ryan swallowed down the bile in her throat and then slapped Vanessa as hard as she could across the face. Her mother's head rocked back, and tears slid down Ryleigh's face when Ryan slapped their mother again on the other cheek before shaking her roughly.

"Vanessa! Wake the fuck up. Right now!"

Her mother's eyes opened, and she glared at Ryan. "Tha'-fuck you hit me for?"

"Stand up!" Ryan swung Vanessa's legs over the side of the bed and yanked her into a standing position.

Her mother's knees buckled, and she fell back on the bed. Ryan glanced at Steve. He made a tsk-tsk noise and stroked Ryleigh's cheek with the knife again.

"Goddammit, Vanessa," Ryan muttered. She grabbed the glass of water sitting on the nightstand and threw it in Vanessa's face. Her mother coughed and choked, her hands waving weakly in the air. Ryan sat her up and pounded her on the back before shaking her again. "Hey, you with me?"

"What?" Vanessa glared at her as drops of water slid down her cheeks. "Whatsyer fuckin' problem, bitch?"

"We are leaving. Do you hear me? Stand up and walk, Vanessa," Ryan said.

"Don't wanna," Vanessa mumbled.

"I don't fucking care." Panic for Ryleigh made Ryan

rough as she dragged Vanessa to her feet. She put an arm around her, thanking God that Vanessa was still dressed and wincing at her mother's stale whiskey breath.

"I hate you so much," her mother slurred.

"I know. Move." She half-dragged, half-carried Vanessa to the bedroom door. She could have cried with relief when Vanessa actually began to walk a little, propelling herself on her own strength as they moved toward the door.

"Wha'she doin'?" Vanessa squinted at the unconscious Lori lying on the floor. She snickered into Ryan's ear. "She can't hold her liquor worth shit. Lori, you stupid bitch, get up."

She tried to kick Lori in the leg as they walked by. She missed and stumbled against Ryan. Ryan glared at her, her fingers digging into Vanessa's waist. "Stop it, Vanessa."

"Shaddup," Vanessa said.

She swiveled her head to stare at Ryleigh. "Ryleigh, baby? Tell Ryan to stop bein' a bitch."

"Mommy, be quiet," Ryleigh said.

Vanessa glared at her. "Don't start bein' like yer sister, you hear me?"

Ryan opened the door, hoping and praying that someone would be in the hallway. It was completely empty and with one last look at poor Lori bleeding on the floor, she stepped out into the hall, dragging Vanessa with her.

Vanessa stumbled along beside her as Steve said, "Walk toward the elevators, Ryan."

"Who's that?" Vanessa said.

"I'm a friend of your daughters," Steve said. "I'm going to make sure you never hurt them again."

Vanessa frowned at Ryan. "What's that asshole talkin' about?"

"Be quiet, Vanessa," Ryan said. They were at the elevators. Relief was starting to wind its way into her belly. The hotel lobby wouldn't be empty. In fact, it would be chocked full of fans and the moment they saw Ryleigh, the shit would hit the proverbial fan. There was no way Steve would try and kill the three of them in front of that many people.

She reached for the elevator button and Steve said, "Nope. Keep moving, Ryan."

"To where?" she asked.

"Around that corner. Quickly, please." His smile was chillingly polite.

Frowning, she dragged Vanessa around the corner. To their right was a service elevator that required a key card to use. Dismay washed over her in slow waves when Steve produced a key card from his pocket and swiped it over the scanner. The light turned green and the doors opened.

Behind them and around the corner, a door slammed. All four of them froze as high-pitched giggling drifted down the hallway. "Oh my God, Rebecca, we look so friggin' hot dressed up like this."

"I know, right? I can't wait for the guys to see us. They're gonna, like, freak out."

Steve put his finger to his lips, the knife pressing a little harder into Ryleigh's throat. He motioned for Ryan to move into the elevator.

Quickly, Ryan dragged Vanessa into the elevator, leaning her mother against the wall as Steve followed Ryleigh in. Keeping one arm around her waist, the knife pressed against her ribs, he used the other hand to swipe the key card then pressed the button.

The doors closed, cutting off the sound of the two giggling girls.

As the elevator moved smoothly downward, Vanessa belched loudly before singing tunelessly under her breath.

Steve's lip curled as he watched her. "She's so pathetic. Just like my mother."

"Who you callin' pathetic?" Vanessa opened one eye and glared at him. "I don't care if yer a friend, you shut up about me."

Steve smiled at her. "I can't wait to cut out your tongue, Vanessa. I'm going to cut it out and then I'm going to make you watch as I feed it to my pigs. In fact, I'm going to cut you apart piece by piece and feed you to the pigs. I'll feed them your eyes last, you stupid bitch, so you can watch as they eat your fucking flesh from your worthless bones. Doesn't that sound like fun?"

Ryleigh was crying again but Vanessa just shrugged before leaning back against the wall. "Sure, whatever."

The doors slid open and Steve indicated for Ryan to step out. She slung her arm around Vanessa's waist, and they staggered into the hallway. It was completely empty and any hope that a stranger or a fan or a hotel employee might see them, died an immediate death in Ryan's chest.

Steve smiled at her. "Employees only hallway. I knew it would be empty this time of night, it always is."

"Who did you hurt to get that key card?" Ryan asked.

Steve scowled at her. "It's hurtful that you think so little of me, Ry-Ry. I didn't hurt anyone. I work here."

"You work here," Ryan repeated.

"Yeah, I'm the head of the maintenance department." The pride in Steve's voice was impossible to miss. "I started off as a bellboy and now I'm the head of the maintenance department. Not bad, huh?"

"Is that how you knew our room numbers? Because you work here?" Ryan said.

"Obviously," he said with an impatient shake of his head. "Let's get moving. This hallway should stay empty, but wouldn't it be just my luck to have a co-worker show up." Steve pointed at the exit door at the far end of the hall. "Walk, Ryan."

She walked. Vanessa was almost out of it again and by the time she reached the door, Ryan was sweating and panting and the muscles in her arm were screaming at her. She pushed open the door, the California heat sent fresh sweat rolling down her cheeks. They were facing a parking lot and she scanned the area to her right, looking for any hotel guests who might be loitering around the public entrance to the hotel. The entrance was deserted, and fresh panic made Ryan's knees wobbly.

Fuck, they were so screwed.

His fingers trembling, Grayson opened the app on his phone and hit map mode. He studied the red light moving across the screen before ducking back inside his room. Too amped up to waste precious seconds grabbing the gun he'd left on his bedside table, he crossed his room and opened the door. The hallway was empty, and he jogged toward the elevators. He turned the corner and ran toward the bank of elevators, calling Ryan's name. The elevators on the left were just closing and he slammed his fist against the wall before sprinting for the stairs.

Relax, maybe she's just going out for…

Out for what? He snarled at his inner voice as he took the stairs two at a time. *She knows not to leave the hotel without me. Something is wrong.*

His tiger growled in agreement as Grayson leaped down the last set of stairs. He landed at the bottom, bouncing grace-fully on the balls of his feet before grabbing the door and yanking it open. Ignoring the startled looks of hotel guests, he ran past the fitness room and the pool and through the lobby to the elevators.

His breath tearing in and out of his lungs, his heart in overdrive, he made a low growl as the elevator stopped at the lobby floor. The soft ding made his claws come out and his fangs dropped as the doors slid open.

The growl died in his throat. He stared mutely at the two teenage girls wearing costumes that mimicked Ryleigh's outfit for the show. They both wore blonde wigs and too much makeup, and they eyed him with the type of disdain only teenage girls could muster.

"Dude, what's your problem?" the taller girl said.

"He's totally gonna wig out," her friend replied. "I can, like, see his fangs."

"Was there anyone else in the elevator with you? Did they get off on a different floor?" Grayson snapped.

"Not that it's, like, any of your business, but no," the first girl said.

Grayson stepped back and the two girls walked toward the lobby.

"Old people are ridiculous," the second girl said with a flip of her blonde wig. "Like, what was his problem?"

Grayson studied his phone, the panic in his gut churning bitter bile up his throat. The red dot was moving steadily to the north and, with his nerves twisting tight, he ran toward the exit at the back of the hotel.

"MOVE FASTER," STEVE SAID IN A LOW VOICE.

"I'm trying," Ryan puffed as she dragged Vanessa across the parking lot. "Vanessa, wake up."

"Stop it," Vanessa muttered. "Tired."

"I know. Just a little farther," Ryan said. She glanced over her shoulder and tried to give Ryleigh a reassuring smile, but it felt stiff and unnatural. Where was Grayson? Surely, she was far enough away by now for the alert on his phone to go off.

He didn't hear it.

"He did," she croaked as she walked, "and don't call me Shirley."

She barked out hysterical laughter as Steve prodded her in the back with his fist. "What did you say?"

"Nothing," she gasped. Vanessa was growing heavier by the fucking second and she actually felt relief when Steve stopped them in front of a silver Corolla.

"Time to go for a ride," Steve said cheerfully.

GRAYSON PUSHED OPEN THE HOTEL DOOR AND RAN OUTSIDE, instinctively moving to the right and out of the range of light shining from the hotel. He was facing the giant parking lot and he scanned the darkness, his pupils narrowing into slits.

A flicker of movement caught his eye and he ran across the parking lot, dodging between the cars until he reached a rusty Dodge Journey with a bumper sticker on the back that read "I Hunt Aliens with the Alien Hunter".

He leaned against the side of it and calmed his breathing before peering around the back. Ryan was shoving a wobbly-kneed Vanessa into the back of a silver Toyota Corolla. Vanessa, groaning softly, leaned her head back on the seat. Her mouth dropped open and he heard her snoring before Ryan shut the door.

The hair on the back of his neck standing up, he bared his

fangs at the man who was standing behind Ryan's sister. Grayson could see the glint of the knife at Ryleigh's throat. He ducked back behind the Dodge so the light from his phone wouldn't be seen and typed out a quick text to Boone.

Back parking lot of hotel. All three being abducted by human male with knife. Get down here.

He shoved his phone back into his pocket without waiting for Boone's response and peeked around the car again. His tiger growled so loudly he could barely hear Ryan when she said, "You have Vanessa and you have me. You don't need Ryleigh, okay, Steve? Let her go, and you and I can go back to your farm with Vanessa. What do you say?"

"I want all of you." The man's voice was soft, and his tiger growled again at the madness in it. "Stop fucking around, Ryan. I told you before that all of you are coming with me. Now get in the car and don't make me ask you again."

"Steve," Ryan's voice was shaky, and Grayson could hear the fear in it, "you really don't need Ryleigh. Just -"

The man slammed Ryleigh up against the car before punching Ryan in the side of the head. She stumbled back and fell on her ass, one hand pressed against her skull.

Grayson pushed away from the car. His body was swelling, his bones cracking and his joints popping. Fur sprouted across his face and his body arched as his spine lengthened. His tiger roared in pure fury and pushed forward, demanding control so he could protect his mate.

With a low growl, Grayson retreated and let his tiger free.

Pain throbbed in Ryan's temple. The high-pitched ringing in her ears drowned out Steve's voice. She tried to focus, blinking repeatedly to clear her blurry vision as Steve knelt in front of her.

Ryleigh was huddled against the car, her hands pressed between her breasts and loud sobs wracking her body. The ringing faded as Steve tapped Ryan's stomach with the tip of the knife. "Get up. If you say one more word, I will gut you like a fucking fish. Do you understand?"

She nodded, her hand still pressed against her aching skull. Steve straightened and rubbed at his temple with his free hand. "I am doing this for *you*, Ryan. For you. This ungrateful bitch act is getting tiresome. Start appreciating what I'm doing for you or I'll…"

He trailed off to a stop, his head cocking to the side as the low rumble behind him grew louder. "What? What is that? Do you hear that?"

He turned and shrieked piercingly as the giant tiger leaped out of the darkness and landed on him. The tiger's weight drove him to the ground and Ryan screamed when Steve, his arms flailing madly, slashed the knife across the tiger's front leg.

The tiger roared with anger and, his head a blur of movement, he tore out Steve's throat. Blood gushed from the ragged hole and Steve made a gurgling sound before clasping weakly at his throat. Blood soaked his hands and Ryleigh retched and gagged before throwing up against the side of the car.

Ryan sat up, staring wide-eyed at the giant tiger as he walked toward her. He bumped her with his massive head, a low purr rising out of his chest.

"Grayson," she whispered.

The tiger purred again, his jade eyes glowing in the darkness. There was a low popping sound, Ryan blinked, and Grayson in his human form crouched in front of her.

"You're hurt," she whispered.

Blood was streaming down his biceps and he gave it a dismissive look before reaching out and cupping her face. "It's fine. Are you okay?"

"I-I'm good. Ryleigh – is Ryleigh okay?"

She tried to struggle to her feet, but Grayson shook his head. "She's okay. Don't stand up yet."

"I need to check on her. I need -"

"Holy fucking shit." Boone's voice carried in the dark parking lot. "How in the motherfucking hell did this happen?"

"Ryleigh? Can you stand up?" Chase's voice was remarkably calm.

Some of Ryan's tenseness dissipated when Chase helped Ryleigh stand. He picked her up and carried her away from Steve's body before setting her gently on the ground. She wrapped her arms around his waist and clung to him, sobbing brokenly as Grayson stroked Ryan's cheekbone.

"I'm fine," Ryan said and then burst into tears.

Grayson sat beside her and pulled her into his lap. She buried her face in his neck, only vaguely aware of his nakedness, as he held her tight and rocked her back and forth. "It's all right, my mate. I have you. You're safe now."

CHAPTER 14

"Cooper?"

Cooper looked up from his computer, his lion purring happily. "Hi, Daisy. Thanks for coming in on a Saturday."

"It's no problem." She set a cup of coffee in front of him, black with four sugars, just the way he liked it.

"I really appreciate it."

"Anytime." She smiled at him and his lion practically rolled onto its back and showed her his belly. "The others are in the boardroom and Grayson is on his way."

"Okay, thank you."

She left his office and he ignored the guilt creeping in, as he gulped down the hot coffee. There was zero reason for Daisy to come into the office today. Unless you counted him barely able to go two days without seeing her.

Fuck.

He scrubbed at the back of his neck. Calling Daisy in on the weekend just so he could see her was a shit thing to do, but he couldn't resist. A meeting at the office was the perfect excuse to have her here, even if she wasn't actually *needed*.

I need her.

I know, be quiet, he scolded his lion.

He was exhausted. He'd spent the night at the emergency room and then the police station with Grayson. At just after five this morning, they'd left the police station and he'd sent Grayson home to get some sleep while he returned to the hotel. He'd spent the morning there before going to the office. He glanced at his watch. It was almost one in the afternoon and his stomach growled. He needed a hot shower, a steak, and a nap – not necessarily in that order.

His door swung open and Grayson charged into his office. "Why is Wes here?" His voice was frantic. "What the fuck, Cooper? You made me go home because you said Wes would watch Ryan. Why the fuck is he here? Who's watching my ma -"

The tiger shifter cut himself off abruptly. Cooper stared at his best friend in stunned silence. "Did you just refer to Ryan Shepherd as your mate?"

"No."

"Yes, you did."

"No, I didn't." Grayson dropped into the chair in front of Cooper's desk. "Answer the question – who's watching Ryan?"

"No one's watching her. The job is over, Gray," Cooper said.

A myriad of emotions crossed Gray's face – anger, worry, relief.

Cooper scrubbed at his neck again. "Fuck, you slept with her."

"I didn't," Gray said immediately. "Cooper, I didn't sleep with her. I know the rules and I followed them."

"He didn't break the rules." Wes had joined them, and the lion shifter sat down in the chair next to Grayson.

"Is Ryan all right?" Grayson asked.

Wes nodded. "I dropped her off at her house just before noon. She's good, Gray. Exhausted but okay. She's tough for a human." He paused. "Her bitch of a mother made both her and Ryleigh finish the conference this morning and meet with the biography guy."

"Jesus," Grayson said. "I fucking hate that woman."

"Why didn't you tell me you were using the tracking bracelet on Ryan?" Cooper asked.

Grayson shrugged. "It was a last-minute decision."

"Was it?" Cooper said.

"What does it matter?" Grayson replied. "It saved her life and the lives of her sister and mother."

"Are you in love with Ryan?" Cooper said bluntly.

Grayson looked away and Cooper leaned forward. "Holy shit. You are in love with her."

"My tiger thinks she's his mate," Grayson said hoarsely. "I haven't even slept with her and my tiger... he's basically claimed her. When that asshole hit her last night... my tiger nearly lost his goddamn mind. The rage and the instinct to protect her was – I've never felt anything like it. I killed a man because he touched her, because he threatened her."

"Not just because of that," Cooper said. "He tried to kill you too, remember?"

Grayson shrugged, glancing at his arm. "Barely a scratch."

"You needed twelve stitches."

"It's fine," Grayson said.

"How did it go with the police?" Wes asked. "Did you call Henry?"

Cooper nodded. Henry Boyson was a leopard shifter and the security firm's lawyer. "Yeah, he met us at the police station."

"Good," Wes said. "What about the Council?"

"They sent a representative to be there," Grayson said. "The police questioned me, then they sent a couple detectives to question Ryan and Ryleigh and Vanessa."

Wes snorted, "Vanessa was in and out of it and could barely answer their questions. She didn't remember shit about what happened. But Ryan and Ryleigh talked to them and both were very insistent that you killed the guy in self-defence."

Cooper leaned back in his chair. "No charges have been laid against Grayson. I spoke with the lead detective about an hour ago. He told me that based on what Gray, Ryan and Ryleigh told them, plus what they found at the guy's farm this morning, that Grayson didn't need to worry."

"What did they find?" Grayson asked.

Cooper stood up. "C'mon into the boardroom. Boone and Chase are in there and I want them to hear this too."

"YOU FEELING ANY BETTER, BABY-GIRL?" OREN KISSED HER forehead and rubbed her back through her robe.

"A little. The shower helped," Ryan said.

"Come sit down." Shay took her hand and led her to the couch.

Ryan sat down, curling her legs up under her and resting her head on Shay's shoulder. Shay kissed her damp hair. "Are you hungry yet?"

"No," Ryan said.

Oren cracked his knuckles repeatedly, a sure sign that he was upset. "I can make you something to eat."

"I'm not hungry," Ryan said. "Sit down, honey."

Oren sat down on the other side of her, resting one big

hand on her thigh. "What about a drink? Do you want a drink?"

She shook her head and snuggled closer to Shay. "Thanks for coming over, guys."

"Of course, honey. How do you feel?"

"Tired, but okay."

Shay touched the side of her head delicately. "How does this feel?"

"A little tender still."

"I'm worried you have a concussion," Shay said.

"I don't." Ryan reached out and took Oren's hand. "I was checked out by the paramedics and Oren did his own exam before I got in the shower."

Oren squeezed her hand. "Just looking out for my girl."

"I know." She smiled at them. "I'm okay. I feel guilty."

"Guilty? For what?" Shay said.

"I should be at the house with Ryleigh. She was frightened."

"She's all right," Oren said. "Saul is with her and so is Mom."

Ryan sat up a little. "Mary went over there?"

"She did," Oren replied.

She blinked back the sting of tears. "I love your mom so much. I know Ryleigh really needs her right now."

"She loves you too," Oren said. "I texted Mom while you were in the shower and she said Ryleigh's okay. She was afraid to be alone while she napped so Mom is lying down with her."

Ryan's shoulders slumped, the tension leaking out of her like air from a punctured tire. "Okay. I'm glad she has support."

"What about Vanessa's assistant?" Oren asked. "Is she out of the hospital?"

"No," Ryan replied. "Lori's doing better, but the doctor wants to keep her until Sunday. She needed ten stitches in her arm, but I guess they're mostly worried about a concussion. Steve hit her really hard. I talked to her on the phone earlier, told her I would come to the hospital, but she said no. She said her best friend was already with her."

They were silent for a few minutes and then Shay said, "Are you ready to talk about what the detective told you?"

Just before Ryan had showered, the lead detective had called her cell phone. She wanted to talk to Shay and Oren about it – *needed* to talk about it – but she'd also needed some time to absorb it all.

She took a deep breath, picking at a thread on her robe. "Nothing too surprising. They went to-to Steve's house and it was actually a farm and he did have pigs."

She shuddered all over and Oren put his arm around her, drawing her up against his warmth.

"He, uh, he had a room that was plastered with pictures of me and Ryleigh. Typical stalker stuff, basically. They found the materials he used to make the heads, he even had pictures of the heads in progress tacked to the wall, and they found another three dead ravens in the freezer.

"Jesus," Shay said. "The guy was fucked in the head."

Ryan nodded. "The hotel staff had no idea he was crazy."

"Let me guess," Oren said. "They said he was quiet and kept to himself."

"Actually, no," Ryan said. "He was really friendly and went to a lot of the staff functions, did tons of socializing with his coworkers. He even held a barbeque at his farm that most of the hotel staff attended. He organized a fundraiser for one of his co-worker's kids who had cancer. They said he-he was *nice* and he was *normal*."

Her body was wracked with more tremors. "The detective

said they're all stunned and-and sad that he's dead. The man kidnapped us and threatened to cut Vanessa up into pieces and feed her to his pigs and they're sad he's dead."

"It's hard for people to see past the person they thought they knew," Oren said.

"I was glad when Grayson killed him. I really was," Ryan said in a low voice. "I was terrified for myself and for Ryleigh, and then when Steve attacked Grayson, I was terrified that Grayson would die too. I felt relief when Grayson tore his throat out."

The dry click of her throat as she swallowed was deafening in the silence. "But now that I know he had friends, that people liked him and are sad that he's dead, I feel terrible. I'm a bad person."

"No," Shay said. "You're not. Just because the guy had friends and did some nice things for his coworkers doesn't make him a good person, Ryan. He let his mother die a slow and painful death. He was going to kill Vanessa and probably you and Ryleigh too. You can't forget that, sweetie."

"His mother –"

"His mother fucked with his head and maybe contributed to him being a sociopath, but she didn't deserve to die," Oren said. "Plenty of people have fucked up childhoods without resorting to what this asshole did."

He cupped her face, being careful of the bruises that still lined both cheeks and made her look at him. "You do not have to feel bad or guilty that he's dead. Do you hear me, baby-girl? He's dead because he tried to hurt you and your man wasn't having none of that."

She didn't reply and Oren kissed her forehead again. "Have you heard from Grayson?"

"No." Even she could hear the dejection in her voice. "Not since they took him to the hospital. I know he's okay.

Wes said he only needed a few stitches and then they took him to the police station to give his statement, but he hasn't texted me or anything."

"Maybe he's still at the station?" Shay said.

"He isn't," she said. "Wes drove me home and I asked him. He said that Cooper had sent Grayson home to get some rest."

"Then he's probably still sleeping," Oren said. "He'll text you when he wakes up."

"I don't know," Ryan said. "The job is done. Grandmother told Cooper at the hotel that we didn't need them anymore and to send her the final invoice. Why would Grayson contact me?"

"Um, because you loves you, you butthead," Shay said with affection in her voice. "Even if he hadn't killed a man to save your life, it was obvious that he is totally gaga over you. He'll text you, honey. I know he will."

"That's just it, he had to kill someone for me. You don't just-just get over something like that, you know? If it wasn't for me, he would never have been put in that position. We haven't even known each other a month yet and we haven't slept together."

"You have a connection," Oren said.

Ryan stared at the blank television screen. She thought they'd had a connection, but what if she was wrong? What if he didn't want anything to do with her now?

He called you his mate.

Okay, that was true, but it was a confusing and scary moment and he had just killed a guy. Besides, maybe shifters called people their mates as a term of endearment, just another version of sweetie or honey. That had to be it. Thinking it was anything else, like maybe that he was in love with her, was beyond ridiculous. Neither humans nor shifters

214

fell in love that quickly, and if they did? They needed to check themselves in to the psych ward.

Well then sign yourself in to the nuthouse, sweetheart, because you are definitely in love with Grayson.

"What time is it?" she asked.

"Almost three." Shay checked her phone. "Sweetie, I really think you should try and eat something. I know you say you're not hungry but -"

The knock on the door made them all stiffen. Oren glanced at her. "Told you he'd show up."

"You don't know it's him," she said as Oren stood. She trailed after him as he headed toward the front door. She paused at the island in the kitchen, clutching at the neckline of her robe and studying Oren's broad back as he opened the door.

Her body sagged, her breath rushing out of her lungs when Oren stepped aside, and she saw Grayson. He walked toward her, his normal confident swagger diminished a little by his hunched shoulders and the nervousness on his face.

She studied him silently when he stopped in front of her. His face was drawn, shadows darkened the flesh under his eyes, and his usual stubble had almost turned into a beard. She wanted to touch him, wanted to throw her arms around his waist and never fucking let go.

Instead, she dug her hands into a tight fist behind her back and said, "Hi."

"Hi. How are you?" he said.

"Uh, good. I'm good. You okay?"

"Yeah," he replied.

They lapsed into awkward silence. Grayson glanced at Shay when she cleared her throat. "Hey, Grayson."

"Hi, Shay."

"Shay-bae, time to go." Oren appeared and took Shay's

hand, tugging her toward the front door. "Ryan, call us if you need us."

Shay looked back at Ryan. "Maybe we should -"

"Time to go," Oren repeated. He opened the front door and pulled Shay outside with him. The door shut with a harsh thump.

Silence descended. Ryan couldn't think of a single thing to say.

"Uh, where's Sam?" Grayson finally said.

"He's still with my grandmother. She said she'd keep him for the weekend," Ryan replied.

"Good, that's good." Grayson studied the fridge, then the dishwasher, and then the microwave like he'd never seen a kitchen appliance before.

She fidgeted from foot to foot, looking like a little kid who needed to pee, but not able to spit a single syllable out. What if Grayson was here to tell her goodbye. What if he was about to tell her that he hated her for forcing him to kill a man.

Fear flooded her lungs, making it hard to catch her breath and turning all four of her limbs into over-cooked noodles.

"Honey," a look of pure guilt covered Grayson's face, "please don't be afraid of me. Please. I swear I'll never -"

"Afraid of you?" She took a stumbling step forward. "Grayson, I'm not afraid of you. You saved my life last night. If it wasn't for you, I'd be dead right now."

"You're afraid." He sniffed the air. "I can smell your fear, Ryan."

"Because I'm afraid you're about to leave and I'll never see you again," she whispered.

His mouth dropped open and a sound that was half purr and half whimper erupted from his chest. "No," he said. "I will never leave you, Ryan."

With a small hoarse cry, she threw herself at him. She smashed her mouth down onto his, kissing him with frantic need. He returned her kiss, sliding his hands around her waist and holding her tight.

She pressed her body against his, licking at his firm lips until he parted them. She slid her tongue into his mouth, moaning when he sucked on it. He pulled back, his eyes already jade and his cock already hard against her belly. She smiled at him and took his hand, tugging him toward the stairs.

"Ryan -"

"The job is over," she said. "I'm not a client anymore."

"I know." He didn't move when she tugged on his hand again. "But we need to talk."

"We do." She pressed up against him again and then licked his throat, loving the sound of his low groan. "And we will. But I need you between my legs and in my pussy first."

"Fuck," he moaned.

"Yes," she replied. "Then we talk. Are you good with that?" She licked his throat again before reaching between their bodies and cupping his cock.

"So good with that," he muttered.

He followed her up the stairs, his hands rubbing and caressing her ass and lower back as they almost sprinted to the bedroom. He turned her to face him once they were in the room, his hands cupping her ass again.

"Naked," she said. "I need you naked."

"You first," he said with a wicked grin that dampened her pussy immediately.

He untied the knot of her robe and pushed it off her shoulders. She was wearing an oversized Denver Broncos t-shirt and a huge grin crossed Gray's face.

"What?" she said. "They're my favourite team."

"Mine too," he said.

"Are you serious?"

"Yep." He reached down and stroked her thigh below the hem of the shirt. "You just might be the perfect woman, Ms. Shepherd."

"Probably," she said.

He laughed and pulled the shirt over her head. The laughter died in his throat and her body trembled at the look on his face. She was wearing just a pair of cotton panties and his hot gaze roamed her naked breasts.

"Beautiful," he murmured before cupping both of her breasts. She shivered, her back arching when his rough thumbs brushed over her nipples. They hardened and he purred loudly. Her pussy ached in response and she squirmed when he tugged on her right nipple.

"Gray, please."

He smiled at her. His fangs were out but she wasn't afraid when he bent his mouth to her breast. His warm tongue teased her nipple and she clutched at his head when he sucked hard. Her hips thrust against him and his purring intensified.

Her panties were soaked now, the material clinging to her and driving her mad. She hooked her thumbs into the waistline and Gray immediately put his hands over hers.

"Let me," he said.

She nodded and he made a sound that was a half purr and half trill and sent her lust into overdrive.

He eased her panties down her legs, crouching in front of her as she stepped out of them. He left her panties on the floor, and she stroked her fingers through his hair as he studied her pussy.

"So pretty," he said with another deep purr before he leaned forward and pressed a kiss against her short dark patch of hair.

She moaned, her hands pulling at his hair. When he stood, she stared at him in obvious disappointment and a grin crossed his face. He stripped off his shirt and then pulled her into his embrace, inhaling sharply when she rubbed her tits against his naked chest.

He leaned down and nuzzled the column of her throat before kissing his way to her ear. "I know you want me to eat your pretty pussy."

"I do," she panted, "I really, really do."

His low laugh made her nerve endings buzz. He cupped her breast, toying with her nipple as he sucked on her earlobe. "I promise to go down on you later, but for now – I need to fuck you, Ryan. I can't think about anything other than how your tight pussy will feel around my dick, and I don't want to taste your pussy when I'm distracted by how much I want to fuck you. I want to make sure your sweet pussy has my," he licked the curve of her ear, "full attention."

"That's fair," she said breathlessly.

He laughed again, not stopping her when she reached down and unbuttoned and unzipped his jeans. "Get naked, right now."

He shoved his jeans and briefs down his legs, stopping to pull off his socks with a languid grace she envied. She licked her lips, staring shamelessly at his body as he stood in front of her.

He was perfection, she decided. He had the lean build of a swimmer with an all over tan – lord, help her, did he sunbathe naked? A light layer of dark hair covered his chest, arrowing down into a thin line below his bellybutton.

And his cock... it was large and thick and beautiful and delightfully hard. Crap... was she drooling? She was possibly drooling.

She wiped her lower lip, relieved when her hand stayed

dry, before lying down on the bed and crooking her finger at him. "Get that glorious cock of yours over here."

"Yes, ma'am." He paused. "Hold on, I need a condom from my wallet."

Before he could grab his jeans, she said, "I'm clean and I'm on the pill."

He froze before staring thoughtfully at her. She blushed a little. She'd never slept with someone without a condom before, but for a reason she couldn't explain, she wanted to take Grayson without anything between them.

"I mean," she chewed at her bottom lip, "if you prefer to use a condom, I totally understand. I'm not going to force you to, like, bang me without one."

A slow smile crossed his handsome face. "Honey, you have no idea how much I want to fuck you bareback."

He laid down on the bed beside her, cupping her breast again and pulling on the nipple. "I'm clean too."

"Then let's get this party started," she said and tried to tug him on top of her.

He purred loudly but didn't move. His hand drifted over the curve of her belly and stroked the tops of her thighs. "No need to rush."

"That's where you're wrong," she parted her legs when his fingers pressed against her inner thigh, "if you don't fuck me soon, I might go…oh God!"

His warm fingers had slipped between her wet pussy lips to brush against her clit. She grabbed his forearm, her hips arching and her eyes closing as pleasure filled her body.

"Oh," she panted, "right there."

"Where? Here?" he said teasingly before rubbing circles around her throbbing clit.

"Grayson!" She dug her nails into his arm, and he purred

to her. The sound was soothing but she needed more. "Don't tease. Please."

"Whatever you want, honey." He kissed her hard, angling his mouth over hers and plunging his tongue deep into her mouth as he rubbed her clit.

She cried out into his mouth, her entire body shuddering and shaking as her orgasm washed over her. She'd never come so hard or so fast in her life and she moaned when Grayson slid one thick finger into her pussy.

He groaned before sucking hard on her bottom lip. He released her mouth and said, "Sweetheart, I am definitely making you come while you're taking my cock. I need to feel you squeezing like this around my dick."

Weak and boneless from her orgasm, she watched through half-closed eyes as he pushed her thighs apart and knelt between them. He propped himself up on his arms above her and the flash of black made her drag her eyelids open. She studied the row of stitches on his upper arm before giving him a worried look. "Maybe I should be on top."

He shook his head. "No, it's fine."

"You might bust your stitches or -"

"No," he said before purring to her. "I want you like this, honey. Under me with those smooth thighs of yours wrapped around my hips. I want you looking up at me as you take every inch of my cock."

Fresh lust exploded in her belly. "Well," she said breathlessly, "when you put it that way…"

He purred again and when his dick nudged at her opening, she spread her legs and wrapped her hands around his forearms. He pushed into her in one smooth stroke, his width stretching her inner walls until she squeezed his arms.

He stopped immediately, staring down at her worriedly. "Okay, honey?"

"Yes," she gasped. "You're just… big."

His adorable smile and loud purr made her lift her head and press a kiss against his lips. "I swear if you purr while you're fucking me, I'm gonna come almost immediately."

He pressed a kiss against one taut nipple. "Whatever you want, honey."

He moved in and out of her with slow, languid strokes that sent pleasure up and down her spine. She wrapped her legs around his hips, squeezing him with her thighs and meeting each stroke with an upward thrust of her hips.

His purring grew louder, the sound filling the room until all she could hear was the deep rumbling sound. When she reached between their bodies and rubbed her clit, he made a low growl of approval.

"That's good, honey. Rub your clit for me."

She rubbed the small bundle of nerves as his strokes turned hard and fast. He was staring at her breasts, his eyes glowing bright jade and a heavy beard on his face. His lips parted, and the gleam of his fangs was bright in the afternoon sun. The sight of his fangs, the feel of his hard cock sliding in and out, the sound of his purring… it sent her pleasure skyrocketing. She cried his name, her fingers rubbing furiously at her clit as her second orgasm exploded within her.

She squeezed around him, closing her eyes and hanging onto him as he roared his own pleasure. Warm wetness filled her, and his entire body tensed as he came deep inside of her. She opened her eyes, watching his face as the last of his orgasm wracked his body.

He collapsed against her, panting and purring. The vibration of his chest against her sensitive nipples made her gasp and he rolled off of her with a low groan. "Sorry, honey."

"'s good," she said. She turned on her side and snuggled up to him, throwing one leg over his and resting her head on his chest. His purring slowed and then stopped, and he stroked her hair from her sweaty face before running his hand up and down her spine.

"That was amazing," he said.

"Hmm," she replied. The two orgasms had relaxed her to the point where she was almost comatose. The stress of the last twenty-four hours and the lack of sleep had finally caught up to her.

"Honey," he said, "we should talk."

"Later," she mumbled. "Sleep now, talk later."

He kissed the top of her head and pulled her even closer. "Whatever you want, my mate."

CHAPTER 15

"Hey, Cooper, do you have a minute?"

Cooper turned away from his office window. "Daisy? What are you still doing here? The meeting ended half an hour ago."

"I know. Do you have a minute to talk?" She hovered in his doorway.

"Of course. Sit down." He sat down at his desk and glanced at his watch. It was just after three and he thought everyone had left. His lion purred to Daisy as she settled into the chair across from his desk. She was carrying a blue file folder that she clutched to her small chest.

"Sorry again about bringing you in today," he said.

"It's really not a problem," she said. "I could use the extra cash."

He didn't reply and embarrassment radiated from her. Clearing her throat, she said, "Not that you don't – I mean, you pay me more than enough, it's just that... I'm not bad with money. I swear."

"I don't think you are," he said.

"Right." Her shame was growing and desperate to make her feel better, he changed the subject.

"What did you want to talk to me about?"

"Oh, um, my research on the manager guy Bert," she said. "It probably doesn't matter now since the stalker has been caught, but I didn't know if you still wanted to hear what I found or…"

She sighed and shook her head. "God, I'm so stupid. You don't want to hear about it. Why would you?"

She stood up to leave and he stood too. "Daisy, wait. I do want to hear it, actually."

She stared at him before sinking back into her seat. "Okay, but why?"

Deciding that "Because I'll do anything to spend time with you," was an inappropriate response, Cooper said, "Call it professional curiosity."

She toyed with the edge of the file folder and he sat down and made a go on gesture before resting his elbows on his desk. His lion purred again when Daisy scooted her chair closer and he got a whiff of her scent. The smell of vanilla always lingered on her and he hadn't yet been able to figure out why. Was it her shampoo? Her body wash? His gaze lingered on her full mouth – lip gloss, maybe?

Only one way to find out. Kiss her.

His lion purred loudly, very enthusiastic about the idea of kissing Daisy. His cock was standing at attention and he was incredibly thankful that the desk hid his lap from her view. Of course, the agonizing pressure of his dick pressing against his jeans was so distracting he could barely concentrate on the piece of paper Daisy was sliding across the desk toward him.

Shifting in his chair, ignoring his urge to reach down and readjust, he said, "What's this?"

"Copies of Bert's banking information," Daisy said. "Lusa got them for me."

"How the hell did she get this kind of information?" he asked. Jesus, the cougar shifter was a better hacker than he thought.

"I didn't ask," Daisy said delicately. "Anyway, they didn't tell us anything other than that he isn't hurting for money."

"That's the goddamn truth." He shook his head and handed back the records. "I should have got into the managing celebrities business."

She smiled before opening a notebook that was tucked inside the file folder. "So, to be honest, even if the stalker hadn't tried to take Ryan and Ryleigh yesterday and we still considered Bert a suspect, I would have suggested we get information on this guy as well."

She handed him a black and white photo. He studied it carefully. It was two men and two women in a restaurant booth. Both men were smoking cigars and the women were sitting between them with their arms around the men's shoulders. They all had big cheesy grins pointed into the camera.

The woman on the right was clearly a much younger Vanessa – he was struck by just how much she resembled Ryleigh – and one of the men looked like a younger version of Bert. If the balding manager had a full head of hair that fell halfway down his back.

"Is that Bert?" He pointed at the long-haired man and Daisy nodded.

"It is. I know it's hard to tell because of all the hair, but it's him."

"When was this taken?" he asked.

"It was 1988. Vanessa had just graduated from high school. She was trying to make it as an actress and was working as a PA for the director of a television series about vampires. Bert was working in the special effects department – it's how they met."

"Okay. Who's the other guy and woman?"

"The woman is Liza Franken. She was a makeup artist on the show. The guy is Corbin Werner. He did set construction for the same show."

"Where did you find this picture?" Cooper asked.

"In an old People magazine. They did this big article on Vanessa when the reboot of the show debuted. They had a bunch of photos of her from before she became famous."

"What I don't get is why she was working as a PA. Beverly was a famous actress, wouldn't that have made it easier for Vanessa to get acting jobs?" Cooper said.

Daisy shrugged. "The People article just said that Vanessa was determined to make it on her own."

"That doesn't track with the Vanessa I met," Cooper said. "She doesn't seem like the type who refuses handouts or anything that will make her life easier. If I had to guess, Beverly refused to help her. For a human, the old lady is tough."

"Maybe," Daisy said. "But what I found interesting is that this guy," she tapped Corbin's face, "was in almost all of the pictures."

"Okay," he said. He was missing something.

"In every picture, Vanessa is draped across him. In the one, they're kissing," Daisy said. "They dated for about a year."

"How do you know that?"

"Okay, so the article named Vanessa and Bert and Liza, but not the guy. I looked up Liza on Facebook and messaged her. I might have told her I was a journalist interested in doing a story about Vanessa's life before the fame. She agreed to talk on the phone with me and gave me Corbin's name as well some information about Vanessa and him." Daisy paused. "But I'm pretty sure that was only because she was completely plastered when we spoke."

"What did she tell you?" Cooper was intrigued despite the job being over.

"She said that Corbin and Vanessa were together for over a year, and it was serious. They even talked about marriage." Daisy glanced down at her notebook. "She said, and I quote, 'but then Corbin got Vanessa knocked up and wanted her to have an abortion'. Vanessa refused."

"You're kidding?" Cooper leaned forward, for once not noticing Daisy's scent. "She has a third kid?"

"According to Liza, she does. She said that Corbin and Vanessa fought bitterly the entire time Vanessa was pregnant and he eventually left her right before she gave birth. Liza said that Corbin moved to New York. Vanessa had a baby boy and then put the baby up for adoption, swore Bert and Liza to secrecy, and never spoke to Corbin again," Daisy said.

"Are Liza and Vanessa still friends?" Cooper asked.

"No, they had a falling out. You know how Vanessa was dating that photographer? Ryan's dad?"

"Yeah," Cooper replied.

"Liza was dating him first. Then she introduced him to Vanessa, and I guess he dumped Liza and he and Vanessa started dating. Liza never forgave either of them."

"Jesus, what a soap opera," Cooper said.

"Here's the thing," Daisy said, "I don't know for certain that I can believe what Liza said. She really was very drunk and the day after we spoke on the phone, she called me again and took back everything she said. She said it was a story that she made up because she hated Vanessa still for taking the photographer," Daisy scanned her notebook, "Jake was his name, from her. Said that Jake was the love of her life and she'd been pissed at Vanessa for years about it."

Cooper leaned back in his chair, rubbing absentmindedly at the scruff on his jaw. "Seems like a pretty elaborate story to make up."

"Right?" Daisy said. "I thought so too. But, here's something interesting." She handed him another piece of paper. "Lusa hacked into Bert's email account. All of those emails that I've highlighted? Those are emails from Bert arranging meetings with Corbin Werner. He meets him every month, sometime between the fifteenth and the eighteenth, without fail."

"For what?" Cooper scanned the messages, looking for a clue.

"Neither of them say in the messages. It's always just arranging a time and place to meet, somewhere in California which means that Corbin's living here again. I did some more digging on Corbin and found him on LinkedIn. He moved back to California almost a decade ago and he's a construction site manager. I emailed him and gave him the journalist cover story and asked if he would be willing to chat with me about Vanessa."

"Did he write back?"

"I got an email back from him this morning. He refused to meet with me, and the entire email was," she paused, "unpleasant in tone. He said some pretty awful things about Vanessa and ended it with saying that he hated her and couldn't wait to piss on her grave."

"So, you were thinking that maybe he was the stalker based on the email," Cooper said.

"Maybe. I mean, it's been a lot of years, but people hold grudges forever sometimes."

He didn't reply and her cheeks flushed red. "I know it wasn't a lot to go on, but -"

"No," he said, "it was good work. If that stalker guy hadn't tried to take them out yesterday, we absolutely would have followed up on this Corbin guy. You did a great job, Daisy. Thank you."

The smile on her face and the scent of her happiness made his lion puff out with pride. He had pleased his mate.

"Okay, well, that's all I had so…" Daisy stood. "Have a good rest of the weekend."

He wanted to beg her to come home with him. He wanted to carry her to his bed and show her exactly how well he could please her. An image of her slender body naked and in his bed popped into his mind. She was so soft and sweet. He would finally find out where that maddeningly enticing scent of vanilla came from. He would finally find out if her pussy could take all of him. She would look so beautiful riding him. He'd make her come again and again, until she realized that he was the only one who could please her.

He shook his head, breaking the mental image of a naked Daisy in his bed. Fuck, his dick was as hard as a fucking stone again and sweat was sliding down his face.

"Cooper, are you okay?" Daisy studied him. "You look flushed and, uh, kind of sweaty all of a sudden."

"Fine," he rasped out.

"Are you sure?" She moved a little closer, and he realized he was about thirty seconds away from jumping over his goddamn desk and kissing her. The daydream about Daisy had gotten his lion completely riled up. It was pushing him to kiss her, pushing him to mark her, and he was so tired of denying it.

"Cooper?"

"I'm fine," he said. His voice was harsh and rough. Not

from anger, but from the sheer amount of willpower it was taking not to touch Daisy. Still, the scent of her concern changed to fear and she backed toward the door.

His erection disappeared immediately, and he stood up. "I'm not angry, Daisy."

"I know," she said as she groped for the door handle. "It's just getting late and I have a... thing so... bye, Cooper."

"Bye, Daisy." He sat down in defeat as Daisy practically ran out of his office.

"SCOOT FORWARD."

Ryan slid forward in the tub. "You like taking baths?"

"I like taking baths with a hot and naked woman." Gray climbed into the tub behind her and sat down in the hot water. He spread his legs around her hips, slid his arm around her waist and pulled her back against him.

She leaned against his chest and he kissed the top of her head. "This is nice. Did you have the largest tub known to man installed, or did it come with the house?"

She giggled and stroked his thigh under the water. "I had it installed. I love soaking in the tub and have a bath almost every night. It was my only real indulgence when I bought the house."

He studied the flat screen television that was mounted on the wall in front of them. "The television is a brilliant idea."

She laughed again. "Trashy reality shows are a thousand times better when you watch them from a hot bath."

"I bet." He kissed her head again before caressing her arms. "I liked waking up in your bed."

"I liked having you in my bed." She twisted her head to stare up at him. "Will you stay the night with me?" She supposed she was being forward, but she didn't care. She wanted Grayson to stay with her.

"Yes."

His immediate response made her sag with relief. He squeezed her arm. "Why do you look so relieved? Did you think I would say no?"

She shrugged. "I wasn't sure. At the hotel during the conference you didn't come by my room in the evenings at all."

He pulled her a little closer, the water lapping around their bodies as they moved. "I wanted to spend the evenings with you, but I thought you would need some alone time after spending all day with thousands of adoring fans."

"They were mostly there for my sister, and normally I would need some alone time, but…"

"But?" he prompted.

Feeling like she was back in high school, she said, "I like you. I like you a lot and I want to spend time with you."

"I like you too," he replied. "I hated not being with you in the evenings." His voice turned dark. "If I had been with you Friday night, you would have been safe. That guy would never have even had a chance to take you from me."

His arms tightened around her and she traced her fingers along his forearm. "I'm sorry."

"For what?"

She rested her head on his chest again, staring at the ceiling. "You had to kill a man because of me."

"Not because of you," he said. "It isn't your fault, I had to kill him."

"Have you killed someone before?" she whispered.

His big body was tense behind her and his reply was clipped, like it had to be forced out. "Yes."

"I'm sorry."

"Me too." He kissed the top of one wet shoulder. "I didn't want to kill that guy last night and I wish to God that it had ended a different way, but he left me no choice. He was going to take you from me. He would have hurt you, honey, and I will never let that happen."

The warmth infusing her body had nothing to do with the hot bath water. She toyed with the rubber bracelet around her wrist. She should have taken it off, she didn't need to wear it anymore, but the idea of not wearing it made her anxious and unsettled. The plain rubber bracelet had saved not just her life but her sister and her mother's lives as well.

"You're still wearing the bracelet," Grayson said.

She nodded, a little angry with herself that she had drawn attention to it. "Sorry, I'll give it back to -"

"No, keep wearing it."

She glanced back at Grayson and he cleared his throat. "I mean, if you want to. You don't have to, but... Jesus, I sound like a stalker now."

She laughed and twisted around so she could plant a kiss against his wet chest. "Maybe slightly, but I'll keep wearing the bracelet."

"Thank you." He cupped the back of her neck and drew her closer, his mouth pressing against hers. She kissed him greedily, relishing his taste and the feel of his firm chest against her breasts.

When she rubbed her tits against him, he groaned, and his hand tightened around the back of her neck. "Honey, wait."

"Why?" she said. "I want to have hot bathtub sex."

He grinned at her, one hand cupping her breast and teasing her nipple. "I'm not against that but -"

Her stomach growled and his grin widened. "But I was guessing you haven't eaten today."

"It's already ten, that's too late to eat."

234

"I'll make something light," he said as her stomach growled again.

She traced her fingers over his collarbone. "Fine. I might be a little hungry. But we could have sex first and then eat."

He kissed her again. "You need to eat. Passing out from lack of food in the middle of sex is not a good thing."

She laughed. "Low blood sugar is nothing to mess around with, I suppose."

"It isn't." He reached around and cupped her ass, giving it a firm squeeze. "C'mon, I'll make you something to eat."

"And then we'll have sex?"

His smile was wicked and warm and set her nerve endings ablaze. Or maybe it was from his hand slipping between her legs to rub her pussy. "Yes, Ryan, then we'll have sex."

She ground against his hand, whining in disappointment when he moved it away. "Be nice, Grayson."

"Honey," he kissed her again, "I'm always nice."

"HOW IS RYLEIGH DOING?" GRAYSON CLOSED THE dishwasher and leaned against the counter. He studied Ryan as she put her phone down on the counter.

"She says she's fine. Apparently, Grandmother went to bed a few hours ago and Vanessa is drunk again."

"Did you want to go over there?" He hated the idea of Ryan being around Vanessa, but if that was what she wanted or needed, he would keep his mouth shut about it and just support her.

To his relief, Ryan was shaking her head. "No, Vanessa is holed up in her room drinking, and Ryleigh's headed to bed. It's fine."

"You sure?"

She nodded before easing her arms around him and kissing his chest. "I'm positive. Weirdly, Ryleigh does sound okay. Like, she's much calmer than I would have thought she'd be."

"You're both pretty calm, considering what happened," Grayson said.

She shrugged, a smile turning up the corners of her mouth. "In show business you learn to be tough pretty quick."

"I bet." He kissed the top of her head, loving the feel of her curvy body tucked against his.

"I told you to leave the dishes and I would put them in the dishwasher," she said. "You cooked, it's only fair that I clean."

"I don't mind."

She cocked her head at him, her smile widening. "Still, you did have to do all the work. Maybe I need to do something to say thanks."

He cupped her perfect breast, the warm weight of it making his cock harden. The smell of her lust intensified, and he groaned when she rubbed herself against his dick. He stroked his thumb across her nipple until it hardened before leaning down and nipping at her neck. "What did you have in mind?"

"Come upstairs and I'll show you," she said.

She took his hand and led him upstairs. She was wearing just her Denver Bronco's shirt again and as they walked into her bedroom and she turned to face him, he realized he'd probably never be able to watch football again without getting a goddamn erection.

She stripped off the shirt and he purred to her. "Your body is incredible."

She smiled and put her hand at her waist, cocking her hip at him. "Thank you. So is yours."

"Come here." His voice was hoarse, his purring so loud, he could barely hear her soft laugh as she walked toward him.

He stared at her tits as she walked, his cock dripping precum and his urge to bury himself deep inside of her a raging fire within. When she reached him, she tugged at the button on his jeans. He slid his arm around her and kneaded her ass as she unbuttoned and unzipped his jeans.

"I want to taste your pussy," he said.

He loved the way she blushed when he talked about going down on her. He nuzzled her ear and said, "I bet you taste so sweet, honey. Lie on the bed and spread your legs. Show me how wet you are before I lick you clean."

She clutched at his arm when he pushed his hand between her legs and thumbed her clit. She was wet, nearly dripping in fact, and he purred to her again. "On the bed, honey."

"Soon," she moaned.

"Now," he replied. He slid one finger into her opening, smiling with satisfaction when she gasped, and her walls clenched around him.

She tugged his hand away, her blush deepening when he licked her taste from his finger. He sucked on her bottom lip then released it with a soft pop. "You taste delicious."

"Stop distracting me," she muttered before shoving his jeans to his ankles. Before he could say a word, she was on her knees in front of him, one hand wrapped around the base of his dick and her tongue cleaning away the precum from the tip of his dick.

He cried out, his hands sliding into her hair and his hips jerking forward. She squeezed the base of him, twisting her wrist in a way that made pleasure snake down his spine. Her warm wet mouth took him in, and his purring grew so loud that she released him and grinned up at him.

"Wow, that gets your motor going, hmm?"

"Please, honey," he begged, "don't stop."

He cupped the back of her head and urged her forward. To his relief, she sucked on his cock again, her lips applying perfect firm pressure as her tongue licked the underside. He stared down at her, knowing his eyes were glowing and a thick beard had grown on his face. It didn't seem to scare her though.

She returned his look, her light blue eyes showing only the same all-encompassing need that he felt. He smoothed her hair back from her face, watching as her lips stretched around him and she took over half of his cock into her wet mouth.

He moaned again, his hips thrusting wildly as she sucked hard. Fuck, if he didn't stop her, he was going to come in her mouth. She licked around the crown before sucking on just the tip. His hips jerked again, and he tugged on her hair.

"Honey, stop. I'm going to come. Please, stop. Please… oh fuck!"

The rhythm of her sucking increased, the pressure of her mouth tightened and with a loud growl, he lost control. He came hard, his hand gripping the back of her head to keep her in place on his cock. Watching her swallow his seed was something he didn't know he wanted until just this moment.

To his delight, she swallowed his come eagerly, her throat working as she took every last bit of him. She licked the length of him, her tongue curling against the slit to get the final drop, and he gasped with pleasure.

She leaned back and licked her swollen lips before smiling at him. "That seemed like a good one."

"Honey," he bent and lifted her to her feet, "you have no fucking idea how good that was."

Without waiting for her reply, he lifted her and carried her to the bed. He set her down in the middle and climbed in after her, pushing her thighs open and lying down on his stomach between them.

He was dying to get a proper taste of her pussy and, ignoring the slight scent of her embarrassment, he bent his head and licked her pussy from her opening to the top of her clit. She cried his name, her hips arching and her hands digging into the bedcovers.

He licked her again, smiling when one hand clamped down on the top of his head and she pushed his mouth against her. All trace of her embarrassment was gone. Her hips were rising, her pussy already grinding against his tongue and his lips. He rested his hands on her inner thighs, pushing them wide and holding her open so he could feast on her pussy.

He licked every inch of her wet lips clean before teasing her clit with the tip of his tongue. His mate tasted like sweet honey and her cries of pleasure and the way she moved in response had his cock hardening again.

He rubbed his dick against the quilt as he sucked on her clit, the pressure sending shivers of pleasure down his back. She was close, he could sense it in the way she moved, in the way she babbled nonsense at him as he sucked and licked her clit.

He kissed her inner thigh and then sucked on her clit again. She screamed his name and wetness flooded his face. He was consumed by the warmth and scent of his mate and he purred happily as he licked her clean.

He sat up and wiped his face on the sheet as he stared down at his beautiful and perfect mate. She was shuddering and panting, her eyes squeezed shut and her hands clenching and unclenching around the quilt.

He rubbed her thigh and she cracked open one eye to stare at him. "Oh my God, that was amazing."

"Good," he said. "Turn over."

He loved that she didn't hesitate. She turned onto her stomach and he admired her ass before cupping her hips and lifting her to her knees. "Spread your legs wide for me, honey."

She parted her legs and he moved closer, nudging at one thigh with his. "Wider, Ryan."

She spread them wider and he smiled before pressing on her back until her upper chest and head were resting on the bed. He studied her body, pulling her thighs even farther apart until he could see every inch of her wet pussy.

"Grayson," she moaned. "I need you."

He purred to her, rubbing the curve of her ass with one hand as he guided his cock to her wet opening. He pushed in, loving the tight snugness of his mate's pussy. She moaned and stiffened when he pushed again. He could go deep in this position and he soothed his mate with trills and purrs, and warm strokes on her lower back until she relaxed again.

"Good," he said before pushing in all the way. She cried out and tried to wiggle away, but he had her firmly by the hips and she couldn't move.

"Grayson," she looked over her shoulder at him, "I'm not sure I can -"

"You can," he said before purring to her again.

She stared at him and he rubbed her ass. "You can, honey. Just relax."

She nodded and took a deep breath. Her body relaxed around him and he made a few shallow thrusts, watching her reaction. She moaned and when she began to meet his thrusts, her curvy body rocking back to meet his, he reached down and wrapped her hair around his fist.

He tugged until she moved to her hands and knees and he pulled lightly on her hair until she was staring up at the ceiling. "Good, my mate."

He fucked her hard and deep, holding tight to her with one hand on her hip and the other in her hair. She met each of his thrusts eagerly, the wet sounds of their coupling filling the room. She squirmed when he changed positions slightly, her pussy squeezing delightfully around him.

"Oh, oh God," she muttered, "I think that's my fucking G spot."

He grinned and pushed into her again, the head of his cock rubbing against the front wall of her pussy. She cried his name, her body shuddering and her pussy tightening like a vice around him. He slid in and out repeatedly, driving her need and his own higher with each stroke.

Her body tensed and she screamed as her orgasm hit her. The squeezing of her pussy pulled his own orgasm from him and he drove in deep, filling her with his come as he climaxed hard.

When he finally pulled out of her, her trembling legs collapsed, and she fell face-first onto the bed. He stretched out beside her and rolled her to her side, brushing her hair out of her face and kissing her mouth.

"You good?"

"So good," she moaned. "You?"

"Never better." He pulled the sheet and quilt up over them and kissed her sweaty cheek. "Do you want some water?"

She shook her head and then yawned. "Less talking, more sleeping."

He laughed and kissed her again. "Good night, honey."

CHAPTER 16

"R yan, please stop asking me if I'm okay." Ryleigh's voice was thin with impatience.

Ryan leaned against the island, switching her cell phone to her other ear. "I'm sorry, sweetie. You just sound off to me."

"Of course, I do. Two days ago, I had a lunatic holding a knife to my throat."

"Why don't you come over tonight. We'll hang out, watch some TV and -"

"No," Ryleigh said quickly. "I'm going to stay home and just relax tonight."

"I could come over there. I told Grandmother I'd pick up Sam on Monday, but I can pick him up tonight."

"No," Ryleigh said. "I want to be alone, Ryan."

"Okay, now I'm really worried about you," Ryan said.

Ryleigh laughed but it sounded forced and unnatural. "You don't have to be. I promise I'm okay, just still a little freaked out and I want some space."

"Maybe being alone isn't the best thing for you right now," Ryan said.

"Saul is stopping by later this afternoon, so I won't be alone. Plus, Mommy and Grandmother are here. Stop worrying."

"Is Vanessa sober?"

Ryleigh's laugh was bitter. "For now. Lori was discharged from the hospital today and she came by to see Mommy. She only stayed for a bit though. They told her she does have a mild concussion after all. Mommy told her she needed her to be at the house tomorrow anyway and Grandmother got mad at her. She told Lori to go home and get some rest. After she left, Mommy and Grandmother had a huge fight, so I imagine Mommy won't be sober for much longer. Anyway, I gotta go, okay? I love you, Ry-Ry."

"I love you too, Ryleigh." Ryan set her phone on the island and stared out the window. It was late Sunday morning and she'd left Grayson sleeping in her bed. He must have been tired. He hadn't moved a muscle when she climbed out of bed.

She rubbed at her aching thighs. She would cook him breakfast for a change, she could handle making some French toast, and then she'd have a hot bath before doing some work.

Or you could fuck Grayson again.

She smiled to herself. Having sex with Grayson was one addiction she was a-okay with it. The stairs behind her creaked and she smiled again when she heard the loud purring. She turned around, "Hey, handsome, what do you think about French toast for... holy shit."

The giant muscular tiger moved gracefully down the stairs. His striped fur gleamed in the sunlight, and his large paws padded silently across the short distance from the bottom of the stairs to the kitchen. A trickle of trepidation went down her spine. She knew Grayson would never hurt her, but just how in control was his human side when he was in his tiger form? She honestly had no idea.

He stopped in front of her, tilting his blocky head to one side. She studied the white in his muzzle and above his eyes. His whiskers were pure white and very long and when his mouth dropped open and revealed his large fangs, she took an involuntary step back.

Her butt hit the island edge and she gripped the island for support as Grayson took another step toward her. He made a trilling sound and then nudged her hip with his head.

"Uh, hey, hi there," she said. "Just, um, felt like being in your tiger form, huh?"

He chuffed and she squealed in surprise when he stood on his back paws and braced his front paws on the island on either side of her.

"Oh shit," she whispered. "Grayson, are you – oh God! Ow!"

Grayson had licked her cheek and the wide scratchy tongue scraped across her bruised skin like sandpaper. He purred and trilled to her and she said, "Um, thank you?"

He chuffed again before rubbing his head against her head, nearly knocking her sideways. She touched his chest tentatively, surprised at how soft the fur was beneath her hand. She winced when one of his thick whiskers jabbed her cheek. He purred loudly and dropped to all fours before rubbing the length of his body against her stomach and hips.

She tightened her grip on the island, trying to stay on her feet as Grayson rubbed against her repeatedly. He rubbed his head against her bare arms and then her thighs below her shorts. His tongue licked her knee and she jerked and then giggled. "Hey, that both hurts and tickles."

He chuffed and purred and made those adorable little trilling noises as he rubbed up against her for nearly five minutes. Finally, he backed away and sat on his haunches, staring at her as she straightened from the island counter.

She stared back at him, blinking when he abruptly changed to his human form. The silence was thick and heavy and starting to get uncomfortable. She pulled nervously at the hem of her t-shirt. "Grayson, I -"

"I'm sorry," he blurted out. "That was – I mean, I shouldn't have…but my tiger, he wanted to…"

"Wanted to what?" she asked.

He scrubbed a hand across the back of his neck. He seemed perfectly at ease with his nakedness and she willed herself not to stare at his dick even though she really, *really* wanted to stare at it. It was so lovely.

"Mark you," he finally said.

"Mark me," she repeated.

Red infused his cheeks and he suddenly became very interested in a spot on the wall to her left. "Yeah. Tigers mark their mates with their scent by rubbing up against them. He, uh, he kind of forced the change when I was only half-awake and then…"

She stared down at herself before sniffing her arm. "So, now I smell like you?"

His blush deepened. "Uh, yeah, but only to other shifters. Humans can't smell it. But shifters will stay away from you because they think you're my – I mean, my tiger's mate. I'm sorry, I tried to stop him, but he can be a bit of an asshole sometimes."

She cocked her head, studying him intently as he fidgeted. Something was off with him. He was usually the very epitome of calm, cool and collected.

As he cleared his throat and looked away again, the truth hit her like Sam barreling into her full speed after a stay at the kennel. Grayson was lying to her. He looked so weird and uncomfortable to her because she'd never seen him lie before.

"Anyway, do you want something for breakfast?" he asked. "I could make…"

He trailed off when she took his hand and led him to the couch. "Sit down," she said and gave him a gentle push on the chest to get him moving.

He sat, sucking in his breath when she straddled him. His dick was already starting to harden, and she pressed her pussy against him. They were separated only by the thin material of her shorts and she ground her pelvis against him as he cupped her ass.

She pressed her mouth against his, pulling away when he tried to deepen the kiss. He scowled at her and she grinned cheekily before stroking his naked chest with her fingertips. "So, this marking thing… how long does it last."

"A few days." He squeezed her ass and kissed her upper chest. "Take off your shirt."

"In a minute," she said. "It was your tiger who wanted to mark me, not you?"

"Yes," he said but wouldn't meet her gaze.

"And it's your tiger who thinks I'm your mate, not you?" She scooted back on his thighs a few inches, then reached down and wrapped her hand around his thick length, stroking him lightly.

"Fuck," he groaned, his hips rising up. "Honey, please."

She tightened her grip and stroked him hard until he was panting, and his eyes had gone jade coloured. When she pulled her hand away, his purring cut out abruptly. "Don't stop."

She smiled at him and slid her hand into her shorts, running her fingers over the wet lips of her pussy. His purring started up again, but when he reached for the waistband of her shorts, she slapped him lightly on the chest. "No."

"I want to see," he growled at her.

"I said no," she repeated. She rubbed her clit, soft little moans escaping her mouth as he stared at the outline of her hand.

"Honey, please," he repeated.

"I'm so wet," she said. "Would you like to see how wet I am?"

"God, yes," he muttered. He reached for her waistband again and she shook her head.

"No, not yet."

He growled at her and she laughed. "No growling at me."

"Give me what I want," he demanded.

"Be good and I will," she said.

He pulled her against his chest, kissing and nipping at her neck. "I'm being very good, honey. Show me your pretty pussy."

"Is lying to your mate being good?" She leaned back and arched one eyebrow at him, her fingers still rubbing lightly at her clit.

His whole body shuddered when she said the word mate and a strange light gleamed in his eyes. "My mate." His voice was rough and guttural and unbelievably sexy. Liquid coated her fingertips and her pussy throbbed with need.

She pulled at the bottom of her shirt with her free hand. When he realized what she was doing, he helped her, cupping her tits eagerly when they were finally bared to him. He rubbed her nipples and she arched her back, moaning when he leaned forward and sucked on one aching nipple.

She slid her hand back into her shorts and rubbed harder at her clit, tempted to just allow herself to go over that pleasure cliff. Instead, she stilled her hand and said, "Stop, Grayson."

His growl was very loud in the quiet, but he stopped and lifted his head, dropping his hands from her breasts. She smiled at him. "That's being a good boy, right?"

"Yes," he said. His cock was dripping a steady flow of precum and she used her free hand to stroke him for a few minutes. His head fell back against the couch and his purring started again. God, she loved it when he purred.

She released him and leaned forward, rubbing her tits against his chest before kissing just below his ear. She licked the curve of his ear as his arms circled around her and he kneaded her ass through her shorts.

"Grayson?"

"Yeah?" His voice was rough again, this time with need.

"Do you still want to see how wet my pussy is for you?" She sucked on his earlobe as he groaned.

"Fuck, yes. Show me, honey."

"I will. As soon as you tell me the truth."

He muttered another curse and she nipped at his earlobe this time. "Tell me, Grayson."

His voice hoarse, he said, "It wasn't just my tiger who wanted to mark you, I wanted to do it too. I want them to know that you're mine."

"Am I yours?" she whispered into his ear.

His growl reverberated against her chest. "Yes. Mine."

Holy crap, that should not have turned her on so much. But the idea of belonging to Grayson, of them being mates, was sending her into a tailspin of lust and need. Feeling a little delirious with desire, she said, "You're my mate, Grayson."

His purring nearly deafened her. His arm curved around her and he crushed her against his chest before kissing her neck. "I'm your mate. I want to see your sweet pussy. Show me."

"Yes, my mate," she whispered into his ear.

Before she could start to remove her shorts, he growled happily, and his hands grabbed the front of her waistband. She jerked in surprise when he easily tore her shorts from the waistband to the crotch. He ripped them apart at both thighs before yanking them off of her and dropping them on the floor.

His big hand threaded into her hair and he pulled her head back before taking her mouth in a hard and demanding kiss. She rubbed at her clit almost frantically, and he leaned back, keeping his hand in her hair as he stared down at her pussy.

"Show me your clit," he said.

Blushing a little, she pushed apart the wet lips of her pussy. He purred at the sight of her swollen pink clit. She cried out, her hips thrusting forward when he ran one rough finger over her clit.

"Mine," he growled again.

He curved his arm around her again, lifting her with surprising ease until his cock was at her entrance. He pushed into her with one smooth motion. She moaned, her fingers digging into his shoulders as he filled her. He was big and thick and perfect, and she loved how full she felt when he was inside of her.

He held her full hips and thrust up and down. She braced her hands on his chest and met each stroke. She bent her head and kissed him, sucking hard on his tongue when he pushed it between her lips. His big hands moved to her breasts, stroking and teasing as she rode him hard.

She reached between their bodies, cupping her pussy and rubbing at her clit as he slid in and out of her aching pussy.

"Good, honey," he breathed as he watched her bouncing

tits. "Make yourself come on my cock."

She moaned and rubbed harder, holding her breath and letting her head fall back when the pleasure washed over her. His hot mouth closed around one nipple and set off another mini orgasm on the heels of her first one.

She arched, her pussy squeezing around him and he released her nipple and shouted her name before thrusting furiously into her pussy. He shouted her name again, the cords in his neck standing out as he came deep inside of her. She squeezed around him repeatedly before collapsing against his broad chest.

Her breath puffed out of her in hot waves, but his purring drowned out the sound of her panting. He stroked her back with long, lazy brushes of his fingers as they both came down from the intense high.

When she could finally speak again, she said, "So, that was really hot."

He laughed and nuzzled her neck. "Agreed."

She straightened and studied his face as she traced the line of stitches across his upper arm. "Do we need to talk about this mate thing?"

"Do you want to talk about it?"

She shrugged. "I don't know. I assume it means, at the very least, that we're dating and exclusive."

He burst into laughter before hugging her hard. "Yes, if you're okay with that."

"More than okay with it. You wanna spend the day with me?"

"I do, and the night, if that works for you," he said.

"It does." She was pretty sure he didn't need a keen sense of smell to know she was happy about it, the goofy grin on her face was more than enough proof.

"Cool. I'll need to go home at some point and get some

clean clothes for work tomorrow."

She kissed his neck. "Let's have a shower and then I'll go with you to your place."

"Sounds good."

When she tried to climb off of him, he held her a little tighter, staring seriously at her. "I didn't mean to scare you when I came downstairs in my tiger form."

"You didn't," she said. "I mean, it surprised me, and I was maybe a little anxious at first, but I got over it."

"I would never hurt you, not in my human form or my tiger form. You know that, right?" he said.

"I do." She pressed a kiss against his lips. "I wasn't afraid, Gray. You can shift to your tiger whenever you want, okay?"

"Okay," he said.

"Good." She poked him in the chest. "Get your naked butt in the shower, mister. We've got errands to run."

SHE WASN'T SURE IF IT WAS GRAYSON PURRING IN HIS SLEEP or the moonlight shining directly in her face that woke her. She'd forgotten to pull the blinds down, and she rolled away from the offending light, squinting at the clock. It was just after three in the morning. Ugh.

She sat up, brushing her hair back from her face as Grayson's purring cut out. He half sat up, staring blearily at her. "My mate?"

"It's fine," she said. "I'm just using the bathroom and getting a drink. Do you want some water?"

"Water, sure, yeah," he muttered before collapsing back on the bed. The purring started up again and she wondered if it was the equivalent of snoring for shifters and if they all purred in their sleep. She'd have to remember to ask Grayson later.

She used the bathroom and then headed down the stairs, automatically grabbing onto the railing to keep from being knocked over by Sam before she remembered he was still with her grandmother. The kitchen was flooded with moonlight and she skirted around the island and grabbed the jug of juice from the fridge. She uncapped it and took a long drink, smiling a little as she recapped it. If Grayson started living with her, she wouldn't be able to do this anymore.

Girl, are you really talking about him living with you already?

She supposed it was quick, but –

The soft *creak* behind her, made her freeze. Clutching the juice jug, she turned slowly. The man in the ski-mask smiled at her, she could see the gleam of his teeth in the moonlight coming in from the window.

"Hello, pretty lady."

His voice was soft and pleasant, but the fine hairs on the back of her neck stood up and her skin prickled. She stared at him in silence as he pointed the gun at her before taking a few steps until he was standing between the kitchen island and the bottom of the stairs.

"Who are you?" she said.

"That don't matter." He studied her body in the dim light. She was wearing just a long t-shirt and her hands tightened around the jug when his gaze lingered on her tits.

"Get out of my home." She wanted her voice to be loud and authoritative, but it was barely above a whisper. She was terrified and every molecule in her body was shrieking at her to run.

"Can't do that, pretty lady. Here's the thing, I'm gonna kill you and I want you to know, it isn't personal. Okay? This is just a job. But," his gaze dropped to her crotch and then her bare legs, "I'm thinking before I kill you, maybe you and me could have a little fun. I've never fucked a celebrity before. What do you say, pretty lady? Should we go upstairs first?"

He took a step toward her and her skin crawled when he winked at her. "C'mon, don't be shy. It might even feel good for -"

His head cocked to the side as the growling started behind him. He turned and squinted at the stairs that were shrouded in darkness. Relief and fresh terror flooded her body as they both stared at the glowing green eyes.

"The dog ain't supposed to be here tonight," the man mumbled to himself before aiming the gun at the stairs.

The bottom stair squeaked, and the tiger stepped into the moonlight. He bared his fangs and crouched as the man screamed. Her heart dropping all the way to her goddamn feet, Ryan chucked the jug of juice at the man. The jug slammed into his upper arm, jerking it to the right just as he fired the gun. The bullet buried itself in the wall next to Grayson, and the man screamed again as the gun fell from his hand.

Grayson roared with rage. The sound vibrated off the walls and Ryan clapped her hands over her ears as the man turned and ran for the front door. Grayson roared again and went after him, the muscles in his large body tensing as he prepared to leap.

"Grayson, no!" Ryan shouted as the man yanked open the door and jumped down the porch steps. He landed in a crumpled heap on the bottom before scrambling to his feet and tearing off into the darkness.

Grayson growled angrily and Ryan sprinted around the island and rested her hand on his massive shoulder. "No, let him go."

He shifted to his human form and glared at her before snarling, "Ryan! What the hell? Why did you stop me?"

She stared up at him, her body shaking and shuddering, and bile rising up the back of her throat. She swallowed the bitter liquid. "I-I couldn't have more blood on your hands because of me. I just couldn't, Grayson. I'm sorry. I didn't want to watch you k-kill another man."

His shoulders slumped and he pulled her into his arms, holding her tight and pressing kisses into her hair. "I'm sorry, honey. I shouldn't have yelled at you."

She wrapped her arms around his waist and buried her face into his naked chest. "I'm sorry too, but I couldn't watch, I mean…"

"I know," he said. "Are you okay?" He lifted her chin and studied her face in the dim light. "Did he hurt you?"

"No." She stared at the gun at their feet and then at the bullet lodged into the wall. "You came down the stairs before he could do anything."

"Thank God I was here," he muttered before hugging her again. The breeze from the open door made her shiver and he pulled away and walked to the door. He examined the door handle before shutting the door and drawing the deadbolt at the top.

When he returned to her, Ryan put her arms around his waist again. She needed his warmth and his solid strength. He kissed her forehead. "Thank you."

"For what?"

He smiled at her. "Throwing that jug of juice."

Her laugh was shaky and weak. "Yeah, I'm a real crack shot."

"It stopped me from getting a bullet to the chest."

She shuddered again. "Please don't talk about you being shot. Okay?" Her voice cracked.

He wiped away the tears sliding down her cheeks before kissing her on the mouth. "I need to call Coop. My phone is upstairs, I'll be right back."

She took his hand. "I'm coming with you."

"All right."

They walked up the stairs and into the bedroom together. He pulled gym shorts on and grabbed his phone from the nightstand. "I'll call -"

It rang in his hand, bringing a startled growl from his throat and a squeak of surprise from Ryan's. He hit the answer button. "Coop? I was just about to call you."

She watched his face as he listened to Cooper. His eyebrows knitted together, and he muttered a curse before rubbing at the back of his neck. "Fuck me. I'm here with her now. What's that? Yeah, I was, um, here with her tonight. She was attacked not five fucking minutes ago. We stopped him, but the guy got away. No, she's okay. Yeah, we'll be right over."

He tossed his phone on the bed. "Get dressed, honey. We have to go."

"What's wrong?" she whispered.

He took a deep breath. "Someone broke into your grand-mother's house as well. Your grandmother surprised him in the hall and -"

"Is she dead?" Her lips had gone numb.

"No, honey. She's okay. Sam attacked the guy, bit him in the face I guess, and it scared him off. Sam's fine too," he said before she could ask. "As is your mother."

"Ryleigh," she whispered. Her terror was so deep, it wasn't just her lips that were numb now. Her entire body was a block of wood.

Grayson's voice was grim. "She's missing."

CHAPTER 17

"Wait, so this guy knew that the dog wouldn't be at Ryan's place?" Boone, his hair sticking up and his voice still froggy from sleep, stared at Sam.

The dog wagged his tail before resting his head on Ryan's lap. She petted his blocky head, only half-listening as Grayson said, "Yes. Ryan said he muttered something about the dog not supposed to be at the house."

"How did he get in?" Chase asked. The cheetah shifter was pacing the large family room.

"Picked the front door lock from what I can tell," Gray said.

"Fuck. We caught the fucking guy. He had fucking dead birds in his fucking freezer." Boone scrubbed his hand through his hair, making it stick up even more, before glancing at Beverly. "Sorry for the language, ma'am."

Beverly waved him off. "I've heard worse. What about my granddaughter?"

"We'll find her," Boone said reassuringly.

Beverly sat down with a thump next to Ryan. "Sweet bird, look at me."

She raised her gaze to her grandmother and Beverly pressed one wrinkled hand against her cheek. "Your sister is all right."

"You don't know that," she whispered.

"I do," Beverly said. "I would feel it in my very bones if either of you were gone."

Ryan winced when she heard Vanessa's angry shouting in the hallway. The door flew open and she staggered in, a bottle of whiskey in her hand.

"They fucked up!" she screeched.

Lori hurried in after her. The jaguar shifter looked tired and unwell, and she touched Vanessa's back. "Vanessa, love, sit down."

"I will not fucking sit down! Not while my child is missing!" Vanessa screamed. She turned around, staggering wildly. Boone caught her by the arm before she could fall, and she glared at him before yanking her arm out of his grip. "You fucked up! You said you caught him! I demand my money back this instant!"

"Your money?" A terrible rage was filling Ryan up, stealing her breath, and making her limbs vibrate. She jumped up off the couch, ignoring Sam's whine of distress, and stalked toward her mother. "Your child is missing, she might be dead, and you're worried about money that isn't even yours? What the fuck is wrong with you?"

"Don't you speak to me that way," Vanessa said. The smell of whiskey washed over Ryan and her rage grew as Vanessa sneered at her. "I am your mother."

"My mother? No, you're not. You're a goddamn monster and you're going to rot in hell for what you've done."

"How dare you, you little cunt!" Vanessa screamed and raised her hand. Ryan flinched but a large hand caught Vanessa's arm before she could slap Ryan's face.

Vanessa squealed as Grayson, his grip tightening around her arm, bared his fangs at her. "Do not touch my mate."

Vanessa's eyes widened, a look of horror crossing her face as she stared first at Grayson and then at Ryan. Her body slumped and she shook her head before whispering, "You-you're sleeping with this thing? How could you, Ryan?"

Grayson dropped her arm and Vanessa immediately drank a large swallow of whiskey straight from the bottle. She coughed and, her voice rough from the burn of whiskey, said, "You're sick. You're the monster, not me."

Lori hurried toward her and put her arm around her shoulders as Vanessa started to sag to the ground. "Love, come with me. Sit down, okay?"

"My baby's gone," Vanessa slurred as Lori led her to the small loveseat across from the couch. "My baby's gone, and I don't know what to do."

"It'll be okay." Lori pressed a kiss against Vanessa's head and sat down beside her. "I'm here for you, I'll always be here for you."

Cooper strode into the room. "Okay, here's what we've got. I just spoke to the security guys at the front entrance and watched their security footage. The guy who broke in scaled the fence on the west side of the property to get out. The security guys saw him running out of the house, but by the time they got to the fence, he was gone."

"How the fuck did he get onto the property?" Boone said. "They've got the cameras running all fucking day and night."

"None of the footage shows him climbing the fence to get onto the property," Cooper said. "The security guys have reviewed all of the camera footage that records the fencing multiple times and there's nothing. As well, the front doors weren't broken into and the security alarm inside the house was turned off with the code."

"What does that mean?" Beverly said.

Ryan's voice was dull. "It means it was an inside job."

Grayson's arm slid around her waist. She was grateful for his support and she leaned against him as Cooper nodded. "Based on Ryan's attacker knowing that her dog wouldn't be at her house, and that this guy got into the house so easily, it had to be someone in your inner circle. Who knows the security code for the house other than family members?"

"The security team at the front, Peter -"

"It wasn't Peter," Ryan said immediately. Grayson squeezed her waist and kissed her temple.

"Of course, it wasn't Peter," Beverly said irritably. "No one would ever think it was Peter."

"Who else, ma'am?" Cooper asked.

"Bert, Saul, and," Beverly paused, her gaze sliding to Lori and Vanessa, "Lori."

"It wasn't Bert or Lori!" Vanessa sat up, her face bright red with indignation. "How dare you accuse either of them, Mother!"

"It's okay, Vanessa," Lori said. "She's just answering a question. It's to be expected that everyone with access to the security code would be a suspect." She glanced up at Cooper. "For the record, it wasn't me."

"Of course, it wasn't you," Vanessa said. "You're better to me than my own goddamn daughters. You would never try and hurt me." Her gaze fixed on Ryan. "Nor would you betray me by sleeping with a filthy animal."

"Shut the fuck up, Vanessa," Ryan snapped. "Say another word about Grayson and I'll -"

"You'll what?" Vanessa said. "Never talk to me again? I'd welcome that, you little bitch."

Ryan shook her head. "You're so pathetic."

"I'm pathetic? You're the one who -"

"Right now, we need to concentrate on who took Ryleigh," Cooper said.

"You're sure it wasn't someone associated with the man who made the heads?" Beverly asked.

"It's possible," Cooper said. "But how would he know the security code to the house?"

Beverly bit her lip. Sam whined again and jumped up on the couch beside her, resting his shaggy head in her lap. Beverly stroked his head, giving him a loving look. "You're a good boy, my Sam. Tomorrow you're getting a special treat of liver, good boy."

His tail thumped against the couch and he licked her hand. Cooper said, "Saul was here earlier, right?"

Beverly nodded. "He was. He spent the afternoon with Ryleigh and left around six."

"What time did Ryleigh go to bed?"

Beverly cocked her head. "I-I don't know. I don't even remember seeing her after Saul left."

"It was him," Vanessa said. "It had to be. He took my baby! I knew that asshole couldn't be trusted."

"Saul wouldn't hurt Ryleigh," Ryan said. "He loves her."

"He's gay!" Vanessa snapped.

Ryan rolled her eyes. "I didn't say he was *in* love with her. I said he loved her."

"It had to be him," Vanessa insisted.

Beverly stroked Sam's head anxiously. "The security guys said that the only cars in and out today were Lori's and Saul's. Maybe – maybe Saul put Ryleigh in the trunk of his car and-and kidnapped her."

"Grandmother," Ryan said, "you know Saul wouldn't do that."

"He might," Beverly said. "How well do we really know him?"

Ryan bit back her reply as Cooper said, "Do you have Saul's number?"

"Yes." Ryan pulled out her phone. "I'll call him, and you'll see how stupid you're all being."

She called Saul, tapping her foot impatiently as it rang in her ear. When he didn't answer, she chewed on her bottom lip. "It's almost five in the morning, he's probably sleeping."

"Maybe," Grayson said.

"Do you know where Saul lives?" Cooper asked.

"Yes," Ryan said.

Cooper glanced at Grayson and Boone before turning to Chase. "Chase, stay here with Beverly and Vanessa. Boone and Grayson, let's go. Ryan, text Grayson the address."

"I'm coming with you," Ryan said.

"No, you're not," Grayson said.

"Bullshit, I'm not." She pulled away from Grayson and glared at him. "You need me."

He cupped her face, rubbing his thumb over her cheek. "I need you to be safe."

"It isn't Saul, okay? I'll be perfectly safe."

Grayson glanced at Cooper who shrugged. "We might need her. Saul will open the door to her and if he does have Ryleigh, we don't want to spook him."

"He doesn't have her," Ryan said. "C'mon, let's go."

THE EARLY HOUR MEANT TRAFFIC WAS LIGHT. IT TOOK THEM less than half an hour to get to Saul's house. It was shuttered and dark, and Ryan hopped out of the car before the three shifters could say anything.

She was at the front door, hand raised to knock, when

Grayson's hand slipped around her wrist and stopped her. "Just wait, Ryan."

"For what?" she asked impatiently. "The longer it takes to prove to you guys that he doesn't have her, the more danger Ryleigh could be in. We need to rule him out so we can move on to Bert."

"You think it's the manager?" Boone raised his eyebrows at her.

"I do now," she said. "It isn't Lori and it isn't Saul, so that leaves Bert." She pulled her wrist free and pounded on the door. "Saul! Saul, it's Ryan!"

The three shifters gathered behind her as she pounded on the door again. "Saul! Open up! Please!"

The door yanked open and Saul, looking weirdly awake for this time of the morning, stared at her. He was wearing a purple silk robe and he finished tying it around his waist. "Ryan? What are you doing here? Do you know what time it is?"

"Can we come in?" She pushed past him and Saul blinked as the three shifters followed her.

"Uh, this isn't really a good time," he said.

His house was a small bungalow with an open floor plan. Ryan paced back and forth in the living room as Saul slid past the shifters.

"What is going on?" Saul's gaze drifted to his bedroom door and then back to her. "Why are you here, Ryan?"

"Ryleigh is missing," she blurted out. "Someone attacked me at my home tonight and there was another guy in the mansion."

"Jesus, what? Are you okay?"

She shook off his concern. "I'm fine. But Ryleigh is missing. Do you know where she is?"

Saul rubbed his palms against his silk robe. "Uh, no. Why would I?"

"When you left the house this afternoon, was she still there?" Ryan asked.

Saul nodded, his gaze drifting to the bedroom door again. "Uh, yeah, of course she was."

Cooper stepped toward him and Saul took a nervous step backward. "You sure about that?" Cooper's voice was a low growl.

"Why-why wouldn't I be?"

Ryan could see sweat gleaming on Saul's forehead as Boone joined Cooper. "Maybe because you took her."

"What?" Nervous laughter spilled out of Saul's mouth. "Take her? I – don't be ridiculous? You think I, like, stuffed her in my trunk or something?"

There was a muffled thud from his bedroom and Ryan's eyes widened. "Saul? What did you do?"

"Ryan, I didn't do anything," Saul said frantically as she stared at the bedroom door. "I swear. Just don't go in my room, okay? Don't... oh fuck."

Ryan had already yanked open the bedroom door. She stepped inside and stared in shock at the bed. "What the..."

"Hey, baby-girl. What's going on?" Oren said.

Grayson crowded in behind her as did Boone, both of them staring silently at the bed.

"Well," Boone said, "this is a twist. I did not expect to see a naked man chained to his bed."

Oren grinned at him before rattling the handcuffs that chained him to Saul's headboard. The sheets were drawn up around his narrow hips and his grin widened. "Hey, at least the sheets are covering little Oren. Well, don't get me wrong, he's not *that* little."

"Oren, wh-what are you doing here?" Ryan said.

"I think that's obvious," Boone said with a laugh.

Saul squirmed past them. He grabbed a small silver key from the top of the nightstand and hurriedly unlocked the handcuffs from around Oren's wrists. The leopard shifter straightened in the bed and rubbed at his wrists.

"Sorry," Saul said to him.

"No biggie," Oren said.

"No biggie?" Ryan said. "My best friend and my hair stylist are… are…"

"Slapping uglies?" Boone suggested.

Saul turned bright red. "It's not, I mean… we're just…"

"He means we get together when we both have an itch we need scratched," Oren said. "It's not serious, right?"

Saul nodded and Ryan slumped against Grayson. "Why did you keep it a secret from me?"

Oren shrugged. "It's not a secret. We didn't go around announcing it, but we weren't hiding it either."

"Can we talk about our sex life later," Saul said. "Who broke into your house?"

"We don't know," Ryan said

Oren frowned. "Someone broke into your house?"

"Mine and Grandmother's house," Ryan said. "They tried to kill me and would have killed Grandmother if Sam hadn't bitten him and scared him away. But the guy who got in knew the security code and now Ryleigh is missing and…"

She glanced at Grayson and the other shifters as Saul groaned. "Fuck, you think it's me."

"We don't," Ryan said.

"We kinda do," Boone said.

"I don't have her," Saul said. "But I did help her get out of the house this afternoon and I know where she is."

"GRAYSON, CAN WE TALK FOR A MINUTE?"

He glanced at Cooper before looking back at Ryan. He didn't want to leave his mate. She was sitting at the table next to Ryleigh and her face was pale and drawn. Ryleigh's boyfriend, a cheetah shifter named Gavin, was sitting on the other side of Ryleigh, holding her hand and listening quietly as Ryleigh spoke to Ryan.

"Gray?"

"Yeah, okay." He followed Cooper out of the kitchen and down a narrow hallway to the living room where Boone was waiting. The cheetah's home was small, but Gray hated being out of sight of his mate.

"I just spoke with Beverly. She's hiring us again as security."

"That's a little obvious, isn't it?" Boone said. "She called you instead of the police after she was nearly killed by a guy."

Cooper just shrugged. "It's official now. That means you and Chase are back on duty at the mansion." He glanced at Grayson. "Maybe we should assign Wes to Ryan."

"No," Gray said immediately. "I'll stop sleeping with Ryan now that she's a client again, but I'm the one watching her, the one keeping her safe."

Cooper rolled his eyes. "For fuck's sake, I'm not going to make my best friend stop banging the woman he loves, even if she's a client."

Gray shoved his hands into his pockets. "Is it that obvious that I'm in love with her?"

"Gracie, my man, it was that obvious three hours after you met her," Boone said.

Grayson scowled at him as Cooper clapped him on the back. "I just thought maybe Wes might be better to do security detail. His judgement won't be clouded by -"

"My judgment isn't clouded," Gray said.

"All right," Coop said.

"It's gotta be Lori or Bert, right?" Boone lowered his voice. "It's someone close to the family and all of them are insistent it isn't the butler dude so…"

"I doubt it's Lori," Grayson said. "She's incredibly loyal to Vanessa and besides, I didn't catch a hint of fear or anxiety when we questioned her at the house earlier."

"True," Cooper said. "I didn't smell any lying from her when she said it wasn't her."

Boone shrugged. "Sociopaths are excellent at hiding their true emotions."

"It's Bert," Cooper said. "Daisy found out some information on him that, well, it's pretty damning."

"What are you talking about?" Gray asked.

He listened in shock as Cooper relayed the information from Daisy.

"Holy fuck," Boone said, "they've got a brother?"

"Keep your voice down," Cooper said.

"You want me to keep this a secret from Ryan? She deserves to know she has a brother," Grayson said. "Both she and Ryleigh deserve to know."

Cooper rubbed at the scruff on his jaw. "Is it our place to tell them?"

"She's my mate," Grayson said.

"Okay, okay," Boone held his hands up, "let's remember that we don't know any of this for certain. The woman called Daisy back and recanted her story, right? She was drunk as hell when she spoke to Daisy, so maybe the entire story is completely bullshit. Did this Corbin guy even confirm that Vanessa had his kid?"

"No. But his email was pretty nasty, and he did say he wished Vanessa was dead. He seemed to have a lot of rage toward her. And he would assume that hurting her kids would be the fastest way to make her suffer," Cooper said.

Boone snorted. "If he wants to make her suffer, he should take her liquor away from her."

"Bert's giving this guy money every month for a reason," Gray said. "It would make sense that he's paying him to go after Vanessa and Ryan and Ryleigh."

"Normally, payments for hits are a one and done thing, not a monthly payment," Boone said.

"He's right. This smells more like blackmail to me," Cooper said.

"Right?" Boone said. "But let's say that they were payments to have them killed. Why would he do that? Bert is still managing Ryleigh. If she was dead, he'd lose out on a boatload of cash."

Grayson shrugged. "Cooper said Bert already has a ton of money."

"We need to figure out if what this woman told Daisy is true and why this Corbin guy hates Vanessa," Cooper said. "Wes and I will talk to Bert this morning, put a little pressure on him and -"

"Bert's gone," Boone said.

"What? Where?"

"Before the Alien-Con, I heard him talking to Vanessa about his vacation. He was leaving for Taiwan on Saturday for three weeks, and as far as I know, he did."

"Fuck," Cooper said.

"Yeah. Hey, if you want to pay for my trip, I'll gladly fly out there and chat to him," Boone said.

"Nice try." Cooper scratched at the scruff on his jaw again. "For now, we're back on security detail. I'll get Daisy to email this Corbin guy again, see if we can get him to change his mind about talking to us. I'll talk to Lusa about digging into Vanessa's past. Maybe she can find something to substantiate the third kid story."

"If anyone can find the skeletons in a person's closet, it's Lusa," Boone said.

"Until we come up with more concrete evidence, keep this to yourselves," Cooper said. "All right, Gray?"

Gray hesitated and Cooper clapped him on the back. "There's no point in telling your mate she has a brother if she doesn't. Right?"

He nodded. "Yeah, you're right. I'll keep it to myself for now."

"RY-RY? SAY SOMETHING, PLEASE."

"Three months." Ryan stared at Ryleigh in disbelief. "You've been dating him for three months?"

"Yes," Ryleigh said before squeezing the blond man's hand – Gavin, his name was Gavin and he was a goddamn cheetah shifter - who smiled at her.

"How did you meet?" Ryan said.

"At a club," the blond man said.

"He didn't know who I was." Ryleigh stared affectionately at Gavin.

"I don't watch television," Gavin said sheepishly.

"I love that you don't watch television," Ryleigh said.

"I love that you love that I don't watch television," Gavin said.

Ryleigh giggled before leaning forward and kissing him. "I love you, snuggle bunny."

"I love you too, tater tot."

Ryleigh giggled again and pushed on his wide chest. "Stop it. You know I hate that silly nickname."

"You love it." He brought her hand to his mouth and kissed the knuckles.

"What is happening here?" Ryan said.

Gavin cleared his throat. "Sorry. I'll give you some privacy to talk. I'll be out back feeding the chickens, okay, Leigh?"

"Okay. Thank you, sweetie. I love you so much."

"I love you too." He kissed her again before walking to the patio door connected to the kitchen. When the door slid shut, Ryleigh turned back to face Ryan, a happy smile on her face.

"Feed the chickens?" Ryan said.

"He has chickens," Ryleigh said. "He raises them for the eggs. He also has his own garden and he grows most of his own food. He doesn't have a car and he bikes or takes public transport. He's, like, really into trying to reduce his carbon footprint on the planet, you know?"

Ryan blinked at her. "Are you serious right now?"

"Look, I know Gavin and I are really different, but I love him, Ry-Ry. I've never felt this way about a guy before. Ever."

"Why didn't you tell me?" Ryan said. She could hear the hurt in her voice and Ryleigh snatched her hand up and squeezed it tight.

"I'm sorry. I should have – it's just… my whole life is on display, you know? It sometimes feels like the entire world knows everything about me, and to have this one small thing that no one knew about… it made it more special and precious. I know my job requires me to live my life in a way that I'm basically an open book to everyone, but I didn't want that for this. I wanted what I have with Gavin to be mine and no one else's. Does that make sense?"

"It does," Ryan said.

"I'm sorry, I should have told you."

"No, you shouldn't have. It's okay, honey. I get it."

Ryleigh took a deep breath. "Thank you. The only reason that I told Saul is because he's my best friend and I needed him to help me to see Gavin."

"Did he really smuggle you out of the house yesterday?" Ryan asked.

She nodded. "Yep. Not for the first time either."

Ryan shook her head. "Why? You could just have a driver take you to Gavin's."

"You know that fans watch for me to leave the house. Half the time now, even if I'm wearing a disguise, the car is always followed by fans or the paparazzi. They'd follow me straight to Gavin's. But they're used to Saul coming in and out and they don't follow him anymore. Hiding in his back seat under blankets was the only way to see Gavin."

"Gavin could have come to the house."

Ryleigh snorted. "Are you kidding me? And risk Mommy finding out he's a shifter?"

"She wouldn't have known. She has no clue about Lori for God's sake."

"In Mommy's defense, I didn't know about Lori either until that crazy asshole abductor said she was one," Ryleigh said.

"Speaking of which, you need to make sure you don't tell Vanessa."

"Are you kidding me? I'm carrying that little secret to my grave," Ryleigh said. "If Lori wasn't around, Mommy would make me do everything for her and," she sighed dramatically, "my life would officially be over."

She squeezed Ryan's hand again. "I didn't mean to worry anyone, but I hadn't seen Gavin since they hired security. I couldn't sneak out of the house without Chase knowing. I missed my snuggle bunny so much, Ry-Ry. I had to see him, and I thought the danger was over."

Ryan rubbed at her forehead. "We all did."

"Are you sure you're okay?" Ryleigh said. "You must have been so scared when that guy broke into your place."

"I'm fine."

"It's a good thing Grayson was with you," Ryleigh said with a soft smile. "You're pretty serious already, huh?"

"Why do you say that?"

Ryleigh shrugged. "I can tell by the way he looks at you. It's the same way Gavin looks at me."

She suddenly smiled dreamily at the ceiling. "Maybe we should do a double-wedding. Both of us getting married on the same day… it would be awesome."

"Ryleigh, focus. Someone else is trying to kill us, and the guys think it's Bert or Lori."

Ryleigh shook her head. "They're wrong. Neither of them would do something like that. Also, what are the odds that we have two crazy-ass stalkers after us? What did we do to have karma kicking our asses like this?"

"Are we so sure about Bert?" Ryan said. "It did piss him off when I quit the show and refused to even entertain the idea of doing the spin off."

"That was years ago," Ryleigh said with a wave of her hand. "He's over it. I'd suspect Lori before I suspected Bert."

"Why?" Ryan asked.

"I don't *suspect* Lori, I'm just saying…" Ryleigh trailed off. "Shit, does this mean we're back on security detail?"

"Yes."

"I won't get to see Gavin again," Ryleigh moaned. "This is the worst day ever."

Ryan bit back her retort. Her sister was being overdramatic, sure, but if Ryan had to go without seeing Grayson, she wasn't sure that her response wouldn't be just as over-the-top and dramatic.

"I'm sure we can figure out something. Sneak Gavin into Grandmother's after Vanessa goes to bed."

Ryleigh's face darkened. "Mommy will never accept him. Gavin says he won't hide who he is and as soon as Mommy finds out he's a shifter…"

"You need to live your own life and not worry about what Vanessa thinks or says," Ryan said.

"If she keeps drinking the way she is, she'll be dead soon anyway." Ryleigh's voice was flat and devoid of emotion.

"We can't help her, sweetie. We've tried and until she wants help…"

"I know." Ryleigh blinked back the tears. "I'm just so afraid of what she'll say about Gavin. I wish I could be strong like you."

"You are strong. If you love this guy, then be with him and screw what Vanessa thinks or says. I know you want her to be a mother, but she isn't, sweetie. She never will be. Just be with the man you love."

Ryleigh smiled at her. "Like you are?"

Ryan swallowed hard. "I do love Grayson. I know it hasn't been very long and I know I sound ridiculous, but I love him. I love him so much and -"

Ryleigh's hand squeezed down on hers and she stared pointedly at Ryan before her gaze swung to the left. Ryan turned around. Grayson was standing in the doorway and her heart sank. Fuck, he'd heard her. The look on his face left no doubt.

How long would it be before he made up an excuse to get away from the crazy woman who was already spouting off declarations of love? She figured two hours, three at the max.

"We should go," Grayson said. "I want to add another

deadbolt to your door and your grandmother has called Cooper twice now to bring Ryleigh home."

Ryleigh groaned. "Oh God, this sucks."

"Are you ready?" Grayson asked.

"Yeah." Ryan kissed Ryleigh on the forehead. "I love you and I'm happy for you. Don't let Vanessa ruin your happiness, okay?"

"Okay," Ryleigh said. "Bye Ry-Ry."

"Bye, sweetie."

CHAPTER 18

"Should we have stopped and picked up Sam?" Grayson followed her into the kitchen.

Ryan dropped her purse on the counter. "No, Grandmother asked to keep him another day and after what happened, I couldn't tell her no."

She opened the fridge and grabbed two bottles of water, handing one to Grayson. She sipped at hers as Grayson drank half of his in two large swallows.

Oh God, could this be any more awkward? She could feel the tension radiating from Grayson. She stared at her nails, trying desperately to think of something – anything – she could say that wouldn't sound completely crazy.

"So, listen, about earlier -"

"Ryan, we should talk about -"

They both stopped and she took another sip of water as Grayson cleared his throat.

"Sorry, what did you want to say?" he asked.

She picked at the label on her water bottle. "What you overheard earlier? It wasn't – I mean – I'm not…"

Shit, she couldn't lie and say she didn't love him. Even if it meant she never saw him again.

"Are you about to say you don't love me?" Grayson walked toward her, placing both hands on the counter behind her and penning her in. "That what you told Ryleigh wasn't true?"

"Grayson, I…" She squirmed under his intense scrutiny, dropping her gaze and taking sudden interest in Grayson's forearms.

"Look at me, Ryan."

She stared up at him, her breath catching in her throat at just how brilliantly green Grayson's eyes were. His nostrils flared slightly as he took a deep breath. "Are you in love with me, Ryan Shepherd?"

"Yes," she whispered. "I am."

The tenseness eased out of his shoulders and he grinned at her. "Good. I love you too."

He kissed her once and then stepped back, taking another long drink of water as she stared at him in shock.

"Did you – did you just say you love me too?"

"I did," he said. "Do you want scrambled eggs for breakfast? I've got a delicious recipe where you add some avocado and -"

"Grayson!" She threw herself at him, wrapping her arms around his shoulders as he lifted her and set her on top of the island. "You asshole!"

"Is that any way to talk about the man you love?" He cupped her breast through her t-shirt and pressed another kiss against her mouth.

She hooked her legs around his waist, drawing him in tight against her until she could feel the bulge of his hardening cock against her core. "I was freaking out the whole way home."

"I know. I could smell it."

"You could have told me that you loved me in the car," she said.

"In my defense, I wasn't sure if you were freaking out because you regretted what you said or because I'd overheard you."

"Why would I regret it?" She smoothed her hand over the small hairs on the back of Grayson's neck.

"Sometimes people say or think weird shit after traumatic experiences. They aren't always thinking clearly."

"I'm perfectly rational," she said. "I do love you and, yeah maybe it's weirding me out a little considering how short of a time we've known each other but…"

"I get it," he said. "It is weird, but when you know, you know. Right?"

"Right," she said.

He kissed her again, angling his mouth over hers as she parted her lips. They kissed slowly, teasing each other with small nips and licks until her pussy was wet and aching and Grayson's dick was a hard length against her.

"Let's go upstairs," she breathed against his mouth.

"You should probably eat," he said. "You'll need energy for what we're about to do."

She laughed and nipped the side of his thick throat. "Don't you worry about me. I've got plenty of energy. Get that sweet ass of your upstairs, right now."

He threaded his hand into her hair and tugged her head back before placing a soft kiss against her mouth. "Whatever you say, Ms. Shepherd."

"I like the sound of that," she said before sliding her hand down to squeeze his ass. "If you're a very good boy and give me multiple orgasms, maybe I'll cook you breakfast for a change."

He lifted her and carried her toward the stairs. "You have yourself a deal, my mate."

"I sent Wes home because it was a waste of his time and your money, Coop." Grayson switched his phone to his left hand before opening the back door with his right. Sam sat at his feet, his entire body trembling as he waited for Gray's command.

Grayson scanned the back yard and inhaled deeply. There were no signs or smells of trouble – not that he expected someone to be lurking in the yard in the middle of the afternoon – and he said, "Go on, Sam."

Sam bolted out the door, racing down the steps of the deck toward the tree in the back corner of the yard. A volley of barks escaped his throat as Frodo the squirrel sat on a high branch and chittered down at the madly barking dog.

"Sam, enough!"

Sam stared over his shoulder at him and Grayson shook his head. "No barking."

The dog chuffed unhappily but ceased the barking. He stared up at Frodo, growling quietly as the squirrel continued to chitter at him.

"Gray, you still there?"

Grayson closed the door. "I'm still here. Sorry. I sent Wes home because I'm staying with Ryan. I get that it's my day off and I'm not expecting you to pay me, but why pay Wes when you don't have to?"

"You sure?" Cooper said.

"Positive. I talked to Ryan Monday night and said my preference was to just stay here with her, even when I wasn't working and that was her preference too."

"So, you've basically moved in?" Coop said.

"Basically."

"So, she's perfectly fine with your mild OCD about lights being turned off and your noisy as hell sleep purring?"

"Perfectly fine," Gray said with a laugh.

"Eh, it's only Wednesday, give her time," Cooper replied.

"You're just jealous that we don't live together anymore," Gray said. He and Cooper had lived together for about a year after Gray first left the military.

"Is it that obvious?"

Grayson leaned against the counter. "I did talk to Wes about coming by tomorrow afternoon. I've got a doctor's appointment. Ryan will be working at the house, but I'm not comfortable leaving her alone."

"Yeah, Wes mentioned that in his text," Cooper said. 'Where's Ryan now?"

"Upstairs in her studio. Why?"

"Daisy got Corbin to agree to meet with her tomorrow afternoon."

"You're kidding?"

"No." Cooper's voice was nearly a growl.

"Why do you sound so pissed?"

"He told her to email him a goddamn selfie. Once he saw what she looked like, he agreed to meet with her."

"Shit."

"Yeah," Cooper grunted. "There's no fucking way I'm letting her meet him without me."

"He might not talk if you're there," Grayson said.

Cooper growled so loudly that Gray had to pull the phone from his ear. "You want me to fucking send her by herself? Is that what you're saying? Because it's not fucking happening, Gray. I don't care if -"

"That's not what I'm saying," Grayson said. "Calm down, Coop."

He waited for Cooper's ragged breathing to even out. When the lion shifter was no longer growling, Grayson said, "I'm just saying that we have to be prepared he might not talk with you there, and if he doesn't -"

"He said something in the email about compensation," Cooper said. "If he thinks we'll give him money for spilling his guts, then he'll talk."

"Jesus, isn't he already getting money from Bert every month?" Grayson asked.

"Some guys can never have enough," Cooper said. "Look, he either talks to us or he doesn't, but there's no fucking way I'm sending my mate to talk to him alone. You can fucking forget it."

"Your mate?"

There was a pregnant pause and when Cooper spoke, embarrassment coloured his voice. "Slip of the tongue."

Unease was sliding down Gray's spine. He knew that his best friend had a thing for the human, but if he was calling her his mate, they were in big fucking trouble. "Cooper, you need to remember that Daisy is terrified of shifters. I know you want to believe that you can change her mind, but she's worked for us for a while now and she's still afraid. If your lion thinks she's his mate, you need to -"

"It was a slip of the tongue, I said," Cooper snarled. "Get off my back, Gray."

"All right."

There was a heavy sigh and Cooper said, "Look, I didn't mean to snap at you, okay? I'm sorry."

"I know," Gray said, "but, Coop -"

"I gotta go. Wes will be there tomorrow afternoon to

cover your appointment. I'll call you once we've talked to this Corbin guy and let you know what he said."

"All right. Bye, Coop." He stared at his phone screen, that same trickle of unease still running up and down his spine. Cooper was holding it together so far, but if his lion thought of Daisy as his mate and Cooper continued to deny it what it wanted, he really would go mad. They needed to live in harmony with their animal side and he'd seen firsthand what happened to shifters who didn't.

He shuddered all over. The job with the cougar shifter had been over two years ago, and the image of the shifter putting the gun in his mouth and blowing the top of his skull off was still etched into his brain.

Ryan's arms slid around him and she pressed her warm body against his back before kissing between his shoulder blades. "You okay?"

"Yeah. Just worried about Cooper. You remember Daisy?"

"Your admin person, Cooper has a crush on her," Ryan said.

Grayson turned to face her, wrapping his arms around her waist and pulling her close. "Cooper just referred to her as his mate."

"Didn't you tell me she was terrified of shifters?"

"Yeah."

"Uh oh," Ryan said.

"He said it was a slip of the tongue."

"Do you believe him?"

"No," Grayson said. "Which is bad fucking news. If Coop's lion think Daisy is his mate and Cooper keeps denying it, it's gonna get bad."

"How bad?" Ryan asked.

"Cooper will go insane," Grayson said. His tiger whimpered at the thought, and Gray buried his face in his mate's neck. "I'm worried about him."

"I'm sorry," Ryan said. "Is there anything I can do?"

"Make friends with Daisy, convince her that she doesn't need to be afraid of shifters, and then get her to go on a date with Cooper?" He raised his eyebrows at her, and Ryan smiled a little.

"Well, I'll give it a go but I'm not sure that's gonna work."

"Yeah, I know." He nuzzled her neck. "How's editing going?"

"Good. Thought I'd take a half hour break and see what you were doing."

"I spoke with Cooper about Wes covering for me while I'm at my doctor's appointment tomorrow."

"He doesn't have to," Ryan said. "I texted with Ryleigh. Chase is gonna sneak her out of the house so she can come by for a visit."

"Sneak her out of the house?"

She shrugged. "He has to. You know the paparazzi are always in front of the house. If they think Ryleigh is in the car, they'll follow her, and I do not want them camped out in front of my house."

"I honestly don't get why anyone wants to be a celebrity," Gray said.

"Me neither, but most of the time Ryleigh loves the attention. Anyway, Chase will be here so you can text Wes and tell him he doesn't need to come by. Okay?"

"It won't hurt to have both of them here," Gray said.

"But not necessary," Ryan replied. "It'll be fine. We won't leave the house and it's not like I'll open the door to strangers. Hell, I won't even open the door to a Girl Guide."

He laughed. "Promise?"

"Promise," she said before kissing his throat. "Now, what do you say we do something productive during my half hour break."

"What did you have in mind?" He reached down and cupped her ass.

"Nothing specific, but I was picturing a 'your face in my pussy' scenario."

He purred to his mate, loving the way it made her smile.

"Come upstairs with me." She traced her hands over his broad chest as his purring grew louder. She squirmed free of his grip and held out her hand.

He took it and smiled down at her. "Yes, my mate."

"RYLEIGH? SWEETIE, WHAT'S WRONG?" RYAN SET HER camera down and jumped up from the couch, hurrying across her living room. It was Thursday afternoon and Chase had brought Ryleigh to visit like they'd arranged. She hadn't expected Ryleigh to be a complete mess.

Her baby sister didn't reply. Her face was pale, her nose was red and swollen, and she had tear tracks streaking down her face. Ryan took her hands. "Sweetie, what happened?"

Ryleigh burst into tears and threw her arms around Ryan's waist, burying her face in her shoulder. "It was so awful. She was so awful!"

"Who?" Ryan stared in bewilderment at Chase who was standing next to Grayson and looking extremely pissed off.

"Your bitch of a mother," he said.

"Chase, enough." Grayson frowned at him.

Ryan led Ryleigh to the couch. "It's fine. He's not wrong. What did you two fight about?"

When Ryleigh just continued to sob, Chase said, "She told Vanessa about her boyfriend."

"You did?" Ryan pushed Ryleigh back and cupped her face. "Sweetie, I'm so proud of you."

Ryleigh hitched in a breath before rubbing at her swollen eyelids. "She said such terrible things, Ry-Ry. She-she was so mad when I told her. She said I was forbidden to see him and when I told her I was an adult and she couldn't tell me how to live my life, she-she just lost it."

"She did," Chase said. "The woman went completely nutso, Gray. She must have broken every fucking glass in the kitchen."

"Where was Grandmother?" Ryan asked.

"She wasn't home. She said she was going stir-crazy, so she asked Peter to drive her to his house to see Mary. I should never have told Mommy about Gavin." Ryleigh burst into sobs again.

"Honey, you had to. If you want a relationship with Gavin, you had to tell her."

"She said I was a mistake," Ryleigh whispered.

"What?" Ryan's body tensed. "She said what?"

"That I was a mistake and a disappointment and if she'd known that I would betray her like this, she never would have had me." Ryleigh's slender body shook with sobs. "What kind of mother says that to her child?"

"Honey, you know that when she's drinking -"

"She was sober," Ryleigh said.

Ryan glanced at Chase who nodded. She kissed Ryleigh's forehead. "I'm so sorry, honey."

"She said she didn't want anything to do with me and that as far as she was concerned, she didn't have any children. I said fine and that I was moving out and I would never speak to her again if that was what she really wanted."

"What happened then?"

Ryleigh swiped at her wet cheeks. "She screamed at me to get out, that she couldn't stand to see my face a minute longer, so I left."

"Have you talked to Gavin?" Ryan asked.

"Yes. He was at work, but he said he could leave and meet me at his place. But I told him I would come here first and then have Chase bring me to his house once he was done work. I didn't want him to see me this upset. I look a mess and all my make-up is cried off."

She hung her head, the exhaustion on her face and the slump of her shoulders made Ryan's heart hurt. Ryleigh raked in a shuddering breath. "Plus, he-he tries to understand about Mommy, but he can't. Not really, you know? Not the way that you understand."

"I know, sweetie," Ryan said. She put her arms around Ryleigh and snuggled her close, kissing the top of her head. "It'll be okay, I promise."

She smiled at Grayson when he stopped next to her and bent to kiss her forehead. "I have to go to my appointment. Unless you need me to stay? I can cancel."

"No, we're good," Ryan said.

"I won't be long." He kissed her again and left the room.

Chase cracked his knuckles before clearing his throat. "I could make some tea. Tea always makes my mom feel better."

Ryan smiled at him. "Tea would be nice. Thank you, Chase."

CHAPTER 19

"For fuck's sake, move your ass!" Cooper slammed his hand down on his horn. The guy in front of him flipped him the bird before lazily making the left turn.

"Asshole!" Cooper shouted out his open window before speeding down the road. He glanced at the clock and cursed again. An accident between a Corolla and a Benz had trapped him for nearly half an hour on the freeway, and he was worried that Daisy was going to try and meet with Corbin Werner on her own.

His phone rang and he hit the answer button on his steering wheel. "Daisy, I'm almost there. Are you still waiting for me in the parking lot?"

"Yes." Her soft voice made his lion purr despite how irritated Cooper was. "But he's here. I saw him walk into the coffee shop almost fifteen minutes ago."

"Okay, I'm five minutes out so just sit tight and -"

"Shit, he's leaving. Cooper, he's left the coffee shop and is headed toward his car. I need to stop him."

"No!" His voice was frantic and loud. "Daisy, do not go

near him without me there. Do you hear me? We'll just reschedule."

"It's fine, Cooper," Daisy's voice was muffled, and he heard a car door slamming. "You'll be here in five minutes, right? Nothing will happen in five minutes. We can't let him leave."

"Daisy, no!" Cooper stomped on the brakes, cursing the red light in front of him. "Stay in your car. Do you hear me? Stay in your -"

"I've gotta go. I'll see you soon."

She hung up and he roared so loudly that the woman in the car beside him stared wide-eyed at him. She hurriedly rolled up her window and then looked straight ahead, her back ramrod straight. The moment the light turned green, she tore off in a squeal of tires.

Cooper raced toward the coffee shop, weaving in and out of traffic and running several red lights. His lion paced restlessly within him, roaring every few minutes and demanding to be taken to his mate.

"I'm trying," he muttered as he ran a third red light. "She's fine, okay? Our mate is fine. Calm down."

He turned into the parking lot like a race car driver taking the final curve. He jumped out of his truck and slammed the door shut. He ran toward the coffee shop, stopping abruptly when he smelled Daisy's scent. He turned, his body swelling with rage when he saw the man looming over his mate.

They were still in the parking lot and even from this distance, he could see the fear in his mate's face. Corbin was a jaguar shifter, Cooper could smell it easily, and from the way Daisy's body was shaking, she had figured out he was a shifter as well. He ran across the lot, stopping a few feet away from Daisy and Corbin. He sniffed the air, scenting both his mate's fear and the heavy musky smell of Corbin's lust only slightly overshadowed by his disgusting body odour.

"Don't play shy, sweetheart. You're even prettier in person than you were in that photo you sent me."

Cooper's rage turned white-hot when the jaguar shifter touched a lock of Daisy's hair. "Why don't you and me go for a drive? I'll tell you everything you want to know and then you can show me your pretty human pus-"

Tamping down his lion's desire to kill the jaguar in front of him, Coop said, "Sorry I'm late."

The jaguar shifter spun around, staring suspiciously at Cooper. "Who the fuck are you?"

Daisy, the scent of her fear tangy and thick, darted past Corbin and toward Cooper.

"I'm the editor for the website," Cooper said.

He'd discussed with Daisy beforehand about his cover story, so you could have knocked him over with a fucking feather when Daisy slid her arm around his waist and said. "And my boyfriend."

He stared down at her, his entire body going stiff when Daisy stood on her tiptoes and pressed her mouth against his. The kiss was brief but even that small contact made his lion happier than it'd been in months. It purred loudly, nearly drowning out the jaguar shifter's voice.

"He's your boyfriend?"

"Yes," Daisy said.

Her slender body was shaking against his and although her fear had lessened, he could still smell it drifting from her skin.

"Why's he look so surprised to hear that?" Corbin said.

Cooper put his arm around Daisy's waist, bringing her up against him. He shouldn't. He *really* fucking shouldn't, but if he didn't kiss her again, their cover story would be blown. Right?

He bared his teeth at the jaguar shifter, letting a low growl drift from his throat. Daisy tensed at the sound and he quickly bent his head toward her.

"It's all right, baby," he said in a low voice before kissing her.

He should have kept it brief, but his lion pushed forward and demanded more. Cooper brushed his mouth across hers repeatedly. He tasted vanilla on her lips, and the sweet taste made his lion purr.

When he detected the faint scent of Daisy's lust, he forgot about the jaguar shifter and forgot he was only playing a role. His lion mewed like a kitten, its excitement growing when Daisy tentatively rested her hand against his broad chest.

He cupped her hip with one big hand, rubbing one thumb along her hipbone as he slicked the tip of his tongue across her bottom lip. To his surprise, and his lion's delight, her lips parted. Her quiet moan made his dick harden until it pressed painfully against his jeans. He slid his tongue into her mouth, touched the tip of her tongue with his and then growled unhappily when Daisy pulled back.

She stared up at him, her cheeks flushed and her eyes bright with both embarrassment and lust. Guilt swept through him and he bit back his immediate apology. Jesus, he'd just tried to shove his tongue down his receptionist's throat. What the fuck was he thinking?

"You two done?" Corbin said in disgust.

"Sorry I'm late, baby." Cooper kept his arm around Daisy's waist. "Traffic was bad."

"Oh, uh, that's okay. Mr. Werner and I were just heading back into the coffee shop. Isn't that right, Mr. Werner?" Although Daisy no longer sounded afraid, she hadn't tried to move away from his side and his lion practically strutted around like he'd solved world hunger.

Our mate feels safe with us, his lion purred proudly. *Kill the jaguar. Show her how strong we are.*

Are you insane? We can't just kill someone. Cooper pushed his lion down and the beast retreated with an irritated snap of its jaws.

"Nah, we're done here," Corbin said. He turned and unlocked his car and Daisy stared up at Cooper with a 'do something now' expression.

"Mr. Werner, are you really willing to throw away a sizeable compensation just because you had to wait a few minutes?" Cooper said.

Corbin turned immediately, shoving the car keys back into his pocket. "How sizeable?"

"Talk to us about Vanessa Shepherd and then we can discuss payment," Cooper said.

Corbin scratched at the grey stubble on his cheek. Cooper guessed he was close to sixty in age, complete with the balding spot at the back of his head and the soft blubbery middle that were the cornerstones of growing older for so many men.

He waited patiently. Daisy was vibrating with nerves against him and he rubbed her hip, happy when it seemed to settle his mate a little.

"Fine," Corbin grunted. "But you got half an hour and then I'm fucking gone. Got it?"

"Half an hour is all we'll need," Cooper said. He took Daisy's hand, smiling inwardly when she held it tight.

The three of them walked toward the coffee shop. If they weren't about to talk to a disgusting shifter who had frightened his mate, Cooper would almost be enjoying the moment. The brush of Daisy's hip against him as they walked, the feel of her soft hand clasped in his... it was everything he dreamed of.

Jesus, dude, are you kidding me? Walking hand-in-hand with your girl is suddenly your new fantasy? Maybe later, we'll go looking for your missing balls. What do you say?

He ignored his inner voice. Holding hands shouldn't make him this deliriously happy, but his lion was acting weird lately. Kissing and touching Daisy made his lion feel normal for the first time in weeks.

They followed the jaguar shifter into the coffee shop and found a table. Cooper pulled out a chair for Daisy, but she said, "I'll get us some coffee."

Cooper pulled some cash from his wallet and handed it to her. With a nervous peek at Corbin, Daisy walked to the long counter. Corbin studied her ass with frank interest and Cooper growled at him.

"Keep your eyes to yourself," he snarled in a low voice.

Corbin held up his hands. "Relax, buddy. Besides, how was I to know she was yours? She sure as hell don't smell like you." He cocked his head and sniffed the air. "Awfully weird that your girlfriend wasn't carrying your scent on her. Or have you not fucked her yet?"

"Shut the fuck up." Cooper slammed his hand down on the table. The din of noise in the coffee shop fell silent and Coop's face reddened when humans and shifters alike turned to look at him. A tiger shifter sitting at the next table sniffed the air before moving her chair further away from him. No doubt she could easily scent Cooper's rage.

He took a deep breath, smiling reassuringly at Daisy who had turned and was staring wide-eyed at him. Fuck, he could smell her anxiety from here. He made himself smile at her again and she crossed her arms over her torso and hugged her elbows before nodding slightly.

He turned back to Corbin, the corner of his lip curling up. "You will show respect to my mate or I will rip all four of your limbs off right here in the coffee shop. Do you get me?"

Corbin's mouth dropped open and for the first time, Cooper could smell fear below the shifter's ripe body odour.

He leaned even closer, letting his fangs drop. "Do. You. Get. Me?"

"Yeah," Corbin muttered. "The price for me talking just went up though."

"Fine, whatever," Cooper said. He had no intention of paying this asshole a dime and the fact that he was stupid enough to talk to them before getting the money just made Coop's life easier.

He leaned back, smiling at Daisy when she set the coffee on the table and sat down beside him. He put his arm around the back of her chair and leaned down to press another kiss against her mouth. "Thank you, baby."

"Uh, you're welcome." One hand darted up to touch her bottom lip. Her cheeks were red, and he could smell her lust again. Sure, it was faint and hardly detectable, but it still made both him and his lion giddy.

"Mr. Werner, if you don't mind, I'm going to record this interview." Daisy fumbled in her purse and brought out a small tape recorder. She set it on the table in front of her. Cooper admired her dedication to the lie as Corbin shrugged.

"Long as I get paid, I don't give a fuck."

"Great." Daisy pressed play on the recorder. "So, tell us how you met Vanessa Shepherd."

"Back in the eighties, we were both working on a tv show. I did construction on the sets and she," he flicked his hand dismissively, "was the PA for the director. We didn't run in the same circles, but we was both friends with Bert. He was the one who introduced us proper like. Vanessa's mother was an actress, but she refused to help her get any acting jobs. Vanessa used to bitch and whine about it, said it wasn't fair. Bert told me once when he was high as fuck that Beverly wouldn't help Vanessa with any acting jobs because Vanessa was a self-entitled bitch and didn't deserve to have everything handed to her on a golden fucking platter. The old woman did help her some though – she was the one who got Vanessa the job as the PA."

"Right." Daisy opened a notebook. Cooper could see her neat handwriting filling the page. He settled back in his seat and sipped at his coffee, perfectly content to let Daisy take charge.

"You were also friends with Liza Franken, is that correct?" Daisy asked.

"Yeah. Her and Bert were fuck buddies for a few months. The four of us would go out drinking together."

"When did you and Vanessa start dating?" Daisy said.

Corbin snorted harsh laughter. "She was a stuck-up bitch the first little while, but eventually she started panting after me just like all the other ladies did."

He leaned forward, his gaze dropping to Daisy's tits. "I got skills when it comes to fucking."

Cooper's hand was sliding up Daisy's back to rest possessively on the back of her neck before he even realized it. She twitched like a startled deer, and he stroked the side of her slender throat with his thumb as he bared his teeth at the jaguar. "Watch your mouth, and if I catch you looking at what's mine one more time, I'll -"

"Yeah, yeah," Corbin said hastily before leaning back. "I ain't hittin' on your girl for Christ sake, just stating a fact."

Daisy turned her head to look at him and Cooper stroked the curve of her jaw with his thumb before nodding. "Go on, Daisy."

He should have moved his hand. Instead he scraped his chair closer until Daisy was practically in his lap and kept his hand exactly where it was. He kneaded the tense muscles he could feel at the base of her neck, enjoying the scent of calm it elicited from her.

Our touch soothes our mate. Take her home so we can show her how we'll please her. His lion was almost pleading with him.

"So," Daisy consulted her notebook again, "the four of you were working on the show together. Vanessa became pregnant and you told her to get rid of the baby. When she didn't, you broke up with her."

The jaguar shifter snarled in anger. "That ain't how it happened. Is that what that fucking bitch Liza told you? Because she don't know shit."

"Why don't you tell us what happened then," Cooper said.

Corbin's hand tightened around his coffee cup. "Look, Vanessa got pregnant and it was bad fucking timing all right? I loved her but we was too fucking young to have a goddamn kid. I might have suggested she get rid of it, yeah, but she freaked the fuck out as soon as I said it. She went on and on about how she never should have slept with an animal like me, that it was obvious that shifters couldn't love the way that humans loved."

He flicked the lid off his coffee cup and stared at the steam that rose into the air. "Like she was any better than me just because she was a fucking human. Sure, maybe she didn't want to get an abortion, but she sure as fuck didn't want the kid either. She was planning on giving it up for adoption even before she told me about it. Stupid bitch. Said it wasn't in her career plans. Like she even had a fucking career at that point, but she was a sly bitch, always thinking about what worked best for her and not giving a shit about anyone else."

Tired of listening to the man spew misogyny and profanities, Cooper said, "Why does Bert Hollings pay you money every month."

Corbin jerked, spilling hot coffee on the table and his hand. He hissed under his breath, shaking his hand out before glaring at Cooper. "How the fuck do you know about that?"

"Why does he pay you?" Cooper said.

An unpleasant grin crossed Corbin's face and he sat back in his chair. "He pays me on behalf of that bitch to keep my secrets to myself."

"You're blackmailing Vanessa over the baby she gave up for adoption?" Daisy said.

"Pretty and smart," Corbin said. He held up his hand when Cooper growled at him. "Yeah, yeah, I know. A guy can pay a girl a compliment, can't he?"

Cooper growled again and Daisy reached across and took his hand, linking their fingers together. His lion settled down immediately. He swallowed down his purr as Daisy said. "It's fine, uh, honey."

Corbin wiped the coffee from his hand onto his pants. "Once Vanessa got famous, I knew she'd do anything to keep our kid a secret. She didn't want anyone to know that back in the day, she had a kid who she abandoned. Hell, she already had a bad reputation, fucking any guy she thought would boost her career, wearing those skimpy outfits on that stupid sci-fi show. Did you know she wanted to be a serious actress? She really thought she'd win a fucking Oscar some day."

He snorted laughter. "As if she'd ever be anything more than a second-rate celebrity. The world finding out she gave up a kid because she didn't give a fuck about it, would tarnish her reputation even more. She tried to pretend she was a good mother with those two little shits she kept, but even then, people knew. They knew she wasn't never fit to be a goddamn mother. Some women just aren't, you know? It ain't in their," he waved his hand vaguely in the air, "in their DNA or sumtin'."

He took a sip of coffee, grimacing a little. "God, this shit gives me heartburn so bad but I still fucking love it. Where was I? Right, the money part." He grinned, showing crooked yellow teeth. "So, all it took was me sending a couple pictures of the kid to Vanessa for her to agree to meet with me."

"Pictures?" Daisy's hand squeezed his. "How did you get pictures?"

Corbin's grin widened. "Oh, so there's some shit you *don't* know. The kid didn't get adopted."

"What do you mean?" Cooper said.

"When my mother found out that I'd knocked Vanessa up, she put a stop to that adoption real quick, let me tell you. Said it was my duty to take the baby even if Vanessa didn't want it. I was some pissed and so was Vanessa, to tell you the truth, but Ma threatened to sue for legal custody if Vanessa didn't hand the baby over."

"She gave the baby to your mother?" Daisy said.

"Yeah, she didn't have much of a choice. She told her bitch friend Liza that she put it up for adoption, but she just handed it over to Ma instead. She was glad to see it go… it was a shifter like me and by that point, she'd decided shifters were the fucking scum of the earth. All because I wouldn't do what she wanted." He rolled his eyes. "I did my own thing, let Ma raise the kid, but then Ma went and died when the kid was four and suddenly, I'm a fucking father."

He stared into his coffee cup before taking another sip. "I

would have given the kid up for adoption only," he stared slyly at them over the rim of his cup, "I realized something."

"That you could get money from Vanessa," Cooper said.

"That's right. Not right away o'course. Vanessa was still a fuckin' nobody at that point, but I figured there might be a chance she would get that stupid Oscar. So, I held onto the kid and waited."

Disgust was radiating from Daisy and Cooper knew damn well it was radiating from him. He didn't need to see the defensive look crossing Corbin's face to know that the jaguar could smell both their disgust.

He made himself give Corbin an approximation of a smile. "So, you've been blackmailing Vanessa ever since she became famous."

"Yep. She bitched and moaned after the show was cancelled, said she didn't have the money no more but when I threatened to expose the kid, Vanessa came around like I knew she would. She probably borrowed the money from her mother. That bitch has money to fucking burn."

"Does Beverly know about him?" Daisy asked.

"Him?" Corbin said. "Him who?"

"Your kid," Cooper said.

Corbin shook his head. "Vanessa didn't have no boy. The kid's a girl."

"Liza said she had a boy," Daisy said.

"She didn't. I should fucking know, shouldn't I? I'm her goddamn father. I fucking raised her."

"Okay, so you had a girl. Does she know Vanessa is her mother?" Coop asked.

"Yeah. When she was sixteen, she was goin' through some old boxes of Ma's that I never got around to tossing. She found Ma's diary and read it in there. She was some pissed at me. Said she had a right to know that Vanessa was her mother. I told her that Vanessa wouldn't give a shit about her. Told her that she had her own two perfect human daughters and that she thought shifters were below her. She didn't care. She told me I'd been a shit father her entire life. Can you believe the little bitch? I raised her, took care of her, gave her whatever the fuck she wanted, and she still talked to me that way."

A beard was growing on the jaguar shifter's face and his eyes had turned bright yellow. "I though I'd beaten the attitude out of her, but you know how it is with some women. Don't matter what you say or what you do, they're always smart mouthin' ya."

Daisy was afraid again and Cooper put his arm around her, pulling her close until she was tucked in tight against his body. He kept his arm around her waist, his hand cupping her hip, his forearm pressing against her flat stomach. She rested her hands on his arm, staring at Corbin as the jaguar shifter leaned back in his chair.

"She was obsessed with Vanessa after that. Started making noises about getting in touch with Vanessa. I told her to stop being such a goddamn idiot, that Vanessa would never have anything to do with her. She asked me why Vanessa kept her two other little brats but not her. I told her it was because she was a shifter and that Vanessa hated her."

He laughed, the sound as nasty as finding a cockroach in your bed. "She didn't want to believe it at first, and I could see how jealous she was of the other two brats. For a while, her obsession switched from Vanessa to them. I'd catch her googling the spoiled rich bitches and shit like that. Hell, she even bought the DVD's of that alien show Vanessa and her kid were on and watched them repeatedly. When the oldest got herself emancipated from Vanessa, she kept going on and on about how awful she was to abandon Vanessa like that, and that the younger one was a spoiled brat. She wasn't wrong, but I got fucking tired of hearing about it, to tell you the truth."

He curled his lip. "I finally gave her a couple of smacks and told her to shut the fuck up. Told her she shoulda been happy that Vanessa didn't have nothin' to do with her. Told her she was a spoiled little bitch too and if Vanessa ever met her, she'd really fucking hate her, and it wouldn't have nothin' to do with her bein' a shifter. She got real upset about it, but it was time she heard the truth, you know? Some of it musta got through to her because she finally stopped her fucking whining about how she wanted to meet Vanessa, how she thought that living with that drunk bitch would be so much better than living with me."

He stared moodily into his coffee, "Still, it didn't stop her from moving out as soon as she finished high school. She don't even talk to me no more."

"You haven't heard from her since she graduated?" Cooper said.

"Nah," Corbin replied. "She won't take my calls and I don't even know where she lives or where she's working. I tried to contact her through Facebook once, but she blocked me."

He scowled at Cooper. "Truth be told, I shouldn't be that surprised. Lori always was a bitch, just like Vanessa."

Daisy stiffened against him and he felt more than heard her gasp. His arm tightening around her waist, Cooper said, "Did you say Lori?"

"Yeah." Corbin took a drink of coffee before rubbing his chest. "Ma named her after her grandmother."

Cooper stared at Daisy. It couldn't be Vanessa's assistant Lori. Sure, she was a jaguar shifter, but her last name was Wilson not Werner."

As if she'd read his mind, Daisy said, "Mr. Werner, does Lori have your last name?"

"She used to. She legally changed it to Vanessa's mother's maiden name when she turned to eighteen. Now it's Wilson or Wilcox or some shit like that. Real bitch move, if you ask me. Just another way for her to be an asshole to the man who gave her everything."

Daisy's body was vibrating lightly against his as she stared up at him. Cooper sat frozen in his seat, his mind whirling.

Shit, they needed to get the fuck out of here. Immediately.

CHAPTER 20

"Go on, Sam. And don't bark at Frodo." Ryan shut the back door, watching through the glass as Sam ran down the stairs of the deck and immediately ran across the yard to the tree. He stared up at it with his head cocked.

Ryan returned to the couch and sat down next to Ryleigh. "You should try and eat something, sweetie."

Ryleigh brushed the dog hair from her pants. She tucked her legs under her, grabbed the blanket off the back of the couch and draped it over her. "I'm not hungry, Ry-Ry. I just want to sit here and feel sorry for myself until I can see Gavin."

Ryan patted her leg. "It will get better. Vanessa isn't good for you. Moving out and getting some separation from her will help you to see that. I promise."

"I know," Ryleigh said. "It's just – she's our mom, you know? I don't get why she can't just be normal."

"Alcohol makes a person do -"

"It isn't just the alcohol," Ryleigh said. "We both keep blaming her behaviour on the drinking, but it's more than that. She never wanted to be a mother, and, like, she doesn't even care about us."

Ryan patted her leg again, wishing she could say or do the right thing. Ryleigh was right and while Ryan had come to that conclusion years ago and made her peace with it, she could still remember how devastating it was at the time. Ryleigh was about to go through some really shitty moments as she grappled with the realization that Vanessa didn't love her, and there wasn't anything Ryan could do to help her sister through it.

"Should I make more tea?" Chase asked.

Ryan smiled at the cheetah shifter. He really was very sweet. "Thank you, but I think we're good for now. Are you hungry? There's plenty of food in -"

All three of them froze when the doorbell rang. Chase jumped out of his chair, his body tense and alert. "Are you expecting someone?"

"No," Ryan said.

"Stay here." Chase withdrew a gun from under his jacket and held it at his side as he moved down the front hallway.

"Ry-Ry?" Ryleigh whispered.

"It'll be okay. I'll be right back," Ryan said. She stood and followed Chase's big body down the hallway.

He peeked through the peephole. "It's Lori."

Ryan slumped against the wall and took a deep breath. "Thank God. Let her in, Chase."

He tucked his gun into the holster at his waist and opened the door. "Hey, Lori."

"Hey. I need to speak to Ryan and Ryleigh."

Ryan couldn't see Lori past Chase's broad back, but her voice sounded weird. "Lori? What's wrong?"

Chase moved aside and Ryan rushed forward, taking

Lori's cold hands and eyeing her carefully. "Hey? Are you okay?"

The jaguar shifter was pale, and it looked like she'd been crying. "I need to speak with you and your sister."

"Of course." Ryan led her to the living room, Chase trailing behind them. "Do you want a drink?"

"Hi, Lori." Ryleigh was texting on her phone and she barely glanced up.

"No, I don't want a drink," Lori said.

"Lori, what's wrong?" Ryan asked. "You look upset."

Lori laughed bitterly. "Yeah, I'm upset."

"What happened?" Ryan asked. "Did Vanessa say or do something?"

"Whatever she said to you," Ryleigh continued to stare at her phone screen, "ignore it. She's pissed at me and taking it out on you. She'll get over it."

"She'll get over it?" Lori's hands clenched into fists. "Do you have any idea how upset your mother is right now? Because of you?"

The venom in Lori's voice sent unease down Ryan's spine. She glanced at Chase. The cheetah shifter was sniffing the air and his big body was tense. In a low voice, he said, "Lori, calm down."

"Do not tell me to calm down!" Lori snarled at him. "This is none of your business, so stay out of it."

"What is your problem today?" Ryleigh finally looked up from her phone.

"My problem?" Lori glared at her. "Your mother is an emotional mess because of you, and you want to know what my problem is? How about the fact that you treat her like shit?" Her gaze turned to Ryan. "Both of you."

"Are you kidding me?" Ryleigh pushed the blanket off

and stood up. "You were there, Lori. You heard what she said to me today."

"Because she loves you," Lori said. "She wants the best for you, and you keep pushing her away like she's nothing, like she's garbage stuck to your shoe. She has sacrificed everything for you and you're such a spoiled little brat that you don't even fucking care!"

"Sacrificed?" Ryleigh's face turned red. "Mommy hasn't sacrificed anything for us. She's used me and Ryan for our entire lives. Moving us around like pawns to advance her career. I have done everything she ever wanted and the very moment I stopped, she turned on me!"

"You're such a selfish little bitch," Lori said.

"Lori, stop," Ryan said.

Lori's pupils flicked to slits for a few seconds and then back to round. "Don't, Ryan. You're even worse than Ryleigh. You abandoned your mother because you didn't like being told what to do."

"No," Ryan tried to keep her voice even, "I left my mother because she was mentally and emotionally abusive."

"Neither of you have a fucking clue how lucky you are. You treat Vanessa like dirt, time and time again, and she still wants you. She still accepts you for who you are and -"

"Accepts us?" Ryleigh shouted. "Have you lost your fucking mind, Lori? Nothing we do is ever good enough for her!

"She is at home right now sobbing because of you! Because you betrayed her and broke her trust by dating that-that shifter!" Lori's face was bright red.

Ryleigh stomped toward Lori and Ryan cringed inwardly. Her sister hid it behind a sweet façade, but she had a terrible temper. Ryleigh was about thirty seconds from going scorched earth on Lori.

"Ryleigh," Ryan grabbed her arm when she stormed past her, "just wait a minute, okay?"

Ryleigh tore her arm free of Ryan's grip and continued toward Lori. She stopped a few inches from her and glared at the red-faced shifter. "In case you've fucking forgotten, you're a shifter too. If my mother knew that you were a shifter, what do you think she'd do? Do you think because you've put up with her shit for the last few years, that she'd say, 'oh well, no biggie, run and fetch me my booze would you, Lori'? Because guess fucking what? That is not going to happen."

"You don't know what you're talking about," Lori said. "Vanessa loves me."

"No, she loves what you can do for her. What she can get out of you. You clean up her puke, you change her sheets when she pisses the bed because she's too fucking drunk to even stand, and you wait on her like a little bitch errand boy." Ryleigh spat.

Ryan stared at alarm in Lori. Her face had gone from bright red to completely devoid of colour and her eyes were glowing bright green. A fine layer of black hair covered both cheeks and across her forehead.

She hurried over and grabbed Ryleigh's arm again. "Enough, Ryleigh."

"Stay out of this, Ryan." Ryleigh yanked her arm free before scowling at Lori. "Believe me, the very second she finds out that you're a shifter, she will toss your ass to the proverbial curb. She doesn't give a shit about you, Lori. She doesn't give a shit about *anyone*. All she cares about is her next drink."

Lori growled angrily before slapping Ryleigh across the face. Ryleigh stumbled back, tripping over the coffee table and falling on her ass.

"What the hell, Lori!" Ryan shouted before scrambling to her sister. She helped her to her feet and brushed back Ryleigh's hair to study her cheek. "Jesus, she's going to fucking bruise. Sweetie, you okay?"

"Fine," Ryleigh bit out before rubbing at her cheek.

"You need to leave," Ryan said to Lori. "Right now."

"You don't deserve her," Lori said quietly. "I was so right - she's better off without either of you. She maybe doesn't see that right now, but she will. I'll make sure she does."

A shiver went down Ryan's spine and she glanced at Chase before saying, "Leave my house, Lori. Now."

Chase stepped toward her and took her arm. "Let's go, Lori."

Lori turned toward him, and Ryleigh snorted in disgust when the jaguar shifter threw herself into Chase's arms and burst into sobs. She slid one arm around his waist, the other arm tucked between her body and Chase's, and clung to him. Chase patted her back awkwardly.

"Are you kidding me?" Ryleigh muttered.

"C'mon now, it's not that bad," Chase said tentatively. "Things will get better."

Lori lifted her wet face to him, the tears caught in the hair that still lined her cheeks. "Things will get better? Is that supposed to make *me* feel better?"

Chase turned red. "Look, Ryan's asked you to leave and -"

There was a muffled bang and both Ryan and Ryleigh jumped. Ryleigh glanced toward the front door. "What was that? A car backfiring?"

"Chase?" Ryan said.

The young cheetah shifter's face had a look of blank shock on it. Lori reached up and patted his cheek before stepping away.

Ryan stared numbly at the spreading patch of red on Chase's stomach. Chase touched his stomach before holding out his bloody fingers to Ryan. "Ryan?"

"Chase!" She darted forward, catching the shifter as he fell. His weight dropped her to her knees, and she heaved him onto his back, staring horrified at the blood that immediately pooled on the floor beneath him.

"Ry-Ry?" Ryleigh whispered.

Ryan glanced up, her stomach doing cartwheels when Lori raised Chase's gun and pointed it at her baby sister's head.

"WE NEED TO GO." COOPER STOOD AND HELD OUT HIS HAND to Daisy. She stood and took it as Corbin stared at them in surprise.

"What the fuck?" Corbin shoved back his chair.

"We're leaving." Cooper led Daisy out of the coffee shop and across the parking lot, for once not thinking about how soft her hand was or how good she smelled. He needed to call Boone immediately and have him –

"Hey! Where the fuck are you going?" Corbin had chased after them.

Cooper unlocked his truck and opened the passenger door as the jaguar shifter grew closer. Daisy made a small 'eep' of surprise when he put his hands around her slender waist and lifted her into the truck.

"I have my car here," she said.

"I'll bring you back later to get it," Cooper said. He didn't trust that Corbin wouldn't follow Daisy back to the office or to her home. Hell, he didn't even want the jaguar shifter to know what kind of car she drove.

"Hey! Asshole!" Corbin grabbed his arm and jerked him around to face him.

"Cooper?" Daisy's voice was full of terror.

"It's fine, baby. Stay in the truck," he replied. He stared at Corbin's hand on his arm before raising his gaze to the jaguar shifter's face. The growl that was starting in Corbin's throat died, and he released Cooper before taking a step back.

"Where's my money," Corbin said.

"There isn't any," Cooper said.

"What the fuck do you mean there isn't any?"

"I lied," Cooper said. "Now, scurry away like the little rat you are."

"We had a deal!" Corbin growled. "You can't fucking do this."

"I can and I am," Cooper said.

Corbin's gaze skittered past Cooper's shoulder to where Daisy sat. His eyes glowing, he said, "Maybe I'll take a different compensation for myself."

Rage, thick and sharp like hot needles poking into Cooper's skin, washed over him. A growl burst from his throat and he grabbed Corbin by the throat, turning him and slamming him up against the side of the truck.

"Do you threaten my mate?" He squeezed Corbin's throat as his fangs dropped. There was nothing inside of him but the rage and his lion roaring to be free.

Corbin's face turned red, his eyes bulging as Cooper's hand squeezed again. His voice thick and inhuman, Cooper said, "I will kill you if you even *look* at my mate again."

Yes! Kill him! his lion growled. *Protect our mate.*

Cooper bared his fangs at the disgusting jaguar shifter. Its human body was rippling, and black fur was sprouting across his face. He would kill the jaguar. Once it was dead, he would take his mate home and fuck her. He would put his cub in her belly and –

"Please stop, Cooper."

Her voice pierced the thick wall of fury that surrounded him. He looked over at his mate. She was leaning out of the open door of the truck and she looked and sounded terrified.

His rage was drowned by a tsunami of shame.

He released the jaguar shifter and stepped in front of the open passenger door of the truck, blocking Corbin from going near Daisy. Corbin fell to the ground, choking and gagging before his body swelled and his clothes tore away with a thick ripping sound. He shifted to his jaguar form and Daisy made a harsh cry of fear that tore a ragged strip from Cooper's heart.

He called for his lion, his big body beginning to swell, but the jaguar shifter, making harsh barking coughs, turned and fled across the parking lot. He leaped over the chain wire fence that ran along the back of it and disappeared down a narrow alley.

Cooper took a deep breath and closed his eyes, holding back his lion as it attempted to take control.

Release me, his lion raged. *He is a threat to our mate. We must kill him.*

She's frightened. If we shift, it will scare her even more. He tried to keep his tone soothing and low as he spoke to his lion. *He won't harm our mate. He knows we'll kill him if he goes near her.*

His lion growled viciously, and Cooper winced, staggering forward and grabbing the side of the truck. It felt like his lion was clawing his mind and insides to shreds, and he groaned helplessly.

Please, don't do this, he begged. *She'll quit and we'll never see her again.*

His lion whined and Cooper could feel its uncertainty. After a moment, it retreated, and the clawing pain eased off. He took a deep breath, ignoring his urge to vomit. Sweat was sliding down his face and he wiped it off grimly with his shirt sleeve, thankful that the fur on his face had returned to his regular stubble. His fangs retracted and he wiped his face again before turning to face Daisy.

She was still sitting in his truck, fear etched into her perfect face.

"I'm sorry," he said.

"Oh, um, that's okay. Are you – I mean, are you all right?"

He nodded and she licked her lips. "Okay, that's good. Should I get in my own car now?"

"No," he said. "He might be watching still, and I don't want him seeing your car or following you. I'll bring you back here later."

"Oh, right, okay."

He reached to shut the door, his lion whining pitifully when Daisy flinched, and her arms jerked up as if she was going to cover her face. She lowered them quickly, but he'd seen the damage he'd done.

His mate was terrified of him. He'd tried everything he could since the moment he met her, to show her that she didn't need to be afraid of him, that he would never hurt her, and in a matter of seconds he had destroyed all of his efforts.

"I would never hurt you, Daisy," he said in a low voice.

"I know," she said, but he could smell her doubt and the fear was still thick on her skin.

He had lost any chance with her.

He had lost his mate.

Crushing despair swallowed both him and his lion.

Whining and whimpering, his lion retreated fully, backing away until Coop could barely feel its presence.

His lion side needed soothing, but Cooper's human side was just as desolate over the loss of his mate. He'd be fucking useless in providing comfort. Hell, he'd be lucky if his lion didn't go goddamn insane over the next couple of months.

Besides, right now, he needed to concentrate on doing his fucking job. He would have plenty of opportunity later to think about his impending madness.

He shut Daisy's door and crossed to his side. He slid behind the wheel and turned on the truck. Years of military life enabled him to completely shut out the realization that he had lost his mate and concentrate fully on the crisis on hand.

Without looking at Daisy, he said, "We need to call Boone and -"

His phone rang and he hit the answer button on the steering wheel. "Grayson, where are you?"

"Hey, just heading back to Ryan's. Are you still meeting with the Werner guy?"

"We just finished," Cooper said.

"What's wrong?" Grayson asked.

"Vanessa didn't put her first kid up for adoption. Werner's mother took the kid and then Werner got custody four years later. The kid wasn't a boy but a girl. It was Lori."

There was silence and then Grayson said, "You're fucking kidding me?"

"No. I was about to call Boone and get him to keep an eye on Lori until I got there."

"Why?" Grayson's voice was surprised. "I mean, it's fucking weird that Lori is working for Vanessa and keeping her identity from her, but can you blame her? Vanessa hates shifters and sure as fucking hell that extends to her own damn kid."

"Corbin said that when Lori was a teenager she was obsessed with Ryan and Ryleigh. Said she wanted to know why Vanessa would keep them and not her. She called them spoiled and she thought Ryan was awful for abandoning Vanessa when she was sixteen."

"Shit," Grayson said.

"Yeah. I know it's thin, but…"

"It's still a possibility," Grayson said.

"Do you want to meet me there?"

"I can. I'm only a few blocks from Ryan's place but I can turn around," Grayson said.

"Okay, hold on. I'll get Daisy to call Boone from her phone and we'll make sure Lori's there first."

He turned to Daisy who was already yanking her phone from her purse. She called Boone and put her phone on speaker, holding it out in the space between them. The phone rang twice and then Boone's voice filled the cab of the truck.

"Hey, Daisy. What's up? Did I fuck up my timesheet again?"

"Boone, it's Cooper. I'm with Daisy and I've got Grayson on speaker on my phone."

"What's up, boss?" Boone's voice went from lazy playfulness to all business.

"We just met with that Corbin Werner guy. He and Vanessa didn't have a boy, they had a girl and that girl is Lori."

"What the fuck?" Boone said. "Lori is Vanessa's daughter?"

"Yes. We think there's a small possibility that she's behind the new attacks on Ryan and Ryleigh. Can you keep her at the house? I'm just going to drop Daisy at the office and then I'll be over to talk to Lori."

"She's not here," Boone said.

"Fuck, where is she?"

"I dunno. She was here, but then Ryleigh told Vanessa she was dating a shifter and Vanessa freaked out. They got in a huge fight. Chase took Ryleigh to Ryan's house and then Vanessa just fucking lost it. She was sucking back the whiskey and ranting and raving to Lori about how awful her kids were. How she was betrayed and shit like that. She passed out, Lori put her to bed, and then she took off. Lori was upset but she told me she just had some errands to run and wouldn't be long."

"Fuck," Cooper said. "Okay, if she comes back, do not let her leave. I'm on my way."

"You got it, boss," Boone said.

"Gray, do you want to meet me there?"

"No."

The hair on the back of Cooper's neck stood up. "What's wrong?"

"I just got to Ryan's place. Chase's car is in the driveway and so is Lori's."

"Stay exactly where you are," Cooper said. "I'm on my way. Do not go in there until I get there."

"If she's after my mate, I'm not leaving Ryan alone with her," Gray growled. "My mate needs me."

"Just wait for me," Cooper said. "We don't know for certain that it's Lori, but if it is, Chase is in there. He'll keep Ryan and Ryleigh safe."

"She is my mate," Grayson snarled. "I'm going in, Coop."

"Grayson, don't. That's a direct order. You keep your fucking ass in that car until I get there. Understand? Grayson!"

There was only silence. Grayson had disconnected the call. Coop snarled in anger. "Fuck! I don't even know where Ryan goddamn lives."

He wanted to rip the steering wheel off in frustration.

"You want me to come over there?" Boone asked.

"No," Cooper said. "Unless you know where the fuck Ryan lives?"

"I don't."

"Goddammit," Cooper snapped.

"Boone? I'm hanging up on you, okay?" Daisy said. "I need my phone."

She ended the call without waiting for Boone to reply. Cooper watched as her thumbs flew over the small keyboard. "What are you doing?"

"I'm logging in remotely to the office network."

"You can do that?"

She nodded without looking up. "Lusa set it up on all of our phones a few months ago. Remember?"

He remembered it only vaguely. He'd let Lusa set it up on his phone but knew he would never utilize it. Embarrassingly enough he usually couldn't even log into the network from his home laptop without fucking something up.

"I just need to pull up Ryan's file… hold on… there. Got it!" She recited Ryan's address to him, and he punched it into his GPS before pulling out of the coffee shop parking lot.

CHAPTER 21

"Ryleigh! Get me another towel! Quick!" Ryan shouted. Ryleigh snatched more dishtowels from the cupboard and brought them over. Ryan layered them on top of the blood-soaked ones and pressed hard.

Chase made a groan of pain and his entire body trembled. Golden-coloured hair was appearing on his face and Ryan could see his fangs when his mouth dropped open and he dragged in a breath.

"If he shifts, I'll shoot him in the head." Lori stood over them. The gun was aimed at Chase and she smiled at Ryan, her finger tightening on the trigger.

"Chase, don't shift." Ryan leaned over Chase, her face only inches from his. "Do you hear me? Stay in your human form."

"Hurts," Chase muttered.

"I know. Just stay still and try not to move."

"Come sit down on the couch with me, Ryleigh," Lori said.

"Fuck you, you stupid bitch," Ryleigh said. She clung to Ryan with one hand, her other hand holding Chase's.

"Watch your mouth," Lori said. "And get your flat ass to that couch before I put a fucking bullet in it."

Ryleigh glanced at Ryan who nodded. "Do what she says, sweetie."

"Always best to do what the person with the gun says," Lori said.

Ryleigh squeezed Chase's hand before standing and walking slowly to the couch. She sat down, eyeing the gun as Lori plopped down beside her.

"Thinking about playing the heroine and grabbing the gun?" Lori said with a giggle that bordered on madness. "Not a smart idea, sweetheart. This isn't the movies and these bullets aren't rubber. I'm faster and stronger than you and I hate your fucking spoiled guts. Killing you will make me happy. Remember that."

Ryleigh paled and sunk back into the cushions as Lori looked over at Ryan. "How's he doing? Still breathing?"

"He needs to be in a hospital," Ryan said. "Please, let me call 9-1-1."

Lori snorted. "No fucking way. Besides, hazards of the job, right, Chase?'

"Fuck you," Chase said weakly before lifting his arm and giving her the bird. His arm wavered in the air before falling to the floor with a loud clunk.

His body went slack and Ryleigh made a hoarse cry. "Ryan? Is he…?"

"He's unconscious," Ryan said. "Lori, please, he's dying."

"I don't care," Lori said.

"Why are you doing this?" Ryleigh whispered.

"I told you, because you're spoiled little bitches who've hurt Vanessa for the last time."

"Did you hire the men to try and kill us?"

"I did." There was pride in Lori's voice. "Truthfully, I've

had a plan to kill both of you for a while now. But then you guys had to go and get yourselves an actual stalker. Talk about bad fucking timing. I'd actually been hoping that idiot who sent the dead birds would do my dirty work for me, but that didn't turn out in my favour did it? Thanks to your stupid mate."

She glared at Ryan. "Although, to be honest, I was grateful to him. Not for saving you and your brat sister, neither of you deserve to live, but he did save our mother, so I suppose he isn't a complete moron."

"Our mother?" Ryleigh said. "What -"

"Do you know how happy I was when Mom said you weren't getting security, Ryan? But then no, Grandmother had to step in and be all, 'no granddaughter of mine will be unsafe'. What a load of bullshit. Anyway, when that moron failed to kill you, I put my plan back in motion. It was actually perfect timing, you know? Everyone thought you were safe, security was finished. Having you killed only a few days after your stalker was stopped... hilarious, right? But I should have realized that Grayson would start fucking you the minute he was,' Lori made air quotes, "done with the job. Every shifter within a ten-mile radius could smell his lust for you, but I crossed my fingers and took a gamble that you two weren't at the 'spend the night' stage."

She shrugged and laughed softly. "My bad."

"You gave the guy the security code to Grandmother's house?" Ryleigh said.

"Obviously. And snuck him past the security guards in almost the exact same way Saul snuck you out. Pretty clever, huh? It was so easy. I just drove right into the garage, shut the door, and let him out of the trunk. He stayed hidden in the garage until it got dark and then let himself in with the key that I gave him. A perfectly simple plan."

Lori swung her gaze to Ryleigh. "But, I gotta tell you, the real surprise was you not being at the mansion. If you'd been in your bed like a quiet little mouse, he would never have had to start searching the house for you. He wouldn't have run into Grandmother in the hall, and he wouldn't have had half his face bitten off by the stupid dog."

She cocked her head. "Where is that stupid dog, anyway?"

Ryan's blood ran cold. "He's in the back yard. Don't you even think about hurting him."

"You're in no position to tell me what to do," Lori said. "But leave the hairy stupid thing out there and we won't have a problem. In fact, pretty sure he's the only one of you assholes who will survive the day. Maybe his presence will help soothe Grandmother. She's bound to be upset by your deaths. Mom will be too, but they'll both have me to help her through it."

"What is wrong with you?" Ryleigh said. "She's not your mother. I don't care how close you are or -"

"Shut the fuck up!" Lori shouted before raising the gun. Ryleigh cringed away and Lori smiled with satisfaction. "You don't know what the fuck you're talking about, you stupid cunt. Vanessa is my mother and I'm your half-sister."

"Ryan?" Ryleigh glanced over at her. "Is this true?"

"Of course, it's true," Lori said.

"She's lying," Ryan said. "She isn't our sister."

Lori scowled at her. "No, I'm not. Vanessa gave birth to me two years before she had you, Ryan. She and my father met on a movie set and fell in love. When she got pregnant, he turned on her, said he didn't want a baby and tried to force her to get an abortion. She refused. She refused because she loved me."

Ryan stared at Lori, her pulse slowing and then suddenly

racing to catch up on all the missing beats. Beneath her hands, she could feel the feeble rise and fall of Chase's body as he laboured to breathe. She eased up on his wound as she tried to process Lori's words.

"No, that isn't true," Ryleigh whispered.

"It is," Lori said. "Vanessa had no choice but to give me to my paternal grandmother. She was doing what she thought was best for me. She was still trying to make it as an actress, and she knew my scumbag of a father wouldn't help her. So, she did the only thing she could... she gave me up so I could have a better life and she could live her dream. She couldn't have known that my grandmother would die when I was four and I'd be sent to live with my father."

"You're a shifter," Ryan said. "She hates shifters. She would never sleep with one."

"Because of my father!" Lori shouted. "He's the reason she hates shifters and I don't blame her. My father was a pig of a man and the way he treated our mother was despicable. I couldn't wait to get away from him. The day I found my grandmother's diary and realized that Vanessa was my mother, was the happiest day of my life. I was someone. I was someone special who didn't have to be defined by the asshole I called a father."

Her face tightened and a low growl slipped out of her throat. "I wanted to tell Vanessa right away who I was, but my father, he-he wouldn't let me. I hated that he controlled me, but he was stronger and sometimes he would hurt me."

The bleak look of pain on Lori's face might have made Ryan feel some sympathy for the jaguar shifter, if she wasn't trying to stop a dying Chase from bleeding out all over her floor.

Lori stared at the gun in her hand. "He told me that Vanessa hated me because I was a shifter. He said she kept the two of you because you were humans and better than me. That even if Vanessa met me, she would hate me because I was a shifter. I didn't believe him."

"You should have," Ryleigh said.

"Shut up," Lori said.

"Did you cry like a little baby when you started working for Vanessa and realized that she did hate shifters? That your father was right all along?" Ryleigh said.

"Ryleigh, enough!" Ryan had no idea why her baby sister was antagonizing Lori.

Lori leaned forward and bared her fangs at Ryleigh before pressing the muzzle of the gun against her forehead. "Listen to your sister, Ryleigh, before I blow your useless brains out. You won't be so pretty with a bullet hole in your forehead and brains leaking out of your skull, will you?"

Ryleigh blanched and Ryan said hurriedly, "Why did you start working for Vanessa?"

She didn't care at all about Lori or her fucked up life, but if talking kept her from killing them, she'd listen all goddamn day.

Until what? Her inner voice whispered. *Until Grayson comes home? Lori will kill him the moment he walks in through the door. You know that. He can't save you. He'll only die trying. There is no way out of this for you or your sister. Time's up, Ryan. And if you don't want your mate to die as well, you better hope that she kills you and leaves before Grayson returns.*

Fresh terror knifed into her heart and she stared down the hallway at the front door.

Please God, don't let Grayson come home. Please.

"I moved out as soon as I graduated. I crept away in the night, like a frightened little mouse, but that was the last time I was scared," Lori said. "It was hard at first, I had to do some things that I'm not proud of just for a roof over my head and food in my belly. But I told myself that our mother went through tough times too and she survived. I would survive as well."

She smiled, a genuinely happy one that sent shivers of disquiet up and down Ryan's spine. "I started working in the film industry. Stupid pointless stuff like working in craft services. I took an admin assistant course and got a low-level job as an assistant to a B movie director. He was a pig, but it was a foot in the door. I volunteered at every *Alien Con.* I did my personal assistant shit work and made sure my name was known among the crew who worked the conference and anyone with any sort of connection to *Alien Con.*"

She brushed at the dog hair on her jeans. "I knew that Vanessa had a nasty habit of burning through personal assistants. I knew that sooner or later I'd meet someone in the industry who would have the right connection and knew the right people. And I was right. Vanessa fired her PA, and wouldn't you know it – someone mentioned my name to Bert. I didn't have as much experience as he usually liked Vanessa's PAs to have, but he was getting desperate. It was growing harder and harder to find someone to work for our mother."

"Yeah, because she's awful," Ryleigh said.

"Shut up," Lori growled. "I won't fucking tell you again."

Ryleigh shrank back against the couch when Lori waved the gun at her. Satisfied, Lori said, "I knew I needed to hide that I was a shifter from Vanessa for a little while. I knew I needed to win her over first and prove to her that not all shifters were horrible. That not all of us were like my father, you know?"

"I know," Ryan said. "But you've been working for her for three years, and you still haven't told her. Because after being around her, you know that Vanessa's hatred for shifters can't be reversed. She can't be convinced that you're good. The hatred runs too deep."

Lori pinched the bridge of her nose. "I'll admit that it's taking me longer than I thought to show her that shifters could be trusted, but it's a work in progress. What I realized the longer I worked for her, is that what I suspected was right. The two of you were ungrateful little bitches who didn't deserve our mother's love. She needs me. She needs me to be the daughter she deserves. And once the two of you are dead, and the only person in her life is me, the one who is *always* there for her, she won't care that I'm a shifter. I'll tell her who I really am, and we'll finally have the relationship we're supposed to have. The one we both need."

"Now I know you're fucking crazy," Ryleigh said. "She never wanted to be a mother – not to you and not to us. We were just the unlucky ones she decided to raise like goats in her little petting zoo."

"Unlucky?" A low growl rose from Lori's chest. "You stupid bitch. You're just proving my point. You had every-thing you could have wanted, including Vanessa's love, and you're still moaning and whining. You have no idea what it's like to grow up without a mother's love."

"You're wrong," Ryleigh said. "Our mother doesn't love anyone but herself."

"She loves her children!" Lori snarled.

"No, she doesn't!" Ryleigh said. "Killing us isn't going to affect her. You aren't going to come in and save her from her despair. She won't be grateful that she still has a daughter even if you are a shifter, because she doesn't fucking love anyone. The only thing she cares about is her precious alcohol and killing us will just give her an excuse to drink more. You kill us and she'll be dead within a fucking month from alcohol poisoning, Lori!"

"I guess that's a risk I'm willing to take," Lori said.

The three of them froze when they heard the key in the lock. Ryan's heart jittered crazily in her chest and the breath cut out of her lungs. "No," she wheezed out. "Oh God, no."

"Looks like your little boyfriend's home. Pity, now I'm going to have to kill him too," Lori said. "Stand up, Ryleigh."

When Ryleigh didn't move, Lori stood and grabbed her arm, digging her suddenly claw-like nails into Ryleigh's arm until she moaned in pain. "Stand up, I said."

Ryleigh stood and Lori moved behind her, holding the gun at Ryleigh's temple. Ryan stared frantically toward the door, her hands pressing so hard against Chase's wound that her arms trembled. The door opened and her heart dropped into her stomach when Grayson stepped into the house.

HIS HEART BANGING AGAINST HIS RIBS, GRAYSON RAN UP THE porch steps. He dug his keys out of his pocket and then paused, forcing two big breaths in and out of his lungs. The idea that Lori was trying to murder his mate was ridiculous. Most likely, she had just come over to tell them how upset Vanessa was.

Running into the house amped up on adrenaline was pointless and not helpful. A person didn't turn into an attempted murderer just because they were jealous.

You've been doing this job long enough to know that isn't true.

Fuck, his inner voice was not helping to calm him or his tiger. He sucked in another big breath and unlocked the door, stepping into the hallway and closing the door behind him.

"Ryan? I'm home. Are you – fuck!"

He pulled his gun from the holster and stalked down the

hallway. Chase was lying in the open area between the kitchen and the living room, his feet nearly touching the island. Ryan was kneeling beside him, pressing a large pile of dishtowels against his stomach. Her hands and the dishtowels were stained in blood and he could smell the fear coating her body.

"Grayson, get out of here! Run!" she shouted.

He ignored her and scanned the room, his tiger growling when he saw Lori. She was standing behind Ryleigh with a gun pointed to the small blonde's temple. She had bent her knees a little and tucked her body directly behind Ryleigh's, her face and head obscured by Ryleigh's head so that he didn't have a clear shot.

Keeping his gaze and his gun aimed at Ryleigh and Lori, he said, "Chase, can you hear me?"

"He's unconscious," Ryan said. "I think the bleeding is slowing down a little, but he's lost so much. I don't – I don't know how he's still alive."

"Aren't you going to say hello, Grayson?" Lori said.

"Hello, Lori." He studied the gun in her hand, mentally calculating the distance between them.

"Don't do that," Lori said. "I'll shoot her in the head before you even get close. You know that I will."

"Put the gun down, Lori." His voice was calm, but fear was sinking into his bones. He eased to the side, hoping for a better angle.

"Put your gun down." Lori's voice was light and weirdly serene.

He kept the gun raised. "No. That isn't happening, Lori. Step away from Ryleigh and put your gun down and maybe you'll walk out of this alive."

"Stop threatening me or I'll kill this stupid bitch right now."

"Grayson," his mate whispered. "Please."

He ignored his urge to look at her. "I can't, honey."

She didn't reply. The smell of her fear was driving his tiger insane. The desire to shift was overwhelming and he held it back grimly.

"Why are you doing this?" Cooper was on his way and Grayson fully intended to play dumb until the lion shifter arrived.

And then what? Lori's got a gun and she's gone full blown crazy. You can smell the insanity on her.

His inner voice was right, but he had a better chance of saving his mate with Cooper then on his own. He just needed to keep her talking.

"It doesn't matter," Lori said.

"Sure, it does." He kept his voice light and easy as he moved his big body in front of Ryan, blocking her from Lori.

"Grayson, don't," Ryan said.

"It's all right, my mate," he said.

"You can't save her," Lori said. "You think you're being noble and brave by taking a bullet for her? I'll just shoot you and then her. She can't live. She doesn't deserve it. Not after what she's done to Vanessa."

"What do you care?" Gray said. "You're just her PA."

"I'm more than that, you asshole!" He heard her take a deep breath and release it, the force of her sigh blew strands of hair against Ryleigh's cheek. "You know what, forget it. You aren't important and I don't need to tell you a goddamn thing. But I want you to know that this isn't personal. Now put your gun on the floor and kick it over to me or I swear to God, I will kill this bitch in front of me."

"Oh God," Ryan whispered. "Gray, please. I'm begging you."

Not even years of military training or the voice in his

head screaming at him to not give up his fucking gun, could keep the gun in his hand. Not when his mate was pleading with him like that.

"You know I don't need a gun to kill you, Lori," he said.

He couldn't see her face, but he heard her growl under her breath. After a beat, he set the gun on the ground and kicked it toward her. Lori stopped it with her foot and straightened her legs, her head popping up above Ryleigh's. She smiled at him, her eyes glowing green and her fangs out. She kicked his gun under the couch and moved the gun from Ryleigh's temple until it pointed at Grayson. In the backyard, he could hear Sam start to bark.

Lori glanced at the window overlooking the deck and back yard. He took a step toward her and she flicked her gaze back to his. "Don't move."

He bared his fangs at her. "What kind of fucking shifter are you? Killing me with a gun? You're weak, Lori. So fucking weak."

She laughed. "You can't goad me into shifting, Grayson. We both know that you're more powerful than me when we're in our animal forms. The gun will work just fine for me, thanks."

"Lori, please don't do this." He could hear the tears in his mate's voice behind him. "Please, I am begging you. Don't kill him."

"I have to," Lori said. "You know that I… oh, for fuck's sake! What is that dog barking at?"

"It's just a squirrel," Ryan said as Sam's barking continued.

"Fucking dogs. They're the worst," Lori said. "Where was I? Right, I don't want to kill you, but I really have no…"

She glanced out the window again as Sam's barking intensified. "Jesus Christ. Do I need to put a bullet in that fucking mutt's brain too? He's gonna have the entire neigh-bourhood over here."

"No!" Ryan said quickly. "No, just let me... I'll go out and tell him to be quiet. Okay?"

Lori rolled her eyes. "Do you think I'm that stupid? You're not going anywhere, Ryan. Go to the door and call him inside."

"He won't come in, not if he's barking at the squirrel. I'll come right back," Ryan said. "You think I'd leave my mate and my sister to die?"

Lori cocked her head and stared at her. After a moment, the silence broken only by Sam's barking, she said, "No, you won't. Fine, go on and shut your fucking dog up. You have thirty goddamn seconds. If you're not back, I'll put a bullet in your mate's brain, and you won't get to say goodbye to him. Got it?"

"Yes," Ryan said. "I need Ryleigh to come over and apply pressure to Chase's wound, so he doesn't bleed out."

"He's gonna die anyway," Lori said. "What's the point?"

"Ryleigh, come over here." His mate didn't even look at Lori. Grayson had a feeling that if Ryan kept staring at the gun pointed at Ryleigh's head, she would lose her fucking shit. He couldn't blame her.

Ryleigh glanced at Lori who shrugged and nodded before stepping back. "Whatever. Prolong his misery, see if I fucking care."

She kept the gun pointed at him as Ryleigh knelt next to Ryan and placed her hands on the blood-soaked towels. Ryan kissed Ryleigh's forehead and stood. Grayson immediately bent his head and pressed a kiss against his mate's cold lips. "I love you, my mate."

"I love you too," she said.

"Get out there and shut that fucking dog's mouth," Lori said. 'Thirty seconds, Ryan."

Ryan stood and walked on trembling legs toward the back door. She paused at the door, giving Grayson a heartbreaking look of fear. His blood pumping and his tiger roaring to be free, he forced himself to smile at her.

"I'll be right back," she whispered. "I promise."

"I know," he said.

CHAPTER 22

"You're staying in the truck." Cooper took the freeway exit going twenty miles over the speed limit.

Daisy shook her head. "I don't want to."

"It's too dangerous," Cooper said.

"You don't know that. Lori could just -"

"She's the one behind the second murder attempt," Cooper said. It was a no passing zone, but he pulled out from behind the Honda and zoomed past, ignoring the driver's madly waving middle finger. The GPS instructed him to turn left at the next light and he flicked on his signal and floored it through the yellow light. He pulled his gun out of the holster on the center console.

"How do you know?"

"Because Gray's at the house and he hasn't texted or called me with an update. Which means he and the others are in trouble." He held the gun out to Daisy. "Take this."

"I don't know how to use a gun," she said.

"When this is all over, I'll take you to a firing range and teach you," he said as he made another left. "In the meantime, this is the safety. Flick it down to turn it off. Point the gun at the chest and squeeze the trigger."

"I can't shoot someone," she said.

"You probably won't have to," he said. "But I want you to take it."

"You might need it," she said.

"We only carry guns to make the human clients feel better, you know that. If there's trouble, I'll be shifting anyway. I'm more powerful in my lion form."

She bit her bottom lip, and he hated that he was making her anxious, but he needed his mate to be safe. She clenched her hands together in her lap before whispering, "Cooper, I don't want to take it. Please don't make me."

The light ahead turned red, and he stepped on the brakes, stopping behind a battered and dented pick-up truck, before leaning across the seat and cupping her face. Fresh sorrow clawed at his insides when she flinched. "Baby, I need you to take the gun. Please."

She cast her eyes downward and sighed, her slender body shuddering. "Yeah, okay."

"Thank you." He made himself stop touching her and handed her the gun. She held it gingerly, like it might grow ragged teeth and bite off her fingers.

"Remember, safety off before you fire. Okay?"

"Okay," she whispered.

"I'll come out and get you when it's safe. Do not leave the truck until I return. All right?"

"Please be careful," she said.

His lion surged forward, bolstered by the genuine concern in Daisy's voice. He swallowed down the purr rising in his throat as the light turned green and he stepped on the gas. "I will. Remember, stay in the truck with the doors locked, no matter what happens. If Lori comes out of the house, duck down and stay hidden."

She suddenly reached out and her fingers wrapped around his wrist. Her unexpected touch held him as immobile as if a cement truck had dropped into his lap. This time he was helpless to stop his lion's purring. She cocked her head, staring at him as the rumbling sound filled the small space. His cheeks turned red and he cursed his lion in his head as the damn thing purred louder.

Shut up! Do you know how humiliating this is?

His lion didn't care about humiliation. All it cared about was that his mate was touching him. It wasn't an accidental brush in the hallway which had happened once about two months after she started working for him. His immediate erection was so noticeable, he'd had to sprint to his office before anyone else saw it. She wasn't touching him because they were pretending to be dating for the benefit of a lecherous jaguar shifter. She was touching him because...

Because she wants us! Because she is our mate. His lion's purring was almost deafening in the truck cab.

Enough! He roared so loudly at his lion that it hurt his own head. *She is afraid of us! We will never be with her. So, just shut the fuck up!*

His lion snarled at him and retreated, his purring cutting out with a jagged cough.

"Sorry," he muttered as she dropped his wrist.

He turned onto Ryan's street as Daisy said, "I really think you need the gun more than me, Cooper. It's ridiculous for me to keep it. You'll be the one in danger, not me."

"Lori may not be working alone," he said as he parked and shut the truck off. "If she isn't, you could be in danger just by being in the truck without me."

"Then let me go with you. I can help."

He shook his head. "No, you can't. Stay in the truck, Daisy. That's an order."

A flash of annoyance crossed her face before she sat back in her seat. "Fine. Don't die in there."

"I'm not planning on it." He slid out of the truck and closed the door, waiting until Daisy leaned over and hit the lock button on the driver's door. He studied his mate's face, as if he hadn't already memorized every perfect feature, before turning and jogging across the street.

He had parked two houses down from Ryan's and, hoping that none of her neighbours were watching out their windows, he cut across their lawns and ducked into the space between Ryan's house and the neighbour's house to her right.

Ryan's backyard was surrounded by a six-foot wooden fence. He moved closer and peered over it, studying the house and deck that were to his left. He could see movement in the bay window overlooking the deck and muttered a curse. Lori was standing near the window and Ryleigh was standing in front of her. The angle was wrong for him to see past Ryleigh's head at what was in Lori's raised hand, but he had no doubt it was a goddamn gun.

"Think, asshole," he whispered as he ducked down so Lori wouldn't see him if she glanced out the window. He needed to somehow let Grayson know he was here but with Lori right by the fucking window, she'd see him before Gray did. Fuck. Maybe if he –

He cocked his head and sniffed the air. He could smell Ryan's dog in the yard and - he tilted his head the other way - hear it snuffling along the fence line. If he jumped into the yard, Sam would start barking and if Cooper was really lucky, Lori would send Grayson out to shut him up. Grayson would see Coop and the two of them would figure out how to take Lori the fuck down before she killed the sisters.

"Pretty thin plan," he muttered.

He moved back to where the fence started at the side of the house before taking a deep breath. Yeah, it was a paper-thin fucking plan, but it was the best one he had. He braced one hand on the top of the fence, bent his knees and, with a little help from his lion, vaulted over the fence and landed on his feet in the narrow space between the side of the house and the fence.

Like he was hoping, Sam came tearing across the yard, a low growl starting in his chest and throat. He skidded to a stop, his head cocked to the side, and studied Cooper.

"C'mon, bark," Cooper muttered.

Instead of barking, the dog's tail wagged, and he made a happy whine. He ran forward and sat at Cooper's feet, panting loudly with a big stupid dog grin on his face.

"Are you fucking kidding me?" Cooper said. "Bark, you idiot dog."

More tail wagging. Cooper bared his teeth at the dog and growled loudly. Sam jerked and backed away, his tail down between his legs and his ears flat.

Cooper growled a second time and then cursed under his breath when Sam's ears returned to normal and he made his own growl before wagging his tail again. He stared at Cooper as if to say, 'now it's your turn to growl', and Cooper could have punched the fence in frustration.

He looked up, studying the window on the second floor, wondering idly if he could make the leap to the sill. It was high but he might be able to make it.

Nope, you can't. Release me. I'll get that stupid dog to bark, his lion growled.

With another low growl and a quick glance at the neighbour's second floor window – Jesus Christ, please don't let them be watching out the window, a public indecency charge was the last fucking thing he needed – he stripped off his clothes and called for his lion.

His lion charged forward and he shifted, dropping to all fours as his bones realigned and his flesh turned to fur. When he was fully in his lion form, he glared at Sam and growled menacingly.

To his immense relief, Sam backed up a few steps, opened his mouth and bellowed out the loudest, sweetest sounding barks that Cooper had ever heard. His lion hissed in anger, and Cooper soothed it, stopping it from leaping forward and ripping out the dog's throat. Sam crouched, not quite brave enough to attack but his barking growing in sound and intensity.

What seemed like hours later, he heard the back door swing open. Footsteps ran down the deck stairs and Ryan ran up to Sam.

Fuck, not Grayson. Was he dead already? Fear shot through his gut. The day that Derek died, he'd made a vow to himself that he would never lose another man in his unit. Thinking about Grayson being dead made his legs turn to water and his throat turn to sand.

"Sam, enough!" Ryan's voice was frantic and rough with fear. "No barking, Sam! No…"

She followed the now quiet dog's gaze, her voice dying in her throat as she studied him in his lion form. He shifted to his human form, ignoring Sam's yelp of surprise, and put his finger to his lips.

Ryan moved closer until she was out of view of the window. "It's Lori," she whispered. "She's crazy and has a gun."

"I know. Is Grayson still alive?"

"Yes, but she's going to kill him. She's going to kill all of us," Ryan said. "I don't know what to do."

He reached down to his pants lying on the ground and fished out his phone. "I'll call 9-1-1."

"We'll be dead before they get here." Ryan glanced at her watch. "I have to go. If I'm not back in thirty seconds, she's putting a bullet in Grayson's brain."

Her voice broke on the last word and she swiped at the tears gleaming on her cheeks.

"Fuck," he said as panic swept through him.

"She's acting crazy," Ryan whispered. "She's our goddamn half-sister and – fuck, I have to go!"

She turned and he grabbed her arm. "You're not going back in there."

"She is going to kill him," she snarled. "She has a gun and she is going to shoot him in the head. Let me go, Cooper."

"She'll kill you too."

"I don't fucking care!" She yanked viciously at his grip. "I'm not letting Grayson die alone. I'm not – shit, what are you doing? Cooper, no! She'll shoot you!"

He shoved her behind him and dodged around Sam before shifting into his lion form. Ryan had left the back door open and he leaped up the back steps, his muscles flexing with pure power as he landed on the deck and charged for the doorway.

He ran inside, ignoring Ryleigh's scream of surprise and Grayson's growl of shock. His lion snarled at the jaguar shifter and Cooper skidded to a stop on the slick floor before crouching. Adrenaline flowed through his veins, lighting up his nerve ends and making his body shake. He leaped at the jaguar shifter as she screamed.

He landed on her just as the gun went off. The sound was deafening, the pain enormous and all too familiar. The jaguar growled out another scream as he knocked her on her ass, the gun flying from her hand and landing on the floor.

His right shoulder had turned to fire and ice, both heat and cold radiating down his front leg. He tried to swipe at the jaguar shifter, but nothing on his body seemed to work properly anymore and he tumbled face-first into the floor.

The pain and the shock made his lion retreat and he shifted to his human form, warm liquid gushing out of his shoulder and down his right arm. He was on his back on the floor and he twisted his head to stare at his shoulder as Lori stumbled to her feet and with a yowl of fear and rage, shifted to her jaguar form.

Cooper stared at the blood pouring from the hole in shoulder. Fuck, he'd been shot again.

"OH FUCK, OH FUCK, OH FUCK," RYAN CHANTED AS SHE chased after Cooper. The giant lion leaped up the deck with a powerful flex of his hind legs and disappeared into the house.

She raced up the steps, tripping on the last one and nearly falling on her face before catching herself on the railing.

"Sam, sit! Stay!" She screeched as the dog ran up the stairs past her. He stopped obediently, plopping his butt down on the deck just to the right of the door. She ran past him, crying out when she heard the gun shot.

Cooper was landing on Lori and he roared in pain as blood appeared on the back of one golden coloured shoulder. It soaked across his fur as he and Lori tumbled to the ground. The gun fell from Lori's hand and skidded across the floor toward Ryan.

Cooper fell onto his back, shifting to his human form, the blood bright red against his tanned shoulder. Ryleigh crouched frozen over Chase, her hands pressing against the bloody dishtowels as she stared wide-eyed at Lori.

"Grayson!" Ryan cried.

He was already shifting to his tiger form, his clothes tearing off and landing in heaps on the floor. Lori yowled and shifted to her jaguar, her clothes landing on Cooper's lower legs. Grayson snarled, baring his fangs at Lori before running toward her.

"No!" Ryan screamed when Grayson's big paws slipped in the pool of blood surrounding Chase. He went down hard, his head banging off the hardwood floor. She heard the snap of his teeth as his jaws clicked together, heard his startled growl as he tried to scramble to his feet.

With another yowl of victory and moving so fast, Ryan could barely track her, Lori leaped across the room and landed with a heavy thud on top of Grayson. He growled and tried to stand, the growl turning to a howl of pain when Lori dug her razor-sharp claws into his back and her mouth opened wide. Drool ran from her fangs as she prepared to rip out the throat of the man Ryan loved.

Ryan dove for the gun that was lying a few inches away. She scooped it up, a litany of gun rules ricocheting in her brain as time seemed to slow. She only had seconds, she knew how quickly the shifters could maim and tear and kill.

"Stop!" she screamed as she lifted the gun and aimed it at the wide expanse of the jaguar's chest. Lori didn't even look at her. Her jaws widening, she screamed her triumph as she moved with deadly speed to tear out Grayson's jugular.

Ryan echoed her scream, the sound barren and bleak, and pulled the trigger. The gun jumped in her hand and Ryan staggered forward, her ears ringing so loudly that Lori's shriek of pain was a muted hum.

The jaguar shifter slid off of Grayson, the fur receding

and her body shrinking, until she was in her human form. With blood pouring out of her chest, Lori collapsed on her back, staring up at the ceiling.

"Grayson, no!" Ryan screamed when the tiger leaped on top of Lori's prone body and crouched over her, his front paws on either side of her narrow shoulders. He stopped and stared at Ryan, growling his displeasure as Lori's blood soaked into his paws.

"Don't!" Ryan said.

She rushed forward as Grayson shifted to his human form and stood. She handed him the gun and grabbed the blanket off the back of the couch, covering Lori up and pressing a big wad of the blanket against the wound on her chest.

"Ryan, what are you doing?" Ryleigh shouted.

"She's still our sister," Ryan said as she applied pressure on Lori's chest.

Blood trickled from Lori's mouth. She stared silently up at Ryan as the front door opened. Grayson who was on his way to Cooper, spun around, his tense body relaxing. "Daisy?"

The slender woman didn't spare a glance at him or anyone else. She ran straight to Cooper, falling to her knees beside him and hesitating only briefly before pulling off her t-shirt and pressing it against his bleeding shoulder.

"I told you to stay in the truck," Cooper said.

"You're not the boss of me," she said.

"Yes, I am!"

"Stop moving," she said. "You're going to bleed to death if you keep moving."

"You could have been hurt," Cooper said. "I told you to stay in the truck so you wouldn't get hurt."

"Yeah, well, I'm not the one shot and lying bleeding on the floor, am I?"

He growled and she paled but then shook her head. "Stop that. Just hold still."

He glared at her before reaching down with his left hand and yanking up a strip of Lori's tattered clothing that rested on his lower legs. He covered his dick with it. Despite the blood loss, he apparently had enough still in his body to turn his cheeks bright red when Daisy's gaze skittered to his crotch for a moment.

Grayson knelt next to Ryleigh. He pressed his fingers against Chase's neck and Ryleigh stared at him in terror. "Is he dead?"

"No, his pulse is faint but still there. Keep doing what you're doing."

He moved to Ryan and crouched beside her. He kissed the side of her head and then her forehead and finally her mouth. "My mate, are you all right?"

"We need to call 9-1-1," she said.

Sirens pierced the air and Grayson glanced at the front door. "Pretty sure your neighbours have already taken care of that. Are you okay?"

"Yeah. Are you? You're bleeding."

He looked over his shoulder at the blood covering his back. "She got me with her claws. Hurts like fucking hell, but I don't think she hit anything vital."

"Thank God," she breathed before resting her forehead against Grayson's. Lori wasn't moving and her eyes had drifted shut but her chest rose up and down in a weak and uneven rhythm.

She kept pressure on Lori's chest and kissed Grayson again, her entire body shuddering at how close she'd come to losing him. "You scared the crap out of me when you slipped in the blood and fell."

"Not my most agile moment." He grinned at her and she stared at him in disbelief.

"You almost died and you're grinning?"

He pressed another kiss against her mouth. "Thank you for saving my life. I love you, my mate."

"I love you too," she said.

"I STILL DON'T BELIEVE YOU," RYAN SAID.

Grayson lifted her hand to kiss her knuckles. "The doctor discharged me, honey. I promise."

"You were in the hospital for less than forty-eight hours. You had multiple puncture wounds in your back that required seventy-two stitches and -"

"Seventy-eight," Grayson said as they stepped onto the elevator and he hit the button for the seventh floor.

"*Seventy-eight* stitches," Ryan said huffily, "and one of Lori's claws came *this* close to severing your spinal cord, but he just discharged you after less than two days."

"I'm fine, honey. I just need to take it easy while I heal."

She snorted at him and he laughed and kissed her forehead. "You're adorable when you're all riled up."

The doors opened and he followed her down the quiet hallway. She switched the flowers she held to her left hand as she stopped in front of a half-open door and knocked lightly.

"Come in."

They stepped inside. The first bed had the curtain drawn around it and they tiptoed past it. Chase's curtain was open, and he smiled at them from the hospital bed. "Hey, guys."

Ryleigh was sitting in one of the visitor chairs next to the bed and she smiled at Ryan. "Hi, Ry-Ry."

"Hi, sweetie." Ryan placed the flowers on the table next

to the others and leaned down to kiss Chase's cheek. "You're looking much better than you did yesterday."

"I'm feeling pretty good today," Chase said.

"Yeah, maybe you should ease off on pressing that pain med button," Ryleigh said with a grin. She squeezed Chase's hand and settled back in her chair as Grayson shook Chase's free hand.

"Thanks for the flowers," Chase said.

"You're welcome."

Grayson glanced at the drawn curtain behind him. "Coop sleeping still?"

Chase shook his head. "Nah, they discharged him two hours ago."

"What?" Grayson said. "I told him to call me when he was getting discharged and I'd give him a ride home. Did Boone drive him home?"

Chase's grin widened. "Nope. Daisy was here visiting when the doctor discharged him, and she said she would give him a ride home. You should have seen the way his face lit up. You would have thought she called him her mate or something."

"I can't believe they discharged him already," Ryan said. "What is it with the doctors in this hospital?"

"He was doing good," Chase said. "It's not like they had to go in and dig the bullet out like they did with me, it went right through him. He has to wear the sling for about a week until the stitches come out, but the doc said there was no permanent damage. Apparently, both of us got pretty lucky."

Ryleigh sighed. "Being shot in the stomach is not getting lucky, Chase."

He shrugged. "Could have been worse. The bullet missed all my major organs and the two of you stopped me from bleeding out."

"Sometimes I really hate how positive you are," Ryleigh said.

Chase laughed. "You're gonna miss me and you know it."

She squeezed his hand again. "I might a little. Gavin said he wanted to have you over for dinner when you're out of the hospital. Okay?"

"I'd like that," Chase said. He glanced at Grayson. "How are you feeling?"

"Fine. Just a few stitches," Grayson said.

"So," Chase eyed his and Ryan's clasped hands, "I was pretty out of it back at your place, but I swear I heard you calling each other mate."

Ryan smiled. "You heard right."

"Oh, well, congratulations. You two moved in together yet?"

Ryan blushed and Grayson cleared his throat. "Uh, we haven't, I mean, it's a little soon and we haven't really discussed whether…"

"What he's trying to say is that no, he hasn't officially moved in yet, but he's putting in his notice for his apartment tomorrow."

"I am?" Grayson said.

"You are," Ryan replied. "You have a problem with that?"

"No, my mate." A small smile played on his lips and Ryan wondered if she'd ever get tired of hearing him call her his mate.

Doubtful, she decided. *Highly* doubtful.

"Have you heard anything about Lori?" Chase asked.

Ryleigh snorted in disgust as Ryan nodded. "Yeah. She made it through the surgery and she's doing all right. I haven't seen her, and I know they have guards posted outside her door, but apparently she is off the ventilator and awake."

She glanced at Ryleigh. "She asked for Vanessa."

Ryleigh shook her head. "That crazy bitch. She doesn't actually think Vanessa would come and see her, does she?"

"Does she know that Lori is a shifter yet?" Chase asked.

"Yes. I told her last night," Ryan said. "I told her everything that Lori said."

Ryleigh sat up. "You didn't tell me you were doing that."

"I didn't want to upset you," Ryan said.

"You shouldn't have had to do it alone," Ryleigh said.

"I wasn't." Ryan squeezed Grayson's hand. "Grayson was with me."

"How did she take it?" Ryleigh said.

"Like we imagined she would. She freaked out and screamed and shouted about being betrayed by everyone in her life. She blamed me and you and then Grayson… oh, and she tried to blame Bert and Peter as well… before she finally just shut down and refused to talk at all."

"Did she at least admit that it was possible Lori was her daughter?" Ryleigh asked.

"Yeah. She said it was probably true, that she did give her up as a baby to this Corbin guy's mother."

Ryleigh paled and she swallowed compulsively. "Fuck."

"Did you think Lori was lying?" Ryan asked gently.

"I don't know. I guess I hoped that she was. The paparazzi is gonna have a field day when this comes out."

"It might not," Ryan said.

"It will, it always does. They already know about Gavin and me. The story broke this morning," Ryleigh said glumly.

"Sorry, sweetie."

"It's all right, I couldn't keep my love for him a secret forever, could I?" Ryleigh said. "Are you going to talk to our crazy bitch of a half-sister?"

Ryan frowned at her. "She's been through a lot, Ryleigh. It isn't her fault that she is the way she is. She had a horrible childhood and had to keep her whole identity a secret from her own mother."

Ryleigh sighed. "Yeah, I know. Will you try and talk to her?"

"I already tried. She wouldn't see me. Maybe she'll agree to talk to me once she's feeling a little better and before they…"

"Cart her off to the nuthouse?" Ryleigh said.

"Be nice, Ryleigh," Ryan said.

"The bitch tried to kill all of us and nearly succeeded with Chase," Ryleigh said. "I don't care how messed up her childhood was, it doesn't give her the right to just go around murdering people."

They sat in silence for a moment before Ryleigh's phone buzzed. She glanced at it, a smile crossing her face. "Gavin is here. I'll come by tomorrow, okay, Chase?"

"Sure. Thanks, Ryleigh."

She kissed his cheek before kissing Ryan's and then Grayson's. "Take care of my big sister."

"I will," Grayson said.

Ryleigh studied him. "Yeah, you will. You guys come by next week to Gavin's, okay? We'll have dinner, play some Pictionary."

"Pictionary?" Ryan said.

"Gavin loves it. Bye, Ry-Ry, I love you."

"I love you too."

They waited until Ryleigh had left before Ryan smiled at Chase. "Is there anything we can get you? I could smuggle you in some real food."

He laughed. "Thanks, I appreciate that, but I'm good. Boone brought me in a pizza this morning and Wes stopped by earlier with a bunch of snacks and stuff. I appreciate you guys stopping by but get out of here. Now that the two of you are mates, if you're anything like my mom and dad, you want to spend time alone together."

"Ouch. Did he just compare us to his mom and dad?" Grayson said.

"You are thirty-two years old," Ryan said. "I mean, that's what 145 years old in cat years?"

He growled at her as Chase bellowed laughter and then grabbed at his stomach. "Shit, don't make me laugh."

"Sorry, Chase," Ryan said.

"It's good. Seriously, get out of here."

"I'll come by tomorrow," Grayson said and shook his hand. "Get some rest, buddy."

Ryan kissed Chase's cheek before taking Grayson's hand and following him out of the room and into the hallway.

As they waited for the elevator, he leaned down and pressed a kiss against her mouth. "If you want to stop by Lori's room and try again, we can."

"I appreciate that, but I don't think she'll see me. Not right now." Ryan rested her head on Grayson's wide chest. "Thank you for being so understanding about it."

"Of course. I love you. I'll do whatever it takes to make you happy," Grayson said.

She smiled up at him. "I love you too. Let's go home."

"Yes," he said, "let's go home, my mate."

EDGE OF NIGHT EXCERPT

(SHADOW SECURITY BOOK TWO)

Daisy hesitated outside of Cooper's office. She rested her hand on the doorknob before pulling it back. God, what was she doing? More importantly, why was she doing it? This weird compulsion to come up with every excuse in the book to see him was, at best, going to be super noticeable by the others in the office if it wasn't already, and at worst, get her fired for being incompetent at her job.

Asking a million questions she already knew the answers to might get her close to Cooper, might feed her sudden craving to be near him, but it would also land her in serious trouble if she didn't knock it off. She lived paycheque to paycheque. If she got fired and didn't find another job immediately…

She shuddered, thinking about the homeless people that lived in a tent city situation only a few blocks from her apartment building. Her apartment might be crappy and scary and possibly on the verge of collapse from mold and water damage, but it was better than being completely homeless.

More importantly, her inner voice whispered, *why are you so determined to be around someone who scares the living hell out of you.*

Cooper would never hurt me.

Her inner voice scoffed so loudly she was surprised Cooper didn't hear it through his office door. *Are you really that naïve? After everything you've been through, you still believe that a shifter might be good. That Cooper wouldn't hurt you the first chance he got?*

If I didn't, I wouldn't have taken this job to try and get over my fear, would I have? she snapped back.

You're playing a dangerous game. One that's gonna get you killed. Cooper and Wes and Grayson and all the other shifters in this office are dangerous. It's like you want *to be murdered by shifters.*

Her heart pounding, she moved away from Cooper's door, her limbs jerking along like a marionette whose strings were tangled tight. She didn't have a death wish, she just needed to get over her fear of shifters. She couldn't keep living life this way. That was why she was trying to spend more time with Cooper. That was why she volunteered to cook him dinner every night last week while he was recovering. It was taking much longer than she thought to conquer her fear and by spending extra time with her boss, she was moving along her own self-therapy.

Or you're really fucking horny and want to get laid.

Inner Daisy almost recoiled in horror at that errant thought. Becoming friends with a shifter was one thing, but sleeping with one? No fucking way.

Oh yeah? Then why do you keep thinking about the kisses you shared? And what about that weird sex dream you had about him two nights ago.

Her cheeks turned scarlet and she hurried down the hallway, almost half convinced that just by thinking about her sex dream in the office, Cooper would somehow find out. She'd woken from the dream both horny and terrified, and certain she was losing her damn mind.

She needed to step back from Cooper and find a different shifter to try and be friends with. One she wasn't possibly, maybe, sexually attracted to, which was really freaking her out because she never once imagined she'd be attracted to a shifter.

Although, maybe sleeping with a shifter was the way to get over her fear. Like, a total immersion/exposure thing. It would be kind of hard to be terrified of Cooper if he'd given her multiple orgasms, right? She thought about his big hands, about the way it had felt when he'd cupped her face and kissed her. God, he was a good kisser. Sure, it had been a little scary kissing him, but when he'd touched her tongue with his, it had…

Enough! You're not sleeping with him. Stay away from him. Something weird is going on with him lately. He's acting strange.

She wanted to pretend her inner voice was wrong, but… well, it wasn't. Cooper *was* acting weird lately. There was something off about him. He'd seemed mostly normal when he returned to work on Monday, if not a little distant, but with each day that passed, he got… weirder. The other day, she'd sworn he was talking to himself as he stood at the copier. And as much as she was suddenly trying to see more of him, she couldn't shake off the nagging feeling that he was trying to avoid her. Not that he'd spent all that much time with her before, but he'd always been nice to her and often asked her to help him with his ongoing computer issues. And she'd thought that after spending every evening with him last week, their tentative friendship would continue at the office.

How wrong she'd been.

He hadn't asked her even once to help fix his computer this week, and she was pretty sure she saw Lusa helping him yesterday. Hurt weaved its way into her stomach and she berated herself immediately. What did she care if Cooper didn't want to spend time with her anymore? He was her boss and that was it.

Thinking she should try and be friends with him, or even more crazy – have sex with him – was insanity on her part.

"Cooper's getting worse."

Boone's low voice stopped her in her tracks. She crept forward a few steps and leaned against the wall outside of the boardroom. The door was partially open, and she strained to hear. Listening in on private conversations wasn't something she normally did, but she couldn't seem to get her feet to keep moving. Her suspicions about Cooper were true, and she needed to know what was wrong.

Maybe she could help him.

"He's okay." Grayson's voice was only slighter louder than Boone's.

"He isn't, man. I know you want to think he is, but he's not," Boone said.

"He's stressed out right now. He needs a few days off to -"

"It's more than that, Gray."

This time it was Wes speaking and his voice was so close to the half-open door, that Daisy held her breath. Shit, he would smell her soon. She knew he would. Still, she couldn't move. She had to know.

"His lion is going mad," Wes said. "If we don't do something soon, it'll be too late."

"What are we supposed to do?" Gray said. The worry in

his voice made Daisy's stomach churn. "We can't make her have sex with him."

"No, but maybe we could talk to her," Boone said. "Tell her about the mate thing and what it's doing to Cooper."

"Are you serious?" Grayson said. "How do you think that conversation will go? Hmm? You think we can walk up to her and be like, 'Oh, hey, Daisy. We know you're terrified of shifters, but Coop's lion believes you're his mate and if you don't have sex with him, he's going to descend into madness and never recover.' Yeah, that will go over real well, Boone."

The breath Daisy had been holding leaked out of her lungs in irregular and patchy sips. Cooper thought she was his mate?

Duh, he called you his mate that day at the coffee shop.

Yeah, because he was playing a part. One you forced him to play because you were being your usual terrified self. He called you his mate because you introduced him as your boyfriend, remember?

"Maybe we can think of a more polite way to say it," Boone said.

"Oh my God, Boone, there is no polite way to tell our goddamn receptionist that if she doesn't fuck the boss, he's going to go mad and we'll have to put him down like a rabid dog," Gray said.

"Calm down, Gray," Wes said.

"Don't tell me to calm down. This is my best friend we're talking about, Wes. He's going crazy and there isn't anything we can do about it. We'll never convince Daisy to fuck Cooper."

"Maybe if we fired Daisy…" Boone said hesitantly.

"We can't," Wes said. "The only thing that's stopped him from going insane already is being around Daisy at work. He's gotten so much worse so quickly because she was spending more time with him when his arm was still in that sling. Daisy went to his place every night and cooked him dinner. His lion got used to it and now that he's recovered and she's not at his house every day, his lion's losing his grip on reality."

"This fucking mate thing is such bullshit," Boone snarled. "Cooper is the strongest guy I know and he's going to be taken down because a woman doesn't love him. It's not fucking fair."

"We have to do something," Grayson said. "You guys are right, he's getting worse. I didn't want to admit it, but he is. I wanted to go over to his place last night and he wouldn't let me. He's getting twitchy and weird and -"

"He spends most of his time talking to his lion," Boone said grimly. "His pupils are almost always slits now. We have to talk to Daisy."

"We do," Wes said. "Which one of us is doing it?"

"Not me," Boone said. "You think I want a sexual harassment charge on my permanent record? Because you know Daisy is going to file one against the guy who tries to convince her to fuck her boss."

"I'll talk to her," Grayson said.

"Take Ryan with you," Wes said. "Maybe hearing it from another human female will help. Maybe you don't have to mention the sex thing. If he isn't too far gone yet, just getting Daisy to spend one-on-one time with him again would help. It would soothe his lion enough to keep it from going mad, right?"

"That's a good idea," Grayson said. "But even if we could convince her to spend time with him, that eventually won't be enough. You know how our cats are. His lion will keep pushing for more and Cooper knows Daisy is terrified of him.

He won't attempt anything sexual with her. He'd rather go mad than scare her like that."

"It's the only and best idea we have at the moment," Wes said. "We get her to spend some alone time with him again and that'll buy us some time until we can figure out what to do."

"Maybe we could introduce him to someone else," Boone said. "Another woman who will make him forget about wanting to fuck Daisy. Maybe, if he gets laid by anyone, that will help?"

"Maybe," Wes said.

A weird sensation burned in her belly. After a moment, she placed it. Holy shit...was she jealous? She heard Cooper's office door open and immediately darted down the hallway to reception. She sat down at her desk, her heart thumping like a rabbit and her mouth dry. She was right. Something *was* wrong with Cooper. He was going insane and she could help him. She swallowed down her jagged laughter.

If she wanted to save Cooper from madness, all she had to do was fuck him.

ABOUT THE AUTHOR

Ramona Gray is a Canadian romance author. She currently lives in Alberta with her awesome husband and her super cute dog. She's addicted to home improvement shows, good coffee, and reading and writing about the steamier moments in life.

For more information about Ramona, check out her website at

www.ramonagray.ca

facebook.com/RamonaGrayBooks

twitter.com/RamonaGrayBooks

instagram.com/ramonagrayauthor

amazon.com/Ramona-Gray/e/B00OD26SAM

bookbub.com/profile/ramona-gray

The Welder

The Electrician

The Landscaper

The Firefighter

The Cop

The Paramedic

Working Men Series Bundles

Working Men Series Books One to Three

Working Men Series Books Four to Six

Working Men Series Books Seven to Nine

Other World Series

The Vampire's Kiss (Book One)

The Vampire's Love (Book Two)

The Shifter's Mate (Book Three)

Rescued By The Wolf (Book Four)

Claiming Quinn (Book Five)

Choosing Rose (Book Six)

Elena Unbound (Book Seven)

Other World Series Box Sets

Other World Series Books One to Three

Other World Series Books Four to Six